SHATTERED LEGIONS

SHADRAK REACHED OVER with his right hand, unclasped the elbow guard and let it fall to the deck. Then he unfastened the clamps in the crook of his elbow and mid-forearm, and tugged the composite plasteel-and-ceramite sleeve off. Parts of the gauntlet were still attached, flapping loose. The buckled wrist seal was impacted into his flesh, and it took a little more effort to wrench it clear. Fluid and flecks of meat spattered the deck.

He stripped away the undersleeve, tearing the fabric. His exposed skin looked as pale as bone, in stark contrast to the mauled mess of his hand.

'How did this happen?' the man asked, eyes wide at the fully exposed damage.

'Horus happened,' said Shadrak.

THE HORUS HERESY®

*Many of these titles are also available as abridged and unabridged audiobooks.
Order the full range of Horus Heresy novels and audiobooks from*
blacklibrary.com

Audio Dramas

Download the full range of Horus Heresy audio dramas from
blacklibrary.com

THE HORUS HERESY®

SHATTERED LEGIONS

Edited by Laurie Goulding

BLACK LIBRARY

*Dedicated to the memory of Chris 'Yvraith' Barton,
one of the original champions of the Great Crusade.*

A BLACK LIBRARY PUBLICATION

Hardback edition published in 2017.
This edition published in Great Britain in 2017.
Black Library,
Games Workshop Ltd.,
Willow Road,
Nottingham,
NG7 2WS, UK.

10 9 8 7 6 5 4 3 2 1

Produced by Games Workshop in Nottingham.
Cover by Neil Roberts.

A CIP record for this book is available from the British Library.

ISBN 13: 978 1 78496 629 4

See Black Library on the internet at

blacklibrary.com

Find out more about Games Workshop
and the world of Warhammer 40,000 at

games-workshop.com

Printed and bound by CPI Group (UK) Ltd, Croydon, CR0 4YY

THE HORUS HERESY®
It is a time of legend.

The galaxy is in flames. The Emperor's glorious vision for humanity is in ruins. His favoured son, Horus, has turned from his father's light and embraced Chaos.

His armies, the mighty and redoubtable Space Marines, are locked in a brutal civil war. Once, these ultimate warriors fought side by side as brothers, protecting the galaxy and bringing mankind back into the Emperor's light.
Now they are divided.

Some remain loyal to the Emperor, whilst others have sided with the Warmaster. Pre-eminent amongst them, the leaders of their thousands-strong Legions are the primarchs. Magnificent, superhuman beings, they are the crowning achievement of the Emperor's genetic science. Thrust into battle against one another, victory is uncertain for either side.

Worlds are burning. At Isstvan V, Horus dealt a vicious blow and three loyal Legions were all but destroyed. War was begun, a conflict that will engulf all mankind in fire. Treachery and betrayal have usurped honour and nobility. Assassins lurk in every shadow. Armies are gathering.
All must choose a side or die.

Horus musters his armada, Terra itself the object of his wrath. Seated upon the Golden Throne, the Emperor waits for his wayward son to return. But his true enemy is Chaos, a primordial force that seeks to enslave mankind to its capricious whims.

The screams of the innocent, the pleas of the righteous resound to the cruel laughter of Dark Gods. Suffering and damnation await all should the Emperor fail and the war be lost.

The age of knowledge and enlightenment has ended.
The Age of Darkness has begun.

CONTENTS

MEDUSON

Dan Abnett

THERE WERE NO surgical lasers available.

A clustered missile strike over Isstvan V had blown out the *Ionside*'s flank from the lateral exchangers aft, voiding eight deployment bays and the port-side apothecarion chambers. The smaller medicae annex on the ship's starboard side was overwhelmed with life-critical cases. Dying legionaries on stretcher boards were lined up along the hallway.

Shadrak had only lost a hand. He reported instead to a makeshift triage station set up in the forward hold. Most of the staff there were frightened serfs drummed up from the ship's crew. Gorgonson of the Lokopt Clan was the only Apothecary present, the only one that could be spared from the chaos of the medicae annex. He looked at the hand.

'Excise,' he instructed the human attendant waiting nearby. 'Clean down to the forearm bones. Leave some tissue for conjunction and graft. I'll be back to fit the augmetic.'

Gorgonson didn't say anything to Shadrak. There was nothing to say. No. There was a great deal to say – just no words with which to say it.

He treated Shadrak like a piece of broken machinery presented for repair, not as a brother, an old friend or a fellow son of Terra. He didn't even make eye contact. He just moved on to the next case, a battle-brother whose helm had been fused to his cheek by a melta burst.

The human was a young ensign, freckle-faced and red-headed. His anxiety made him seem like a small boy compared to Shadrak's bulk. 'Seat yourself, lord,' he stammered, gesturing to a commandeered suit-room recliner that had a metal service trolley positioned beside it.

Shadrak didn't much care for the term 'lord'. He was a captain, and that word alone was more than sufficient. But he was too tired to correct the serf, too empty. He felt like the tombs of Albia that he had visited as a child: vast and enduring, but long since robbed of the precious things they had once contained.

Using his good hand, he took off his helm and placed it on the deck. Then he unstrapped his weapon belt, so that the harnessed gladius and bolt pistol would not encumber him when he sat. The belt had loops for reload clips. They were empty.

The recliner creaked under his armoured weight. He set his boots on the foot rest, leaned back and placed his ruined left arm on the trolley. It would have been palm up, if he had still had a palm.

The attendant stared at the wound. The hand was missing most of the fingers. It was a bloody mitten of blackened meat, with broken knucklebones protruding like twigs. The wrist was misaligned. The composite ceramite sleeve of Shadrak's iron-black armour was mangled at the cuff, the torn ends stabbing into his flesh.

'Is there pain?'

Truth be told, Shadrak hadn't been aware of any pain – not physical pain, anyway. The *other* pain was too immense, too entire.

Surprised, he answered, 'No.'

'I have no anaesthetic,' the man added reluctantly. 'I have some numbing agents, but resources are so–'

'Just do it,' said Shadrak. His body had autonomically shut down a great number of his neural receptors at the moment of injury. His left hand didn't feel much of anything anymore. It was just a dead weight, like a piece of kit he couldn't unbuckle and remove.

'There are no surgical lasers either,' the serf apologised. Shadrak saw he was wiping a manual bone-saw with a sterile swab. The man's hands were shaking.

Under other circumstances, in other wars, Shadrak would have been amused by the sheer pathos of the situation. But his capacity for amusement was as empty as the tombs of Albia too.

He sighed.

'You'll never get through the vambrace with that,' he said. The man looked as though he was about to panic. 'Do you have medical training?'

'I am a junior gunnery officer, lord,' the man replied. 'But I have my corpsman certificate.'

Again, the 'lord'...

Shadrak reached over with his right hand, unclasped the elbow guard and let it fall to the deck. Then he unfastened the clamps in the crook of his elbow and mid-forearm, and tugged the composite plasteel-and-ceramite sleeve off. Parts of the gauntlet were still attached, flapping loose. The buckled wrist seal was impacted into his flesh, and it took a little more effort to wrench it clear. Fluid and flecks of meat spattered the deck.

He stripped away the undersleeve, tearing the fabric. His exposed skin looked as pale as bone, in stark contrast to the mauled mess of his hand.

'How did this happen?' the man asked, eyes wide at the fully exposed damage.

'Horus happened,' said Shadrak.

He rested his arm back on the trolley. The man approached, gingerly, puffing counterseptic onto the wound from a flask, his hands still shaking. He took a grip on the bone saw, and consulted an anatomical diagram he had called up on the display of his data-slate. Shadrak knew that the man was dying to ask what he had meant, but didn't dare.

He rested the saw's serrated edge against Shadrak's flesh just below his torn wrist. The skin was covered in spots of fast-clotted blood. The serf swabbed them away, and then made the first draw.

There was pain, of course, but it seemed minor and distant.

Shadrak sat back and let it pass over him. He stared at the hold's gloomy roof, into the darkness beyond the hanging lumens. He let his mind fill with memories – memories from before the pain. He tried to recollect something as far from it as possible. Before this minor discomfort, before the greater injury of the dropsite, before Medusa, before the Gorgon, before the Great Crusade…

He thought of Terra, and the last years of the Unification Wars. He thought of his first days as a Storm Walker, serving under Lord Commander Amadeus DuCaine in the theatres of Afrik and the Panpacific. Back then, justly proud of their fresh, gene-herited might, none of them had known what the Storm Walkers would become, or what revision of structure and loyalty they would have to undergo. And even once they had known, they had embraced it wholeheartedly. It had not been a matter of reformation or repair, though fates knew that the X Legion were especially resilient when it came to repair.

It had been a matter of ascendancy.

It had been a blessing. To be called to your primarch's side, to become one of his. Shadrak had cast off his Terran surname, a mortal vestige that had fallen into disuse anyway, and taken the name Meduson to demonstrate and affirm his allegiance to his new home world.

He had become Shadrak Meduson of Clan Sorrgol, Captain of the Tenth Company. The Storm Walkers of Unification had become the Iron Hands. They had expected nothing but glory in their future. Even if calamity chanced to overtake the Iron Tenth on the field of war, it would be a glorious calamity in the Emperor's service.

None of them had ever anticipated this inglorious ruin. None of them could ever have imagined such a measure of raw treachery.

None of them could ever have expected this scale of loss and pain.

'I'm sorry,' the man said.

Shadrak opened his eyes.

Despite his clotting factors and vascular shunts, the top of the trolley was running with blood. It was dripping off the edges and making a rectangular, splatter-pattern halo on the deck. The flesh of his wrist was marked with several bloody hesitation wounds. When the young serf had finally found some confidence and purpose, he had opened a gash like a gasping mouth, but the bone was barely nicked.

The man's hands were shaking more than ever. 'Your bones are very… very strong, lord.'

Shadrak saw that he was sweating.

'They were made that way,' he replied, sitting up. 'Give me that slate.'

The serf handed him the data-slate, and Shadrak reviewed the anatomical graphic as dispassionately as he might check a mechanical diagram. He made a note of the bone formation, compared it with what remained of his wrist, took note of blood vessels and tendon assembly and paid heed to the recommended link points for structural and neural grafting.

'I'll do it,' he said, handing the slate back. 'It'll be quicker.'

The man slowly offered him the bloody saw, but Shadrak had already leaned over the side of the recliner and drawn his gladius. He set the edge of the blade along the clumsy guide cut that the bone saw had scored, paused, and struck his ruined hand off with a single, swift blow. It bounced off the side of the trolley and landed in the pool of blood on the deck. The serf hesitated, as though he felt it would be polite to pick the severed hand up and return it to Shadrak. Then he remembered himself, dropped the saw, and hurried forward to attend with clamps and wadding.

'If it's going to hurt anyway,' said Shadrak as the man worked, binding the stump tightly, 'it's better that it doesn't linger too.'

Good advice, he thought. *Applies to so damned much.*

GORGONSON RETURNED AN hour later and inspected the wound.

'Do this yourself?'

'It seemed for the best,' Shadrak replied.

'You're no surgeon,' said Gorgonson.

'Never claimed to be. But your man there was intent on whittling me down until I was nothing but a spinal column and a rictus.'

Gorgonson frowned. 'We're doing the best we can, given the circumstances.'

'Well, he made more of a mess of me in ten minutes than the damned Sons of Horus could manage in a week.'

Gorgonson glared at him. 'Don't even joke,' he hissed. 'Damn you, Shadrak. Don't even say the words aloud.'

'You don't think I'm angry?' asked Shadrak. 'I'm beyond rage. I'm in another place entirely. White heat and boiling blood. I'm going to butcher and burn every one of the bastards. Give me my new hand so I can get on with it.'

Gorgonson hesitated. They had known each other for twenty-four decades. Like Shadrak, Goran Gorgonson had been a Storm Walker, a son of Terra. They had fought through the Unification Wars side by side. At their ascendancy, Goran had elected to join Lokopt, the clan that most remembered and celebrated the Terran aspect of the founding. But he had changed his name to Gorgonson in honour of the primarch.

'Anger's not going to get us anywhere, earth-brother,' Shadrak said quietly, 'except deader than we are already. Anger's a blindfold, a fool's motivation. I reserve it only for killing blows. We need cool heads and clear minds. This is survival, repair, rebuilding. Terra only knows, we're good at repair – we excel at it, so this should play to our strengths.'

'They're calling a council,' said Gorgonson.

'Who's they?'

'The clan-fathers.'

'A Clan Council?' Shadrak asked. 'What in Terra's name for? This isn't a matter of bloodline and heritage.'

'Isn't it?'

'The clan-fathers are proposing to assume command? *Collective* command?'

'I suppose so. In the absence of...' Gorgonson paused. There were words that were going to be too hard to say, names that were going to be too hard to utter. 'The clan-fathers take control, for now. Isn't there comfort and assurance in that? They are veterans who understand–

'A Clan Council is the last thing we need,' said Shadrak. 'Command by committee? Pointless. We need positive, singular leadership.'

'I didn't know you had aspirations of command,' Gorgonson remarked.

Shadrak thought about that for a moment. The notion came as a surprise.

'I don't,' he replied. 'I've never considered it. I just know we need something now. *Someone*. We're dead without it. Just a shattered rabble.'

Gorgonson sighed. 'Any Apothecary, even the best of us, will tell you that you can graft on a new hand, but you can't graft on a new head.'

'Then we'll have to learn how,' said Shadrak.

A servitor beside Gorgonson was holding the augmetic on a tray.

'Nothing fancy,' said the Apothecary, reaching for a scraper and a neuro-fuser. 'I have no juvenat packing left either, so you'll have to let it bond by itself. Don't test it. It'll be weak. For months, probably. Let it bed in and heal.'

Shadrak nodded.

'Just fix me up,' he said. 'I'm sure I'll have many weeks of calm and leisure to get the healing done.'

Gorgonson started working. 'Is he dead?' he asked quietly.

'Yes.'

'You know this?'

'Amadeus told me,' said Shadrak. 'It was confirmed from the surface.'

'Lord Commander Amadeus is dead too,' murmured the Apothecary.

'Yes. I saw it. But his word lives. The Gorgon is dead, and our step-father Amadeus is gone too. So we can lie down and die with them, or we can learn to graft heads.'

It took eight weeks for the Council to assemble. That meant eight more weeks of running. The Gorgon's martial policy had always been to fight and move on, but this was not the sort of moving on that Shadrak approved of.

They gathered at Aeteria, a lonely rock of sulphurous waste and tainted pink skies on the edge of the Oqueth Sector.

Twenty-nine ships hung low in the heavens, including two Salamanders vessels and three Raven Guard. They seemed ghostly, like dark thunderheads behind the wispy banks of cloud. They were survivors of Isstvan, all of them.

It wasn't much of a council. Only five clan-fathers were present. The fate of the others was unknown, though intelligence data reported that the forces of the Iron Tenth had scattered after the massacre, put to rout. Many of the Raven Guard and Salamanders had fled too. Purge-fleets of the Sons of Horus and the Emperor's Children were reported to be razing system after system in an effort to obliterate any survivors before they could regroup. No reliable figures were available, but it was possible that all three Legions had been reduced to mere thousands.

'We have been... shattered,' said Lech Vircule, Clan-Father of Atraxii, rising to his feet. They had gathered in the courtyard of a ruined monastic structure, built in the Age of Strife and abandoned, like Aeteria, generations before. The lonely walls echoed his words.

'But not broken,' answered the Clan-Father of Felg, Loreson Unfleshed. 'There will be others, like us, meeting in secret as we do now. We are disconnected, but not lost.'

Vircule shrugged.

'We cannot regroup or coordinate,' he said. 'Lines of communication are cut or disadvantaged. No one dares show himself or attempt an open signal. With the traitors abroad in force, any glimpse of us will result in unstinting prosecution.'

'Our structure allows for this, lord father,' said Augos Lumak, a captain of Clan Avernii. He was one of the few members of the gene-sire's favoured to have made it out of the massacre alive. 'Our clan structure, as ordained by the Gorgon, will serve us well. Independent units of command, interlocking. We can survive, by dint of our individual commands, and reassemble.'

The Atraxii clan-father nodded. 'That is to be hoped. Only when unified can we turn and fight back.'

'Then we will never fight back,' said Shadrak Meduson.

There was a silence, filled only by the moan of the wind across the lagoon.

'You spoke, captain?' said the flesh-spare Loreson.

'Quite clearly, lord father,' said Shadrak. 'The accursed Warmaster, may fate smite him, will not give us grace to regroup.'

'We do not need his grace.' The clan-father's voice was a synthetic growl. 'Or his permission.'

'As he did not need our grace or permission to slaughter us, and to murder our gene-father and stepfather alike,' said Shadrak. 'We are not alone in this. Salamanders and Raven Guard stand with us.' He gestured to the ranks of the other Legions present. 'Our brothers of the Eighteenth and Nineteenth follow different martial philosophies. We could learn, learn *mutually*. We could learn to fight in new ways, marry the iron force of the Tenth to the stealth of the Nineteenth and–'

'Our brothers of the Eighteenth and Nineteenth are welcome here,' said Vircule of Atraxii.

'Our losses match yours in scale and grief,' said a Raven Guard captain named Dalcoth. 'We must combine resources–'

'You are welcome here,' Vircule repeated, cutting him short.

'But our words are not?' asked Dalcoth. There was a bitter grin on his lips.

'In time, of course,' said Karel Mach, the Clan-Father of Raukaan. 'But this is Clan Council business and words. Our way of war is not yours, sir. We will not stoop to sly hit-and-run tactics.'

'Stoop?' asked one of the other Raven Guard officers.

'I meant no insult.'

'On the flight here, we spent time discussing operational needs with your captains,' said Dalcoth. 'Meduson of Sorrgol agreed with my proposal that a hybridisation of tactics might avail us of–'

'Captain Meduson should know his place,' said Vircule.

'He was not the only officer of the Tenth who thought so,' said Dalcoth.

'But I was the loudest, so I speak for the notion here,' said Shadrak.

'Eight weeks aboard the survivor ships, crammed in with brothers from other Legions. Of course we talked. It is self-evident that–'

'Know your place, Meduson,' said the Clan-Father of Atraxii more firmly. 'Know your place, Terran-born.'

'I know my place well enough,' said Shadrak. 'It appears to be somewhere on a sulphur-stinking waste at the end of the galaxy. Any delay is going to weaken us further. We are not, and we will never be, what we once were. The Raven Guard are ready to fight. Guerrilla tactics, if necessary.'

Dalcoth nodded.

'The Salamanders too,' said Shadrak.

Nuros, the most senior legionary of the XVIII Legion present, nodded in turn.

'This is Clan Council business,' said Loreson Unfleshed.

'It would seem that the Council does not *know* its business,' replied Shadrak. 'When we lose in war, we are returned to the enclaves and are rebuilt. We are made better than we were before. But that luxury is not open to us now. When we lose on the field, away from an enclave, what do we do?'

'We repair as best we may,' said Karel Mach. 'Battlefield fixes. We make the best of the resources available to us.'

'That is our situation now,' said Shadrak. 'And what is available to us? The good brotherhood of our fellow Legions. The chance to learn, to alter ourselves, and to remake ourselves in ways that the traitors are not expecting.'

'Enough!' barked Jebez Aug. Aug was an Iron Father of the Sorrgol Clan, hailing from Medusa. With his venerable status came great influence. 'You shame our clan with your outspoken remarks, Terran-born.'

'I speak only with respect,' said Shadrak.

'You have shown the Council precious little respect,' said Aan Kolver, the Clan-Father of Ungavarr.

'Indeed, because you have warranted none,' said Shadrak. 'I speak with respect to our gene-sire.'

'Escort the captain from this place immediately,' said Vircule to Aug. 'He needs time to level his head and dull his tongue.'

'WHAT ARE YOU playing at?' Aug asked. Shadrak could feel the Iron Father's anger radiating out like a force field. They stood on the caustic shoreline of the sulphur lake. Acid vapour swirled like battlefield smoke.

'What? We bite our lips now? Even now, in this predicament?'

'Sorrgol has no clan-father here,' said Aug. 'You shame us in the company of–'

'I shame you?' Shadrak shook his head. 'Is that really what matters now? The shame of speaking out? Fates above, we are shamed enough! The clan leaders are groping around, trying to recover something we have lost forever. By the time they reach a decision, we will be discovered and slaughtered. Or if they reach a decision, it will be the wrong one, and we will be slaughtered anyway!'

'We need unification, Shadrak,' said Aug. 'For morale alone.'

'I agree. But under one warleader, with one purpose.'

'One leader?' Aug laughed bitterly. 'Who?'

'You, perhaps?'

Aug spat and looked away.

'No one wants it,' said Shadrak. 'None of us. Not a single captain, not a single Iron Father. That's why the clan-fathers have taken the lead. They are projecting a sense of security, of unity, through our blood heritage. A reassurance in this time of loss through the bonds of fraternity. But it's a group decision, so that no one shoulders the burden alone. No one bloody wants it! That's why no one has stepped forward and called the rally around him.' He looked at Aug. 'No one wants to be seen as trying to replace the Gorgon. No one wants to replace Amadeus DuCaine. No one wants to be seen as that impertinent or disrespectful. I understand it.'

He paused.

'But we need to raise the storm again. No one wants the command.

No one wants to appear so arrogant as to imagine that he can assume the primarch's role. But it's not a matter of want, or pride, or vainglorious ambition. It's a matter of necessity.'

'This talk will get you killed, Terran-born,' said Aug.

'No!' Shadrak snapped, pointing towards the monastery. '*That* talk will get us killed.'

He lowered his hand. The augmetic graft had not fully healed and still ached abysmally. The violence of the gesture had jarred it.

'I have it on good medical authority that you can't graft on a new head,' he said.

Jebez Aug uttered a dry laugh. He shifted his flesh-spare frame and wiped his mouth with the back of his hand. 'You don't need to be a medical authority to know that,' he replied.

'I'm not suggesting that anyone pretend to be the Gorgon. I'm not proposing that anyone presumes he can command as well as Ferrus Manus, or attempt to be such a master. I am simply talking about focus of authority. One mind, one will, one iron drive strong enough to compel us for long enough to...'

'To what?'

'Do what needs to be done.'

'Which is what? Survive?'

'No.' Shadrak looked out over the misted lake. 'You can't graft on a new head, but you can cut off an existing one.' He turned to the Iron Father. 'We need to focus long enough to get Horus. To cut off his head. We decapitate the traitors. We do to them what they did to us. We shatter them, and scatter them to the winds. We end this treachery.'

After a moment, he added, 'Then we can die, for all I care.'

EMBARKATION HAD BEEN ordered. Stormbirds and lifter ships rose from the surface of Aeteria and soared up to the waiting warships.

Shadrak had been posted to the strike cruiser *Iron Heart*. They were to escort the flotilla's flagship *Crown of Flame*. Iron Father Aug gathered the officers of Clan Sorrgol while the ship prepared to make way. The clan-fathers had instructed the respected veteran Aug to take command.

'I believe we have Meduson to thank for this,' he said.

'What have I done now?'

'Our clan has the weakest numbers after Avernii,' said Aug, 'so we have been told by the Council to absorb the overspill into our formations. We are to coordinate with the Salamanders and Raven Guard squads as they are brought aboard, too.'

'So we are bastardised while the other clan-companies stand more or less intact?' asked Captain Lars Mechosa.

'No one's intact,' whispered Shadrak.

'I'd ask you to watch your words, brother,' Augos Lumak said to Mechosa. 'You absorb my Avernii too. Do we make you bastards?'

'No, you make us fatherless,' snarled Mechosa. 'Where were the favoured Avernii at Isstvan? Saving the Gorgon? Why, no! They were dying at his feet.'

'Damn your eyes!' Lumak cried, rising from his seat.

'Sit down, Lumak!' Aug shouted. 'Captain Lumak of Avernii! Sit yourself down! This clan-unit is mine to command.'

'Then bring your foul-mouthed dogs to heel, Iron Father!' Lumak snapped. 'If you expect me to recognise your authority, then you damned well better exercise it and put Mechosa in his place.'

'Captain Lumak–'

'Or I'll do it,' Lumak added.

'Oh, really?' replied Mechosa. 'I would love to see you try, you toothless cur.'

Lumak reached for his sword, but another hand clasped over his before he could draw the blade.

'Don't, Lumak,' said Shadrak through gritted teeth. 'I mean it. Don't.'

'Let go of me,' said Lumak, looking Shadrak in the eye.

'Yes, let him go!' mocked Mechosa. 'I yearn for some sport.'

'Do not unsheathe your blade,' Shadrak whispered into Lumak's face.

'Not in here. Not like this, against a brother. Once it's drawn, it cannot be put away.'

'You Sorrgol bastards,' growled Lumak, 'covering for each other, dishonouring the–'

'My loyalty to Clan Sorrgol becomes more frayed with each passing hour,' said Shadrak. 'I would rather cut it and cast off my chosen name of Meduson. I would go back to my Terran birth name. My loyalty is only to the Tenth, and to the memory of the Gorgon.'

'Then unhand me,' said Lumak.

'We're in the middle of a civil war against traitor Legions,' said Shadrak slowly. 'Is this really time to start another one, inside our own?'

He looked at Mechosa.

'Apologise,' he said, 'right now.'

Mechosa looked down and hesitated.

'Civil war is the greatest crime humanity has known,' Shadrak said to him. 'Brother betraying brother? The very thought sickens me. What about you, Mechosa? Or are you of that disposition too? Do you find it a matter of nothing to draw arms against your own?'

Mechosa looked up, his eyes burning brightly. 'Damn you, Shadrak,' he said.

'Already good and damned,' Shadrak replied. His grip on Lumak's sword hand had not diminished.

'I'm no traitor,' said Mechosa.

'Then stop acting like you're about to become one,' said Shadrak.

Mechosa cleared his throat.

'Brother Lumak, I apologise for my words. We have endured too much. Tempers are weak… Ahh, I make no excuses. There was no call for that.'

Lumak looked at Shadrak. 'Unhand me, brother.'

Shadrak released his grasp. Lumak let go of his sword grip, walked around the table and offered his hand to Mechosa.

'I would that all of Avernii had died, and more besides, if we could have saved the gene-sire,' he said. 'You were not there. You did not see. We did not shirk. We gave all we could. It was not enough. That fact will haunt me until the day I die, surrounded by the butchered corpses of traitors.'

Mechosa took his hand.

'I do not doubt it. I would gladly join you in that death.'

Shadrak sat down as the officers retook their places. His graft throbbed from the effort of keeping Lumak's hand in place.

A thin thread of watery blood sobbed from the cuff of his armour.

A FIST THUMPED on the outer hatch. Shadrak rose, rebinding the blood-soiled wrap around his wrist. He was stripped to the waist, his torso and shoulders showing a hundred old scars. His flesh was inlaid with augmetic circuitry. On his right side, his entire rib-wall was an augmetic plate grafted to his flesh-spare bone. That had been part of him since the Battle of Rust.

'Come!' he called.

His quarters were small and cluttered. Space was limited on the *Iron Heart*.

The hatch opened with a scrape of metal on metal, and Jebez Aug stepped inside.

He looked around.

'Your chamber is no better than mine,' he remarked.

'What do we need more than a deck to sleep on?' asked Shadrak.

Aug smiled. 'I sleep standing up.'

'Are we underway?' Shadrak asked. He knew that they were. He had felt the yawing slip of translation an hour before. His question had been a soft way of asking where they were going.

Aug nodded.

'I need a Hand Elect,' he said, cutting right to it.

To recompense Aug and Sorrgol for becoming a bastard clan, the Council had declared him acting warleader of the fleet under their authority. In practice, this simply meant he was responsible for the clan-fathers' protection. But however compromised a warleader's role was, a warleader always needed a reliable deputy.

'You're asking my advice?'

'I considered Mechosa, of course, because of his record, but he's an ill-tempered brute.' Aug paused, and idly scratched the back of his shaven head. 'I also considered Lumak, as a gesture of good faith towards the Avernii. After today's altercation, I can't favour one without offending the other.'

He looked at Shadrak.

'By the way, my thanks for that,' he added. 'You defused a bad moment.'

'I spoke my mind, Iron Father. That's all.'

'As a Hand Elect should.'

'Me?'

'Yes, sir, *you*, sir.'

'No one likes me,' said Shadrak.

'One of your most appealing qualities. You have been pretty blunt about your demand that somebody steps up and take the reins of authority.'

'Yes, but not me. I have no ambitions above line command.'

'Wasn't that your very point?' asked Aug. 'No one wants the responsibility? The Gorgon's gone, and none of us want to suggest we could take his place.'

'Yes.'

Aug sat down on the cot.

'Shadrak, you're Terran-born. That means that we Medusans, no matter how brotherly we are, either think you're superior because you were gene-reared before us, or dismiss you as not actually Medusa-born true-stock. You favour the welfare of the Salamanders and the Raven Guard more than most. You seem to understand them and liaise with them better than others. You speak your bloody mind all over the place. The clan-fathers despise you. And you're the only man I know who seems to have a clear and singular vision of what we should be doing.'

'Which is?'

'Focusing command and killing that bastard Horus.'

'So you *were* listening to me.'

'Shadrak... for the dubious reasons I've just enumerated, you seem to me to be the wisest choice. I can't think of a better Hand Elect, not when it comes to helping me keep what's left of this clan in line.'

'I suppose the Hand Elect would get a privileged look at our line orders?'

Aug reached into his thigh pouch and produced a data-slate. He tossed it to Shadrak. who caught it, instinctively, with his left hand, and winced.

'What's the matter?' asked Aug.

'Graft's still healing. The augmetic's fine. The flesh is weak.'

He speed-read the slate's summary.

'Several aspects of this I don't like already,' he said.

'I knew you wouldn't,' said Aug.

'Can I consult the other Legions? Share this with them to get tactical feedback?'

'My Hand Elect can do just as he damn well pleases,' said Aug.

DALCOTH, NUROS AND their seniors slapped their fists to their breastplates as Shadrak entered the chamber.

'No need to salute,' he said.

'I think there is,' said Nuros softly. 'You are the Hand Elect. Discipline and respect remind us we're not dead.'

They took their seats around an oval table. Shadrak placed the data-slate in front of him.

'You've seen the data,' he said.

'Troubling,' said Dalcoth.

'Enlighten me.'

'You know already,' said Nuros.

'Doesn't hurt to hear someone else say it.'

'Your clan-fathers are all transiting together on the *Crown of Flame*.'

'The Council stays together,' says Shadrak.

'And forms one nice, big target,' said Dalcoth. 'Idiocy.'

'Clan Council business and Clan Council words,' said Shadrak. 'They are collectively our leadership, now. No one has pre-eminence. They stay together. Consider them as one being – our leader.'

'And one big target,' Dalcoth repeated.

'How did the Tenth ever conquer worlds?' asked Nuros.

'Brute force,' said Shadrak. 'And rigid discipline. It served us well. Superbly well. But we always had the Gorgon and DuCaine to remind us when to break the rules. Now we haven't got the numerical strength to deliver any great degree of force, and we're hidebound by the traditions of our Legion. The Clan Council has always gathered in times of need, to maintain a sense of union and solidarity, especially in the absence of the primarch or the lord commander. I think the custom was all well and good when those absences were temporary.'

'Your Legion must *unlearn* their old ways,' said Nuros.

'I know.'

'Or one of you must step up,' Dalcoth added.

'Jebez Aug has been named as warleader for this endeavour,' said Shadrak.

'An honorific only,' said Nuros. 'That is, if I understand the obscure and shifting lines of allegiance and fealty within your Legion. Jebez Aug answers to the Clan Council. He is only as much of a warleader as they will let him be.'

'I know that too.'

'You should also know,' said Dalcoth, 'with respect, I'm not sure how long the Eighteenth or the Nineteenth can stay with the Tenth Legion formations while this attitude prevails. Singular vision of war leadership is essential, even if it is then divided between autonomous splinter fleets.'

'A council can only advise,' said Nuros. 'It can't command. How long will it take them to reach any tactical decision in the heat of combat?'

'Longer than usual,' said Shadrak. 'No one wants to make the call. Unless we can learn to graft heads back on.'

'What?' asked Dalcoth.

'Nothing. No matter.'

'Let's move on,' said Nuros.

'Oh, let's,' agreed Shadrak.

Dalcoth tapped the slate's screen. 'And this is what we're doing? This is our undertaking?'

Shadrak nodded. 'Sub-vox communiqués have been received. Coded. Iron Tenth battle-cant. There's an Iron Hands flotilla waiting in conceal-ment in the solar shadow of Oqueth Minor. They have Raven Guard forces with them. They're awaiting reinforcement. We're moving to join them. Council's orders. United, we'll form a reasonably serious battlegroup.'

'If I was Horus,' said Dalcoth, 'and I was hunting the remnants of my enemy, I'd want to lure them out of hiding. I'd pretend to be a friend and call for help.'

'Is that Raven Guard tactics?' asked Shadrak.

'Sometimes.'

'Do the traitors know Iron Tenth battle-cant?' asked Nuros.

'Why should they?' asked Shadrak.

'Why *wouldn't* they?' asked Dalcoth. 'We study each other. We all do it. We observe the strengths and weaknesses of our fellow Legions. You can be sure as hell the traitors have done it. How else did they over-whelm us so entirely at Isstvan? We trusted them, and they were right inside our comm-nets.'

'Fulgrim and your gene-sire were good comrades of old,' said Nuros quietly, 'as close as any brothers. There was trust there. But Fulgrim cut off the head of Ferrus Manus without a moment's hesitation. By comparison to that foul act, how little do you think he would have agonised over stealing your ciphers?'

'So this is a trap?' asked Shadrak.

'No,' said Dalcoth. 'We're saying it *could* be a trap.'

'I invite your recommendations,' said Shadrak.

'IF IT COMES to a boarding action, or a counter-boarding response, we'll do it the old way,' said Jebez Aug. 'Tubes. Launches. Ship-to-ship teleportation requires a vast expenditure of power, and it's notoriously unreliable. We're likely to lose a fifth of our forces to an unsecured teleport during combat.'

'Don't worry,' muttered Shadrak, 'they'll mainly be Raven Guard.'

'Your humour grows ever darker, brother,' said Aug.

'Are we going to employ their expertise or not?'

'The clan-fathers will never approve it.'

'They don't have to. You have command. This ship is yours. You are the acting warleader.'

'Is this the true advice of my Hand Elect?' asked Aug.

'You'd better hope so,' replied Shadrak.

Aug pursed his lips, and then nodded.

'Good,' said Shadrak. 'Next, tighter field control on the shields.'

'Useless against long-range fire.'

'But perfect for close quarters, which is what this is going to be if it happens. Next, all ship munitions set for impact detonation rather than timed or ranged. Next...'

SHADRAK HAD NEVER even made it onto the surface of Isstvan V. The clan-companies of Sorrgol had been in the second line with Amadeus DuCaine, an orbital reserve for the Gorgon's main assault.

They had seen the horror blossom across the world below in disbelief. Then it had become a frenzy – first to extract any of their brethren still alive, then simply to fight their way clear. Ships had flamed out all around them. The heavy kill-ships of the IV and XVI Legions had come in gunning, raking their way across the orbital line.

The *Ionside's* escape had been stalled by the cluster strike across her port side. With the drives off-line, they had been boarded. The Sons of Horus had poured in through the breach, hungry to take the killing to a personal level. They had fought in corridors where the decks were streaming with blood. They had fought in voided compartments where the space around them was full of spinning debris and wobbling bubbles of gore and fluid.

Shadrak made war with a bolter in his right hand, and a gladius in his left. His aim had always been better right-handed, his speed and strike superior with his left. That was where his strength and dexterity lay.

He'd just emptied the last of his bolt-rounds through the faceplate of an enemy legionary when the plasma blast mutilated and cooked his left hand. He had picked up his fallen gladius and fought on right-handed.

Not long after that, the frantic teams of enginseers had relit the cruiser's drives and, with a series of desperate and unsteady burns, they had torn free of the enemy ship grappling them.

On the bridge, dripping blood that wasn't all his own, Shadrak had taken the last message from Amadeus DuCaine.

His old friend. His commander from the very start.

'The Gorgon's dead!' DuCaine had yelled at him over the link, the image of him fracturing and breaking up.

'My lord?'

'He's dead! He's gone! Fulgrim butchered him! They're all dying, Shadrak! It's a bloody massacre! An obscenity!'

'My lord, move your ship clear of the line!'

'Too late, boy! The drive's gone for good. Hull plates are splitting. They're inside with us! Bastard bloody—'

The image had blinked away for a second. Then it had come back.

'—ember Rust!'

'Say again, my lord.'

'I said, do you remember Rust? Fates, you were there! You were one of the first, Shadrak – one of my Storm Walkers from the very start! Emperor's bloody own!'

'Yes, my lord.'

'Then don't you forget Rust, boy! Don't you lie down and die! Not ever! You know what kind of horror that horde-fight was! Millions of the greenskin bastards! But we raised the storm. We raised the bloody storm! We prevailed!'

The lord commander's voice had become a brittle screech. Shadrak had not been sure if it was through pain, or the strangling distortion of the vox.

'My lord? Lord Commander DuCaine?'

The image blinked on and off, choppy and broken.

'Raise the storm, Shadrak! Raise the bloody storm, my boy! Tell the Tenth to raise the storm and take every last one of the bastards to hell!'

The image had vanished. The screen had fuzzed with white noise.

Then there had been another, final blink. Amadeus DuCaine was screaming.

'Don't you forget me–'

Dead air.

Off the bow of Shadrak's wounded cruiser, the lord commander's warship had blinked out like a dying comm-link, and been replaced by the heat and light of a newborn sun.

TRANSLATING OUT OF the warp, the survivor fleet decelerated towards Oqueth Minor. It was a pale, baleful star.

'Contacts!' the Master of Detection announced. 'Thirty ships!'

'Code match?' asked Jebez Aug.

'Codes confirmed.'

'Of course they are,' muttered Shadrak.

'Profiles?' asked Aug.

'Pattern match. Several types. All Legiones Astartes fleet-craft.'

'Which is in no way an assurance,' Shadrak whispered to the Iron Father.

'Ramp up visual resolution,' Aug called.

'Standby, commander... Hulls read as blackened. Fire damage. No visible insignia or serial numbers.'

'You don't like this, do you?' Jebez Aug said to Shadrak.

'I haven't liked much of anything since my eighth birthday, warleader,' Shadrak replied.

'Is Dalcoth prepared?'

'He is.'

'I'll lead them if it comes to it.'

'No, warleader. That's the Hand Elect's job. Your place is here.'

'Our flagship is hailing,' reported the Master of Vox.

There was a long wait.

'Codes exchanged. Cipher confirmed. Lead ship is identified as the *Master of Iron*. Clan-Father of Borrgos commanding. The Council is greeting.'

Aug tapped his fingers on the console impatiently. 'Come on, come on...'

'Request for our flagship to draw alongside the *Master of Iron* so that the Council can be united,' reported the Master of Vox. 'The request has been accepted by the clan-fathers.'

'Batteries to power?' asked the Ironwrought Master of Ordnance.

'We dare not risk anything so provocative,' replied Aug. 'But ready the mechanical autoloaders. I want all weapons at my discretion inside ten seconds, if it comes to it. You understand me?'

'Aye, sir.'

'The flagship is under *our* protection,' Aug reminded everyone.

On high resolution, they watched the tortuously slow progress of the *Crown of Flame* as it drew alongside the *Master of Iron*, and secured mooring lines and anchors.

'Council is boarding,' advised the Master of Vox.

They waited again.

'Report?' asked Aug.

'Nothing, sir.'

'It's been ten minutes. Report.'

'Vox is dark, sir.'

'There will be ceremonials,' said Mechosa. 'This is a great day, after all.'

Shadrak was about to warn him about tempting fate, but the Master of Vox cut him off.

'Acoustic echoes,' he said, straining at his augmetic ear plugs, one hand clamped to the side of his head.

'Origin?' barked Aug.

'From inside the *Crown of Flame*. Flattening the signal. I'm trying to wash it to get a clean signature. It sounds like... cheering.'

'I told you,' smirked Mechosa.

'Cheering,' the Master of Vox repeated, and then halted. 'And *gunfire.*'

'Arm the batteries!' Aug roared. 'Shields! Ahead half! Battle stations!'

'Contact group is arming weapons!' the Master of Detection yelled. 'Gun ports opening! Their batteries are charging!'

A light licked up inside the *Crown of Flame*. It stuttered, then grew brilliant, lancing out from every port and launch bay. The flagship began to buckle, as if it was being twisted and wrung out by huge, invisible hands. The hull split and geysers of fire rushed up through the cracks, forming great plumes of burning gas and interior atmospherics.

'Target and fire!' Aug yelled. 'Target and fire!'

The *Iron Heart's* deck shivered beneath their feet as the main batteries began to spit. The blackened enemy ships were already purring forwards and unloading storms of ordnance. Space lit up in a blinding flicker show.

Close quarters, Shadrak thought.

The rest of the warleader's fleet was firing too. Formation against formation, point-blank in starship terms. The flagship was already dead, a burning ruin slowly tumbling away from the enemy's mooring lines and showering incandescent dust, ash and debris into the void. The cruiser alongside the *Iron Heart* shuddered and tore open under the enemy bombardment.

'Get us closer,' Aug ordered. 'Gut them!'

'Raise the storm,' Shadrak whispered.

He looked at the main oculus screen and shuddered. Hololithic projectors upon the prows of the approaching enemy ships had lit up, unfurling bright banners of light.

Each one, in gold and red, revealed the searing Eye of Horus.

The screen blinked.

'Intercept signal!' the Master of Vox called over the general chaos of voices yelling orders.

'Keep firing!' Aug shouted.

'Intercept, sir!' the Master of Vox repeated.

The screen blinked again. A face appeared. It was cold and expressionless, framed in black armour. There was no mistaking the Cthonian aspect of the features: a true son of Horus.

The vox crackled as the image spoke.

'I am Tybalt Marr,' he said. 'You are declared an enemy without reservation. Your extinction is my undertaking. I offer you a plain choice, in simple respect of our old fraternity. Surrender now, and be rewarded with a swift and relatively painless death, or fight on and receive the most excruciating doom imaginable. You have thirty seconds to answer.'

Jebez Aug looked at Shadrak. 'Hand Elect?'

'My warleader?'

'Board the bastard. Bring me his head.'

'Gladly. What are you going to do?'

'I'm going to answer him.'

Shadrak ran to the bridge exit, calling out commands into his vox-link.

Behind him, he heard Jebez Aug open a channel and then begin the most profane stream of invective ever uttered by one of the Iron Tenth.

It was as furious and blistering as the void-war around them.

THE SHIP-TO-SHIP FIGHTING was as intense as any that had occurred above cursed Isstvan. There were fewer ships, but they were so closely packed it was as though they were being swept by artillery bombardment from batteries of monstrous guns. Ships burned. Everything shook. Light-bursts bloomed so brightly that they overwhelmed legionary auto-senses. Rail guns spat. Laser batteries and hull mounts streamed ropes and stutters of light. Hard-round cannons hosed shell loads into shields and hulls, or countermeasured rushing shoals of missiles.

Aug drove his fleet directly in amongst the enemy ships, maximising the effect of his tightly calibrated shields and impact-detonating warheads.

He had been designated warleader, the escort protector of the flagship, and thus, according to structure, was de facto second-in-command to the Clan Council.

And the Council was gone.

'Are you ready?' Shadrak asked as he entered the teleportarium.

Dalcoth nodded. 'All four bays are set and ready for transfer, Hand Elect,' he replied.

Shadrak eyed the mix of battle-ready Raven Guard and Iron Hands on the transmission platform.

He opened his vox. 'Warleader,' he said.

'*Speak,*' Aug replied.

'Request permission to divert power to the teleportation systems. The main batteries will be deprived to the extent of forty-four per cent for the next two minutes.'

'*Permission granted.*'

Shadrak looked at the Master of Transfer as he took his place on the platform beside Dalcoth who drew his bolt pistol.

'Do it!' he ordered.

THEY LOST NINETEEN of their force in the transfer, transmitted atoms scattered like dust by the enemy shielding, or befouled by materialisation inside the dense hull plating.

The interior of the XVI Legion warship smelled of smoke and blood. The lighting was on red reserve, with primary power diverted to weapons and shields.

Coming out of the winding shock of teleport, Shadrak glanced around to get his bearings. Immediately, he saw two Raven Guard planted deep into the deck by mis-materialisation. Both were dead, blood streaming from their dislocated neck seals.

'Move!' Dalcoth yelled.

Shadrak ignited his visor's preysight. The corridor became a luminous green cave. He saw streaks and ribbons of glare as gunfire erupted.

Sons of Horus, night-black in green wash.

Target one. His flickering overlay crosshairs darted. He put a mass-reactive round into a faceplate at ten metres. The traitor's head detonated in a flash that Shadrak's auto-senses read as whizzing shards of ceramite and hot, cooking chunks of bone.

Parts of the ceiling blew out. Fizzling power cables slithered out, jerking like snakes. Dalcoth engaged two of the Sons of Horus, gutting one with his chainaxe, then twisting away from the toppling figure in a neat sidestep to blast a bolt-round into the chest of the other.

The legionary flew backwards, crunched off the wall plating, and left a liquid smear of blood and pulped organs on the panel as he slumped onto his side.

Another came at Dalcoth. Shadrak stepped in and sheared the traitor's head in half cross-wise with his gladius. Blood jetted into the air as the half-headless warrior took a couple of stumbling steps and then collapsed.

Despite the binding and bracing, Shadrak's left wrist stung with the jarring impact of the blow.

'Forward!' he ordered.

Iron Hands Terminators in Tartaros-pattern wargear led the way along the spinal hall, heavy flamers hosing ahead of them. Breacher legionaries flanked the group, their panoplies locked. Shells and bolts rebounded from the shield wall. Then Shadrak heard the shriek of multi-meltas and felt the chest-pummelling thump of heavy bolters.

Heavy contact. The heaviest.

Shadrak passed the fallen form of a Salamander who had been shredded by a volkite caliver. He loosed off mass-reactives into the defensive lines ahead of him. Something energy-laden and sensitive detonated, throwing bodies and deck plates into the air.

'*They have force superiority!*' Nuros voxed.

'Agreed,' Dalcoth cut in. 'If our objective was to take the ship, it is no longer viable.'

'We've barely begun!' snapped Shadrak. 'Are you suggesting we abort?'

'Hit and run tactics,' Dalcoth replied. 'We hit, we run. That way, we live to fight again.'

'Sometimes, with respect, your tactics sound like cowardice,' replied Shadrak. 'How did you Raven Guard ever conquer worlds?'

'By knowing when to fight and when to retreat. It's called tactical restraint.'

'Abort denied.'

'Then select a new objective, Hand Elect!' Dalcoth's voice was temporarily drowned out by gunfire.

'We could loop back to the drive chambers and attempt to trigger an overload,' Nuros voxed. *'My assault group has sufficient charges.'*

'Denied. Objective is now Tybalt Marr's head,' said Shadrak.

'How is that strategic?' yelled Dalcoth.

'It's symbolic. It matters.'

'How did the Tenth ever conquer worlds…?'

'Exactly like this,' replied Shadrak Meduson.

SHADRAK MEDUSON OF the Clan Sorrgol, Iron Tenth, Terran-born Storm Walker, did not achieve his objective.

Not that day, at least.

He was denied by circumstance, by fate, and specifically by a Sons of Horus Terminator that Shadrak's visor display identified as Xorn Salbus.

Shadrak, supported by Raven Guard and Iron Hands Breachers, fought as far as the enemy ship's main bridge interlock. Terminator life-guards met him there, appalled and astonished that the loyalists' boarding effort had cut so far and so deep.

Volkite and bolter fire sliced into the boarding party. Bodies, and body parts, began to pile up in the narrow entrance to the interlock annex. There was turmoil, a deadlock of wicked crossfire.

In cover, returning fire, Shadrak felt his vox chime.

It was Aug. *'Shadrak!'*

'My lord!'

'The day has turned against us, captain. Abort your efforts and jump out.'

'Negative. We are too close. I can smell Marr's fear-sweat!'

Shadrak ducked back, and slammed home a fresh clip.

'I repeat, abort,' voxed Jebez Aug, *'We've crippled seven of their ships, for the loss of nine of ours. But a relief force flying Third Legion colours has*

just translated into the system. They're eighteen clicks out and closing fast. Shadrak, we're outnumbered four to one now. We can break and run, or we can die.'

'My lord...'

'Aren't they the tactics your Raven Guard friends recommended? We've hurt them, and hurt them properly. Let that be enough. Abort and withdraw now, or we leave without you. I'm breaking the grapple lines.'

'Abort. Understood,' Shadrak voxed back.

He knew it was the right decision. In the fever of close combat, his blood was up, and that was clouding his judgment. A full measure of vengeance was never going to be taken in a single day. He had to live, so that he could avenge again.

Still, the temptation to press on just a few minutes longer and take Marr's head as a trophy...

His vox chimed again. This time, it was Mechosa.

'Meduson! Hand Elect! Promise me you're aborting the raid now!'

'Mechosa?'

'The Iron Heart's *bridge is hit! Two salvos. Warleader Aug is dead. I–'*

A roar of blast wash and static drowned out his voice.

Aug was dead. According to the ordained structure, after the Council and the warleader, Shadrak was, by default, next in command succession.

He was warleader now. He had to go where he was needed before the entire hierarchy collapsed in disarray.

'Abort! Abort now!' he yelled. 'All boarding squads trigger abort!'

'Abort confirmed!' Dalcoth called.

'Confirmed!' voxed Nuros.

Further responses echoed in from the X Legion's own boarding officers.

Shadrak fired to cover his men as they fell back. He moved clear of the heavy iron bulkhead so that the teleport could get the cleanest possible lock on him.

The air was thick with smoke and blood mist. A black-plated Terminator loomed out of it.

Xorn Salbus.

The Butcher Salbus, whose reputation for brutality had spread beyond the ranks of his own Legion long before he had turned traitor.

The monster swung his chain-blade.

Smaller and lighter, Shadrak evaded, emptying his clip into the giant's chest plating. Salbus reeled back in a fireball of exploding mass-reactives. Blood dribbled from his peppered, punctured chest, but he remained on his feet.

Shadrak didn't wait for the Terminator to swing his blade again. He lunged forwards and drove his gladius tip-first into the breastplate where it was compromised.

The plating caved like honeycomb. The gladius cleaved through Salbus's chest, clean through, until Shadrak's plunging fist was buried half a forearm deep in the warrior's oozing, throbbing innards.

Salbus shuddered and began to sink. Shadrak tried to pull his hand and sword free. They were wedged tight by the inward-punched ceramite plate.

Sons of Horus were closing all around him. Shadrak saw them, shadows in the smoke. Dalcoth and others were desperately voxing his name.

He pulled again, unable to relax his grip on the gladius in order to slide his hand free.

Salbus fell to one side, dragging Shadrak down with him, who fought to release himself.

One of the Sons of Horus emerged from the smoke, but was immediately blown off his feet. Nuros appeared, blasting into the choking vapour with a captured volkite caliver. There were two of the Iron Tenth boarders and a Raven Guard with him.

'Come the hell *on!*' Nuros yelled.

Shadrak wrenched again. 'Trigger the extraction!' he ordered. 'Go!'

He pulled as hard as he could. Pain flared up his arm, white hot. He felt flesh tear and graft bonds shear.

He pulled his arm free, and left his augmetic hand behind in Salbus's chest.

✠ ✠ ✠

WITH THE LOSS of one more ship, the loyalists broke from the void battle and made a jump at emergency velocities. They left a half-mauled enemy fleet and a debris halo of burning hulls in their wake.

JEBEZ AUG WAS not dead. The strike on the bridge had taken his right arm and leg, and ruptured several organs. But he had survived.

'He will make recovery in time,' the Apothecaries told Shadrak, 'but it will be months, and he will be more flesh-spare by the end of the process.'

Shadrak sat at the Iron Father's bedside, watching the vital monitors flicker.

Aug stirred.

'Shadrak…' He smiled weakly. 'Did you bring me the head?'

'I failed to do that, warleader,' Shadrak replied. 'Another time.'

'We tasted some vengeance today,' murmured Aug.

'Too little, and at a terrible cost. But it is a start and, if nothing else, we have learned what we must do from here on. We have learned what it means to be shattered, and the path we must follow if we are to achieve our vengeance.'

'Singular focus of command,' said Aug.

'Yes, that. For this force, and for any broken unit like us. But more than that. We must learn to pace ourselves. Tactical restraint. To hit and run, and not to be greedy and trust in overwhelming power as of old. We must learn the tactics and techniques of those thrown in with us and respect them. We must take our iron and alloy it with the mettle of the others who were shattered alongside us. We must mix our broken strength with other broken strengths to forge a new, unbroken edge.'

'Spoken like a warleader,' whispered Aug.

'I am Captain of the Tenth Company, my lord, and you are living yet.'

'In some degree,' Aug smiled. 'Shadrak, I will not be fit for command for a long while yet. These days are too crucial. The line of authority must be constant and unwavering. There must be continuity.'

'Yes, but–'

'You know this is the truth of it, Shadrak. You have always been sharper on tactics than me. See the truth of it now, and do not fight me on this. I am too tired to beat you into submission.'

Shadrak smiled. It was the first time he had truly smiled in a long while.

'I see the truth of it,' he replied. 'But I want it recorded that this is not something I ever asked for.'

Aug nodded.

'That will be recorded. Shadrak, those who aspire to command are seldom the ones best fit to take it. Since Isstvan, you have proven yourself to be the most clear-sighted of us all. The right hour chooses the right man. The right man emerges in the right hour. This is your time, Shadrak. The Tenth Legion needs you. Consider it destiny, if you will. And it may be unwanted by you, but you are the one who must seize it. You are not presuming to take the Gorgon's place – the void he left has called you to this duty. No one will oppose you, or they will answer to me. Help me up.'

Shadrak eased Aug a little more upright with his good hand.

'Witness this!' Aug called out.

Dalcoth, Nuros, Lumak and Mechosa entered from the outer chamber.

'My last act as warleader is to name Shadrak Meduson as warleader of this battle group. Bear witness, and honour him with your loyal service.'

They nodded and slapped their fists to their chestplates.

'I will need a good Hand Elect,' Shadrak said, rising. He looked at the others. 'I will need the finest force captains too. I want the four of you, and any men, officers or line troops, that you choose to recommend. This is a moment to trust on experience, not the rote of seniority.'

He raised his fist in the old salute of Unity.

'My first act as warleader is to name Iron Father Jebez Aug as my Hand Elect. If you will serve, brother, and suffer the indignity of our reversal.'

'No indignity, but I am not fit,' said Aug.

'You will be. Until you are on your feet again, these four will jointly serve in the role of Hand Elect as a… What is it they call it again?'

'A Mournival,' said Dalcoth.

'Ah,' said Shadrak. 'Just so. But I dislike that term. You are the four quarters of this whole, until Jebez Aug is remade.'

THEY LEFT THE chamber to let Aug rest.

'Go to the bridge,' Shadrak said to Mechosa. 'Open the wide-band comms, and send a direct signal. Iron Tenth cipher. For the attention of Tybalt Marr, son of Horus. Let the message read, "Days will pass. Years perhaps. But know this, traitor. I will raise the storm, and I will find you, and I will take your head. This I swear by the blood of the Iron Tenth and the memory of my gene-sire. Shadrak Meduson, warleader." Understood?'

'You would put your name to this?' Mechosa asked. 'Why?'

'Because a shattered Legion of survivors inspires no dread,' Meduson replied. 'So we will give them a name to fear. Each strike we make, each blow we deliver, we will leave my name in blood until it breeds in them a terror for their very souls. The Sons of Horus are no match for the wronged sons of Medusa.'

GORAN GORGONSON CLEANED the ruptured stump and began his repairs. Ceiling fans breathed cold air into the apothecarion chamber.

'Is there pain?' Gorgonson asked.

'None at all,' replied Shadrak.

The Apothecary showed him the new bionic he was about to graft in. 'A better design. Superior function and strength. *If* you let it bed in this time.'

'I can't promise anything,' replied Shadrak.

Gorgonson lit the surgical laser to excise splintered bone. He had alloy mixed ready to remodel the bone ends and make them fit to receive the graft.

'What was your name?' he asked as he worked.

'What?'

'Your birth name, earth-brother. From before. Before you were Meduson, before you and I were made Terran-born Storm Walkers.'

'Smyth,' said Shadrak.

'Smyth?'

'You were from Solar Stellax as I recall, Goran. Smyth is a name all too common in Old Albia where I was raised.'

'But you appreciate the deeper meaning? A worker of metal? A craftsman with a forge?'

'I do. I seem to have a fondness for symbolism.'

'You've forged something powerful today, Shadrak.'

'I will forge better tomorrow, Brother-Apothecary,' said Shadrak Meduson, 'and the day after, and, even better still, the day after that. Give me my hand, Gorgonson. Make me whole and give me my hand, so that one day soon I might close my fists around the throat of Horus Lupercal and choke him until his filthy light goes out.'

AFTER THE REPAIR was finished, Gorgonson left Shadrak alone.

His arm bound to his chest, the new warleader rose from the surgery cot, and walked to one of the chamber's thick-lensed ports.

He stared out. He saw only infinite blackness.

He knew that somewhere in its enfolding embrace, lost and scattered in the darkness, were the souls of the ones that had lived, souls that he would struggle to unite until death claimed him.

And out there too, blacker than the void by far, were the treacherous souls of the ones he would destroy.

UNFORGED

Guy Haley

'It's DEFINITELY DOWN there?' asked Jo'phor.

Hae'Phast checked his hand-held auspex. The screen displayed the topography of the area in tightly-bunched lines. Where the ravine split the land, the lines gathered into one thick band. A red dot pulsed at their centre, a Salamanders Legion designation screed hovering over it.

'The reading is clean, Jo'phor. A Stormbird, designation Warhawk VI. One of ours. All the codes are correct.'

'How far down?'

Hae'Phast removed his helmet and scratched at his face. The lines of his coal-black features were etched with pale grime, and his beard reached past the lip of his plastron. The last weeks were a blur of frantic escapes, scavenging, furtive dawn marches. Time had become a meaningless value that their suit systems enumerated. Their armour was battered, the colours unrecognisable, stripped down to dirty metal, or scorched black.

'Hard to tell,' he said. 'There might be a ledge down there, could be on that. It might be down at the very bottom – that's two kilometres.'

'We have to ask ourselves, assuming it is whole, then how did they get it down there?'

Hae'Phast grunted. 'It's not that narrow. I knew a veteran pilot attached
to the Twelfth Chapter. He could thread a needle with a Thunderhawk.
I don't see many places that are any better to put down without alert-
ing the traitors.'

Jo'phor stared into the ravine. Noon had passed three hours ago.
The bottom was lost in shadow. Midnight lurked there, unconquered
by the sun.

'It is a suitable place to hide a Stormbird.' He blinked several times,
his eyes gritty with tiredness. They had gone past the point where the
gifts of the Emperor could help them. Not since his transformation
had he been so sorely pressed. He knew it was even harder on the
neophyte, Go'sol.

'I don't see how it matters,' Jo'phor said. 'Either it is an extraction
team, or it is a trap. We can go down there or we can walk away. A
simple choice.'

Hae'phast slid forward on his belly to gain a better vantage, but he
saw no more than Jo'phor did.

'We might die if we do, or we will die if we don't,' Jo'phor continued. 'Is that our choice, between probably and certain death? Or are
we losing focus, brothers. Are we giving up?'

Hae'Phast's face set. The light of his eyes, low as embers these last
days, flared angrily. 'Never,' he said.

Sulphurous winds blew out of a grim sky. Mountains of black granite
stretched away in every direction, the land between faulted by gaping
chasms. Somewhere to the south was the Urgall Depression, although
where *exactly* Jo'phor was no longer sure. That was a good thing. The
chaotic terrain baffled their auspex and armour systems. If they found
the mountains difficult, so would the traitors.

They had seen no one else for days. Jo'phor sometimes entertained
the idea that they were the only living things on the planet. At other
times, when the sorrow overwhelmed him and the world took on a
distant, brittle quality, he thought that they might all be dead.

There were similarities between Isstvan V and his home world of

Nocturne. Both were landscapes crafted by volcanic upheaval, but Nocturne heaved with furious vitality. Isstvan's heart was cold and still, its surface nigh on lifeless. Up in the mountains, the air was so bitter that even the world's meagre apportionment of low order vegetation would not grow.

If Nocturne were to die, it would be like Isstvan V. Jo'phor could not imagine a more fitting hell for his Legion.

Away to the south, a straight line gave away the location of one of the ancient xenos highways. Who they were and what had happened to them was lost to prehistory. They were dead too, their works mere monuments to the futility of existence.

Jo'phor looked away from the canyon to the rest of his pitiful squad. 'I can't make this decision. Brothers?'

The four of them looked at each other. Hae'Phast curled his lip. 'I say let's do it. Better a slim chance than no chance at all.'

'Go'sol?'

The Scout thought a moment. 'Hae'Phast is right,' he said. He had abandoned the honorifics due to the others several days ago. He had proven himself to them time and again. In their eyes at least, he was a neophyte no longer. 'What choice do we have?'

'Donak?' said Jo'phor.

The last of their number was silent. His features were so tense they were like a clay model that had been carelessly crumpled before firing. He did not speak. As far as the others knew, he was unable. Only Donak could have told them, but he had not uttered a single word since he had joined them. His eyes flickered as they danced from face to face. He nodded once, and drew his knife.

'Then we are decided,' said Jo'phor, sliding back from the edge. 'We go down.'

THE DESCENT WAS arduous. The ravine's side was a twisted mass of boulders and grotesque rock formations. The mountains were young; their rock had been rapidly formed and was as fragile as glass. The trek took

hours. The weight of their armour caused seemingly solid rock to give
way beneath them. Several times they doubled back to find a safer way,
until they came to a place where they had no alternative – a vast scree
cone, high as a mountain itself, the far side blocked by a cliff that pre-
vented them from skirting the top.

'I don't like the look of it,' said Jo'phor. 'The material looks unstable.'

'It is unstable,' said Hae'Phast. He threw a rock into the centre of
the scree. It stuck fast, but a portion of the slope slipped dangerously
around it.

Loose rock and sand mantled the slopes as far as they could see
downwards. The execresences of lava that made up the upper slopes
were buried beneath it.

'We're not turning back,' said Hae'Phast. 'We're almost there.'

They stood precariously, legs locked against the treacherous black
stone.

'I'm lightest,' said Go'sol. 'I don't have full battleplate, so I'll take a
line.'

'You don't have to do this, brother,' said Jo'phor.

'Yes, I do.'

From their utility pouches, the Space Marines pulled out emergency
rappels – fifty metres apiece of string-thin high tension cable. Go'sol
linked them together, then bound one end around his waist. Hae'Phast
drove his combat knife into a cleft in the rock and tethered the other
end to its hilt.

Cautiously, Go'sol crabbed his way across. Shattered stone skittered
away from his feet as if startled. The Scout froze, his fingers spread,
ready to grab for any purchase he could. He looked as though he were
trying to placate the mountain itself.

But the debris moved no further, and Go'Sol went on. Shortly after,
he made the other side.

Hae'Phast tested the rope after Go'sol hauled it taut. 'That's as good
as it'll get.'

'I'll go next,' Jo'phor offered.

A hand grabbed his arm. Donak shook his head and pushed past him.

His great, armoured weight sent miniature avalanches slipping down the mountainside. He slid on the material all the way across, almost losing his footing towards the end. Only the line saved him.

He announced his arrival with a single vox-click.

'Now me,' said Jo'phor. He checked the knife.

'It will hold, or it will not,' said Hae'Phast gruffly. 'Cross, brother.'

Jo'phor gripped the line. It seemed ethereally slender, almost impossible to feel through his gauntlets. The drop below was staggering. The slope was so steep that its integrity must have been at the utmost limit of material tolerance. He went slowly.

By the time he joined Donak and Go'sol at the foot of the cliff, it was dark.

'Hae'Phast,' he said, risking the vox.

'*On my way.*'

The line twanged with Hae'Phast's every step. The light from his helm became steady as he fixed his eyes on his destination.

He paused. 'Brothers. There is–'

He never finished.

The line went slack. Jo'phor switched to light amplification in time to see Hae'Phast fall, his arms windmilled. He toppled backwards, tumbling head over heels, dislodging rolling curtains of stone as he tried to dig in with his hands. But he could not hold on, and slithered away into the dark.

A rumble heralded the avalanche. Hundreds of tonnes of rock sheared away. Hae'Phast's helm lenses flashed once more in the gloom, far below, and the mountainside followed him.

As the thunder of the fall subsided, Jo'phor searched the night.

'Do you see him? Could he have survived?' Go'sol whispered desperately.

In the green-tinted, static-laden view that Jo'phor's helm provided, he saw nothing but settling dust. Hae'phast's vital signs were flat.

'No,' he said. 'He is gone.'

From there, the way was easier.

✠ ✠ ✠

JO'PHOR PUT HIS head around the corner carefully. He had his boltgun in his hands. The ravine floor proved wide enough to take a gunship, bringing the slippery rush of hope. They were close enough now for his battleplate's short-range sensors to pick up the locator signal. He had a thumbnail map active in the top right of his vision plate, the beacon there pulsing red. A bight floored with black sand greeted him. On the other side was a crag. He pulled his head back in.

'Is it there?' asked Go'sol hopefully.

'There's a spur of rock. The signal's coming from behind that,' said Jo'phor. 'Even if someone's watching, we should be able to get across without being shot at.'

'We should try signalling them. We should turn our identification markers back on. If there is someone here, and they're friendly–'

'We have few friends left on this rock,' interrupted Jo'phor. 'Chances are it's a trap. We'll have to risk it.'

'And if it's not?' said Go'sol.

Donak, as always, said nothing.

They ran across the sand, eyes upon the cliffs and scree around them. As they rounded the corner, Jo'phor's hearts sank.

There was no gunship.

The locator beacon was genuine, but there was no sign of the Stormbird that once housed it. The apparatus was propped up against the rock face. Above it three words were scraped onto the rock, almost luminously white in the dark:

WELCOME TO PURGATORY.

The air cracked gently – the characteristic report of a legionary sniper rifle. Jo'phor spun around. Go'sol collapsed, shot cleanly through the head.

A second shot caught Donak in the arm. He fell sideways, sprawling for cover.

Jo'phor threw himself to the side as a third shot spacked into the ground exactly where he had been standing. The Emperor's gifts came alive, supercharging his metabolism. Time slowed. Conscious thought receded. What little was left of his humanity was submerged. The alterations to his mind bypassed his frontal lobe, reaching under it for the more primitive, efficient systems it overlaid. Before he knew it, he was running, his body and armour working in tandem. He functioned optimally despite his weariness. He was a weapon, forged to the Emperor's design. His helm's auto-senses switched to thermal and highlighted three heated paths through the cold night, still coherent though warped by air currents.

A las-weapon's discharge track.

Another round flared across his lenses. He had his bolter up to his shoulder, laying down a suppressive burst as a figure moved to engage him from behind another boulder. The warrior was forced to duck back.

He could see them now – five traitors betrayed by plumes of hot air vented by their armour's cooling plants. They were visible to him as writhing columns that flattened themselves out six-point-four metres up against a cap of cooler air, their tops dragged into cirrus shapes by sluggish laminar flow at the thermal boundary. His racing mind tracked them all. He fired on fully automatic the moment he saw a cooling vent protrude over a rock.

His infravision flared as the nozzle was caught and detonated, the blasts of other shells bursting all around it. The traitor was flung around by the hit, and his hand appeared bright in the false-colour image as he steadied himself. This Jo'phor missed, but by then he was bounding up the slope, using the talus that sheltered the traitors as stepping stones. Donak had gained cover and was firing from behind Jo'phor, keeping the enemy pinned down.

So be it. If they were to die, let them take a few more of their treacherous kin with them.

Bolt fire blasted the fragile rock into pinging shards all around him, the rest of his foes abandoning caution as he closed.

He reached the rock sheltering the first Space Marine and scrambled over the top, slaying him with three fast shots, gun pointed down as he leapt across the gap to the next boulder.

The vox clicked. *'Stop! Stop!'* came a frantic voice.

Jo'phor detected cowardice. His hatred for those who had slain his father, betraying the great dream, howled in his mind and blotted out all else. Let them beg for mercy. He had none to give.

The next traitor was ready for him. Bolter shots raked across his breastplate. Two were deflected, but two more penetrated the cabling on his front. Gas hissed. Power was abruptly cut to his left leg. He sagged, off balance. The foul taste of Isstvan's unfiltered air filled his mouth. The fifth blasted through the joint at his shoulder, embedding itself deep inside his chest. The bolt blew, shredding both his hearts and his lungs.

His armour contained the explosion. Somehow he survived, but his time was ending. He fell forward, coughing blood into his visor.

A figure appeared from behind a rock twelve metres away. Jo'phor's eyes widened.

A Salamanders unit identification rune pulsed in his viewplate.

The legionary threw down his sniper rifle and broke into a run. 'No… *No!'* He reached Jo'phor and caught his arm. 'Brother! What have we done? Cease fire! Cease fire all of you – they are ours!'

Other ident-runes blinked into life, smeared out by Jo'phor's fluids. *Iron Hands.*

The Salamander wrestled Jo'phor's helmet off – the world was already dimming as it clanged off the rocks. The Salamander held up Jo'phor's limp head with cold metal gauntlets.

'Brother! Brother!' The warrior's voice was anguished. Such pain. It was no terrible thing to be leaving all this behind, Jo'phor realised. 'No, stay with us! Stay with us! What have we done?'

Jo'phor could no longer see. A fearful roaring filled his ears. Through it, Jo'phor heard Donak bellowing wordlessly into the desolate night.

He felt a sense of vague disappointment, but his war was over.

IMMORTAL DUTY

Nick Kyme

I have erred, and so I must atone.
I lived when I should have died, and so I must become Immortal.

– Oath of the Immortals

ON MY KNEES, I faced the ship's deck. The contorted faces of my brothers stared back, frozen in their last tormented moments.

My name is Ahrem Gallikus and I am Immortal, but this was the day that I was supposed to die.

It was my right. My destiny, one that I alone set in motion long before the fields of our greatest ignominy. Long before Isstvan.

A chill pricked the skin at the nape of my neck, between the black adamantium gorget and a closely shorn scalp of coal-dark hair. At first I thought it was the starship's atmospheric recirculation lacing the air with frigidity, until I realised it was the axe blade poised in judgement.

Mercifully, the edge remained enervated or I would surely have been dead already. But then why imbue it with an actinic sharpness when a simple heft and cleave will do the job just as well?

Logic. Efficiency. Temperance.

Forged together, these words were our creed. A bond of iron, I always believed. Where was this alloy in our father when he needed it most? Again, as they often did in those days of bereavement and grief, my thoughts turned to melancholy.

'Ahrem,' uttered a voice from the shadows surrounding me, as sharp as the naked blade against my flesh. 'Tell us.'

He used my given name, the one afforded to me by the chieftain of Clan Gaarsak, and it grated in my ears. He had no right to use that name.

'I am Legionary Gallikus, Order Primii,' I replied with minimum respect. Back then I saw it as needless theatre, all of this.

'Gallikus, then,' uttered the voice a second time, the irritation in its timbre unmasked. 'We have questions. You will answer them.'

The axe blade descended incrementally, nicking my skin to draw a bead of blood. I saw my breath fog in the cold, stagnant air; felt the thrum of the *Obstinate*'s impulse engines resonating from the lower decks; heard every minute adjustment of my interrogator's posture in the low, predatory growl of his armour.

I was at peace, ready for my duty to end. My immortal duty. I lowered my head a fraction in gentle supplication.

My interrogator took that as an indication to proceed, which it was. In a way.

'Tell us of the *Retiarius*.'

The name of that vessel put fire in my veins, banishing the cold of the hangar deck as my mind was cast back to hot halls, crimson and black. Sweat, blood, death... it all collided in a moment of searing recollection. It did nothing to warm the frozen flesh of the battle-brothers who stared back at me, dead eyes fixed wide in their decapitated heads.

I wondered briefly if the method of execution was meant to be symbolic, ironic or inadvertently in bad taste.

'Tell us what you remember.'

I remembered fire in the upper atmosphere of Isstvan, and hell reigning across the heavens. But this was amorphous, an impression only. An emotional response.

I considered the possibility of sanction if I had admitted that. Emoting is supposed to be anathema to the Iron Tenth. I am sometimes led to wonder if life itself is, too. Instead, the first memory hit me. It felt like a mailed fist, but sang with the thunder of a battle-barge's opening broadside...

'BLOOD OF MEDUSA!'

Mordan was seldom given to such outward expression, but our path to the *Retiarius* was proving volatile.

Harnessed in the assault ram's dual prows, my brothers were giving off the same, albeit unspoken, sentiment.

Katus gripped his breaching shield double-fisted and held it across his chest like a totem. The bionic eye he wore in his right socket flared with nerve-induced auto-calibration.

Sombrak ground his teeth. He was my shield-brother and did it before every battle. It was loud and discordant because his jaw was cybernetic. Most of us were patched up thusly, our broken bodies rebuilt so that we could wage war one final time.

This was my eighth 'final time'. Fate could be cruel like that.

Azoth was the last brother I knew well, though in all there were ten souls armoured in Medusan black in the hold. The rate of attrition was grievous amongst our ranks, and I soon found little need to learn names.

Of all my brothers, those known and unknown, Azoth was the most prone towards rhetoric. When we were made Immortal, our father stripped us of rank and title. Reforged, our new calling was a badge of shame to all in our Legion, and we lost our old identities. I believe that Azoth had been a *Frater Ferrum* – an Iron Father – before he fell from grace. He still had the gaps in his armour where they had unbolted his servo-arm. Whatever he had been before, now he was our sergeant.

He called out to us, bellowing against the tumult within the hold.

'Forlorn hope! Our ranks have never been breached. Be steadfast.' I could hear the servo-grind of his gauntlet as he gripped the haft of his thunder hammer. 'Be resolute. Our dishonour demands it of us. Death awaits. We do not fear it! For what is death…?'

'To those who are dead already!' I roared in unison with my brothers.

He had a way with words, old Azoth. I think I will miss him the most.

Warning klaxons sounded, coinciding with a rush of crimson light flooding the low ceiling above us. We were close, but that was no guarantee of us reaching the *Retiarius* intact.

Over thirty assault rams were cast out into the void, all ridden by Medusan Immortals. I doubted that even half would make it through.

A Caestus was a durable vessel, fashioned specifically for this purpose. It was fast too, but the sheer amount of weapons fire erupting between the two larger vessels across the gulf of space was intense.

Great tracts of the void separated the *Gorgonesque* and the *Retiarius*, littered with silent explosions like scarred nebulae, and immense clouds of rapidly dispersing shrapnel. To us, aboard our diminutive assault ram, it was a long and perilous journey. To those two great behemoths, it would be regarded as close range.

As our hull shuddered with every close impact, the inertial suppression clamps held us steady. I closed my eyes and imagined our destination.

I had seen the *Retiarius* before, during the Great Crusade. Back then it had been an ugly, hulking vessel, well-suited to its brutish occupants. Its flanks were stained azure and dirty white, the echo of legionary war-plate. Slab-nosed and upscaled with muscular fighter bays and ablative armour plating, it was reminiscent of a pugilist in the form of a starship.

I felt our punch resonate through the Caestus's hull, a glass fist striking a jaw of steel. Were it not for the magna-meltas burning furiously to soften the *Retiarius*'s formidable hide then we would have been dashed to wreckage in an eye-blink.

As it was, we bit deep. Our glass fist had shards, and these had cut the outer flesh of the much larger vessel.

We broke through amidst an evaporating cloud of ferric smoke, our small assault ram having bored through the starship's hull and clamped securely in place. Disgorged onto a dark, semi-lit hangar we had little time to get our bearings before counter-boarding troops arrived to try and repel us.

'Lock shields!'

Azoth bellowed out the command, but we had already begun to form up.

It was an archaic tactic, reminiscent of the Romanii or Grekans of Old Earth, but it was effective. Much about war endures, fraternal conflict being foremost in my mind as we breached a vessel that we had once considered to belong to our allies.

But it was mortal armsmen and not our erstwhile brothers in arms, the World Eaters, that we faced upon that deck.

A strong, determined fusillade hit us first, hot las raining in from hastily erected weapon teams and broken firing lines. We held, soaking up their fire, taking everything they threw at us without flinching. Then we pushed on, moving as one, the aegis of our breacher shields impenetrable to the brave men and women who had come to stop us.

Despite their obvious disadvantage, the *Retiarius*'s mortal troops went in close. Three further assault rams had struck this section of the ship and all four squads came together before the armsmen hit us. Their solid shot weapons and mauls proved fatally ineffective.

The feeble momentum of their attack was dispersed when they shattered against our shield wall, and we absorbed the impact before returning it tenfold. Medusan war-oaths cut the air as cleanly as any blade.

And almost as deadly.

The mortals quailed before our seeming inviolability and fury.

I battered my first opponent, letting the blood from his broken skull spray against my shield before I finished him. The stomp of my foot was all it took, and suddenly I was pushing forwards with my immortal brothers. I shot a second through the cheekbone, his face erupting into mist as the mass-reactive shell exploded. I barged a third, splitting ribs. A fourth fell back in front of me against our advance and I severed his neck with the edge of my breacher shield, barely noticing the blood wash against my armoured boot.

Our purpose made us ruthless. A blockade around Isstvan's upper atmosphere was preventing the X Legion from reaching its father, with the *Retiarius* just one of the vessels impeding our path. Our mission was simple. Our Iron Fathers had been clear. Destroy the ship by any means possible. If that meant our deaths, so be it.

Inexorable, inevitable, we crushed the counter-assault forces from the *Retiarius*. Then we cut down the weapons teams, then the deckhands, until every crewmen in sight was slain. It was an honourless but necessary act.

After this, we broke ranks to quickly neutralise the rest. The deck was slick with enemy blood, but it was hard to discern in the dull light.

'Where are we?' asked Mordan.

'Aft of the enginarium, I think,' I replied. I knew a little of the vessel's layout, in so far as it would adhere to extant expeditionary fleet schemata. 'In one of the smaller hangar bays, near the ship's outer skin.'

A relatively small chamber with a low ceiling and bare deck plate underfoot, the hangar would have been used to cloister the *Retiarius*'s various smaller interdiction craft. For now, it was empty of starfighters and assault craft, the World Eaters having disgorged their entire complement to duel with the Iron Hands vessels attempting to break through the blockade. Instead, ammo hoppers and riggers crowded the narrow space. Rigging chains hung down from overhead pulleys, gently swaying in the aftermath of the battle. Steam plumed from vents in the walls, and it was sweltering. A pervasive, animal heat lathered every surface in a fine veneer of sweat. It stank.

The vox-feed in my ear crackled. Communal channel. As expected, the voice of Brother-Captain Udris of the *Gorgonesque* came through the void-static.

Azoth told him that we had successfully made ingress and were moving deeper into the vessel. Resistance had been minimal.

We all knew that would change.

'The blockade?' asked Sombrak, when Azoth had finished receiving his orders from the *Gorgonesque*.

'Still intact,' Azoth replied. 'We'll know if it isn't. These halls will be filled with fire, the walls will shatter and we'll be cast to the void. For now, they stand. So we must sunder them. The Avernii are dying below us, brothers.'

'I would have liked to stand with the Gorgon one last time,' said Katus, his head bowed.

Azoth clapped a gauntleted hand on his shoulder. There was an underlying anger in the former Frater's tone. At the betrayal unfolding on Isstvan or the stripping of his rank, it could be either or both.

'Aye, Katus. So would I, but we have our lot and it is here aboard the *Retiarius*.'

We moved out, leaving the dead to fester in the heat.

As soon as our breach had been detected by the bridge crew, the *Retiarius* locked down its bulkheads and sealed all blast doors, seeking to contain us in a non-vital part of the ship.

While two of my brothers with lascutters went to work cleaving open the blast door to the hangar, the rest of us adopted a defensive posture. Azoth took me aside. His mood was grim.

'No word from the other squads,' he told me. 'Cunaeda, Vorrus, Hakkar...' he shook his head. 'Thirty-three assault rams went out. Currently, I only know of four that reached the *Retiarius* and they stand in this hangar. How far is the enginarium?'

'It's relatively close,' I said, recalling the schematics eidetically, 'but there are warrens of tunnels and chambers beyond those doors before we reach it.'

Azoth nodded, looking to my side rather than at me, as if I had just confirmed what he already knew in his gut. He spoke with some resignation. 'This was always a suicide mission...'

Of all the Immortals I had known and fought beside, Azoth seemed
the least sanguine about dying to restore his impugned honour. Or
perhaps it was dying with what he felt was his honour *still* impugned.
Azoth was brave, the equal of any Iron Hands legionary – including
the noble Avernii – but I suspected his fervent wish was to return to
the order of Iron Fathers before he fell in battle.

But we were ghosts now, all of us, our honour as incorporeal to us
as smoke. We had erred, and so we had to atone, or so the oath went.

The blast door from the hangar went down, heralded by a resound-
ing clang as it hit the deck on the other side.

More gloom, more visceral darkness. Sweltering heat struck us like
a fist, even more palpably than before. Impulse droning from the
nearby enginarium was deafening. The thunderous report of broadsides trembled the deck underfoot and the walls shook with vibrational
recoil. Petrochemical stink merged with the actinic aftertaste of recently
discharged laser batteries wafting upwards from the lower decks.

A starship at war was as brutal a battlefield as any, but the *Retiarius*
deserved infamous acclaim for its severity.

The power-armoured warriors who came at us from the sweat-drenched
shadows were testament to that.

First blood went to the World Eaters.

Clad in beaten up war-plate, festooned in spikes and studs, the
sons of Angron looked worthy of their name. Blood and grime tarnished them, lending further ferocity to an appearance where no more
was needed. Froth bubbled up through their rebreather grilles and
fever-sweat scented the air. Savage, snarling, brutal – I saw animals
coming at us from the shadows, not men. Their martial prowess was
daunting, even to us.

An Immortal I did not know cried out, shield arm hanging slack
with his vulnerable shoulder joint cut and the tendons beneath it
severed. A second blow went from left clavicle to right hip. After over-
coming inertial resistance, the two body halves slid apart and spilled
my brother across the deck.

A plasma pistol at close range evaporated the head of another Medusan who reacted too slowly. Three more in the front few ranks were savagely gutted. Chainblades – both swords and axes – growled bestially.

Like an animal that was suddenly aware that it had been wounded, we recoiled. First we closed the breach from the door, keeping our enemy on the far side, so they couldn't spill out and surround us. Then we fought back.

A strong push that was as much about Medusan tenacity and grit as it was the durability of our breacher shields saw us gain a footing in the first corridor section beyond the blast door. Our enemy yielded to us, surrendering ground without choice, but then trammelled any further progress with ferocity and sheer weight of bodies.

It was impossible to count, but I reckoned twice our number thronged the warren of corridors before us. We breached, every legionary in our foresworn company, and then the sons of Angron hit us like a hurricane of swords.

Hot sparks flashed angrily off the edge of my shield as it met the burring chainblade of a World Eater. My enemy was unhelmed, revealing a face puckered with scar tissue and metal piercings. A chain looped from his ear to his nose and a spiked bar skewered both cheeks. Tattoos that looked like kill-tallies marked his neck, though the darkness made it hard to tell for sure.

I mashed my shield into his body and he staggered, grunting. Pressing my bolt pistol into the purpose-forged groove of my breacher shield, I shot him almost point-blank in the throat. Skull fragments and red matter rattled against my faceplate as the World Eater's head exploded.

Grimly, I advanced a step.

We all did.

Azoth rallied us.

'Hold steady!' he roared. 'Shields as one!'

They hit us again, raging, foaming at the mouth like rabid dogs. I felt the frenzied, repeated axe strikes against my shield resonate down to my shoulder. It burned and a numbness born from excessive muscular tension spread into my arm.

Azoth was unrelenting. 'Hold!'

A few more seconds of battery passed before he said, 'Now… heave!'

Unified, ordered, strong, we advanced and threw our aggressors back. Their killing lust made them fearsome but profligate with their effort. One man, however skilled and ferocious, cannot hold back a tide. A hundred men, if acting individually, will find themselves similarly disadvantaged.

After their initial wild flurry, the World Eaters were struggling to break us down. After herding them from the breach in the blast door made by our lascutters, we found ourselves several metres into the warren of corridors. Compared to the hangar it was confined, but wide enough for six shields abreast.

'Form ranks!'

Azoth was trying to impose further order. Unable to match their ruthless fury, it was the only way to break the World Eaters.

Thrust to the front, I was shoulder-to-shoulder with Mordan and Katus. The former was an arch fatalist who had surprised us all by living this long. The latter was a zealot who believed that strength came from adversity, and who revelled in his Immortal calling. Different though they may be, the mutual determination bleeding off my brothers was both infectious and galvanising. Behind us, I could sense Azoth's desire to be a part of the fighting rank, to prove that his shaming had been unjust. His shield was against my left shoulder guard, stalwart and unyielding. Sombrak had the right, as staunch as an iron buttress. Not once had I seen him ever take a backwards step in combat.

As well as our former ranks, our clans were also scoured from us. To be Immortal is to be alone, but despite this abject form of penitence I felt as closely bonded to these warriors as if they were all from Gaar-sak and not spread the length and breadth of Medusa.

The World Eaters hit us hard with a renewed strength born of rage. Bloodied, they carried on unbowed, proving as tough and determined as we knew them to be.

I had seen their war-making first hand, not as an enemy but as an ally.

I earned my shame that day on Golthya, during the Great Crusade, not long after we were reunited with our father…

Inside the *Retiarius* we reached as far as a cross-junction before our progress was arrested. A hulking Dreadnought almost filled the corridor ahead of us with its sheer bulk. Our sudden stall also prompted World Eaters to attack us from either flank. Our steady advance was stopped at the nexus of the junction, forcing us into an arrow wedge.

Katus and three others stormed the monstrous war engine.

One of its weapon arms was missing, and I suspected it had been in the midst of ground deployment preparation when we breached the vessel. Instead, it had been reassigned to stop us getting any further. Sombrak carried a melta-charge. So did three other Immortals in the boarding party. Allowed to detonate in the enginarium deck, these incendiaries would wreak havoc on the *Retiarius*.

Leading with his shield, Katus took a bruising blow that dashed him against the wall. His power pack ruptured and the small explosion threw him forwards into the Contemptor's lightning claw.

He spat blood. It sprayed the inside of his helm and leaked out through a crack in his faceplate. He was dead before he hit the ground. Bolt-shells caromed off the Contemptor's armoured hide from the other three Immortals who had charged with Katus, but they were no more than irritants. The Dreadnought battered two of them down with its claw, gouging one through his shield and crushing the other under its armoured foot when the Iron Hand lost his footing.

The fourth Immortal was Mordan, the only one to be alone out of the group that had gone forwards to engage the monstrous Contemptor.

He wasn't alone for long. A renewed shield wall rushed up to join him.

I tried to suppress a twinge of envy at my brother's glorious death as I advanced on the Dreadnought. It swung again, blood boiling on its energised talons and filling the corridor with the stench of burned copper. Mordan and I put up our shields as one, but I felt every pound of the Contemptor's piston-driven force rattling down through my body. It put us both on our knees.

'Your mistake...' I snarled, as Azoth waded into the gap left by Mordan and staved in the Dreadnought's head with his thunder hammer. Sombrak's volkite speared it through the chest in the same coordinated attack. It staggered as if unable to comprehend the immediacy of its own demise and fell back into an inert heap of metal.

The Dreadnought's death barely registered with the other World Eaters. They were of the killing mind now and would not relent until either they or we were dead. For the first time since we had boarded the *Retiarius*, the thoughts of the Iron Tenth and the World Eaters aligned.

We rode the storm of their fury. Without the Contemptor to break our ranks, the close confines of the corridors suited us.

'Take it!' shouted Azoth, now part of the front fighting rank where he belonged. 'Take everything they've got!'

Hammer blows pummelled our collective defence, but we held. The shield wall held and we were able to advance.

The base of my shield scraped the floor with every hard-won step. My shoulder burned from having to thrust it into the reverse side of my shield to keep the enemy from overrunning us. Our strength came from cohesion. If one link failed then our entire chain would unravel.

They hit us; we hurled them back. Each time we stood firm and absorbed the punishment, the World Eaters became more frenzied in their attempts to break us, and more reckless.

It took over eighteen minutes for us to kill every warrior-berserker in the warren. By the time it was over, blood slicked the walls, and drenched the deck beneath us, and we emerged into the next chamber weary but victorious.

I had expected to see the enginarium. What we found was something quite different.

A wide slope led from the corridor section's upraised bulkhead. We barrelled out onto it, maintaining good order and swiftly redressing our ranks in the process. It led to a pit, little more than a hollow basin of bare, bloodstained metal. It had been recently cleansed but some marks remained, the indelible legacy of a Legion's bloodletting.

More of our Immortal brothers were waiting for us in the pit, impaled from groin to crown on ugly iron spikes. I counted thirty and balked at the realisation that so few of us had even reached the *Retiarius*, let alone died on it.

I heard the clenching of fists in impotent wrath, the muttering of vengeful oaths against the World Eaters. I kept my own emotions buried, but felt the deepest stirrings of hate begin to flare like a hot, angry welt against my pride.

Azoth had been right in his assessment – this was a suicide mission.

Glory and honour were not the rights of the damned, and we were damned men. Our shame had made us that.

My shame had condemned me to that fate. On Golthya.

It had been a bleak, ugly world. We were arrayed against the kethid, a hairless, perversely humanoid alien species who had, like so many others during the coming of Old Night, subjugated the native human populace. Deep into the yawning mouth of Jreth Valley, we deployed clouds of phosphex to kill the grey-skinned aliens, but the kethid had fashioned anabatic winds through their crude science. It turned our deadliest, most loathsome weapon against us.

How we burned, the green flame flaying our flesh and turning our iron to nought but charred matter...

Croen died first, our company's vexillary. Then Laeoc, Garric, Maedeg... until there was only me, Sombrak and a handful of others left. Our flank had been crippled and we too surely would have died were it not for the berserkers clad in blue and white that descended from on high.

We fought with them, but only in a supporting role. It was meant to be our victory. The World Eaters lauded us for our courage. I stood at the shoulder of Varken Rath, a legionary of singular skill, who thanked me personally for my efforts. Sombrak and the rest of our surviving iron-kin made similar sword-brothers.

Alas, our father did not see it thusly. I have wielded a breacher shield ever since.

I have often reflected on the cruelty of that and how the battle of Golthya mirrored that aboard the *Retiarius* in both its desperation and ferocity.

At the edge of the pit on board the *Retiarius*, the World Eaters were waiting for us. Unlike the ones we had defeated in the warren, these men were armoured more like gladiators.

I knew them. I had seen them emerging from the burned metal teardrops of their deep insertion pods, through the dissipating phosphex mist that had claimed over half my company before the alien kethid attacked.

Savage, even back then, the Rampagers were much changed.

Unhooded, they wore their facial tattoos openly. Chains and thick veils of iron ringlets accented their white and blue power armour, the spikes entwined between the links presaging a darker aspect to come. Head to foot, they were swathed in gore, baked hard over their war-plate by the *Retiarius*'s immense enginarium heat. Without needing it confirmed, I knew in my marrow that the blood was Medusan, wrung from the tortured bodies of our brothers in the pit.

One of the Rampagers stood out amongst the rest. He nodded towards us, I thought. Then I realised he was actually gesturing to me.

'Gallikus...' his voice boomed across the echoing space, resonating off the pit and the shattered breacher shields lining its walls. 'Well met.' It almost sounded genial, a greeting.

It was, of sorts. Or rather, a challenge.

It was Rath. There could be no mistaking my former comrade in arms. It was blunt nomenclature for a genhanced instrument of war that was anything but. He was an exemplary swordsman and wielded a blade in each hand as if to prove it. I needed none. He had gutted kethid on those blades like they were swine. Falax, they were called, or so Rath had told me.

'If you want to reach the enginarium then this is the battleground you must cross to do it,' he said, calmly gesturing to the pit where they had staked our brothers out to die. He nodded to me again. 'I'll give you a good death. You've earned that right.'

I wanted to crush him. For his unintended condescension and the barbarous way his kin had treated mine. I almost heard our sword-bond break in his casual laughter.

'Some yet live!' cried Sombrak, who jabbed a finger at an Immortal twisting on his metal spit.

'Blood of Medusa!' Mordan's gauntlets cracked as they clenched tighter around the handle of his shield.

Rath was smiling. All the Rampagers were smiling.

Azoth had seen enough.

'Kill them! Avenge the fallen!' he roared, and every Iron Hand in our slowly dwindling company drew swords and mauls.

For what the Rampagers had done, we would have our vengeance at close quarters.

Our desperate assault was over. All we had left was retribution and, some believed, a last chance for honour. Our immortal duty.

To their martial credit, the World Eaters waited until we were half-way across the pit before they rushed to engage us.

Then we clashed. There was no order to it, no unity. Just blood.

We outnumbered the Rampagers two to one, but in the first eight seconds of the battle those odds were slashed drastically.

As I closed on Rath, briefly allying with Mordan to bring down one of the Rampagers and watching the World Eater gut one of my brothers in return, I considered the very likely fact that we had been allowed to get this far. That we had been drawn here for the prospect of a good fight. Perhaps Angron needed his psychotics to have their blood up before he unleashed them?

That arrogance would unstitch them, I decided.

Rath and I met in the centre of the arena. I still had my shield – it would be a vital barrier against my opponent's twin falax – but had drawn a gladius in lieu of my holstered pistol.

Blade to blade. Honour demanded no less.

At first, Rath seemed to appreciate the gesture but then his face locked up in an expression of pure, agonised rage. His eyes widened, the spontaneously rupturing veins turning the sclera a deep, visceral red. No trace of the man remained; now there was only a beast.

For almost three minutes he hacked into my shield as I mustered a desperate defence. He only stopped when Sombrak tried to wade in and relieve me. Despite his murder-blindness, Rath reacted on instinct. He half-parried Sombrak's thrust and let the blade pierce his side. With the other falax, he cut off Sombrak's head.

I sagged back, too exhausted to take advantage of Rath's distraction. My breacher shield was split down the middle, the arm holding it numbed to lead. I watched Sombrak's body slump to its knees and his head roll away into shadow.

Then Rath turned, exultant with the kill, and came again for me.

No martial quarter was given this time. Rath was drunk on murder-lust.

His falax came in high and I twisted to let my shoulder guard take the blow. It found the vulnerable join between the metal plates of my armour and cut all the way down to the mesh beneath, cleaving through to my flesh. Blood welled instantly. I felt it seep into my armpit and gum around my chest.

The second blade I blocked, turning it aside before aiming a stabbing thrust that sank my gladius two thirds of the way into Rath's midriff.

It was a debilitating wound, meant to slow and eventually incapacitate. Rath showed no sign of either. We were up close. I could smell his charnel breath. A savage headbutt smashed my faceplate, cracking the retinal lenses and sending the glass splinters back into my face. An elbow strike put me on one knee before Rath brought the falax round into my flank where it lodged like a nail.

I screamed. He roared.

The end was near, my immortal duty almost dispensed at last. I saw my breacher shield, smashed apart and discarded on the deck. Other shields and the bodies of my brothers had joined it.

We should never have broken our ranks, given in to hate and fury. Ours was a colder creed, one of reason and the inviolability of tactical logic. We had erred, and now our atonement was due.

Head bowed, I felt a chill progress through me. It matched the cold disembodied sensation of my cybernetics.

But the blow did not fall. My neck and head remained attached.

Instead, I heard the klaxon drone of emergency sirens as the arena was flushed with red urgent light.

Azoth had fought his way from the pit. He was wounded, and his thunder hammer was bloody, but he still stood. He was venting the chamber, releasing everything into the void.

The World Eaters had not cleansed the pit before. They had purged it in the vacuum of space. My brother had found the mechanism and did so again, only with us and our enemies present.

In the few seconds I had left, I saw the grim resignation on Azoth's face. This wasn't how he had wanted it to end.

Then I was yanked out by the venting pressure. I felt light and not just because of the absence of air and gravity. Rath's last defiant roar was stolen in that rushed exhalation, pitched into silence in dark and starless space. He swung for me, out of compulsion from whatever fuelled his rage rather than petty impotence, but the slow cut of his falax missed its mark.

Las flashes cut through the darkness, spearing us on their incandescent beams. Rath was shredded, so too were my brothers. I saw Azoth impaled through the chest before I was struck a glancing blow.

I spun, fading in the endless void, just another piece of debris.

The vista of the battling starships expanded before me, terrible and beautiful at once. Broadsides carved through kilometres of space. Explosions bloomed, abject in their quietude. The *Gorgonesque* was listing, her engines dead, her shields and armour stripped bare.

Her warp drives going critical was like the dawning of a miniature sun, a silent flash of awesome light that seared my retinas. I rode the resulting bow wave of pressure, my armour crystallising with hoarfrost even as I felt the explosive burn of the *Gorgonesque*'s dramatic last breath.

'I REMEMBER LITTLE more after that,' I told my accusers, the *Obstinate*'s black deck resolving before me as I left the memory of the *Retiarius* behind, 'save waking in your apothecarion and being marched to this hangar bay for summary judgement.' I could not keep the bitterness from my voice.

'You believe you are being treated harshly, Legionary Gallikus?'

I declined to reply, my head bowed with the cold weight of the axe blade upon my neck. The dead stares of my decapitated brothers frozen on the deck seemed mocking. And I was about to join them.

'Before you kill me,' I said at length, 'tell me, did we break the blockade?'

My accuser came forwards into the light. I heard some gesture he made, the whirring of old servos in a wrist or elbow, and felt the pressure against my neck ease. I looked up into the face of an Iron Father, but not one that I recognised.

He was badly scarred and his left cheek and part of his skull shone dully in the half-light. A tight grey beard like wire wool was shaved into a spear-tip on a jutting, imperious chin. The venerable Iron Father looked down upon me like I was the dirty oil he had to scrape from his weapons.

'We failed,' he replied. 'We were weak.'

There were two others with him, a Salamander and one of the Raven Guard.

'This is barbaric...' I heard the son of Vulkan mutter, despite the low hum of the *Obstinate*'s impulse engines partly masking his voice. His eyes flared like burning coals.

The Raven Guard gently raised his hand, warning the Salamander to silence, and they stepped back as one. This was Iron Hands business, conducted in the Medusan way as our father had taught us.

I was finding it hard to process the situation, the incongruous presence of the other Legion warriors, the mood of fatalism emanating from the Iron Father. Then there was the last figure in the room with me, my would-be executioner, one I felt I recognized and that stirred a disquiet in me that I could not explain at the time.

'Then what are our primarch's commands? Is Horus defeated? Is Isstvan still contested?' I had so many questions. 'What of the *Retiarius*?'

The Iron Father shook his head, sadly. 'It's over, Legionary Gallikus. You were the sole survivor of the attack on the *Retiarius*. The war for Isstvan is done. We lost...' He paused, as if to telegraph the blow that was coming so I could be ready for it. 'Ferrus Manus is dead.'

'Dead?' I tried to rise from my knees but a strong hand held me down. 'Release me!' I snapped, turning to meet the haunted eyes of an old friend. For a moment, I let slip my other concerns. 'Azoth?'

He gave no recognition of the fact I had just spoken his name. I thought he had died and yet here he was, aboard the *Obstinate*. But something was very wrong. His flesh looked cold, gelid, like the severed heads in front of me. Azoth's fire had been extinguished. Ice filled his veins and countenance. A dead man stood before me with the axe, dead and yet animate, bereft of any sense of cognition that would mark him out as the warrior I once knew.

'What have you done?'

'What was necessary. Horus defeated us, scattered us. *Shattered* our Legions.'

Looking back at the Iron Father, I saw he held my breacher shield. It had been reforged, made whole, even as we ourselves had fractured.

'You have erred,' he said, 'and so you must atone...'

I took the proffered shield, stunned into silence by the revelations I had just heard.

The Iron Father met my gaze and I saw the determination in his eyes, the bitterness and soul-shriving desire for revenge.

'*Such is the fate of all Immortals...*' uttered a voice behind me. The voice of Azoth, the echo of our damnation.

GREY TALON

Chris Wraight

It was a lucky ship, one upon which the fates smiled. Its hull had been laid down on the forge world Aphret in the one hundred and thirtieth year of the Crusade. Seventeen other destroyers had been completed in the same series, their superstructures filled out to the same template, each one also destined for Legion fleets.

This one was number seven, a good number, free of the defects that were always found in early-run models. As war fronts had multiplied and the Mechanicum worked to ever-more punishing schedules, such defects were possible whatever the magi might have claimed.

From Aphret's orbital shipyards it was delivered to the distribution hub at Tallameder for fitting out and ritual dedication. Legion brokers crawled over the void-docks in huddled packs, observing, noting, checking and scheming. They knew the consequences of returning to their masters bearing lower-quality materiel than their rivals, and so bidding was fierce.

The Luna Wolves had a reputation. They were tough, dragged to maturity on Cthonia with none of the refinement of, say, Fulgrim's agents. Ship captains from other Legions whispered that Horus had insiders throughout the requisition bureaucracy, and as a result his own fleet had the edge. That might even have been true, although ship captains whispered all sorts of things.

The unmarked ship was snapped up by a Legion agent named Flak Trakus, along with five more of the series. He said he liked the looked of number seven. All were quickly marked with provisional XVI Legion iconography, before being escorted under low burn to the Luna Wolves' forward base at Ipheriax Tertius for trials. Two failed to meet the Legion's exacting standards, leaving four to be given the full livery.

The ships' induction was overseen by Ezekyle Abaddon, deputising for his primarch, who remained at the cutting edge of the Crusade. The First Captain did his duty perfunctorily, eager to be back at his master's side. He looked – so observers reported at the time – deeply bored.

Number seven was named *Grey Talon*, and given to the command of what had been the 19th Chapter of the Luna Wolves. Its first legionary captain was Lucial Vormar, a Cthonian with ambitions to rise within the Legion and an enthusiastic lodge member right from the inception of the quiet orders. The *Talon* was small by the standards of the fleet, slotting between a pure torpedo boat and a line frigate. Such vessels were often referred to as destroyers, though the forward lance mounted under the main prow shield was uncommon for the class, making it weapon-heavy for its void displacement. The configuration performed well during seventy years of constant warfare, and it was only returned to its home berth twice for refit and overhaul. Four more captains and two more shipmasters took the helm during that period, each of them using it as a springboard for greater things.

Soon the *Talon* had reinforced its reputation as a fortunate ship, one that promised advancement for its crew, and it found a regular place in actions across the ever-expanding battlefront of the Great Crusade.

By the time of Isstvan III, it was under the command of Hierek Mon, a member of Vormar's lodge with an enviable kill-tally and a reputation for void flair. He defied orders to remain on a high-orbit blocking station and entered the bombardment zone in the wake of Angron's disastrous intervention, earning the ire of the Legion command. His reward was to be placed in a suicidal position during the fleet deployment for the subsequent inferno at Isstvan V, given little cover and expected to atone for his zeal in death.

Once again, though, the *Grey Talon* defied expectations, riding its ever-present luck during the ruinous battle over the scrap-filled void space. Mon almost survived the entire encounter, poised to rejoin the main warfleet with honour restored, but for the intervention of a fleeing Salamanders boarding party on a captured lander. The loyalists used it to break into the destroyer as she came about, and after a brief but brutal action took it from within.

Mon died on his bridge, screaming out curses as his limbs were hacked from him. During the confusion of the loyalist withdrawal, the *Grey Talon* managed to clear the system and enter the warp, its innards still riddled with close-quarters fighting as the Salamanders assumed full control.

It was renamed after that, given the title of Nocturne's primary city, *Hesiod*. Other refugees were found and taken on board, including Bion Henricos of the X Legion and the renowned White Scars Librarian Targutai Yesugei. The ship was drawn into a new kind of war, running the shadows, hunting down isolated advance-packs of the enemy and cutting their throats. It was dangerous work, testing the good fortune that had by then been burned into the ship's spars.

The end almost came under the broadsides of the Death Guard frigate *Mind's Resolve*. With the charred orb of Prospero below it, the *Hesiod* was surrounded in a corona of fire, knocked off-beam and rolled into macro-cannon range of three more cruisers. Its fortune held out, though, arriving in the shape of the main White Scars battlefleet. The fighting swept over it, dragging it spinwards, leaving it listing but still airtight. By then Henricos was its commander, cheated from the death he had confidently expected and left to brood as his powered-down ship drifted silently from the battlesphere.

The *Hesiod* was retrieved six hours later and pulled into the V Legion's ambit. Tech-crews discovered then that the engine-chamber had been punctured and that it had been only minutes from destruction. The White Scars had laughed at that. Henricos hadn't – he knew the reputation of the ship, the one it had carried since its hull had been laid down, and did not see survival as something necessarily to aspire to.

With the last of the Salamanders dispersed throughout the fleet, Henricos was joined by new White Scars on the bridge. The ship's name was switched again, restored to *Grey Talon* as it had been before, and its colours reverted to those of the Sons of Horus. Its ongoing role was decided even before the policy came down from the Khan himself – it would be an infiltrator, a chameleon, a snake in the shadows. Outright warfare, openly declared, was no longer an option.

Henricos never left the bridge during the refit. He worked obsessively, driving the menials to extreme lengths to refashion the engines and realign the weapons. Those who saw him during that time sent shocked reports back up the V Legion hierarchy.

He was like a devil, they said. A tortured spirit.

Perhaps that was why they sent Hibou to him, to act as some kind of exemplary punishment. That was possible, though not likely. The primarch had doled out penance in sorrow rather than rancour.

Moreover, Hibou knew to what manner of ship he had been assigned. It had cheated death before, and might do so again, whatever odds it sailed into. They had all told him that – Nozan, Torghun – trying to improve his mood before they were sent on their own death-missions. Even in the face of their great error, locked down by the shame of it, they could still see a path into the future. A way back, if fortune smiled on them.

And the *Grey Talon* was a lucky ship, they said. One upon which the fates smiled.

FOR A LONG time after boarding, Hibou Khan did not leave his cell. He felt the vibrations as the plasma drives keyed up, thrusting the ship clear of the already dispersing White Scars fleet. Some time later, this changed to the high-pitched whine of warp engines, followed by the lurch of entry into the aether. After that was the eerily quiet passage through the immaterium, punctuated only by the creak and snap of the *Talon*'s flanks.

It felt like they had been in the warp for a long time. The campaign on Chondax had been a near-constant series of jumps, bridging the vicious combat-phases on the system's far-flung worlds. He'd had plenty of time back then to consider the Legion's place of dishonour, to listen to the words of Hasik Noyan-Khan, to talk to fellow members of the lodges and take in their grievances. The fighting had become almost secondary to the question that had come to dominate discourse in the brotherhoods.

What next?

And the answer to that had been: *the Warmaster*. Distrust of Imperial command structures had become so absolute, so ingrained, that aligning with Horus had come to seem not so much as prudent as inevitable. The entire Legion admired Horus. They knew of the regard between him and the Khan. Out of all the Eighteen, only the Thousand Sons had been closer, and relations with Magnus's sons had been conducted largely through the Stormseers.

So it had been natural. When he was in the mood to find excuses, Hibou would remember that. On other days, when the shame made him want to ram his face into the metal walls of his cell until the blood ran, he would remember the warnings of his heart, the tremors of unease when the transmissions came in from beyond the veil around Chondax and the strange light in the eyes of some of his fellow loyalists.

Loyalists. None of them had been loyalists. That term was now reserved for those who had cleaved to the Throne, while those who had been drawn to Horus's magnetic presence had been cast into the darkness, reviled as traitors and consorts with *yaksha*.

That had never been part of the draw. No one had shown them the destination at the end of that path, and if they had done so the revolt would have been snuffed out long before it could have threatened the Legion's cohesion.

It made him nauseous to think how close they had come. The vid-captures from the *Vorkaudar*, the Word Bearers ship captured by Yesugei, had made the implications plain.

It would have started with a vow. The vow would have been made in good faith.

At times, musing on that, Hibou regretted not taking the death-oath, the *tsusan garag*, which would at least have sealed his pact and left no room for reconsideration. If he had done so, he would now be dead, his hearts pierced by the primarch's own blade. As it was, he had been left the path of penance – to cleanse his soul by taking the fight ahead of the main fleet, striking with no hope of survival, carrying the anger of betrayal back to its heart.

He was of the *sagyar mazan* now. They would find absolution only by returning the pain to its origin – to blood the arch-traitor as he had blooded them. Deeper, more sharply.

But there would be weeks before he could unleash his blade again, and until that moment he had to negotiate the inner warrens of the starship with a soul who hated him almost as much as he hated the ones who had cast their lot with damnation.

Sighing, Hibou Khan adjusted his robe over his armour, and made to leave his cell. It could not be put off forever. If they were to fight together, they would first have to learn to speak.

HENRICOS WORKED ON the machine. He had been working on it since the day he had been taken on board by Xa'ven. In contrast to the *Vorkaudar*, it was a good, clean machine, one that he could engage with and improve. The Sons of Horus had not fallen quite so deeply into debauchery as the Word Bearers, at least not by the time of the Dropsite Massacre when the ship had been taken over, and the metal remained unsullied. It smelled of them still – the fusty pelts they wore, the Cthonian hides – but it functioned more or less as a machine should.

For as long as he worked, he could forget the anger. If his hands, bionic and organic, were occupied then they did not itch to carry a weapon. In any case, there were no weapons on board that were worthy of his adoption. He still had his Medusan bolter, though no blade to go alongside it. The White Scars had offered him dozens of their own, and it had been hard not to laugh at them for that. Their metalwork was capable enough but they had fouled the metal with sweeping Chogorian runes, and the shafts were too basic, too unaugmented. Nothing they had offered him had had the same heft and killing potential as a true Medusan zweihander, and so he had rejected everything.

He leant over his navigation station, staring at the images on the vid-feeds. He had been looking at the scan for hours, and his eyes were beginning to have trouble focusing. He could have let the cogitators take the strain, but they were poor on detail, and detail was everything.

The task consumed him. By the time he sensed the other presence on the bridge, it was hard to guess how long he had been there.

Damned Chogorian stealth.

'What do you want?' Henricos rasped, never taking his eyes from the screen.

Hibou Khan drew closer. Henricos could smell him too – old ceremonial oils on his ceramite, the last gift from his brothers in the Legion that had banished him. That had been sentimental and a waste. Henricos would have killed them all and recycled the gene-seed and weapons. Why trust a part that had already failed?

'I do not know our trajectory,' said Hibou, in accented but reasonably fluent Gothic. It seemed that not all of them had the same impediment as their storm-witch.

'And?'

Hibou stiffened. 'We are destined to fight together. Perhaps I should know something of your plan.'

Henricos let a long breath slide out of his clenched lips, then stood up. 'Nine of you. All traitors. You will know the plan when I tell you.

Until then, you would do well to keep your mouth closed and your eyes away from my scanners.'

To his credit, Hibou absorbed the spite. His tanned face, marked with the pucker of self-inflicted scars, flickered by just an infinitesimal amount.

'If we had been traitors, we would be dead,' he said.

Henricos could feel his humours darken. Even looking at the White Scar made him angry, just as almost everything else made him angry. 'I do not wish to do this now,' he muttered.

Hibou stood his ground. 'We have been in the warp for a week. I would train, if I knew what I was training for.'

Henricos turned on him. 'What do you need that you do not possess? You have your blades. All fighting is much the same.'

'You truly believe that?'

Henricos drew closer. 'So what fighting have you seen, White Scar? Greenskins?'

It was so easy to bring it back – the skies above the dropsite, flared red, streaked with the contrails of falling assault claws. There had been seven primarchs in that slaughter. *Seven*. The killing had been industrial.

'I know you underestimate us,' said Hibou evenly. 'Do not think that this will anger me. We are used to it.'

'Damn you!' spat Henricos, clenching his metal fist. 'Underestimate you? I know the damage you can do.' He edged even closer, his sour breath washing over the scarred face before him. 'Tell me why I should even suffer you to look at me. I fought as the Gorgon was being cut apart. I fought as my Legion was being cut apart. I have fought every second since, and will fight until fate stops my hearts, and you. *You*. You were not even sure who the enemy *was*.'

Hibou did not respond, but Henricos could see that he wanted to strike him. A nerve had been touched.

'We were wrong,' the White Scar said, softly. 'We erred. We will pay the price.'

'Aye, we all will,' Henricos said, his voice edged with disgust.

He had never doubted, not for a microsecond. Ferrus Manus had never doubted. There had never been room for it – they had the assignment, and they executed it. That was why Horus had gone for them first. Of all the Legions, the Iron Tenth had been the most steadfast, the only ones not plagued by ambitions beyond the most efficient prosecution of war.

There were moments when he took pride in that. Mostly, though, the thoughts just summoned the blind rage back, so he shoved it down, burying the memory in the work schedule that made his servos stutter and his eyes scratch.

'Get away from me,' Henricos said. 'I will summon you when I need you. Until then, just stay away. You make me…'

In another age, he might have said 'sick', but the Iron Hands did not sicken, for what was broken was quickly replaced.

'…angry.'

And that was true enough, though hardly remarkable anymore.

HIBOU DID AS he was bid. There was no point in antagonising the Iron Hand further, for who knew where his rage would take him? Hibou adopted the same tactic his Legion always did – withdraw, pull away, conserve strength for another pass. He tried not to let his ever-lurking shame cloud his emotions, for that would make him duller, less able to react when the time came. But that was not easy, for the shame was infinite and did not diminish.

He walked down the corridors of the ship, feeling its otherness with every step. He had only ever gone to war on vessels of the *ordu*, with their clean lines and bright livery. This ship was stained by the temper of its original masters – crude edges, dark shades. It was a blunt-edged weapon. The ongoing sense of dislocation surprised him, and he made a mental note to attend to it in his meditation.

The *Grey Talon* was sparsely inhabited – a mix of servitors, a skeleton crew of menials from the White Scars, and no doubt some old XVI Legion serfs who had managed to avoid Xa'ven's purge and now kept their heads down in the dingy corners of the bilge levels. In the absence of proper numbers, it was Henricos who kept the whole thing together, stringing automated mechanisms into line, restoring burned-out systems, reviving dormant machine-spirits. The furious pace of work was all that kept him from lashing out at living targets, and that was welcome enough.

Were all Iron Hands the same, Hibou wondered, with that mix of sullen fury and morbid obsession? Impossible to tell. He had never fought alongside them before, and did not expect the current experiment to last long enough for him to form a settled opinion.

He reached the practice cages, where Teji was already limbering up. Hibou drew one of the blades from the racks, watching his opponent idly.

He had not known Teji before. The young warrior had been just one of many lodge members across many brotherhoods: each of them seduced by the same words and tiptoeing the precipice of damnation without knowing it. The Khan had ruled that kill-squads of the sagyar mazan be composed of strangers, lest the bonds of old brotherhood return and kindle fresh insurrection. A sensible precaution, but in truth hardly necessary. They all knew how close they had come, and what they had to do to redeem themselves.

Teji had been from the Brotherhood of the Red Sun, one of the many under Jemulan's command. He had reached Ascension just before Chondax, joining the fleet in the last reinforcement wave from Chogoris before the veil fell. Not long in which to make a choice that would cripple his future forever.

Hibou entered the cage, bowing. Teji returned the gesture, and brought his blade into guard. The weapon was as blunt as Hibou's, and wouldn't have hurt even a mortal badly. Damage was not the point of the exercise, though – it was balance, speed and reaction.

'Did he speak to you?' asked Teji.

Hibou shook his head. 'I made the first move. He will make the next.'

Teji smiled. 'Maybe.'

The sagyar mazan had become closer during the voyage, all nine of them, but wariness still remained. They were an artificial unit, pushed together only by a shared culpability, which in itself was a poor foundation for vengeance. Combat would test their weak links, either welding them firm or shattering the whole.

'Begin, then,' said Hibou, and the two of them swept into movement, parrying, jabbing, using the blades with all the fluidity of their training. In seconds, the cage became an arena of Chogorian art, a crucible of swordsmanship.

Immersed within that, the divisions seemed trivial. The doubt, the guilt, all of it became invisible, sublimed by the dominant physicality of combat.

So they fought one another, enjoying the release. They knew, though, that when the blades were lowered again it would all come back, vivid like the shuddered recollection of dreams.

He was back on Medusa, trudging beneath lightning-scored skies, feeling the primordial cold pressing in upon his skin. Somewhere up in the gloom, invisible beyond the night-dense clouds, the iron band of the Telstarax hung in orbit, ruined and echoing – a grave-marker of another age.

He had never seen it, but it had always been a figure of Medusan myth – the ancient torc that marked the world from the void, shackling it in metal. He had never seen the primarch Ferrus Manus either, but knew that he was there too, somewhere. A mortal Telstarax of sorts, both guardian and destroyer, forging the planet's sons into new weapons and purging the last morsels of weakness from their privation-hardened bodies.

He had walked for ten days as the dull Medusan sun had it, drinking little, eating little, his boots kicking up black dust and caking his layered synth-fabrics. His breather-mask had picked up a fault and clicked when he inhaled, letting in the gritty taste of spoil-dust. His land-engine was just a memory now, grinding its way south with the rest of his clan. The dirty smoke-plume had hung on the horizon for a long time before being lost in the smog, but he had never turned to look for it.

On the eleventh day, the tower rose up before him – colossal, clad in plates of ink-black iron. He heard the boom of engines under the earth, and felt the shiver of the solid rock underfoot. Walls loomed away from him in geometric layers, star-shaped for siege, crowned with guns as vast as his old tracked home.

He thought he had reached the Sorrgol citadel then, but he was wrong, because the tower before him was only the smallest of many spires, a mere sentinel over the southern gates. Beyond it stretched forges, burners, smelters and extractors, kilometre after kilometre, linked by webs of iron pipework and covered in a cloak of carbon vapour.

Before the gate stood Ferrus Manus, a titan in charcoal armour, invincible and eternal in his watch over the citadel. Except that he was wrong about that too – the guard was just a legionary of the Tenth, the first he had ever seen, though to a youth's awed eyes it might just as well have been the primarch himself.

He felt his head go light at last, and struggled to keep his feet. The gate-watcher gazed down at him with eyes that glowed dull red amidst a slope-grilled helm.

'I come to serve,' he said, proudly, belligerently, daring the warrior above him to refuse.

He thought he heard a faint whirring, like optical instruments. The legionary might have been considering the words, or was amused or irritated by them, but with the helm in place his emotions were unreadable.

'So I see,' the legionary eventually replied.

The gate cracked open, pulled back by immense cylinders. He swayed on his weary legs, catching sight of the furnaces beyond – the fields of metal and the boiling, underlit clouds.

The legionary gestured for him to enter.

'Have you the spine, child?' he asked, his voice a tinny, machine-filtered snarl. 'Make it to the tower, and they will test you further.'

He was afraid then. Desperately afraid. His throat was dry, his hands cold with sweat, and it was hard to make his legs move. The legionary waited, silent again, as unmoving as the walls around him.

He wanted to move. He could see the great tower within, a jagged blade at the heart of the foundries, glistening like the slate edges of mountains.

He wanted to move.

HENRICOS WOKE WITH a jerk. He had fallen asleep over his station on the bridge, slumped on a scanner console. None of the crew had dared to wake him.

He lifted his head, wiping a line of drool from the smeared screen. How long had he been out? Seven minutes, by his armour's chronos. That was his sleep-pattern now – a few moments here and there, islands of unconsciousness between the long work shifts.

The lapse was shameful. He was on the bridge, surrounded by those who had marked his weakness and would now be wondering how much longer he could last.

Work harder.

He tightened his shoulders, feeling the shift of armour-plate over tight muscle, the pain of limbs that had been cramped and compressed for too long.

He looked down at the screen. It was covered with phosphor-trails of warp-wake projections, overlaid on a cartographic grid of dizzying complexity. He had traced the last two trail patterns over that, marking the passage of the *Grey Talon* through the maze of the aether.

He studied the incoming signals, making allowances for the known ghost reflection from the augur array. Blinking to clear the last of his fuzziness, he remembered where he had got to before unconsciousness had crept up on him. He activated a new scan-sweep and watched the screen fill with data. It had taken five hours to prepare the algorithms, just as it had done for all the other searches. At times he wondered whether he had forgotten how to do it properly.

It had been Jebez Aug who had hammered the technique into him, drilling the procedures by rote under the shadow of constant discipline. 'Others may be faster,' the Iron Father had been fond of saying to him. 'Others may even be stronger, but none are more methodical.'

Aug, no doubt, was dead. It was likely now that the entire clan had been wiped out, either at Isstvan or in the aftermath. All of them, lost in the inferno. The old lessons had not helped them then, but they had all gone into that situation blind, forgetting their own maxims in their haste to reach the enemy.

Ferrus, too. The blindest of us all.

The lens before him throbbed with fresh runes, and Henricos snapped back to full attention. He reviewed the multi-layered tangle of trajectory markers, twisting away within stylised warp-conduits.

For a moment, he saw nothing.

Then a glimmer. A faint trace, just visible over the range of possible warp-paths.

He could almost imagine Aug with him again, leaning over him, uttering a rare grunt of satisfaction.

Henricos checked, to be sure, then opened a channel to Hibou. There was no avoiding the meeting now.

'Khan,' he said, keeping it to the point. 'Ready your squad and meet me on the bridge. We have our target.'

HIBOU STARED AT the screen, wondering exactly what he was supposed to be looking at. He was adept at reading tactical displays of a dozen kinds, but Henricos had created a mosaic of overlapping nonsense on the pict-feeds, one that even a Mechanicum magos would have struggled to process.

'You see it?'

'I do not,' said Hibou, bracing himself for fresh scorn. 'Please, show me.'

Henricos snorted in exasperation, then zoomed in on the image. 'Forget three dimensions – the warp operates differently. We alter standard scan algorithms and course settings to cover the greatest area in the shortest time. The result is an organic pattern, developed by my clan's Iron Father on Medusa, and takes into account the underlying movement of aether conduits. We are not in physical space, so we do not move as if we are. The equations are... complex.'

Hibou could believe that. The screen was crammed with trajectories, half of which meant nothing to him. 'You mean this,' he said, pointing to a ship-marker set several hours in *Grey Talon*'s wake.

'No. Look at its movements, the same as ours – it is a mirror. A ghost. Consider it an artefact of the scanners and ignore. The target is *here*.'

Henricos gestured towards a faint blip on the extreme edge of the display. Hibou frowned.

'That is not a ship-marker,' he said.

Henricos rewarded that with a sarcastic smile. 'Astute. A ship-marker is not what we seek.' He zoomed in further, increasing the granularity of the sweep. 'This is a warp-wake – the sign of deep passage. Count yourself lucky, White Scar. None of your Legion could have detected this.'

Hibou let the insult slide. He was used to them. 'How far?'

'I can bring us within strike range. But remember this is not physical space. We must track it, using the search-pattern, waiting for them to drop out, then we fall upon them. I can materialise on top of it, in its shadow. They will have only seconds to respond.'

'They will not see us coming?'

'Not unless they were schooled to recognise an algorithmic pursuit. That is unlikely.'

Hibou detected the sullen pride there and let Henricos enjoy the moment. The Iron Hands had had precious little to celebrate, and if their warp-tracking prowess was grounds for arrogance then they were welcome to it.

'Which Legion, then?' Hibou asked. 'Can you tell me that?'

'Look here.' Henricos zoomed in further, exposing the wound in the warp gouged by the prey-ship's engines. 'Three salients, aggressively pitched, characteristic of Draco-series drives – an old configuration. These were favoured by one Legion only, so either that is a Sons of Horus ship, or you may have my eyes.'

Hibou felt eagerness stir just at the name. 'Can we take it?'

'No idea, not until we break the veil. But it cannot be much larger than us, and we will be on it before it knows we are a threat.' He looked up at Hibou, and for the first time there was a crooked grin twitching at his lips. 'You wished to know the plan. Here it is. We are in their colours – that will give them a moment's uncertainty. We board before they can raise shields, take the command bridge, disable it. The guns on the *Talon* can do the rest.'

Hibou nodded. The schematics were already beginning to untangle in his mind, and he could half see the route that the Iron Hands legionary was proposing.

'And you will take the *Talon*'s helm,' he said, planning how he would deploy the boarding party.

'I will not,' growled Henricos, slamming the screen away on its angled mount and resuming the hostility that bubbled just under the surface of his humour. 'I will be with you. We will need all the blades we can muster.'

That anger was directed now – no longer at those he was forced to serve with, but at the real enemy, the ones who had unambiguously chosen treachery.

'Side by side, then,' said Hibou, smiling dryly.

'If you insist,' muttered Henricos, turning back to the data. 'As long as we kill and as long as we hurt them, I care not.'

IT WAS TWELVE more hours before the target ship made signs of dropping from the warp. For most of that time the kill-team waited in the holds of the gunship *Golden Dagger*, primed for rapid hangar exit. Boarding torpedoes had been considered and rejected – they would be coming in too fast to guarantee a fire-angle – so they trusted the manoeuvrability and speed of the Thunderhawk to get them across the void gulf.

After launch, the *Talon*'s mortal crew, under the command of a stoic Chogorian bridge officer named Omoz, would keep the destroyer as close as possible, drawing any incoming fire while the boarding parties infiltrated the hangars.

Henricos waited impatiently, locked in the gunship's forward hold, Hibou's White Scars in restraint cages on either side of him. Streams of data scrolled across his visor feed, giving him every detail of the final approach. Both vessels were still in the warp, but the target had now changed course dramatically and was slowing for exit. The *Grey Talon* pursued it along the twisting lines of the Sorrgol pattern, operating on the automatic guides he had set in place before taking position.

'Start launch cycle,' he muttered, keeping an eye on the evolving timings.

The Thunderhawk's thrusters roared into life. Ahead of them, glimpsed through grainy pict-feeds, the hangar door locks slammed open.

'*Warp-bubble punctured ahead,*' reported Omuoz over the comm. '*It is coming out.*'

'Remain tight on it,' warned Henricos, frustrated that he could not be in two places at once and fly both ships. He had tried to relax – the V Legion pilots who steered both the *Talon* and the gunship were as good as any he'd ever seen – but it was still hard to trust outsiders. 'Five kilometres, real space. No more.'

It was insanely close, a warp exit virtually on top of their enemy's, but it had to be that tight or they would lose the fractional chance.

Golden Dagger rose from the apron on booming cushions of downdraft, hovering a metre clear. A second later, the *Grey Talon* ripped free of the aether's clutches. As soon as it had cleared the rift, the hangar's void-doors ground open amidst a smudge of straggling Geller remnants.

'Now!' cried Henricos.

The Thunderhawk hit full speed, hurling him back against his restraint harness, and shot out into the void. The target hung just ahead of them on the augur screens, emerging from the last of its warp rift just as the *Talon* was cleared, angled away and with its running lights low.

'Shields?' demanded Henricos.

'*Not yet,*' reported Omoz, his voice commendably calm.

The enemy ship raced towards them. Henricos saw then how big it was – a line frigate with a full battle-lance – and cursed under his breath. It would already be scanning the *Grey Talon*, sending hails, running checks against fleet ledgers and picking up the incoming gunship. The subterfuge of their XVI Legion livery was painfully slight.

'Get us in now,' he voxed to the *Golden Dagger*'s crew.

They sped under the shadow of the frigate's hull. Rows of hangar bays, all of them barred, swam up into the viewers. The Thunderhawk's battlecannon loosed, sending shells screaming into the nearest void-doors. Hull plates exploded under the impact, disintegrating in a welter of spinning adamantium.

'Faster!' roared Henricos, knowing that the void shield arrays would now be powering up.

The gunship swooped for the aperture, blasting through at a steep pitch, scraping the edges of the hangar entrance before shuddering to a full-stop and coming to rest on a violent bloom of downthrust. The sponson-mounted heavy bolters opened up, spraying in twin arcs from the ingress, raking enemy ships locked on the deck rails and shredding any crew caught out on the apron.

Disengaging his restraint cage, Henricos slammed the ramp release. 'Out, out, out!'

They spilled from the holds, accompanied by the howl of released atmosphere and the blare of alert klaxons. Behind them, the gauze of atmospheric containment fields finally slid across the shattered hangar entrance, now too late to do anything other than trap the infiltrators within the hull.

Hibou raced ahead, making for the hangar's inner doors. The Khan had a power sword with a florid dragon carved into its crackling edge. Henricos followed him with his bolter at the ready, scanning for incoming targets.

The first opposition came from the ship's mortal crew. They reacted quickly, forming up at the intersections of the corridors leading up from the hangars and laying down concentrated fire. All of them were from a hard world and had lived lifetimes of combat, so they performed admirably.

Yet it didn't help them. The White Scars were astonishingly fast, crashing aside the opposition before it had time to get established, whooping and yelling as they laid about them with their blades. Henricos had never seen them in action as squads before, and he could admire the seamless interaction between them – a warrior would sway out of the way to allow another to fire, then dart back into contact, aware the whole time of the flight of bolter-rounds and the whirl of steel around him.

'The flesh is weak!' Henricos roared, watching the enemy die, listening for the wet slap of flesh splitting and the echoing rip of the mass-reactive shells going off. That gave him pleasure, the first he had taken since the similar slaughter on the *Vorkaudar*.

The Scars joined him in viciousness. They hit recklessly, aiming for pain, and their cries were edged with something more raw than he had heard before. It was a kind of frenzy, with each kill seeming to spur them deeper into it.

They were the sagyar mazan, the penitents, and they fought like it.

Henricos and Hibou led them onwards, carving twin passages towards the command bridge. The pace quickened, and they stormed through crew halls and armouries, leaving a long trail of slicked blood behind them. The decks shook as heavy impacts rocked the hull – the *Talon* firing, stressing the void shields and keeping the enemy crews busy.

The boarding party tore up through the levels, hurling grenades into choke points, charging through them with the flesh-scraps still flying. The White Scars' armour became streaked with red splatter-patterns across the ivory. Henricos's own iron-black plate barely reflected the gore, though he was as steeped in it as the rest of them.

By the time they had reached the wide assembly chamber below the bridge, the real enemy emerged, pushing past their own battling crew to get at the invaders, issuing Cthonian kill-challenges from brass-edged augmitters.

The Scars scattered instantly, spreading out across the chamber's marble floor and racing for the cover of the supporting columns. Bolter-fire crisscrossed the open spaces, shattering rockcrete and throwing a powder haze across the hall. Henricos thudded up against a three-metre-wide pillar, feeling the stone of it tremble as the mass-reactives exploded.

He waited two seconds, letting his cover absorb the fusillade, before charging out again – keeping low, trusting his armour to take the hits. By then the Scars were moving too, flitting like gore-speckled ghosts between the columns. They danced through an oncoming storm of bolter-rounds, spinning as they came within sword-reach to give their blades more speed.

Henricos lumbered by comparison, coming up against the bulk of a Sons of Horus warrior in dark, sea-green plate. Both bolters fired simultaneously – Henricos was hit on the shoulder, his enemy in the chest. The impact of the Iron Hand's round caused the greater damage, throwing the traitor back by a hand's width.

Henricos pressed in fast. He fired again, cracking his enemy's faceplate, then piled in with his gauntlets, punching rapidly and hard until he heard the wet crack of a breaking spine. As the warrior fell, Henricos grabbed his power maul – finally something he could relish using – and pressed onwards.

By then the noise in the hall was hammering, a mix of vox roars and explosions. More Sons of Horus charged in, adding to the lattice of shellfire.

Henricos's mind suddenly shifted back to Isstvan – the last time he had faced the XVI Legion in numbers. He remembered the desperate stands on the ridges at the edge of the depression, watching as waves of the enemy advanced, the bloody dust kicked up into a boiling cloud of rage.

He was hit again, a bolt-round smacking into his knee joint before exploding against the covering plate, and he staggered in the charge. A traitor got close to him with a chainaxe, and Henricos whipped his crackling maul around to block the challenge. They were coming in from all angles now, pushing the boarding party away from the hall's far end and driving them back towards the exposed centre.

'For Ferrus!' he bellowed, lashing out and driving the maul deep into his enemy's neck before kicking the choking adversary aside and launching himself at the next. They had to keep the momentum up, break through to the bridge before they were dragged into a drawn-out melee, or the chance would be gone.

By then the Scars were fighting with an almost berserk energy, their battle-challenges more like screams. Henricos saw a Sons of Horus legionary literally torn apart by two of them, his body sliced at the armour joints by whistling bladework. The Warmaster's own were just as vicious – a few metres away, an ivory battle-brother was dragged to the deck, his back broken and his helm-plate smashed.

Henricos limped over to avenge the kill, but was slammed to the ground by a bolt impact, the third to hit him. He skidded over, his armour scraping against the marble. He made to rise, and only then realised what damage had been done – blood was cascading down from his stomach, foaming around the ragged edges of the hole in his armour.

He spat, furious at the setback, and switched to his bolter, snapping the muzzle up to fire. But his vision blurred from pain, and he missed the target. An enemy legionary sprinted towards him, swinging a power axe around his head to generate the down-force for a killing strike.

Henricos tried to rise, to get his maul up to block the blow, but he never got the chance. A White Scars legionary smashed into the charging traitor, blocking him bodily and sending them both careering across the deck. They rolled together, hacking madly, until the White Scar managed to pin him. With a deft twist, he plunged his curved sword deep into his enemy's gullet, ripping upwards to tear out his throat. Then he was up again, falling back to Henricos's position, drawing a bolt pistol and firing out into the throng.

'Khan…' acknowledged Henricos, still struggling to rise.

Hibou crouched beside him. 'Can you fight?'

Henricos snarled, knowing the answer but unable to get the words out. He would be lucky not to bleed to death where he lay. 'The bridge… is within range…'

That, technically, was a lie. The assault had stalled, and the bodies of four White Scars lay motionless across the chamber floor. The rest were falling back towards his position, pursued by twice that number of Sons of Horus.

Hibou kept firing, trying to slow the oncoming traitors. 'I do not think so. We will end more of them yet, though.'

Henricos reloaded his bolter and took aim. As he did so, the entire chamber rocked, as if buffeted by a hull breach. For a moment he dared to hope that the *Grey Talon* had broken through the void shields, though the thought did not last long – the ship did not have the weaponry, and even if it had there were no more troops aboard that could have turned this battle.

'Die well, brother,' he snarled, taking aim at an advancing group of Sons of Horus and opening fire again.

He didn't expect his shots to do more than hinder their inevitable onslaught, but his shells seemed to multiply in mid-flight, hitting the targets in a whole volley of mass-reactive destruction. The advance crumpled to a halt amidst a roiling wave of explosions, sending the Sons of Horus reeling backwards.

Startled, Henricos looked around, and only then detected the acrid tang of teleport discharge. Seven leviathans in Terminator battleplate stalked out of disintegrating warp-frost spheres, clad in a mix of Gorgon and Cataphractii suits, laying down a heavy curtain of fire from twin-linked bolters and combi-meltas.

Their plate was black, pitted with bare metal scratches, the edges picked out in white. He saw Medusan emblems on the pauldrons – cogs, fists, skulls. They were all clans he recognised, ones he had fought alongside or been rival too, including his own – Sorrgol, bearing the wrench-and-cog sigil, just as he himself wore.

The White Scars reacted quicker than he did, joining the new assault, adding their speed to the advance of the Terminators. Henricos remained locked down by the shock of recognition.

We were all dead...

Hibou sprinted back into the melee, joining his brothers in the counter-attack, crying out in the outlandish tongue of his home world. As Henricos struggled to regain his feet, cursing at the sluggish recovery of his flesh, a shadow fell over him.

He looked up into the red-eyed glare of a Legion deathmask. He might as well have been back on Medusa – gazing up, stupefied, at the anonymous legionary he had thought was Ferrus Manus.

'Bion Henricos,' came the familiar voice of Shadrak Meduson, once captain of Sorrgol's Tenth Company, but now so much more. 'Ensure you do not die here. I will have need of you.'

MEDUSON HAD ARRIVED in the X Legion strike cruiser *Iron Heart*. The warship was many orders more powerful than either *Grey Talon* or the XVI Legion frigate – which was named, somewhat ironically, the *Inexorable Conquest* – so it had been able to render down the enemy ship's shields in two colossal broadsides. The Terminator bridgehead was just the start – more troops were sent over in boarding rams, spilling into the narrow inner passages and clogging them with slaughter.

With such numbers, the assembly hall was quickly taken, followed by a swift and brutal assault on the bridge. The enemy, as could be expected, fought to the end, but it was Meduson who ended it, decapitating the ship's captain with a single savage swipe, mirroring the death of his gene-sire amidst the metallic choler of the assembled Iron Hands.

Hours later, the ship was secured. Five of the White Scars' kill-team still lived, including Hibou Khan. Henricos came closer to death than he felt comfortable admitting, but the hated flesh-components responded to the challenge, aided by the knives of the *Iron Heart*'s medicae teams.

By the time the last of Meduson's troops returned to the strike cruiser he was on his feet again, and was there when Meduson himself returned to the ship's council chamber. The room was hexagonal and of night-black iron, rising up into a shaft like a foundry vent and filled with the grinding hum of engines.

'Henricos. You did as you were bid,' the warleader noted.

That was as much congratulation as he was likely to get from Meduson for staying alive. It already felt unusual, having grown used to the courtesy and deference of the Chogorians, to be plunged back into the blunt manner of his own Legion.

'It was an order,' said Henricos.

Meduson stood alongside four others – two Iron Hands, a Salamander and a Raven Guard. It seemed that the hybrid army sent to Isstvan still endured, at least in scraps.

'Many clans,' said Henricos. 'Many Legions.'

'Forged into one. We are gathering in numbers again.'

Henricos could admire the sentiment. A nagging part of him thought it mistaken, but there could be no arguing with rescuers. 'Others of Sorrgol?'

'Jebez Aug lives, though I command the clan. Much has changed – you will be told all these things. What of you?'

Henricos told them of the flight from Isstvan, the encounter on Prospero, and the penitents of the V. Shadrak Meduson listened intently, absorbing the data like a machine, scouring it for anything he could use.

'Then that was a ship of my Legion?' asked the Salamander, sounding genuinely interested.

'For a time,' said Henricos. 'Though it has been many things.'

'And the Khan remains loyal?' pressed Meduson.

'Completely. His Legion has mobilised for war. Even now he will be engaging the enemy.'

'But those you fought with – they were traitors?'

Henricos paused. 'No. They were not.' He struggled to find the words. 'There was… insufficient data.'

Meduson did not look convinced. 'You vouch for them?'

It felt strange, to be defending Hibou and the rest, but now that they had fought together it was harder to maintain outright hostility. 'They are atoning.'

'So be it. If they can fight, I can use them.' Meduson looked at Henricos carefully. 'You can see what is happening here. The strands are being pulled together, winding into cords of greater strength.'

'And that is wise?'

'Why would it not be?'

Henricos glanced across the faces in the room: three of them ashen, one bone-pale and another dark. 'While we hunt apart, we are hard to detect. And when we come together, we can be seen. We cannot defeat this enemy through strength – they have more of it.'

'Yet there are things we can achieve,' said Meduson. If the challenge to his strategy irritated him, he made no sign of it. 'I have marked a soul for destruction and I have bound the warriors under me to this cause. If we do no more than this, it will have satisfied honour.'

Henricos did not much like the sound of that, but knew better than to press the matter. If Meduson was motivated by vendetta than that would at least be *purpose*, and he himself had been working without that for too long.

'Count yourself fortunate,' Meduson said. 'You were fated for death on that ship. Now you will fight on.'

Fortunate. Of course.

'But it was not fortune that brought you,' said Henricos.

Meduson snorted a dry laugh. 'So you worked it out.'

'The sensor-ghost, mirroring our every move. You were watching us.'

'Aug detected you. He recognised the Sorrgol search-pattern and replicated it, mimicking a scanner-artefact, something we have done many times. Consider *that* your luck in this – if he had not counselled us to wait and to observe, we would have destroyed you as a Sons of Horus vessel.' Meduson sounded amused. 'Aug admired the way you ran the algorithm, though he was disappointed that you did not investigate the ghost.'

Henricos felt the barb. The White Scar had seen it, and he had not. 'I was in error. I will learn from it.'

'See that you do. This will be a war of deceptions, and they are as apt to it as we.'

Henricos bowed. 'So what now?'

'Our fleet has another ship. We are used to the process now – purge the crew, instate our own and add the guns to our arsenal.'

'You are rebuilding the Legion, brother?'

Meduson shook his head. 'No, but we are more than scattered clans now. That is the lesson here.'

'And if there is no Tenth, I guess you are no longer captain.'

'Warleader. That is all.'

Henricos could have commented on that. He could have remarked that there had already been an idea in which many Legions were subsumed under a single commander, with a title that was not so far away from this new one. He might have noted that this had not apparently ended well and that the parallels were worth noting...

Of course he did not do this. Meduson's quiet command was evident. The suicide mission that Henricos had willingly embraced was now part of something greater. He was no longer alone amidst the warriors of other Legions, and he had the chance to do more than petty damage to those he hated with such perfect clarity.

He should have been happy. That should have doused the anger that still burned through his every vein.

'Then you will join us,' said Meduson, in a way that was more observation than command.

'On one condition,' Henricos replied.

Meduson looked at him warily.

'Name it,' he said.

Medusa's skies were never open. There were never starlit nights – just the turmoil of toxin-heavy vapour banks, jostling, boiling and murmuring in the dark.

He limped from the southern gate towards the citadel's heart. All around him the forges worked, tended by ranks of silent guardians with faceplates of beaten metal. Factory spires rose from the installation's twisted entrails, each one crusted with the panoply of the machine – valves, intakes and conveyors. Between them were the great shafts, plunging away into the planet's core, welling up rust-red from the violence unfolding in their deep wells.

He dragged his bandaged feet through streets thick with dust, his jaw clenched tight against the pain and the hunger. The walls were far behind now and he had not seen another armoured guardian, just mortals like him in black climate suits, all consumed by the spine-breaking labour of the forges. He had been told to enter, but did not know the way. Amidst the smog, the spark-spills and the biting cold, it was hard to see more than ten metres ahead, let alone locate the path to the citadel's heart.

He knew even then that this was the test. Others must have done what he was doing – left the precarious safety of the clan land-engines and stumbled over the plains towards the strongholds. Maybe most of them died on the way, their bones picked clean by the icy wind. That was the kind of selection Medusa specialised in, the one that made its children harder than adamantium.

He lowered his head, clutching his collar to keep the chill out. There was no point in peering ahead through the gloom, so he just focused on putting one foot in front of the other keeping his muscles moving in rhythm.

It must have been many hours before the ground started to rise and the path switched back between stairways of new-cut stone. Inner walls rose up around him, vaster even than those on the perimeter. He saw a great sigil made from polished slate – a circular cog device, centred on a stylised wrench-head. It was huge, more than thirty metres in diameter, and embedded in a cliff face of stone that seemed to tower up into the turbulent heavens themselves.

Before he was even fully aware of it he was climbing steeply, breathing heavily, feeling the air grow more coarse and cold. His eyes were slits now, screwed against the dust. Something was bleeding – he could feel the hot trickle down his chest – but he kept putting one foot on each new step before him, inching his way upward.

Only once did he look back. He saw the plains stretch away from him far below, webbed with metal and punctured with gas-pluming wellheads. He saw concentric rings of walls, as solid as the sacred mountain, each one studded with defence towers. When the lightning whipped across the obsidian landscape he saw the detail there, picked out in neon, markers of a manufactory of infinite power and strength.

He never remembered the final ascent, the one that ripped the skin from *the soles of his feet and made his lungs burn. He must have passed through many portals, each one opened for him by the machine-guardians of that place who recognised a supplicant and allowed him passage.*

By the time his senses returned he was in a great hall, lined with iron columns and lit with orange sodium lamps. He had fallen and was on his knees, but he still shuffled onwards, knowing that he would either reach the place of testing or die like an animal.

He looked up, blinking through the filth-smear across his eyes. There were bodies all around him then – skeletal figures with metal parts embedded in their ghostly flesh, spidery amalgams of mortal and machine, and dwarfish attendants that scuttled between the legs of the greater constructs around them.

And then there were the Lords of Medusa, clad in blackened iron and attended by scores of robed menials. They were looking down at him. He could hear their mask-filtered breathing, scraping like the wind of the plains over stone.

One of them came closer, stooped, and took his chin in one gauntlet.

He lifted his head, painfully, trying not to wince. Just as at the gate, he heard the whirr of instruments. He was being scanned, judged and assessed.

The iron knight before him said nothing until the scans were complete. The grip on his chin was ice-cold.

'Pass the gate,' said the knight, 'and your trials will be eternal.'

He could feel his heart beating weakly.

'You will be Sorrgol. None will own you but us. When you learn secrets, you will never share them. You will fight alone, you will take no allies. We are the Iron Tenth, and we are alone. Outside this place is weakness. We alone are strong.'

He believed those words as soon as he heard them. A fierce joy kindled in his breast, and for the first time he became sure that he would survive to take the trials.

'You will never trust. You will never dilute your strength by fighting along-side another who is not of Medusa. We are the Iron Tenth. We alone are strong.'

There was moisture on his cheeks. He would listen, he would learn. He would break free of the shackles set upon the world by fate, and see the iron collar in all its void-set majesty, and to accomplish this he would absorb every maxim given to him.

He would learn. He would believe.

'*You understand this?*'

'*I… do,*' *he rasped, his lips dry and bleeding.*

'*Then repeat it. Say it, and never forget it.*'

'*We are the Iron Tenth,*' *he said, burning with both pain and pride, yearning for nothing more than it to be true.* '*And we alone are strong.*'

HE FOUND HIBOU down in the *Talon's* practice cages. The Khan had been working near-constantly since the assault on the *Inexorable Conquest*, believing that faults in his kill-team's tactics had led to the failure. Unlike Henricos, he could take little satisfaction from the arrival of Meduson, since his actions had done nothing to bring it about. The redemptive mission he had embarked upon had brought him neither deserved victory nor honourable death, leaving him dependent once again on the intervention of others.

Henricos watched him for a while, remaining in the shadows. The White Scar fought just as he had done on the frigate – a blur of speed, far surpassing anything that the common warriors of the X Legion could summon. There was a virtue in that, just as there was a virtue in the more solid techniques that the Medusans had been schooled in.

Eventually the Khan stopped, glistening with sweat, panting heavily. He must have been working for hours. Henricos came to meet him at the cage's entrance, offering him an oil-stained cloth.

'I did not think to see you again,' said the Khan, wiping his brow.

'You thought I'd take a place on the *Iron Heart.*'

'It is a fine ship.'

They walked together, heading for the chamber's exit. 'It is a long time since I was on a Medusan vessel. Perhaps I remember them differently.'

Hibou raised an eyebrow, and the movement made the scar on his cheek twitch. 'Then you are staying on the *Grey Talon?*'

Henricos shrugged. 'This is a lucky ship. And I do not trust you to fly it.'

'That may be wise – you have fouled half the systems.'

They reached the exit, and Hibou paused at the doorway. 'Teji is dead. Three others. Their blood was wasted – we would have lost the action.'

'That is war.'

'We must do better.'

Henricos nodded. 'We will.'

He reached over his shoulder and drew a sword, the first he had carried since Isstvan. It was no curved piece of Chogorian steel, but an augmented-function Medusan zweihander, the length of a mortal man, riddled with power feeds and linked disruptor field generators. It was the kind of weapon he had dreamed of owning again, far better than a bolter or a borrowed power-maul.

'Next time we fight, I will be at your shoulder with *this*. A single strike can carve a legionary in two.'

Hibou looked at the longsword cautiously. The heavy construction was the antithesis of everything that his own Legion practised in weaponry. 'Impressive, certainly,' he said, doing his best.

Henricos laughed. 'It was the condition of my taking Meduson's command. That, and captaining the *Talon*. I see potential here. I see a melding of philosophies.' He sheathed the sword again. 'Your kind move a blade fast. You could teach me how to do that.'

Hibou didn't manage to hide his surprise. 'Teach you?'

'And the reverse.' Henricos hit the door release, and the blast-panel slid back. 'Meduson is serious. He's going after the Sixteenth now, right to the top. You are correct – we need to find a way of doing better. Perhaps this is it.'

'That is madness.'

'In all likelihood, but what strategic use is sanity now?' Henricos fixed Hibou with a steady glare. 'If the chance comes, I will take it. I will look on the Warmaster's face as I end him. Will you be beside me then?'

Hibou stared back warily, seemingly unable to decide if he was being mocked. 'You will never get the chance.'

'You're probably right.'

'But if you did...'

Henricos waited patiently. In the end, though, Hibou never finished the sentence. The Chogorian's eyes moved back to the hilt of the zweihander.

'So how does it handle?' Hibou asked.

Henricos stepped back from the door and unsheathed the blade again. He nodded over to the practice cage.

'Draw your own blade,' he said, wondering how well his wounds would hold up if things got too strenuous. 'I will demonstrate.'

THE KEYS
OF HEL

John French

'The true danger of the unknown lies not in its existence, but in knowing that it exists.'

– Kyril Sindermann, in his speech to the Symposium of Nessus

What are the Keys of Hel?

I sleep and the question rises in my thoughts like the moon above a black sea. I do not know what the question means, and if I know the answer then it is lost to me.

My limbs are a dull echo on the edge of my awareness. My thoughts move with creaking slowness through my mind.

I see a face of dead flesh, its lips moving though no words come. I feel the cool flash as a blade punches through my ribs.

Pain skitters down my nerves.

The clink of chains.

WAKEN.

Warm blood. Thickening beat by slowing beat.

I see...

Nothing.

Thoughts are echoes. Have I had them before? Have I asked this question before? Is this slow cycle of consciousness a wheel turning without end, repeating again and again?

I know who I am. My name is Crius. I was Lord of the Kadoran. I am the banner bearer of the X Legion. I am the emissary of Ferrus Manus. I am the Iron Hand of the Crusader Host. I am all this. But these are answers to questions I have not asked.

Where am I?

Am I still beneath the mountain? Do I lie still in the gaol of the Emperor for the crime of being a loyal warrior in a war of betrayal? Is the coldness of this sleep a prison?

More questions, but still not the right question.

WAKEN.

I see a face. It is set in golden-yellow armour, and it looks down upon me. A black cross on a white field, and the clink of chains

Friend...

The word comes to me, but I do not know why. What is a friend? I am not a creature of friends – of brothers, perhaps, but not friends. I am one of a kindred. We are bound by what makes us strong, by the flesh of our father.

Father...

Pain, bright like a fractured sun. I am the pain and it is my world. I am not alone here because it is here with me.

Why is the pain here?

Still not the right question, but closer. Much closer.

The pain is rising now, spinning around me, flaying the numbness of sleep.

What is this?

The pain is everywhere. The world is not blank now. It is white. Blinding, cutting, burning white.

And the pain is growing. It has a shape. It has a head now, and arms, and a hole that beats where there should be hearts.

The figure of pain reaches for me.

Why is it here?

It is pulling me in.

Why does it want me?

What is it?

WAKEN.

And I wake.

The connections snap into place down my spine. Pain flashes along nerves and cables. My limbs become my own, dead flesh and machine answering with icy snarls.

I know what I am.

I open my eyes. Light pours into my world. Projected data bathes the chamber before me. Vapour rises from ice-clogged machines. I feel the snaking sensation as the flesh and machine fuse to my mind.

I step forwards. Ice falls from me in brittle scales. Pistons extend and snap my limbs into place. Energy crackles along conduits and I hear iron fingers flex. The pain is everything. Every sensation is a colour of agony.

I am a son without a father. I am a warrior risen from the edge of the grave of all he knew, and all that created him. I am the dead in a war of fools.

What are the Keys of Hel?

I am the answer.

I am a life stolen from the dark, and lived in oblivion.

I walk from my tomb, and behind me my brothers wake from their own sleep and follow me to war.

THE FIRE ROARS and we fall. A shot hits the drop pod's carapace and peels off a petal of burning armour. The air rushes out. Flames roar in the spill of atmosphere and then vanish. We are tumbling, the view beyond flicking past in snatches. I see the starforts sitting at the centre of webs of light, great burning spiders hanging above the blue sphere of the world below. I see our ship, the *Thetis*, sinking into the pool of fire pouring from them. She is bright with the blood of her wounds, liquid metal and glowing gas spilling from her bulk as she scatters more and more craft into the well of gravity.

I am still clamped to the drop pod's core. Nine stand with me. We are silent as our world spins and spins. There is no air in the pod now. A sensation registers cold on the bare flesh of my face. I neither blink nor move.

I can feel the echo of the animating waves pulse through me, stronger than the beat of blood, sharper than ice-laden air.

A wall of gouged armour fills the split in the pod wall. The muzzles of vast guns shout silently into the distance. We spin and spin. Explosions throw shards of metal through the pod. I feel one strike my armour and bury itself deep. The sensation passes.

The drop pod's thrusters fire. Our spin is a blur, then a scream of thrusters fighting to steady us. They fail.

The pod strikes the starfort.

Force slams through. A wall buckles inwards. Sheared edges slam into the warrior next to me. He dies for a second time. Black pearls of stagnant blood and oil rise from him as the pod bounces back up from the starfort's surface. The thrusters are firing at random. Lights begin to pulse in time with an alarm that no one can hear. We are hit again, spinning, rolling and glancing over ravines and cliffs of armour.

A plate rips from the pod and I can see the great, crenellated ring of the starfort extending away. Pods and gunships hurtle towards it, and the fire of a thousand guns rises to meet them. The *Thetis* is no longer sinking through the starfort's bombardment. It is drowning in an inferno.

This is the end.

We will not waken again. Here we perish. This is the last battle that we have snatched from the jaws of death. It is not an end of renown and glory. It was never going to be. All things end. All ages pass, and even the deathless may die.

Our pod leaps high above the starfort's skin, and I know that we will slam down again. I can see the buttresses and ridges of antennae waiting for us, ready to mash the pod to splinters and spill the wreckage back into the void.

'Fire,' I call, and the machines in my throat catch the word and carry it to my brothers. They move like sleepers still half in a dream. We fire our weapons.

Beams and shells rip the shell of the pod from us, and we are loose from the wreckage, diving towards the fort.

We strike the hull. The impact shudders through me as my armour mag-clamps to the fort's skin. Bones crack in the remains of my flesh

I rise, pistons straightening, and I feel my weapons arm with a tingle of shifting agony.

A hatch blows outwards from the outside of the starfort. Five Death Guard roar into the vacuum in their void-harnesses.

I fire and my brothers follow. They are like me. They died on battlefields from Isstvan to Greydoc and have slept in cold dreams at my side. Most still dream, the echoes of life just tatters. They follow, and they know the pain of this un-life, but they are spared the thoughts that remain to me.

Rounds and beams skid from the Death Guard's armour. A volkite strikes one in the gut. The beam burrows through a join in the plates and into his flesh. He becomes instantly still. The impeller of his harness pushes him upwards for a second and then cuts out. Then a jet of steam and powdered flesh explodes from the wound and spins him over and over. The rest land. There are four now. They wait until they are on the surface of the fort's hull to fire. Strings of plasma cut through us. The Death Guard shake as the recoil tugs at them. Another of my brothers falls, his body and armour hanging in a shredded ruin, swaying from where his feet are still clamped to the hull.

I charge at them. My boots ring and lock as they strike the hull. My brothers come with me, loping forwards. A bolt-round hits my shoulder, explodes and shears off layers of piston casing and cables. The impact registers somewhere far off and remote, a sliver of information that does not belong to this moment. The hammer head snaps out from my arm and locks into my hand. The first Death Guard stops firing and a film of cold energy sheathes the shield on his wrist. I raise my hammer, and behind and above me the *Thetis* looms and glows, like a spear tip hot from the forge fires.

The Death Guard does not wait for me to strike. He slams forward, his shield high, his muscle and armour cannoning into me while my blow is still unfolding. I reel, one foot clamped to the deck and the other loose. His chainsword comes up, tip first, the teeth a silent blur, and I have an instant to know that it will hit and that there is nothing I can do to prevent it.

The chainsword slams into my torso. I feel the cutting teeth bite into the ceramite, and their roar suddenly vibrates through my armour and body. There is a second of resistance and then blood, oil and shreds of dead flesh are churning into the vacuum as the blade saws upward. I feel it, but with a slow, drawn-out delay.

I have a jolting instant to see all around me, to see our drop pods and boarding craft disintegrating into motes of fire, to see the *Thetis* rock in her wrapping of explosions, to see the human troops pouring from the starfort's hatches, guns ready, their movements slowed by void suits. And I have long enough to know that we have reached the end of our war. We will be no more after this. We will end. I am not sorry. Ours was a war fought from beyond death. It was a war of obliteration not victory, and its end always lay in a moment like this, in fire and ruin.

My eyes find the helmed face of the Death Guard as he prepares to rip his blade from my chest.

It will end now.

But not without a price for our destroyers.

I punch my left hand forwards, metal fingers splayed. My fist closes on the Death Guard's gorget and I yank him close. He is fast, but my strength is not that of flesh. The chainblade is buzzing in the ruin of my chest. His face plate crashes into my shoulder. His eye lenses shatter and the air inside his helm vents outwards with a mist of blood. I would like to think that he feels shock, that he feels doubt and panic, and the cold realisation that retribution has found him. He won't though. The only thought running through his skull will be that he has to kill me. I know this. It is what I would have thought. They made us alike in that respect.

He recoils. The chainsword rips down. My hammer activates as I strike, and strike, and strike, until red meat and blood scatters with the slivers of his armour.

I stand still, suddenly cold and without the pain that tells me I am still in the land of flesh.

Data is cascading past my eyes like blood flowing from a wound. Somewhere beyond the runes I see the lights of battle. I turn my head up to see the *Thetis* fall as I know she will.

And a vast, black shape cuts through the lattice of fire. It is another vessel, smaller than the *Thetis* but still vast – a dagger compared to her scorched hammer head.

Fresh flowers of bright, cold light open across the blackness. A great dome of light erupts on the other side of the starfort, and a second later the tremor hits.

The scrolling data in my eyes stops.

I hear a voice calling to me in tones of static, but I am no longer a thing that hears or replies. I am falling backwards away from the world above, falling back to the jumbled memories of life and the questions that only the dead ask.

What are the Keys of Hel?

They are a dream that ends and wishes it had not. They are what happens when life runs out and hate endures.

WAKEN.

I am standing beneath the burning dome of the heavens.

WAKEN.

I am watching the world become a receding dot. Beneath and behind me the blank dream of true death rushes up to catch me as I fall.

'Waken.'

It is a voice that calls me. I obey it. I waken to the slow unfolding of pain that is the return from the dreams of ice.

I know the face that greets me. It is a face of blank iron with slots for eyes. It is the face of Phidias, my resurrector, my brother amongst the living. Interface sockets dot his armour and a mane of interface cables hang down his back like a cloak.

I try to speak, but the connections between my mind and body are not complete.

Phidias gives a single shake of his head, as though hearing what I was about to ask.

'We endure still, Crius. The battle was won, the enemy destroyed.'

A spider of pain climbs my throat and I can speak.

'How?' I ask.

'You were found and taken from the void.' He pauses. 'I made you again.'

I track the sensations as my body becomes mine again. It is different. The beat of blood is fainter, the tingle of flesh more distant. The cold thrill of metal presses into my awareness where before there had been the warm pulse of muscle and nerves. I have lost much, but I do not feel weaker. I feel stronger.

'No,' I say, forming the word slowly. There is still ice on the remaining flesh of my face. 'How did we prevail?'

Phidias looks at me for a long moment. He is calculating, processing data and possibilities.

'Another ship came to our aid.'

'Another ship?'

'Its arrival caused the enemy to miscalculate its key defensive choices. That cost them everything.'

'What other ship?'

'They have been looking for us, following the messages we sent into the warp to bring the enemy to us. They have been seeking for some time. Or so they claim.'

'Who are they?'

'The ship is the *Daedalus*.'

I hear the word, and at the back of my awareness I feel something move – a twitch, like the fingers of a hand beneath a shroud.

'Do they know I am here?'

'No,' he says with a brief shake of his head.

'Is the *Daedalus* still bound to the same clan?'

He nods. I wish that I could close my eyes to think, but I cannot. Data blinks across my vison as I consider. After a moment I speak one of the key questions aloud.

'If they do not know I am here, then why were they seeking us?'

'They say that they have been seeking all they can find of the Tenth Legion. There is a gathering of might, an attempt to mend what is broken so that we may be whole again.'

I pause. There is no point speaking of the delusion of such an idea. I think of Rogal Dorn, of Sigismund and the Imperial Fists squatting on Terra in hope of being able to face down the tide of treachery. I think of the hunger for hope that took me from Terra to find the shattered remains of my Legion. The nobility of such motives does not make any of those actions any less futile. There is only one reason to fight now, and that is to take the measure of vengeance from this universe before it is ashes.

'Why have you woken me, Phidias?' I ask, and the master of the *Thetis* nods again as though acknowledging that we have reached the point he was waiting for.

'Because they have asked to meet the chiefs of our force, and because they are not fools. The *Thetis* is still being repaired and will not be able to run. Once they realise what I have done and what you are, we will have to destroy them before they attempt to destroy us. Unless we can reach a point of balance.'

'You wish to avoid death at the hands of our kin. Does the manner in which we end still matter, Phidias?'

'Yes. It does.'

I am silent. I do not know if I feel the same way he does. I do not know if I feel anything. At last I nod.

The Kadoran. The *Daedalus*.

Pearls of ice fall from my face as I shrug from my wrappings of frost. My clan. My ship. Two shards from a life I no longer live.

'Very well,' I say as. 'Let us go and speak with my clan-brothers. Let them see what has become of their lord.'

What are the Keys of Hel?

They are the fires taken from the mountain. They are what should not and must not be. Only in the last days of humanity, when law has no meaning, should any think to break the locks placed upon them.

These are those days.

THE REPRESENTATIVES OF Clan Kadoran wait for us. Twenty warriors – armoured and armed, their weapons ready – stand beneath the wings of their gunships on the deck of a hangar bay. Around them, the jumble of our scavenged assault craft fill the gloom like the half-gnawed leavings of a carrion beast. It is hot, or so the data tells me. I feel neither cold nor heat anymore. They will have noticed that, as they will have noticed the damage to the *Thetis*'s hull, and the quiet which radiates from the darkness of the ship. They wait and wonder exactly who, and *what*, they have found. I know this. It is a mirrored moment, an experience repeated from my past but this time seen from the other side.

We watch them for several seconds, but they do not see us. Beside me stands Phidias, and to either side of us, stretching away into the gloom, two hundred of our silent brotherhood. At last Phidias steps forwards and I go with him. Our brothers remain where they are, unseen and unmoving.

The Kadoran react as they see us. Guns come up and volkite calivers and plasma blasters shrill as they rise to a firing charge.

We stop. Stillness extends into the space and silence. The moment has a feeling of stolen familiarity.

'I am Soter. I am Clan-Father of the Kadoran.'

I look at him and he looks back. His armour is battle marked, but the marks are like scars over healed flesh, and beneath them his armour purrs with smooth efficiency. His helm is clamped at his belt, his head bare. A strip of steel-grey hair runs down the centre of a scalp dotted with cog studs. His eyes are his own, but the flesh of the right-hand side of his face is a sculpture in circuitry and chrome. He radiates calm and strength.

I know him. I know him very well. His eyes move between Phidias and me in a single sweep of movement. Lights flicker beneath his right eye, but his face shows nothing. He waits, and when we say nothing he speaks again.

'We are come to you as blood of the same Legion, and to call you to gather with our kin. Who are you, and of what clan?'

'I am Phidias, master of the *Thetis*.' The words are uninflected, a blank gift of fact.

Soter gives the smallest nod, and then turns his gaze to me.

'And you?'

'It is I, brother,' I say, even though I know that my voice no longer sounds like the one they would remember.

He stares at me. Everything is very still. I feel a pulse in the air and know that vox transmissions are flicking between Soter's entourage. Their guns do not lower.

'Lord Crius?'

I take a single step closer, aware of the piston creak of my frame as I move.

'It is a long way from old wars, Soter, and longer since I was lord of anything.'

He continues to stare.

'We did not know you lived,' he says at last.

I do not respond to that. 'Why are you here?' I ask instead.

He pauses for a second, and I can feel him considering his answer. That was always his strength, both in battle and in strategy. Logic and strength were the pillars of the X Legion's might in war, but in Soter there was a vein of instinct rarely found in those of our blood. It was one of the qualities that allowed him to rise above his peers, and triumph where others fell. It was one of the reasons – in the limited form we are given to such sentiment – that I liked him. And now I could tell that his instinct was holding his tongue, telling him that something was wrong.

'I came looking for any of our Legion who might endure.' His eyes move between Phidas and me. 'I came to summon all I found.'

'To what end?'

'For war.' He leaves off both my name and the title he had previously given me. It is not an accident. The Iron Hands do not make small errors.

'War is everywhere, Soter. There is no need to gather to find it.'

'The Legion will be drawn together again,' he says.

'*He is dead!*' I hear the dry voice roar into the vast space. It is a thunder-crack of rage, bitterness and pain. It is my voice. I feel the bulk of my body flex, as pistons and cable feeds twitch. When I speak again my voice is quieter, but I can still feel the edge in it, the emotion which has come from somewhere I cannot see within myself. 'Ferrus Manus fell, our father is no more. We are broken. The Legion is no more. Nothing can change that.'

'We are strong. We endure, and we can be reforged.'

'We are not strong enough, brother. We are the remains, the echo which has yet to fade.'

'You refuse, then?' he asks, and I hear the suspicion in the words. I take another step forwards.

'That you ask is a courtesy I appreciate. But you know already that we will not be a part of the false dream you chase.'

Our gazes are locked, and in that moment I know that I was right and that he has deduced what I am now. I wait to hear his next words.

'What have you done?' he asks, and I hear the voice of the young Medusan warrior who I chose from a throng of shivering humans, and who became a warrior at my side and bore my banner for six decades of conquest and war.

'I have become the vengeance of the fallen,' I say, and behind me my brothers in death step from the gloom.

What are the Keys of Hel?

They were the seal placed by our father upon all the principles and knowledge that should never be applied. Few outside the Legion knew of the ban placed by Ferrus Manus on the Sarcosan Formulae, the Progression of the Seventh Gate, and the Ophidian Scale. Even amongst his sons few knew more than the name and, of those who did know, most grasped only shadows of dark possibility. Cyber-resurrection, ghola, death and life bound by field, woven by metal and sung by axioms of the unknown. Created by man in the Dark Age of Technology, or by alien hands under cruel suns, their origin does not matter. They are the evolution that our father placed beyond our reach, the lock upon a gate to a denied realm.

I have walked through those gates, and now I step between stolen moments amongst the living. I walk with fire, pain and hatred for all that has brought me here, and for all that has been lost.

And as I persist I think of my gene-father. Of the warrior who died, who fell and who allowed himself to be weaker than the universe.

And I know now – with every pulse of false life – that he was right.

'HOLD!' SOTER'S SHOUT cuts through the buzz of fire-ready weapons.

I watch him. He has not taken his eyes off me. His warriors freeze. He had not needed to call out – he could have held their fire with a sub-vocal command. But he had spoken it aloud, and I knew as I looked at him that it had been so I could hear it.

Beside him one of his warriors flicks a gaze across the lines of the dead. I recognise him: Taurus, a sergeant in the 167th. I had raised him to that rank. He had been a fine warrior, hard and unyielding as a worn anvil. I realise that I no longer think of them as *my* warriors. If I look further, and let memory and logic flow, I will recognise more of them. They once followed me in war, knelt to me as their lord, and I had called them brothers. That is gone now. We are separate, two shards cleaved from a broken sword falling away from one another.

'We did not come here as enemies,' he says. He looks carefully at the dead ranged behind me. I read the gesture and shake my head.

'I do not threaten, Soter. This is honesty. We cannot be a part of what you attempt. You know that. You need to understand.'

He shakes his head once.

'That you could do this...'

'There is nothing to protect. We are what we are. The Legion cannot be remade, and we are no longer with you. We are this age's last children. Go back to your dreams, Soter, and leave us to ours.'

Soter is utterly still. He is calculating, running the situation through logic and reason, searching for the decision he will have to make. The living flesh of his face shifts almost imperceptibly. He is about to speak.

'You have broken the decrees of our father,' he says. Behind him, Taurus and the rest shift imperceptibly. They are holding themselves on the razor-fine edge before violence. 'You have passed beyond. You have turned your back on Ferrus Manus. You are not of the Legion. You are its shame.'

And there is a paused instant, as though the second that has just passed and the one that is to come have yet to join. He is right. I know that he is right. The words are true, but they also do not matter. The warriors facing me come from a different world, a world that is not the cold sleep of death and the pain of waking.

'Kill them,' says Soter.

Gunfire blazes through the dark. Haloed beams of light spear into armour and explode cold muscle. Plasma screams as it blasts metal into vapour. Soter's Iron Hands are spreading out amongst the hulls of the assault craft, firing as they pull back towards their own gunships even as the ring of dead warriors closes. None of my brothers fire back.

'Hold your fire, Soter!' I call. He has leapt away and is firing at the slow shapes of the dead. He has not fired at me, though. He had the opportunity, in the long moment when he faced me, his weapon in his hand as the dead stepped into the light. He could have poured bolts into my head until it was pulp and bone.

He did not fire. Iron Hands do not make such errors. He had chosen not to fire.

'Soter,' I call and stride forward. The air is thick with the streaked light and tattered shrieks of gunfire.

'You are an abomination,' he calls.

They are halfway to their gunships. The craft's heavy bolters are stitching the gloom into a sheet of explosions.

'Leave us,' I call, as rounds explode across my armour. I rock in place. 'End this and go.'

'This ship will burn,' he calls and raises his bolter. Its muzzle is a frozen circle of black in my sight. 'We will purge you from us.'

'I cannot allow that,' I call. 'You will end here and we will endure.'

'So be it, then,' he says, and squeezes the trigger.

The bolt never leaves the barrel. A sharp edge of plasteel and lightning cuts the weapon in two, and a ball of shrapnel bursts from it.

Soter is turning fast, but Taurus's second blow cuts the front from his skull, and the third shatters his chest plate and ribs.

Soter falls.

'Cease,' Taurus calls, and the warriors beside him put up their weapons. He turns and looks at those whose brother and leader he has just killed. Again there is the itching pulse of vox traffic, felt but silent to me, passing between them.

Then he turns back to me. I cannot read his posture; he seems just as all of the X Legion can at times, unmoving, poised between detachment and fury.

'My thanks,' I say. He twitches.

'We will leave,' he says. 'You will not try to prevent us. You will not stand against us.'

He turns and walks away. I can still see the sheen of Soter's blood on his armour, splattered red reflecting black in the dim light. The rest fold in around him, taking the places of a warrior guard of a clan-father.

'You claim his place by taking his life?'

Taurus pauses and turns back, and in that motion I can sense the loathing he is carrying just beneath the surface of control.

'That was always the way. The old Medusan way. He made the wrong choice, the weak choice, the choice of flesh and sentiment, not iron. If he was stronger I would not have been able to kill him. Death is the consequence of weakness.' The blank gaze of his helm is fixed on me, and I hear the unspoken implication in his words. 'What you have done is not gain strength. It is not inevitable. It is weakness.'

'Then why leave us unpunished?' I ask.

He laughs, a growling roll that sounds utterly inhuman, and utterly without humour.

'Destruction is forgiveness. I will not sacrifice the strength of our clan to undo what you have done. You are living the punishment for your own heresy, and I will not spare you from it.'

Taurus turns his back, contempt sharp in every line and movement. He begins to walk towards the waiting gunships

'And him?' asks Phidias looking down at the shape of Soter on the deck between us. Taurus turns and looks at the bloody ruin of his former lord.

'He stays with you,' he says.

What are the Keys of Hel?

They are a voice growing fainter as the past walks away from us. A key is a beginning, but once the door is open those beginnings are forgotten. We walk through and leave what brought us there behind. We become the present.

We become the inescapable now.

SOTER WAKES. I am waiting for him when he does. He looks up at me. He no longer has a true face. Lenses and tangles of wire sit at the front of a skull of chrome. I watch the lenses twitch, watch the hand rise and the digits flex.

'Welcome, brother,' I say.

'It...' he begins, and then stops as though the buzz and click of his voice has surprised him. 'It is... pain.'

'Yes,' I say. 'It is.'

He rises, each limb moving one at a time until he is standing.

'Will this end?' he asks and his eyes are not looking at me but at the exposed flesh of his right hand, waiting for its skin of armour.

'Yes,' I reply. 'When we wake no more.'

He looks for a moment longer at his still fingers, and then nods.

What are the Keys of Hel?

They are the reward for our weakness. They are the cruelty of iron. They are all we have left.

DEEDS
ENDURE

Gav Thorpe

'COMMENCE BOMBARDMENT!'

A second passed.

Then another.

Still there was no sign that the command of Spearhead-Centurion Kratoz had been heard. The gun decks of the *Phorcys* remained suspiciously silent. On the ship schematic in the lower right corner of the main screen the status display showed the battle cruiser's torpedo tubes still loaded.

The Iron Hands' commander turned artificial eyes on his fire control officer, Khrysaor, glinting yellow in the dim light glowing from the panels and screens of the strategium.

'Sergeant-at-arms, why have we not opened fire?'

'Forgive me, but our firing solution has been compromised. I was attempting to recalculate.'

'Compromised? Explain.'

'Our companions, spearhead-centurion. The Salamanders' vessel has moved into close orbit, coming between us and the surface of Praestes. If we open fire they will be in the path of our ordnance.'

'They are in the way? Is Ari'i an imbecile? Does he realise what he is doing?'

'I would suggest, commander, that he is entirely competent from our recent experience. Adjusting for navigational error would not bring the *Hearthfire* so close. I would have to conclude that the intercession of his ship is deliberate.'

'Blocking our fire on purpose? I see. Truly the flesh is weak. Ari'i is mad, not stupid. Let us see if sanity can prevail.'

ON BOARD THE frigate *Hearthfire* Pyre Warden Ari'i of the Salamanders considered the possibility that he had just sacrificed the life of nineteen fellow Space Marines, as well as his own, in a pointless gesture. It was an outcome not lost on his second-in-command, Sigilmaster Aka'ula.

'With much respect, my lord, we have no guarantees that the Iron Hands will not simply open fire regardless.'

'I do not recall the pyre warden offering guarantees when he asked that we remain with him after Isstvan,' answered Sergeant Hema from the navigational controls. 'Can not even the most prodigiously-talented artisan find that his final blow quite unexpectedly shatters the blade he has diligently forged?'

'They will not fire,' Ari'i assured them. *Not yet*, he added silently.

'They have no sense of brotherhood, my lord, not as we understand it. They cannot be trusted to act in a rational manner.'

'A grave error, Sigilmaster,' replied Ari'i. 'The Iron Hands are exceptionally dedicated to their code, and reason and rationality are prized amongst Medusa's sons. I am hoping that my irrational act will force them to reconsider. I take it as a good sign that we are still alive to have this conversation.'

The command chamber of the *Hearthfire* fell silent as the trio of Space Marines waited for the Iron Hands' response.

A shrill tone drew their attention to the sensorium controls. Hema was closest, turning from his position to tap out an inquiry into the console's keypad.

'Aggressive sensor sweep, localised,' he announced.

'From the *Phorcys?*' asked Aka'ula.

'Yes. It's a target lock.'

'A bluff,' Ari'i told them, having not moved a centimetre from his place at the central command array. 'Centurion Kratoz must know that we realise he has enough firepower to destroy us in a single salvo, even without a dedicated target lock. He is simply making a point of it.'

'Detecting energy surge in the *Phorcys's* weapon batteries.'

'Spearhead-centurion, I submit that it is inadvisable to open fire at this juncture.'

Kratoz ignored his subordinate's protest and considered having Khrysaor replaced. He offered the sergeant-at-arms one last opportunity.

'All power to starboard armament, weapons officer. Prepare to open fire on target vessel.'

'As you command, spearhead-centurion.' The screens flashed with the redistribution of the main reactor output to the starboard energy grid. 'I submit that we cannot conclude one hundred per cent that the *Hearthfire* will not have opportunity to return fire. Salamanders vessels are famed for being up-armed.'

'They have nothing that can penetrate our shields.'

'I further submit that our target on the surface is stationary and hence not going to depart any time soon. You could request that they remove themselves from our line of fire.'

Kratoz could no longer glare, not with artificial eyes, and it was an expression he missed on occasions such as this. Despite his borderline insubordinate tone, Khrysaor was correct in his assessment.

'Very well. Comms officer, hail the *Hearthfire.*'

The comms-link display situated to Kratoz's left crackled into life, the screen filling with static for several seconds until the connection was established. A blurry, monochrome image appeared on the display, becoming more focused after another few seconds. In grainy grey and white, Ari'i's pitch-black skin seemed flat and unmoving. The hoop of ornamentation he wore through his right brow was like a ring of white and his eyes a light grey, though in reality Kratoz knew they were a disturbing scarlet. There was a four millisecond delay between Ari'i speaking, white teeth showing on the screen, and his bass voice coming from the speaker grille beneath.

'*Centurion Kratoz, I trust there is a solid reason for why your ship seems to have locked its weapons onto my vessel.*'

'Why in the name of the Gorgon are you getting in my way? Move aside and allow the *Phorcys* to open fire on the target.'

'*I cannot do that at the moment, my ally. I am still not convinced that yours is the justified course of action.*'

'You are not convinced? I have gigatonnes of destructive potential pointed at your vessel, that is all the convincing that is required. Move your ship out of my way!'

The brow-piercing swayed as Ari'i frowned.

'*You misunderstand, spearhead-centurion. Perhaps you have forgotten in the six months since our introduction, so let me remind you that I am a praetor of the Emperor's Legiones Astartes. I do not explain myself to officers of a captain's rank, no matter how impressive their battle-honorific. Or is it the case that the Iron Hands no longer care for chain-of-command and rank protocol between Legions? Has the loss of your primarch also stripped you of any adherence to the discipline and order for which your Legion was rightly famed?*'

Ari'i's words burned like the acid-etched geometric designs on the back of Kratoz's hands, deliberately spiteful and yet utterly vindicated. Kratoz touched the fingers of his left to his forehead in apology.

'My error, kinsman. I spoke in anger. As the Gorgon taught us, the flesh is weak. Shall we let more rational, calmer heads prevail over the vagaries of the heart? I would very much appreciate if you would come aboard the *Phorcys* to discuss the ongoing action against Praeneste.'

'*Your invitation is welcome. Both of our vessels will hold station for the moment. I will prepare to come aboard at once.*'

Kratoz nodded and signalled to the comms officer to cut the link. The screen stuttered into grey and then turned blank, reflecting the spearhead-centurion's gaunt features where Ari'i's face had been moments before. His eye lenses looked like circles of pure white against a haggard mass of creased skin.

'Prepare to receive the pyre warden and his party,' Kratoz told his command crew, before his voice dropped to a mutter. 'Perhaps in person he'll be more tractable.'

KRATOZ INSPECTED THE conclave chamber, ensuring nothing was amiss or out of place. The Thunderhawk had already docked and the Salamanders were making their way under an escort led by Khrysaor. The main table was a long rectangle of chrome polished to an almost blinding sheen, gleaming in the pale blue light of the strips overhead. At the table's centre was a plate of diorite carved in representation of the Iron Hands' Legion icon. Kratoz took a moment to consider the faceted white-and-grey stone. Harder than granite, it had been chosen to represent the unyielding nature of the Gorgon's code, a code that Kratoz had tried to uphold in the months since he had left the Isstvan System, his primarch dead, slain by the traitor Fulgrim.

It was difficult. To confide in his subordinates would be an unseemly act of weakness. It was his rank to lead, to be not only the spearhead-centurion but the spearhead itself. Where he went the others would follow. But who could he follow? The Gorgon was dead. The Legion... Was there a Legion without its primarch?

There had been anarchy, conflicting orders, death and destruction everywhere. He had acted. He had led. The preservation of warriors and materiel had been his primary concern. Warriors and materiel that was now of use in the fight back against Horus.

So why did he feel guilty? Why did he feel like a coward?

'The flesh is weak,' he whispered, running his gauntleted hand over the diorite.

'*We shall be at the chamber in thirty seconds,*' Khrysaor warned over the vox. '*In attendance with Lord Ari'i, Captain-Sigilmaster Aka'ula and Sergeant Hema.*'

'These Nocturnean names make me worry I'll choke on my own tongue.' Kratoz took his place at the head of the table and sat down. 'Very well, I am ready.'

He waited, immobile, quelling the doubts and frustration with the straightforward facts he would present to Ari'i. In the last few seconds before the Salamanders arrived he was settled again, confident that he pursued the correct course of action.

The doors slid open and Khrysaor entered first. Like Kratoz he was clad in battleplate of black, trimmed with silver. The sergeant-at-arms had extensive bionic remodelling of his left arm and shoulder, replacing the limb that had been lost fighting orks on Duraseth. Although Khrysaor always maintained that he was perfectly integrated with the artificial limb, he sometimes had the habit of clenching and unclenching his robotic fingers repeatedly in times of stress, as he was doing now. Kratoz thought again of dismissing his subordinate but chose not to – better that he had some moral support against the three Salamanders than none at all.

Kratoz hated himself for momentarily questioning his authority on his own ship, and it was perhaps his sour expression at this that greeted Ari'i as the Salamanders commander crossed the threshold. Taken aback, the pyre warden stopped a stride inside the doorway, head tilted slightly to one side in surprise.

To cover his momentary embarrassment. Kratoz rose to his feet and bowed, right fist held to his forehead.

'Welcome aboard the *Phorcys*, my lord,' he intoned solemnly as he straightened, glad that his artificial eyes could not further betray his flustered mood. Kratoz gestured towards the empty bench that ran down one side of the narrow table facing the briefing displays.

'My aides-de-militant,' said Ari'i as his two companions joined him. The first was nearly a head taller than any of the other Space Marines, his flesh like carved ebony, crisscrossed with scars that covered almost every part of the exposed skin. He wore a tabard of scaled reptilian hide over his dark green armour, mottled dark red and brown like dried blood. 'Sigilmaster Aka'ula.'

'Sigilmaster? I am not familiar with the rank,' said Kratoz, inclining his head towards the Salamanders legionary.

'Mostly an honorific,' Aka'ula replied, seating himself close to Kratoz. 'I was a record-keeper. My rank is as company captain.'

'And this is Sergeant Hema,' Ari'i continued, indicating the third member of the visiting party. Save for his broader cheeks to Kratoz the sergeant was physically indistinguishable from his officer. His armour, on the other hand, had been heavily modified, based on an old Mark III suit with external reinforcement, additional plates and visible boosted muscle-systems and pneumatics.

'You like it, my friend?' said Hema with a grin, raising his arms and turning first to one side and then the other to show Kratoz the battle-plate. 'They call me a superstitious fool, but I could never abandon this armour. It saved me many times before they introduced the Mark Four and I couldn't part with it.'

'Impressive,' Kratoz conceded. 'And the internal systems?'

'Fully upgraded to the latest autosensor suites and black carapace interface, my friend.'

'Perhaps when this current situation has been successfully resolved you might spend some time with my armourers. I am sure they would be intrigued to learn more about what you have done.'

'Of course. What I know you shall know.' He cast a pointed look at Kratoz as he sat down. 'We are on the same side, are we not?'

Kratoz ignored the question as he sat. The conference was a delay he would have preferred to have avoided. Every minute before they acted risked the success of their mission at Praestes.

'We were agreed that the World Eaters facility on Praestes had to be destroyed. I believe you said it was an ideal target for our next mission.' Kratoz held up a hand as Ari'i looked to interrupt. The praetor nodded for Kratoz to continue. 'I do not wish to throw your words back at you, kinsman, that is not my intent. There is a threat here. It must be neutralised. Not only is the recruiting citadel creating the World Eaters that we will face on the fields of battle in the future, they have begun to use their psycho-lobotomisation techniques and cyber-netic augmentations on a wider swathe of the populace. The creation of legionaries is a time-consuming process but all too soon Praestes will flood the galaxy with tens of thousands, perhaps millions of aug-mented, merciless, fearless human soldiers.'

Ari'i listened to this with an intent look and when Kratoz was finished the Salamanders commander stood up, placing his hands on the table.

'I do not object to the destruction of the citadel, but to the manner employed. The main structure is shielded against laser and telepor-tation, we know that much from our earlier scans. Using weapons batteries and torpedoes will cause immense collateral damage to the surrounding area. To destroy the World Eaters you would annihilate the city of Taurius and kill millions of Imperial citizens.'

'Citizens in league with the World Eaters,' countered Kratoz. 'Praestes has been a fief world of Angron for decades. Do you think they will stop supporting the World Eaters if we merely ask them?'

'I know for certain they will not support us if we kill their families and flatten their capital!' Ari'i banged a fist on the table, leaving a sizeable dent. Kratoz took a deep breath, resisting the urge to berate his superior for such offhanded vandalism. 'When Horus is defeated, every world we turn against the Emperor must be brought back to the Imperial Truth. We can neutralise the threat at Praestes without turn-ing three billion people against the Imperium.'

'I am only a simple spearhead-centurion,' Kratoz said, also rising to his feet. 'I will gladly leave such lofty matters of strategy to you, my lord, but I must apply myself to the immediate concern.'

'Which is?' asked Hema.

'The prosecution of the war against the traitors that have sided with Horus,' Kratoz answered. 'There is a valuable target vulnerable to attack beneath us and I will destroy it. You speak of the longer term? If we allow the facility to continue to produce warriors it threatens any chance we have of victory. The traitors cannot be allowed to use the civilians of the Imperium as a means of avoiding vengeance.'

'Vengeance?' Ari'i said the word quietly, leaning toward Kratoz, his eyes become crimson slivers. 'That is simply another word for revenge.'

'What of it? Do you not wish to hurt those that have so hurt us? It is not ignoble to strike back at those who have betrayed all we fought for. They have killed our primarchs, destroyed whole Legions of their brothers. You would allow them to escape punishment for a few million people? Do not claim that throughout the whole of the Great Crusade innocent blood never once stained the hands of the oh-so-noble Eighteenth Legion!'

'When unavoidable, we killed the innocent to secure compliance,' Ari'i admitted. 'But only then. It seems to me that perhaps your desire to punish the World Eaters extends to those that, through no decision of their own, supported Angron's Legion in the past.'

'You are wrong,' added Hema, glowering at Kratoz. 'About the primarch. Vulkan lives, and when we are reunited with him we will have to look him in the eye and be proud of our conduct in his absence.'

'What alternative course of action would you submit?' asked Khrysaor before Kratoz could retaliate with more venomous words. 'If we are agreed on the objective, perhaps we should concentrate on the means.'

The spearhead-centurion allowed his subordinate to quell the tension, taking the time to restore some equilibrium to his own thoughts. It was just too galling for the Salamanders to be so righteous, but there was still potential for them to be useful allies.

'The praetor does not have to issue explanations, only orders,' snapped Aka'ula. 'Be thankful he has indulged you thus far. You will stand down until you receive such commands.'

'I think you overestimate his authority,' Kratoz said slowly, trying hard not to let the Salamander's words goad him into another outburst. 'The inter-Legion codes were left in bloody tatters in the Urgall Depression. The simple fact is that you have a frigate with twenty legionaries on board, while I have a battle cruiser with more than two hundred, plus considerable materiel.'

'Such threats are unnecessary, spearhead-centurion,' said Ari'i, sitting down.

'It was a statement of fact, not a threat. If I wish to conduct an orbital bombardment of Taurius I will do so.'

'And I cannot force you to do otherwise, but I hope that I can steer your thoughts to another solution.' Ari'i sighed and leaned back, turning his gaze to Khrysaor. 'Did you know that I once met your primarch. Fought alongside him, in fact.'

'I was not aware of that,' admitted the sergeant-at-arms. 'It is a great honour for you.'

'It is, it is indeed. He told me that he admired the artisanship from Nocturne, and that we should be proud of our heritage as makers and warriors. Simple words, but coming from Lord Manus it was the highest praise I had known that had not come from the lips of Vulkan.'

'And the point of this nostalgia?' snapped Kratoz, who had only briefly met the Gorgon amongst a thousand others during his induction, and never exchanged words with him. 'Do you seek to drag authority from a chance encounter with our dead father?'

'I hope to help you see that we have more in common than divides us, but you seem intent on confrontation. Tell me, son of Medusa, why do you wish to antagonise me in such fashion? Have you something to prove?'

Kratoz kept his tone matter-of-fact, as though he was debating the best way to wire a power unit or strip an engine for maintenance. It helped him to make his points with precision, finding comfort in the exactitude of his statements.

'It is your condescending manner that aggravates my mood, kinsman. I am afraid your Legion is notorious for its sanctimony on occasion. Today you have demonstrated why that reputation was earned. Mercy and the protection of innocents are worthy ideals to uphold in times of plenty. The Salamanders could choose to sacrifice as many of their own as Vulkan wished to uphold such ambition.' The centurion's voice turned harsher despite his effort, the thought of recent events too much to hold back the emotion. 'The universe has changed! We stand on the precipice of annihilation and you would have me toss my warriors over the edge for the sake of a few million civilians? We will mourn their loss, but nobody else will. There are trillions more that require our protection. The Gorgon might not have passed on his wisdom to me in person, but I have followed his teachings. He taught us that in war, a pragmatist will always defeat an idealist, because a pragmatist will do whatever needs to be done. We live in pragmatic times, Pyre Warden Ari'i of the Salamanders. We can no longer afford the luxury of ideals.'

'If we are not fighting to protect our ideals, for what cause *do* we fight?' asked Hema. His armour wheezed as he turned on the bench to look at his commander. 'I cannot see that we will resolve this dispute any time soon. Perhaps a moment of reflection for all of us and then we shall reconvene?'

'As the Medusan saying would have us believe, the wisest head often sits on the shoulders of the least rank,' said Kratoz. He bowed his head to Ari'i and stepped away from the table. 'Let us not take too long, the enemy are aware of us and even now I fear they make preparations against our design. I will have refreshments delivered and we will speak again in ten minutes.'

'Refreshments' transpired to be thick slabs of ship-bread spread with lumpy protein paste and jugs of recycled water, which remained untouched on the table. Considering the circumstances – fresh food had not been a priority in the last half-year – Ari'i convinced himself that Kratoz had made the offer with sincerity.

'It's beyond me why you allow Kratoz to speak to you in this manner,' Aka'ula said after a few minutes.

Ari'i raised his hand to silence the Sigilmaster.

'Remember where we are. Keep a tight hold on your tongue for the moment.'

They waited for their hosts to return, each alone with their thoughts. After ten minutes, to the second, the doors opened and Kratoz stepped into the chamber with Khrysaor close behind. As the spearhead-centurion seated himself, looking with a grimace at the uneaten food, Ari'i spoke up.

'An orbital attack is not only wasteful of life, it is the least effective means we have at our disposal. Only a total saturation bombardment will guarantee the implantation facilities are destroyed beyond reconstruction. We cannot expect resupply, so a good proportion of your ordnance will be expended in the attempt.' Ari'i leaned his elbows on the table, the metal creaking beneath the weight. 'A ground assault not only reduces collateral casualties, it ensures total success with the minimum use of our most scarce resources.'

'A ground assault? Against the World Eaters? I would estimate the garrison of such a citadel at three to four hundred, and we have no information regarding how many of the lobotomised soldiers they have thus far created. Even if we were against the legionaries alone, they are in a prepared position. Between us we do not have enough force to complete an assault.'

'However, we will try,' said Ari'i.

'Why?' Kratoz looked at the Salamanders, incredulous. 'We give up the lives of our warriors to protect traitor lackeys? It makes no sense, morally or tactically. No, praetor, your plan is simply unacceptable.'

'Are you not ready to die for the Emperor?' asked Aka'ula, rubbing his stubbled chin. 'Has the Iron Hands' honour vanished so completely?'

'It is not a question of honour, Sigilmaster,' Khrysaor answered quickly, cutting off his commander's retort. 'Practicality demands that we assess the benefits and costs of any strategy, and the costs of the pyre warden's strategy do not warrant the potential costs.'

'Honour?' growled Kratoz. 'Where was the honour of the Word Bearers? The Iron Warriors? The Sons of Horus? The Gorgon and his Avernii veterans fought with honour and it earned them their graves. Do not lecture me on honour, son of Vulkan. Where was your master when the Gorgon confronted the foe?'

'You need to ask such questions because you were not there,' replied Aka'ula. 'How convenient that you should arrive late to Isstvan when you should have been beside your primarch when he led the attack.'

Kratoz paled, jaw tightening. Again Khrysaor responded first, but his demeanour was as livid as his superior's.

'The vagaries of the warp robbed us of the opportunity to prove ourselves on Isstvan, but they do not explain how it was that your ship was so close to the edge of the system when we arrived. The calculations are easy enough to make and show that you must have quit your holding orbit of the fourth world within hours of the drop taking place. Why did the *Hearthfire* flee so soon, my lord?'

Hema and Aka'ula both were on their feet in an instant, demanding apology for the accusation. Kratoz's ranted reply was lost in the shouting.

'Enough!' bellowed Ari'i, once again slamming his hand onto the table, the crash of ceramite on metal filling the chamber. He stood slowly, taking a deep breath. His glare was directed at his fellow Salamanders more than the Iron Hands. 'This is not how we conduct ourselves. Ever. Centurion Kratoz, accept my apology for any implication that you have been anything less than a stalwart warrior of the Emperor.'

This mollified Kratoz a little and he once again touched his forehead in apology.

'My lord praetor, with the utmost respect let me continue the petition. It is pointless to risk our lives in a direct confrontation with the World Eaters when orbital attack will bring equal success.'

'I will consider your views, spearhead-centurion.' Ari'i walked the length of the table and extended a hand, which Kratoz shook hesitantly. The praetor held him there for a few seconds, looking deep into the artificial eyes of his counterpart. 'I do not throw away the lives of warriors needlessly, but sometimes sacrifice is required to uphold a greater truth. Be assured that I have made no final decision and I will give your concerns the full weight of my thoughts.'

'If you are not prepared to accepted my plan immediately, I must be content with such assurances.' Kratoz led Ari'i to the door and signalled to Khrysaor. 'Sergeant-at-arms, escort our visitors back to their

gunship. Pyre Warden Ari'i, I await the conclusion of your delibera-
tions. I hope they do not take long.'

WHEN THE CONTINGENT was back aboard the *Hearthfire*, Ari'i summoned
his legionaries to attend him, leaving orders with the bridge that the
navigational officers should continue to hold course between the
Phorcys and Praestes. The Salamanders convened on the upper mess
deck, standing in a circle so that all could see and address one another.

It was a small command by the standards of a lord praetor, but Ari'i
valued it as though it was a task force of ten cruisers and twenty thousand Space Marines.

'We were delivered from the firestorm of Isstvan by fortune and the
command of our primarch,' Ari'i began. 'It is a chance to wage war
against Horus that many of our Legion were not given. It must not
be thrown away with rash action, but we should not be so timid that
opportunity to inflict harm on our foes is squandered.'

He looked around the circle of Salamanders and saw fierce pride in
the expressions of his black-skinned warriors.

'You understand the situation that we face, and the options that have
been laid before me. I know that you are loyal and will follow my lead
into the heart of Mount Koranua itself, but we are few and before I
make my final decision I would hear your thoughts, pay heed to your
guidance. I will lead, but I will not be a tyrant.'

'You cannot allow Kratoz to bully you into accepting his strategy,'
Aka'ula began, lifting his fist to his chest in salute as he spoke. 'If you
defer to his demands now, all authority is lost.'

'If you do not,' ventured Tu'atta, repeating the Sigilmaster's gesture,
'you risk alienation. We can accomplish more in concert with the Iron
Hands than alone.'

'Kratoz has a point,' added Hema, giving respect to the others with
his salute. 'He has far more men than us, and his ship has greater firepower. Perhaps we need him more than he needs us.'

'We will show him the error of that view,' countered Sergeant Marsoon.

'If we do not act with conviction now, what is the point having Kratoz as our superior in all but name? Better that we show him our true strength and fail than to continue to hide it for no future gain.'

'Iron Hands seek only revenge,' Aka'ula snarled. 'They act out of destructive spite and will do so again and again to our destruction unless you can leash Kratoz to your authority and guide their passions to a more worthy end.'

'You must lead.'

The words were quietly spoken, but they came from Vestar, who rarely spoke to anyone. Though uncommon, his observations always contain sound insight. All eyes fixed upon the Nocturne-born legionary.

'Kratoz has lost his father and fears to replace him. You cannot replace the Gorgon, but you must assume command here.'

Ari'i accepted this with a nod, and others spoke, but the words of Vestar stayed at the forefront of the praetor's thoughts. When all had spoken, their fists lifted to the plastrons to show as such, Ari'i smiled.

'Whatever occurs, I could not have asked fate to deliver to me a better company of brothers than stand beside me now,' he told them. He moved around the circle, touching forehead-to-forehead with each of the Salamanders as a sign of respect.

When he had returned to his place Ari'i took a deep breath, his demeanour solemn undiminished.

'I do not seek the preservation of life for its own sake, but I will not weigh the lives of innocents against the worth of a Space Marine. Loyalty, honour and respect cannot be calculated, measured and balanced by logic engines, they can be judged only by the hearts of men. The countless trillions we fight for may seem an uncountable mass at times, but we must remember that they are us – they are humanity. The seed of each is our future, potential leaders and warriors and great saviours of our people. The Emperor created us to fight, and to die if needed. There is no easy route to victory. We must tread the steeper trail to the summit of the mountain, and some of us will fall along the way. But believe me, the view from the top will be all the grander for the effort!'

Led by the pyre warden, the Salamanders raised their fists and swore anew their oaths of fealty, to Vulkan and the Emperor. And so the sons of Nocturne began their preparations for battle.

'SENSORS, REPORT POSITION of the *Hearthfire*.'

Kratoz knew the command was superfluous – the officer at the sensor banks would notify him the minute the Salamanders frigate moved out of the way – but nearly an hour had passed since Ari'i had departed to make his decision.

'Still holding position relative to our orbit, spearhead-centurion.'

'Gunnery, lock all weapons on that frigate!'

Khrysaor turned to look at his commander, his expression conflicted.

'You wish to open fire on the Salamanders' vessel, spearhead-centurion?'

'The senses of a legionary are famed across the galaxy, sergeant-at-arms, and yet twice now in the last few hours your hearing appears to be deficient. If Ari'i does not move his ship out of the way in the next ninety seconds, I'll blast him out of the way. Do I need to send you to the apothecarion?'

'May I submit an alternative course of action, spearhead-centurion?'

'Does it involve listening to Ari'i lecture me endlessly on protecting innocent lives and adherence to duty and my moral obligations?'

'No, spearhead-centurion.'

'Very well, submit your proposal.'

Khrysaor left his post to approach his superior and spoke softly.

'Contact the *Hearthfire* and request an audience with the praetor.'

'I'm disliking this plan already, sergeant-at-arms, but continue.'

'He will accept your request. We travel by gunship to the *Hearthfire*, and take with us a full complement of legionaries. Once aboard the Salamanders ship we can commandeer the vessel and steer it out of the way ourselves.'

'You want to commence a boarding action against the *Hearthfire*? Your hearing really has deteriorated, Khrysaor, or perhaps your memory. Why would I risk boarding when I can simply annihilate them from afar?'

'The Salamanders will not offer resistance, spearhead-commander. They will be outnumbered and Ari'i will see that the death of warriors from either Legion serves only the enemy's purpose. Faced with such direct action, the Salamanders will comply.'

The plan had some merit, not least because despite his threats, Kratoz was not comfortable killing his fellow legionaries. His anger dissipated by Khrysaor's intervention, the spearhead-commander could see the benefits of a peaceful resolution to the impasse.

'Very well, make the necessary inquiries with the pyre warden. I will assemble the boarding force myself.'

THE CRACKLE OF cooling metal accompanied the thud of boots as Kratoz descended the assault ramp of the Stormstrike gunship. He had expected Ari'i or one of his senior legionaries to meet him, but instead found a solitary member of the *Hearthfire*'s unenhanced crew standing to attention, hands by her side. She was middle-aged, perhaps fifty years by Terran-standard, and wore a dark green dress coat bound tight at the waist with a thick black belt, a sash of reptile hide across her torso – perhaps denoting she was of some higher rank amongst the Legion attendants. She raised her fist sharply to her chest in salute as the centurion stepped down to the deck of the landing bay.

'Where is the lord praetor?' the Iron Hands commander demanded.

'He is currently engaged with another matter,' the aide replied. 'I am Mehhet Ulana Vacol, primaris deck officer of the *Hearthfire*. I have full authority in the absence of the lord praetor.'

'Absence?' Kratoz waved away his own question. 'It doesn't matter, I can tell you as easily as Ari'i. Guide me to your main bridge, I am taking command of this vessel.'

'By what authority, spearhead-centurion?' If the woman was surprised or nervous she was remarkably adept at hiding it. 'This is a vessel of the Eighteenth Legion, and it is commanded by a praetor-echelon officer.'

Kratoz sent a signal over the comm and his legionaries marched from the Stormstrike, footfalls thunderous on the bare metal of the deck. The Iron Hands formed two ranks behind their leader, moving in perfect unison like fifty black-and-silver automatons. For the moment their weapons were lowered, but Kratoz was sure his intent was clear.

'I am not used to repeating myself, Primaris Deck Officer Vacol. This frigate is now under the auspices of the Iron Hands. It is currently interfering with my mission and will move aside. I demand to see the lord praetor.'

'He is on his way,' Vacol told him, glancing towards the massive blast doors that split the hangar from the adjacent landing bay.

A rumble of hidden gears caused Kratoz to turn in the same direction, in time to see the huge portal rumbling open and a blaze of light from the adjoining flight deck flooding between the receding doors. Twenty figures were silhouetted against the light, far bulkier than any normal Space Marine. As his eyes adjusted, Kratoz recognised Terminator armour, but unlike anything he had seen in a long time.

The war-plate of the Terminators was far broader and taller than standard legionary power armour, and these had an additional exoskeletal frame carrying slanted plates of extra armour, all decorated in the dark green livery of the Salamanders. Their left hands were fashioned in a variety of powered fists, claws and chainblades designed for close combat, anti-armour assault and bulkhead-cutting, and in the right they carried an assortment of weapons ranging from simple combi-bolters to triple-barrelled autocannons, plasma chargers and rocket launchers, and one carried an immensely rare long-muzzled volkite culverin.

Yet it was not these amendments that amazed Kratoz. The Iron Hands had numerous experimental suits of Terminator armour with modified heavy weaponry and ablative shields. What stole the curse from Kratoz's lips was the additional weapon systems mounted across the backpacks and shoulders of the Terminators. A plethora of armour-piercing missiles, lascannons, multi-meltas and a conversion beamer were all pointing in his direction. Each was quite literally a walking tank.

The voice of Ari'i emanated from the external vocaliser of the lead warrior.

'Spearhead-Centurion Kratoz, welcome aboard the *Hearthfire*. These suits were designed by Vulkan himself and we were about to transit them to the surface of Isstvan when the massacre began. The primarch gave me a direct order not to allow them to fall into the hands of the traitors, hence our swift departure.'

Ari'i swung first to the left and then to right, looking at the row of warriors behind him.

'You mentioned something about trying to take my ship from me?'

If the situation had not been so fraught Ari'i might have enjoyed the moment of hesitation before Kratoz reluctantly raised his hand in salute and bowed his head to the approaching pyre warden. The Salamanders commander had not intended to humiliate his counterpart in this fashion, it had been happenstance that Kratoz had launched his ridiculous coup as Ari'i and the others were about to board their gunships in the neighbouring launch bay.

'I expect you to return to the *Phorcys* immediately.' Ari'i raised his power fist and pointed to the Stormstrike. 'And take your legionaries with you.'

'What a waste,' replied the centurion. He waved a hand at the Terminators, shaking his head slowly. 'Vulkan entrusted you with his work and this is how you use it? Even with these armoured suits you cannot take the World Eaters' fortress alone. Be thankful that there will be nothing for the enemy once I have annihilated the city after your deaths. It is not the armour or weapons that makes the warrior, it is the spirit. You will fail. Your sentimentality will be your undoing. The flesh is weak.'

'I have heard you say that phrase on several occasions since our first encounter. I am not sure that you really understand what it means.'

'You may have spoken with the Gorgon but do not think to school me in the teachings on my own primarch!'

'Perhaps I must if the lesson was not learned properly,' Ari'i snapped back. 'What you say, the flesh is weak, is only part of the saying. In forgetting the end you have lost the meaning. Vulkan said it in praise of Ferrus Manus, after the One Hundred and Eighty-Fourth Expedition when our Legions jointly liberated the ork-dominated worlds of the Shoxua Cluster. The fighting had been fiercer than anything we had expected. Your primarch said in jest that his arm was tired from killing so many orks, and Vulkan retorted with "the flesh is weak, but deeds endure". It was a celebration of what they had achieved, and a remark that even primarchs can die but what they do will last beyond their lifespan. It was a message of humility, not condemnation. Flesh is weak because it knows it must come to an end, and so we must rise about the concerns of flesh and leave a legacy that others will be proud to inherit. Ferrus Manus understood that. He was a harsh master, an unforgiving ally, but he was also a maker of things – a builder, not a destroyer.'

Kratoz stepped back, shocked by Ari'i's words. In a moment he had recovered, his confusion quickly turning to irritation.

'Another lecture,' snarled the centurion. 'It doesn't matter what you say, the only thing you are going to leave behind on Praestes are corpses.'

Kratoz spun away, shouting for his men to embark onto the gunship. He followed them up the ramp and paused at the top to look back with a last shake of the head. Ari'i returned to his warriors and ordered the launch bay sealed again. As they lined up to board the dropships, he paused at the foot of the ramp.

'Reconsidering your choices, my lord?' Hema asked, stopping next to him. The old sergeant had tried to insist he could accompany the squad in his Mark III armour but had eventually relented and donned one of the modified sets of battleplate. Even so, Ari'i could tell at a glance that Hema had already started making adjustments, shamelessly thinking he could refine the primarch's work.

'Perhaps I am victim to a different sort of hubris, Hema,' Ari'i admitted. 'If we fail, Kratoz will level the city anyway. What then of our sacrifice? Am I just wasting the wargear and time the primarch gifted us?'

'That's the problem with legacies, my friend,' said Hema as he started up the ramp. 'You're never around to see which sort you've left.'

THE STRATEGIC DISPLAY of the *Phorcys* showed the positions of Ari'i and his Terminators, the signal routed to the battlecruiser via the comms-network of the *Hearthfire*. From a dozen speakers around the strategium the voices of the Salamanders' vox exchanges surrounded Kratoz. He listened intently, torn between wishing failure upon the self-righteous pyre warden Praetor and admiring Ari'i's bravery and dedication. Not to mention the skill and firepower of his squad, who had already stormed the outer barbican of the citadel and were cutting their way to the power plant housing located near the east wall.

'Hema, watch your left flank, there are more of those psychotic scum up in that gun tower.'

'Tracking five power armour thermal plumes on the wall ahead. Engaging with tempest missile fire.'

'We need a chainfist to get past these security doors. Abanta, cover me while I cut through.'

On the display the flashing icons of the Salamanders moved closer and closer to the heart of the citadel, but they were massively outnumbered despite their prowess and superior firepower. Every few minutes one of the flashing sensorium returns would wink out, the life-signs of the warrior no longer detected. Twenty-three minutes after arriving on the surface, an energy spike registered on the scanner, denoting a significant explosion.

'Spearhead-centurion!' Kratoz turned at Khrysaor's uncharacteristically excited exclamation. 'The shield generator. It has been disabled.'

'Full power to laser batteries,' Kratoz snapped. 'Lock targeting array on the citadel.'

'While the Salamanders are still inside, spearhead-centurion?'

'Stand aside, sergeant-at-arms,' insisted Kratoz, his anger at being countermanded for a third time almost too much to bear. At that moment his ire burned sharply more than fiercely, turning his words to an icy whisper. 'I will lay in the target coordinates myself. Issue the stand-by for battle readiness.'

There was no further protest from Khrysaor. He stood back from his panel, allowing the spearhead-centurion to take his place at the weapons targeting controls. Kratoz looked up at the strategic display and listened to the terse conversations across the vox. Two more Terminators had died in the last few seconds, surrounded by a small army of lobotomised psychopaths, leaving only twelve to fight their way into the facility core.

He looked at Khrysaor with unblinking lenses, hand hovering over the button that would issue the fire command to the gun decks, torpedo bays and laser turrets.

'The flesh is weak, sergeant-at-arms. Remember that.'

'PRESS ON! FIGHT on for Vulkan and the Emperor!'

Despite his exhortations, Ari'i knew that the battle was lost. The momentum of the initial assault had drifted away and the advance had become bogged down by the sheer quantity of soldiers being thrown into the path of the Terminators. His triple-barrelled autocannon cut a swathe through a heavy gunnery team setting up a lascannon in a doorway to the right, the explosive shells turning the weapon to a mangle piece of metal, the flesh of the gunners splashed across bare ferrocrete. He turned the autocannon onto three World Eater legionaries firing at him from a trench ahead and simultaneously activated the mind impulse unit of the primarch-forged battleplate to fire the heavy bolter mounted over his shoulders.

The Salamanders Terminators strode onwards through a tempest of fire, lasers and bullets deflected by their additional armour plating, shells and mortar bombs showering them with shrapnel and broken ferrocrete as explosions engulfed the advancing squad.

The killing ground between the outer fortifications and the keep was filled with the living and dead, a carpet of Praestan corpses underfoot as he advanced. Their guns were proving insufficient so the citadel's garrison poured from sally-ports and armoured doors with knives, mauls and chainswords. They threw themselves at Ari'i and his warriors, the World Eaters implants buzzing in their temples, oblivious to the fact that their swords and dirks were as effective against his Terminator plate as a gnat's bite. Ari'i's power fist hissed with energy as he smashed aside his foes, sweeping them away in bloodied pieces.

His suit's sensors flared a high energy warning a moment before something brilliantly white flashed for an instant just a few dozen metres ahead. A gun tower that had been raking machine gun fire across the squad exploded into molten droplets, showering red-hot rain onto the defenders and Terminators alike. The shrieks of the unarmoured soldiers quickly merged with the ongoing cacophony of battle.

'Orbital laser!' Aka'ula shouted as another pale line seared down through the gate tower of the keep. 'Damn Kratoz, he couldn't even wait until we were dead.'

Ari'i looked up and saw dark blurs descending towards the ground.

'Torpedoes,' he muttered, not quite believing Kratoz had finally acted. Even the Terminator suits would be no defence against ordnance designed to breach the hulls of battleships.

If it spelled the end for the Salamanders, it also heralded destruction for the World Eaters. Ari'i contented himself with the thought that had he not taken out the shield generator, the *Phorcys* would be using mass drivers and anti-ship missiles rather than pinpoint laser strikes. There would be deaths in the city, but far fewer because of the Salamanders' actions.

The quiet, confident voice of Vestar broke through the fog of confusion and disappointment that clouded Ari'i thoughts as he watched the dark smudges growing larger above the citadel.

'Those aren't torpedoes.'

Pinpricks of fire became the recognisable flare of retrorockets firing. The torpedoes resolved into drop pods, several dozen of them. As they slammed into the rockcrete of the killing ground, some petalled open discharging flurries of explosive warheads that slashed bloody holes through the World Eaters' slave-soldiers. Squads of legionary warriors poured from others, bolts, plasma and laser fire adding to the torrent of deadly fire. A second wave of larger craft hit the ground a few seconds later, their armoured skins shed by explosive charges to reveal Predator tanks, Vindicator siege tanks and a Dreadnought.

The Salamanders parted to allow the Iron Hands armour to form an attacking lance point directed towards the inner fortifications. Lasers, whirlwind missiles, autocannon shells and a storm of other ordnance converged on the keep, lighting it with dozens of detonations and slicing energy beams.

A Predator tank slewed to a halt beside Ari'i and he looked up to see the command hatch in the blocky turret flip open. Helmetless, Spearhead-Centurion Kratoz emerged from inside the tank. He raised a fist to his forehead and then cupped his hands to shout down over the din of growling engines and the crash of a citadel wall falling under the bombardment.

'Your flank is secured, push forward, lord praetor. I should not have doubted the strength we gain from righteous conviction. Let us leave a worthy legacy together. My thanks for setting me back on the right path. Deeds endure!'

THE NOOSE

David Annandale

'You are marred,' Lord Commander Ariston said.

Theotormon was silent. There was nothing he could say, Ariston thought. Not before that self-evident truth. The captain of the Emperor's Children strike cruiser *Tharmas* stood in Ariston's quarters aboard the battle-barge *Urthona*. His flaws were an affront. No doubt conscious of this, Theotormon kept his peace so as not to give further insult.

Ariston was conscious of the irony in his words. They were surrounded by flaws. His irony was deliberate. He revelled in it. Yet it was a false one, for he was justified in upbraiding Theotormon. The tapestry series that covered his walls had once been exquisite in its flawlessness. It was *The Tribute of Europa*. Millennia-old, it depicted the birth of the Emperor's Children – brought to heel by the Emperor's Thunder Regiments during the Unification Wars on Terra, the nobles of Europa offered up their youth in service to the Emperor. The sequence was a movement from justified defeat to glorious fealty, culminating with the first warriors of the III Legion marching under the banners of the Palatine aquila.

Or so the tapestries had been. Now they were slashed by an elaborate cross-hatch of knife strokes. Nailed to the marble wall behind the hangings were the bodies of remembrancers who had spoken out when the great enlightenment had come upon the Legion. Their flesh had been torn with the tapestries, and their vitae had run down and stained the woven fabric. Thus the art of the enemy bled and died. The destruction of the perfect possessed an even greater perfection.

But it still wasn't enough, was it? The ordinary, completed flawlessness of the atrocity fell short of the transporting sublimity he sought. The blood had dried and blackened. The suffering was over.

But the bleeding should not end. The cries should not fall silent. Blind to the truth that had come to Fulgrim, the enemy should know only pain and more pain.

That would be better; that would be closer to true perfection.

Theotormon's flaws, on the other hand, were the mundane, unforgivable ones of failure. His flesh and his armour were disfigured by his own hand, but his ship had been scarred by another's.

'This is the tally of the encounter in the Hamartia System,' Ariston said. 'The battle-barge *Callidora* destroyed, its escorts, the *Infinite Sublime* and the *Golden Mean*, lost as well. And when a full fleet answers the call for help, not only are two more ships lost to mines and the *Tharmas* damaged, but the enemy escapes. Tell me again, captain, what enemy is this?'

'The Iron Hands.'

'The Iron Hands.' Ariston paused, pretending to sort through his memories. 'I *was* under the impression that we had shattered them at Isstvan. Perhaps I was wrong. They must have been able to field a number of formidable squadrons to hurt us that much.'

Silence again. Into it fell the distant screams of the tortured. The exploratory desolation of the flesh never ceased aboard the *Urthona*. There was so much to learn, so much to experience. Mortification's supreme ecstasy beckoned just beyond the horizon of knowledge. The cries were now part of the air of the battle-barge. They rose and fell with the rhythms of lungs, of hearts. They were the sound of the new soul of the Emperor's Children.

'How large was the squadron?' Ariston pressed.

'They used a single strike cruiser,' Theotormon said. 'The *Veritas Ferrum*.'

His voice was flat. Ariston didn't know if the care with which he kept emotion from his voice was due to shame or anger at being made to answer for the disaster.

Ariston hoped it was both.

'One strike cruiser,' he said. 'Which then escaped.'

Theotormon nodded.

At the end of another long silence, Ariston repeated, 'You are marred.'

'I am, lord commander.' Theotormon barely hid his resentment.

'But from excess comes wisdom,' said Ariston. 'The flaw is the foundation of future perfection.'

'I do not understand.'

'Clearly not.' This was why a commander's role was also one of instruction. 'We will extinguish the last sparks of the Iron Hands resistance.' A simple statement of fact. Based on the estimates of the portion of the X Legion to have escaped Isstvan, the squadrons that were accompanying the *Urthona* were enough on their own to exterminate the Iron Hands. 'But we will not waste resources in searching the galaxy for the hiding places. They will come and offer themselves up to us for the slaughter. Thanks to you. Thanks to your flaws.'

'I see.'

'Do you?'

'You will put the *Tharmas* out for bait.'

Ariston smiled. The razorwire he had threaded through the contours of his lips scratched at his flesh, re-opening wounds. The taste of his own blood trickled down his tongue.

'Are you helpless?' he asked. 'Are you that badly flawed?'

Theotormon's left fist tightened. 'We can still fight,' he said. 'We have lost half the starboard guns. Our Geller field is unstable. Any jumps we make must be small, and we can't do many.'

'Hardly bait, then,' Ariston said.

He was lying. They both knew it. When the fleet coming to the aid of the *Callidora* had encountered the mine field left by the *Veritas Ferrum*, not all the ships had been damaged. And some had been hit more severely than the *Tharmas*. The rest of the fleet had pursued the Iron Hands through the immaterium. And lost them. Ariston's squadrons had joined up with the wounded vessels later, and he had singled out the *Tharmas* for a reason. He would construct the perfect trap for the Iron Hands, and the *Tharmas* was the perfect bait. It was strong enough that it could put up a convincing fight. But its injuries were such that Ariston thought it very unlikely it could prevail against a strike cruiser or larger ship. That was the prey Ariston sought. Let Theotormon pick off any minor targets that swallowed the lure.

The lord commander strode to the ornate desk dominating the port side of the chamber. Human limbs were fastened to its legs. He picked up a vellum star chart and showed it to Theotormon. 'Here,' he said, pointing to the Cyzicus System, a short jump from Hamartia. 'You can make it this far, I believe.'

Theotormon nodded. 'I believe so.'

'You are fatally marred if you do not. Make for Cyzicus. Then call for our help.'

'And I call until the enemy appears,' Theotormon said.

'Yes.'

'My redemption has a high cost.'

Ariston frowned at the resentment. 'You are fortunate to have this opportunity,' he said.

THE DELIUM SYSTEM had a name only because it existed, and for no other reason. It was uninhabited. Its four planets were all gas giants. None of their moons were colonised. And yet, it was a hostile system; Khalybus suspected that he and the ragged fleet he led had found the most hostile corner of it.

Fleet. He felt a jab of anger when he remembered what that word had meant to the Iron Hands before Isstvan V. It had meant more than a single strike cruiser and a handful of frigates and destroyers, all of them damaged to a greater or lesser degree. He knew he was lucky to have even that much at his disposal. Of his fellow captains with whom he had managed to make contact after the disaster, he was one of the few to have escaped Isstvan with more than a single ship.

Luck.

Escape.

Hateful concepts. They should have no place in the experience of the 85th Clan-Company of the X Legion, or aboard the *Bane of Asirnoth*. They should have remained abstractions. Things that enemies relied upon, only to be fatally disappointed when the Iron Hands shut down every destiny except total defeat. But he knew *luck* and *escape* now, along with other, equally foul terms.

Defeat. Treachery. Flight.

Then there was that other concept, the worst of them all: *Ferrus Manus is dead.*

Like so many of his brothers, he refused the experience of that one. Though its shadow fell over every moment of his existence, and every decision he made, he shunned it. He would not think about it. None of them could.

Khalybus had enough to think about on Galeras. The moon was a study in geological anguish. It was in close orbit around its planet. The gravitational forces of the giant tore and pulled at it. The crust distorted, rising and falling with an ocean's tides. Volcanic eruptions racked the globe, throwing ash plumes hundreds of kilometres into the air. The surface was layers of congealed lava flows. Galeras had no indigenous life forms, but in its constant violence and change, it had its own form of life. Landing on Galeras had been a challenge in itself. The construction of a base was madness.

Khalybus walked along the outer wall of the madness, inspecting the work. The modular fortification had to be modified if they were going to last more than a day on Galeras's heaving crust. The flesh was weak, yes, always, but sometimes iron could become stronger if it took on

some of the characteristics of the flesh. Flexible plasteel seals joined
each segment of the walls, given them a degree of flexibility. Khalybus
stood motionless, feeling the microquakes send vibrations up from
stone, through the walls, and through his boots. Both his legs and
his right arm were bionic, and the faint thrum ran along their length.

The base was on the crest of an isolated hill. Beyond the walls
the land dropped away in a steep slope. The ground was uneven yet
smooth – the succession of flows gave it the contours of melted wax.
Ash fell from the sky, an endless blizzard of grey. Visibility was a few
hundred metres at best. Though the base's location had been dictated
by priorities other than defence, its position was a good one. It would
take a very determined and powerful siege to triumph over what was
being constructed.

Also a mad one. For who would want to contest possession of a
worthless satellite in a strategically irrelevant system?

This was not a world for the sane to inhabit, not even the sons of
Medusa. The Legion's home world put all of its life forms through brutal tests, but it *did* still support life. He had faith that the Iron Hands
could sustain a foothold on Galeras indefinitely, but there were few
reasons to do so.

Few reasons. There was, however, one in particular.

Khalybus turned to face the interior of the base. The hab units were
along the periphery, and there weren't many. Even with rebreathers,
the mortal serfs of the 85th could not survive long on the surface. The
construction of the base and its operation was the work of the legionaries. The central block had been completed, and the project within
was proceeding well. Smoke, steam and sulphur vented from its chim-
neys. From the interior came the heavy, syncopated beat of machinery.
Deep booms and the harsh cracks of splintering rock blended with the
endless thunder of the distant eruptions.

Two legionaries emerged from the block. One was another Iron
Hand from the *Bane of Asirnoth*, Raud. The other was Levannas, a
battle-brother of the Raven Guard contingent that had been part of

the desperate flight from Isstvan V. Altogether, there were now two squads' worth of XIX Legion warriors aboard the *Asirnoth* and its escorts. Khalybus knew that some Salamanders had also been picked up by his brothers, but there had been none within reach during his own retreat.

Raud and Levannas spotted him and strode towards the wall. Khalybus waited. When they reached the iron staircase up to the parapet, Levannas hung back, walking more slowly so that Raud would reach Khalybus first.

'I take it you have news, sergeant,' Khalybus said.

Raud saluted. 'A message from the *Asirnoth*. The auspex has picked up a distress beacon. It appears to be from the Emperor's Children strike cruiser *Tharmas*.'

'Appears to be?'

'Full confirmation is impossible,' he admitted.

Khalybus hadn't expected otherwise. This was the new reality of war in the Imperium. He couldn't trust anything to be what it appeared.

Still, this might what they had been seeking. 'Where is it?' he asked.

'The Cyzicus System.'

That was a piece of data hard to ignore. Close enough to the Harmartia System to be convincing. Khalybus had not spoken with Atticus since they had conferred along with Plienus and Sabenus by remote lithocast, but a short time ago there had been a signal burst from him. It had been linked to a mine, set to be released upon detonation. It was a proud curse directed at the Emperor's Children, but it had been received by the *Bane of Asirnoth* as well. It was Atticus's way of telling his brothers that he was still in the war without jeopardising his location.

There had been no word from Atticus since, and no detection of the enemy.

The immense storms that had surged through the immaterium made communication almost impossible and travel perilous. The risks needed a high prize. The *Tharmas* might be it. The vessel's location made sense. Khalybus could picture it limping just that far from Harmartia.

Levannas joined them. 'What do you think, captain?' he asked.

Levannas had become the liaison between the Raven Guard and the
Iron Hands. His qualifications for the role appeared to be an instinc-
tive diplomacy, since he was not an officer by rank. There were none
who had escaped with Khalybus.

'It is clearly a trap,' Khalybus said. It was difficult to speak of strategy with the Levannas. The Raven Guard and the Salamanders had
not *betrayed* his primarch, Ferrus Manus, but they had not marched
with him as they should have either. He knew Levannas believed in
the decisions of Corvus Corax. He knew that there was nothing to be
gained in shunning the warriors of the XIX Legion.

Trust, though, that was different. He could not trust.

Yet he had to, or at the very least not refuse to hear what Levannas
had to say. What was left of the Iron Hands must now engage in a new
form of warfare. As much as he resented having to admit it, even to himself, this was a form with which the Raven Guard was more familiar.

'Yes,' Levannas said. 'It is a trap. That does not mean it will be a successful one.'

'The Emperor's Children do not do things by halves,' Raud said. 'It
will be a good trap.'

'I would be insulted otherwise,' said Khalybus. 'Even more insulted
than I am by the methods we must use.'

Raud muttered, 'Strike from the shadows, then scuttle back.'

Levannas smiled to show that he was not offended.

'The only dishonour,' he said, 'belongs to the traitors. The shadows
are true, brothers. If you understand them, they have an honesty that
is missing in the light.'

As the Raven Guard spoke, it seemed to Khalybus that the crepus-
cular light of Galeras dimmed around him. He was standing in the
open, as they all were, but he became harder to see. His hard features
became difficult to make out behind the ashfall. His stillness took on
the characteristics of an absence. He was in and of the shadows, and
that, Khalybus saw, was indeed a truth. In withdrawing from sight,
Levannas revealed his core reality to them.

Khalybus looked at his own right arm. He moved the fingers that had not been flesh and blood for over two hundred years. He considered his own truth – the truth of the Iron Hands that he must safeguard more jealously than ever before.

'We are not you,' he said to Levannas. 'And we will not become you.'

'I would never suggest that you should,' Levannas answered.

'We still can't attack directly,' said Raud.

'I know. We all do.' He eyed the central block of the base. 'So we must find a new way to fight that is still true to our primarch.'

'Then we will head into the trap.' The upper half of Raud's skull was metal. There was still flesh on his lower jaw, though, and he could just about form the approximation of a smile.

'Well, they're hardly going to come to us, are they?' asked Khalybus.

THE LOGICAL MOMENT to spring the trap would have been at the Mandeville point of the Cyzicus System. Khalybus had the *Bane of Asirnoth* at full battle stations, ready to open fire the second after transition to real space. He would not let the Emperor's Children have an easy kill. He had no illusions about such a battle's outcome, though. If the *Asirnoth* were unable to flee back into the warp, it would not survive a prolonged encounter. The strike cruiser had been damaged over Isstvan. Some repairs had been made, but there were limits to what had been possible. The void shields were some way from full strength. There hull had been compromised, and the sites of those wounds were painful weaknesses.

The first hard reality of Khalybus's gamble: it was easily within the power of the Emperor's Children to annihilate any single ship that took the offered bait.

The second hard reality: he had no choice but to take that bait.

He stood in the lectern above the bridge of the *Bane of Asirnoth*. Nothing appeared in the oculus. The system was quiet except for the distress beacon of the *Tharmas*.

'Auspex?' Khalybus asked.

'We have picked up the radiation from the *Tharmas*'s engines,' Seterikus said. 'No other vessels within range.'

'Which doesn't mean they aren't here,' said Raud. He was at the weapons station, at the forward end of the bridge.

'Of course they're here,' Khalybus said.

But they hadn't attacked. They were remaining hidden. Why? Because killing the *Bane of Asirnoth* would be insufficient. The traitors had bigger prey in mind.

So do I, he thought.

'It would be disappointing if they were not. Set course for the *Tharmas*.'

The III Legion strike cruiser was about a third of the way from the Mandeville point toward the system's sun. Czysicus was an old red star. It had swallowed up its inner planets hundreds of millions of years ago, leaving only the outer gas giants and the frozen planetoids of its Kuiper belt. Czysicus was as dead as Delium, though it was now alive with the anticipation of war.

Khalybus kept the first stage of the approach to the *Tharmas* slow and cautious. There was no point in trying to disguise the *Bane of Asirnoth*'s presence. The *Tharmas* and whatever other Emperor's Children vessels that waited concealed in the system already knew that they were here, but he wanted time to detect the rest of the enemy force, if he could. He wanted a feel for the full nature of the trap.

Still nothing. Only the endless broadcast of the enemy cruiser's beacon.

Khalybus saw Levannas looking at him. The Raven Guard had taken up a discreet position on the bridge, near the back wall, just below and to the right of the lectern. He was out of the way, but visible if the captain wished to speak to him.

'Well?' Khalybus asked. 'What do you see in the shadows here?'

'I'm sure I see the same things you do, captain. They are waiting for us to engage.'

'At which point they will wound us, force us to retreat, and follow.'

'Yes.'

Which is what we've been expecting all along, he thought. The absence of an initial attack was confirmation of that theory.

Khalybus nodded to himself. 'We have no choice but to play their game,' he announced. 'But we will beat them at it. Full speed ahead, full barrage. I want that verminous ship destroyed.'

The background hum that was the sum of the *Asirnoth*'s machinery of life increased. Its vibrations became more intense. Khalybus felt the ship's anger as though it were his own. Its life and his were on a continuum.

This was part of what it meant to be one of the Iron Hands – not just to understand the strength of the machine, but to *be* the machine. When he was aboard the *Bane of Asirnoth*, when he commanded its course and its actions, there was no absolute demarcation line between his being and the ship's. The helmsmen of other Legions experienced that blurring when the mechadendrites fused them to their vessels. But every warrior of the X Legion walked the path towards the unbending power of the mechanical. The machine had a discipline, a focus and a clarity that was foreign to the flesh. The *Bane of Asirnoth* was an extension of his will, a force multiplier of his own strength. It was his right arm reaching out to crush his foe. And he, and all the legionaries aboard, repaid the machine's gifts by moving closer and closer towards complete identification.

Ferrus Manus had shown them the way. He had not been given the time to complete his journey – *though he was not dead, he could not be dead* – and it was their duty to redouble efforts to complete the pilgrimage. Now, more than ever, they needed the rigour of the machine.

Standing a few steps behind Khalybus in the strategium, Cruax said, 'And so, as we expected, we will strike and we will run.' His machine voice sounded more cold and hollow than ever.

'Yes, Iron Father.' Khalybus did not look back. 'But more than that, as well.'

'I know. My concern remains. What will this strategy cost us? How much is it shaped by strangers to our philosophy?'

Khalybus glanced down at Levannas. Circumstances were forcing the Iron Hands to learn from the methods of the Raven Guard. But those lessons would not alter the core of the Legion. 'Do you doubt me?' he asked Cruax, quietly, keeping the exchange between the two of them.

'I have doubts about where this path is leading us. The Legions who abandoned our primarch on Isstvan have nothing to teach us.' There was no tone in the voice of the guardian of the Iron Hands' soul. The anger was in the words.

Khalybus shared it. He wanted Cruax to understand that he had not made his decisions lightly.

'What choice do we have? If we wish to fight on, then we must adapt.' He looked back at the other warrior. Cruax's servo-arms were folded behind his back. Of all the legionaries aboard the *Asirnoth*, he was the one most fully transformed. Khalybus wasn't sure if he had any flesh left at all. 'What we are about to do,' he said, 'is true to the Iron Hands. It will be precise. It will be rigorous. It will succeed on those merits.'

Cruax said nothing. Khalybus faced the oculus once more.

'IT'S THE BANE *of Asirnoth*,' Enion reported. 'Captain Khalybus.'

'Thank you, equerry,' Ariston said. Not the *Veritas Ferrum*. A shame. Revenge on Atticus would have been a pleasing, violent symmetry. But perhaps Khalybus would be the key to the other captain as well. Ariston watched the trajectories of the strike cruisers plotted on the tactical screens.

'We could take them apart now.'

'We could,' Ariston agreed.

Enion hesitated, expecting an order. Ariston amused himself by not giving it.

'There is no need to put the *Tharmas* at risk,' said Enion.

'The imperfection of Theotormon's command needs to be chastised,' Ariston told him. 'Emphatically. And more to the point, are we going to satisfy ourselves with a single strike cruiser? Not even the one that destroyed the *Callidora*?'

'No, lord commander.'

'No,' Ariston repeated. 'We will use these Iron Hands to take us to their brothers.'

'They aren't fools.'

'True. So our mistake must be perfect. They must believe they have thwarted us.'

THE TWO SHIPS went to war. They opened fire at virtually the same moment. They were as big as mountains, as long as cities. Their movements were too massive to reflect the urgency in the wills that drove them. They struck at each other with torpedoes and cannons. Their weapons had speed, but the wills were faster yet, the hatreds more furious. The ships turned on each other with majesty, with the grace of monuments. There would be no evading the wounds of the duel. Instead, they engaged in the lethal, gradual dance of manoeuvring to be the first to strike the greatest injury.

The oculus flashed with the energy discharges of the void shields. Khalybus heard the damage reports. He saw, below him, the tell-tale red of the runes appearing on the screens monitoring the cruiser's health. He had little need to hear or see either. He could feel how his ship fared. Its body was his.

But it had his will, and it would not stop before it had torn the life from its enemy.

The *Bane of Asirnoth* was cutting across the prow of the *Tharmas*. The Emperor's Children ship presented a smaller profile, but Khalybus was able to strafe it with the full thunder of the starboard armament. The *Tharmas* fired forwards, and Khalybus saw the weakness – most of its torpedoes and shells were coming from the port side.

'Get us around to their starboard flank,' he told the helmsman, Kiriktas. 'They don't want us there.'

Kiriktas complied. The *Asirnoth* began its turn, still at full speed. The *Tharmas* tried to counter. It did not have to move as far or as fast to keep the *Asirnoth* away from its vulnerabilities. But its movements were hampered, and it revealed its second weakness.

'Their engines…' Raud began.

'I can see,' Khalybus said. He saw more than that. He saw the inevitable result of the dance. The Emperor's Children had already lost. They had lost the moment the nature of their wounds had become visible. There was nothing the traitors could do to stop what was coming. He hoped they realised this as completely as he did. He wanted them to experience the closing down of possibility, the unstoppable approach of execution.

They fought to the end, though. They fought hard to take the *Asirnoth* to oblivion with them. The *Tharmas*'s guns concentrated their fire on a single point amidships.

'Shields going down,' Demir called. 'Hull integrity compromised.'

'Vent and seal,' Khalybus ordered. 'Full energy to the starboard shields.'

'Contacts!' said Seterikus. 'Multiple signals moving in.'

'From what direction?' Khalybus asked.

'All of them.'

'Brother-captain,' said Demir, 'our port flank will be vulnerable.'

'We have time.'

Demir paused, then said, 'So ordered.'

They had time, Khalybus told himself. He would create it himself if necessary.

The *Bane of Asirnoth* completed the manoeuvre. The two ships were flank to flank. The distance between them became an irrelevance. The *Tharmas* was still fighting, but it was dead.

'Fire,' Khalybus said.

The *Asirnoth* struck with a full broadside, and then again. It hit the *Tharmas* with better than twice the force that the III Legion ship could summon. Khalybus grimaced as he felt the *Asirnoth* shudder. The shields flared again, and even with the boost in power, some of them collapsed. Demir was calling out damage reports, but Khalybus tuned them out. He focused on the *Tharmas*. His concentration followed ship-killing ordnance across the void. He had committed the *Asirnoth* to this action, and by the Throne, this act of justice would be complete.

Under the bombardment of massive shells, the void shields of the *Tharmas* flared like suns, then fell into darkness. The torpedoes slammed through the hull, and then there was a new light. It began as a pulsing crimson. That was the firestorms scouring the ship's corridors. It grew brighter, building in pain and intensity. It became the plasma cry of a dying ship. The *Tharmas* cracked wide open. Its fore and aft halves began to move independently even as they were swallowed by the growing fireball. The immense ship was dwarfed by its explosions. Cascading shockwaves reached out across the void.

'Get us clear,' said Khalybus, but Kiriktas was already altering course, putting the *Asirnoth* into a straight run, taking off on a tangent from the arc it had been making around the *Tharmas*. 'Redistribute shield energy, Brother Demir.'

Even as he spoke, the first torpedoes from the rest of the fleet hit the *Asirnoth*'s port flank. The jolt was a big one. Even before Demir spoke, Khalybus knew the injury was serious. The vibrations of the ship had carried the shock to him. The pulse of the ship's life stuttered. Khalybus wondered if he'd been wrong. This didn't feel like an attack to wound. The Emperor's Children were coming to kill.

'We've lost two banks of port cannons,' Demir said. 'Secondary damage from exploding ordnance. There is a breach across the loading bay. Fires are spreading.'

'Do what is necessary,' Khalybus said. Demir did not need to be told what to do. The order was confirmation that, as captain, he understood the losses that were occurring, and the further toll that would be paid. How many battle-brothers had been near the bay and had been propelled into the void? Had they lost any gunships? How many serfs had been incinerated by the fires? Questions whose answers were, in this moment, irrelevant. What mattered was the survival of the ship itself, and its ability to continue the war. Second by second, that was the only consideration, if there was to be any hope of reaching the end game of this campaign.

'Can we afford the greater loss ahead?' Cruax asked, as if reading his mind.

'If there is a way of avoiding it, I will take it,' Khalybus said.

The *Bane of Asirnoth* shuddered again. Tocsins wailed.

'There will not be,' Cruax said.

'The Emperor's Children will suffer worse,' Khalybus promised.

But only if the *Asirnoth* escaped this system.

'Helmsman Kiriktas, make course for the Mandeville point. Brother Seterikus, what are the positions of the foe?'

'Still on the outer edges of the system. The ships on the far side are closing. The ones closest to the Mandeville point are not advancing.'

'They know we have to come to them. Then let us do so. Full speed. All forward batteries fire.'

This was the hardest gamble he would make in the Czysicus System. It was also the one move that was open to him. The Iron Hands could not evade the net being drawn around them, and they could not fight an entire fleet. There was a tremble in the *Asirnoth*'s vibrations now. Khalybus doubted his vessel could fight a single enemy with any expectation of survival. There only flight or death now. And so the strike cruiser ran in the teeth of the trap.

'Brother-captain,' Seterikus reported, 'we are making for the battle-barge *Urthona*.'

'Then let us give them cause to worry,' Khalybus said.

'This is desperate,' Cruax muttered.

'So is this mission. So is our war.'

'I understand, captain. But is the desperation one that is true to us?'

'It is,' Khalybus said. 'We knew this was a trap. The risk is a calculated one. That the odds are against us makes it no less calculated.'

'Good,' said the Iron Father.

The *Bane of Asirnoth* ran straight for the *Urthona*, cannon shells and torpedoes racing ahead, as if they might clear the void of incoming fire. The *Asirnoth*'s profile would be reduced from the perspective of the battle-barge. Khalybus saw the irony in using the same tactic against the enemy that had done so little for the *Tharmas*. But the Iron Hands had speed. That, and the faint hope of luck, was all they had to see them through to escape.

Calculated, Khalybus thought. The word was all the more bitter for being true. He and his brothers had been pushed to this extremity by treachery. All the Iron Hands had now was the calculated risk in its most dire form.

The guns of the battle-barge and its escorts flashed.

ARISTON SMILED AS he turned from the tactical screens to observe the display in the oculus. The clockwork toys of the X Legion were behaving with perfect predictability. They did as he expected, when he expected. He could mark time with the beats of their manoeuvres. There was no art to their warfare. It was mechanistic. He had never understood their commitment to that approach. When they had fought side by side, he had appreciated the pulverizing victories they achieved, but found their methods uninspiring. Now he had a different perspective. Now he would use their plodding dullness as a medium for his art. He had the canvas prepared, and they would travel across it, marking it according to his will. A creation on this scale would be a source of delicious sensation, he was sure, especially at its moment of fruition, when the Iron Hands took a great leap towards final extinction.

'Annihilation,' he said to Enion, 'has a piquancy that should be tasted more often, don't you agree?'

'Quite so, lord commander.'

Did Enion agree because he felt he should, or because he truly did understand what Ariston meant? The equerry was an intelligent officer. He had been demonstrating a growing aptitude for the intricacies of sensation, and the nuances of pain. Hooks and wires linked the corners of his eyes to his shoulder plates. Every time he turned his head, he opened his flesh again. He appeared to be eternally weeping tears of blood, though he had slit the corners of his mouth into a fixed grin. Perhaps he did have some conception of the exquisite nature of Ariston's plan.

'Hurt them,' Ariston ordered his officers. 'Make them believe their moment has come. But do not kill them.'

✠ ✠ ✠

'At least we made one of them move,' Raud said.

A frigate to port of the *Urthona* was engaging in evasive action, rising above the plane of the battle. The battle-barge did not deviate in its course. Its ranks upon ranks of guns blazed, shaking the void with silent thunder. The *Urthona* was twice the size of the *Bane of Asirnoth*, but there was still arrogance in its unwavering slow approach. It was not invulnerable to the strike cruiser's attacks.

They know how badly we've been hurt, Khalybus thought. He saw mockery in the *Urthona*'s indomitability. The Emperor's Children were holding up a mirror to the Iron Hands. *Look*, they were saying. *This is how you once went to war, and we have taken this from you.*

The *Ariston* shuddered again as the enemy shells struck its prow. The shields bled off the worst of the impacts, but the kinetic force of projectiles a dozen metres long was such that heavy blows ran along the spine of the vessel. The armour on the prow crumpled.

A torpedo flashed across the top of the hull and struck the base of the superstructure. The impact shook the bridge with the force of an earthquake. It knocked the mortal crewmembers off their feet. The legionaries remained standing, though Khalybus knew they were bracing for the inevitable. It would not take many more barrages of that scale to doom the *Asirnoth*. If the rest of the fleet started hitting them, the end would come in seconds.

'Helmsman,' Khalybus said, 'our need to escape grows pressing.'

Kiriktas summoned more power from the engines. The background hum of the *Bane of Asirnoth* became a snarl. And beneath it was the deeper, coiling tension of the warp drive building up for the jump. The juddering and the stuttering spikes in the vibrations became stronger too. Khalybus spared a thought for the stability of the warp drive, the integrity of the hull, and the strength of the Geller field. Then he put the concerns to one side. The *Asirnoth* would survive the jump, or it would not.

First it had to survive *until* the jump.

'Ten seconds,' Krikitas announded.

Another barrage from the *Urthona* hit. Somewhere, iron shrieked. A chain of explosions, building on each other, rattled down the spine of the ship.

It seemed to Khalybus that he was holding his vessel together through willpower alone.

Well enough, then. He had plenty to spare.

Reality shuddered and tore. The *Bane of Asirnoth* jumped into the warp.

THE WOUNDED SHIP vanished from the physical realm. It left behind dissipating energies – some from its own injuries, some the whispers of insanity that bled in from the warp. Ariston saw perfection in the damage done to the strike cruiser. The Iron Hands would, he judged, survive the journey through the empyrean, though they would be tested. It would be a much more difficult one for them than for the Emperor's Children, even if they weren't limping.

He opened a communications channel to the entire fleet. 'All ships, follow behind the *Urthona*,' he said. 'We shall let our quarry guide us through the immaterium.'

The battle-barge made its jump minutes after the *Asirnoth*. Its drives had been powering up during the entire confrontation. The length of the Iron Hands' lead meant little, though, in the warp. There, space collapsed and time contorted. Neither had any objective meaning. Dark simulacra took their place, alongside the illusion of matter, the insistent presence of dreams, and the being of dark intelligences.

The warp was a storm. It convulsed with a fusion of delight and fury. Waves of non-being rose to infinity and crashed upon the mad creatures who thought they could navigate the domain of the gods without their leave.

For the chosen few, however, the way was made clear. The *Urthona* passed between the vortices of destruction. The Emperor's Children would travel the seas of unreality without hindrance. Enlightenment had taken them to the wisdom hidden in the furthest extremes of sensation, and that light shone on their paths through the immaterium. The powers that ruled in the warp were one with Horus's war against the Emperor.

The *Bane of Asirnoth* was caught in a tempest. Their Navigator would be all but blind. Where was the Emperor's light to guide them?

Nowhere. Occluded. Swamped by the great ruinstorm.

'The enemy will be lucky to make short jumps,' Enion commented.

'Luck has little to do with it,' said Ariston.

'I don't understand.'

'We are here to follow. We want them to reach their destination. Our masters wish it too.' He smiled. 'Their journey won't be easy, but they will reach safe harbour.' His smile became broader yet. 'Which we will then burn.'

THE SHUDDERING OF the *Asirnoth* grew worse after the translation to the warp. The stresses of the immaterium were less direct than a bombardment, but they were more insidious. The death of the real surrounded the vessel, and sought to erode its existence.

'Are we being followed?' Khalybus asked Seterikus.

The legionary shook his head in frustration. 'I can't tell, brother-captain.' He turned from the auspex display. 'They could be right on top of us and we wouldn't know.'

'They are here,' Levannas said. 'Depend upon it.'

'I am.' If they weren't, the Iron Hands would have won a tiny victory, one hardly worth the sacrifice. He addressed the entire bridge. 'We cannot see the enemy, but we must assume that they can see us. All efforts must now be put toward evasion.'

'The longer we stay in the warp...' Raud began.

'I know, brother. I wish we had a choice.'

'If we manage to lose them,' Seterikus asked, 'what have we accomplished?'

'We won't lose them. But we can't underestimate them. If our evasions are a facade, they'll know. We must try everything in our power to shake them.' He paused, waiting. There was a question his brothers would be asking themselves. He wanted one of them to articulate it. Speaking it aloud, and having it answered, was important. Not for the success of his strategy, but for the morale of his clan-company.

Raud spoke first. 'Brother-captain, it would appear that our strategy is predicated on the assumption of our own failure.'

'It is,' Khalybus told him, still speaking to them all. 'This is our weakest moment. We know this. So do the traitors. Knowing exactly what our relative strengths are is crucial to the prosecution of war. We will be rigorous in all things. Even in this necessary failure. It is from this precision that our victory will come. Do any of you think we can deceive the Emperor's Children? No? I swear to you, brothers, that we can. But we will deceive them with the truth.'

He looked back at Cruax. The Iron Father nodded.

'Perfection,' Khalybus said. He faced the bridge again. 'Perfection. The Emperor's Children believe the concept is theirs. But recall the weapons that Ferrus Manus and Fulgrim forged on their first encounter. They were both perfect. Our route is not theirs, and our perfection will *smash* theirs.'

He paused for a moment.

'After all,' he added, 'they failed to stop us from entering the warp in the first place.'

TRACKING THE *Bane of Asirnoth* was a pleasure in and of itself. It was, Ariston thought, like watching the scurrying of an insect across a sheet of parchment. The insect could change direction all it wanted, but it remained as visible at the end of its efforts as it had been at the beginning.

The warp was not parchment. It was obscurity and madness. The strike cruiser made sudden course corrections, taking advantage of the very storms that threatened the ship with destruction. Ariston pictured how the manoeuvres must appear to the Iron Hands. They sailed down current after current of insanity, making ever more random choices, risking with every decision the dissolution of coherence.

They must, he thought, find it impossible to believe that they could be detected in this raging insanity of non-space.

The *Urthona* had no difficulty tracking its quarry. If the chase had been through the Czysicus System, and the *Asirnoth* had been leaking radiation, the pursuit could hardly have been simpler. The art lay in keeping back. 'I will personally execute the captain of any vessel that is detected by the enemy,' he announced to the fleet. They were all eager for the blood of the Iron Hands. So was he. But there must be enough blood. There must be all of it.

So the fleet followed. The distance between it and the X Legion ship was a fiction where space was a lie. But the vessels were all real. They had presence, an intensity that affected the warp and was detectable by the other ships. Ariston held his force back. He reduced to zero the intensity of the fleet's presence with respect to the *Bane of Asirnoth*. The strike cruiser faded to a dim perception. It could still be tracked, but it hovered on the edge of disappearance. To the Iron Hands, beset by the full force of the warp storm, the Emperor's Children would be invisible.

Enion said, 'We run the risk of losing them.' The *Asirnoth* was travelling down yet another turbulent current.

'We do not,' Ariston replied.

'But if they should...'

Ariston cut him off. 'What they do is irrelevant. They have been lost from the moment they took the bait. Our actions are what matters. I will not sully the perfection of our art by rushing forwards in blind eagerness. *That* is the risk. When we mar the work by accident instead of purpose is when we fail. That was Theotormon's crime.'

And he had been punished.

Hours of ship-time passed before the *Bane of Asirnoth* at last translated from the warp. Ariston was surprised its captain had risked a jump this long and turbulent. His ship was badly damaged. It must be on the verge of losing structural integrity.

The *Urthona* followed. The fleet re-emerged in real space.

The system was another dead one.

'Delium,' Enion said. Ariston liked the symmetry with Czysicus. Chance had reinforced the aesthetics of the trap. They were running their prey to ground in a corner of the galaxy as empty and hopeless as the one where the chase had begun.

Good.

The *Bane of Asirnoth* was leaking plasma. It left a trail so easy to follow it was almost insulting. If Khalybus was trying to hide, Ariston really would take offence.

He wasn't. They found the strike cruiser at low anchor over Galeras. Observing the auspex readings, Bromion called out, 'Strong energy readings from the moon. The enemy has established a base.'

'So they've chosen their gravesite,' Ariston said.

In the oculus, the *Bane of Asirnoth* became more clear. Its injuries were extensive. Fires shone through the fissures in the hull. The cruiser's silhouette was deformed, sunken. It was a chewed bone.

Ariston pointed at it. 'We will march on the base. But first, rid my sight of that sad wreck.'

The Iron Hands fired back. Once. Ariston was surprised they managed even that.

The *Urthona*'s void shields shrugged off the single broadside. It responded with a devastating barrage of torpedoes and cannon fire. It was joined by every ship in the fleet. They surrounded the *Asirnoth* and seared the void with the power of the Emperor's Children. The cruiser vanished, the explosion of its ruptured warp drive indistinguishable from the firestorm that caused it.

The fire of the *Asirnoth*'s death still burned, a miniature sun, when the drop pods began their descent on Galeras. The near orbit of the moon was crowded with ships. Their hulls disgorged a metal hail that pummelled the surface. The plains below the Iron Hands base filled with legionaries in armour the colour of luxury and violence.

Ariston stood at the base of the hill as the host gathered before him. He turned to Enion at his side. 'The point is not just the victory,' he said. 'There is a lesson to be taught as well.'

The Emperor's Children would roll over the Iron Hands with an unstoppable wave. They would smash the foe with an echo of their own machinic war, and in the irony of that gesture would be the excess of true art.

The rows of Space Marines disappeared into the murk of the atmosphere. The drop pods were vague silhouettes. Further out came the snarl of the tanks brought down by dropships. Ariston could not see them, but their strength was at his command. Their shells would hammer the walls of the base while the legionaries marched on it.

'Brothers,' he voxed to them all, 'the Iron Hands have fled, and now they cower. Shall we complete their humiliation?'

He was answered, exulted in the clamour of his warriors. This was war converted to sensation, and sensation weaponised.

The march began.

The Iron Hands base was barely visible at the crest of the hill. At first, it was a smudge, a blurred mass of black. It wasn't until Ariston was halfway up the slope that the details began to resolve themselves. The lines of the wall sharpened even as they were battered by the Demolisher shells of the Vindicator tanks. It was only then that the cannons on the walls answered back. That surprised Ariston. The Iron Hands had given the Emperor's Children all the time they needed to land and assemble. Ariston's army was beyond any numbers that Khalybus could possibly have behind the walls, but to wait this long to return fire was a compounding of errors.

At his side, Enion frowned. 'Are they really this stupid?'

'I find that hard to believe.'

'A trap of their own?'

'Likely.'

'But how? What could they hope to do?'

Ariston didn't know. For the first time since the arrival of the *Bane of Asirnoth* in Czysicus, he felt a flicker of unease. He tried to imagine what the broken, depleted Iron Hands could possibly use to counter his advance. He failed, and that failure disturbed him, because the abject collapse of the X Legion was even harder to imagine.

Ariston watched for a mine field or an ambush. Both would have been possible. The volcanic smog of the atmosphere was so thick, that even with his preysight he would not have seen an attack until it was too late.

But even a successful ambush would barely have slowed the advance. And there was nothing. Just the cannons on the wall.

Their shells punched craters into the hill. Legionaries disintegrated. The guns took their toll, though it was a small one. And one by one, they fell silent as the tanks drew nearer, concentrating their fire, and smashing the walls down.

There had been no further defensive barrages for several minutes by the time Ariston crossed the ruined fortification lines. Ahead was the centre block of the fortress. The smaller prefab structures close to the walls were burning.

'Where are they?' Enion asked.

Ariston was wondering that too. Whatever was buried in the rubble would remain hidden, though he saw what looked like the remains of servitors here and there. There was no trace of the Iron Hands, and there was only silence from the heart of the fortress ahead.

Was the ambush yet to come, he wondered? No. Even with the greater concentration of his forces in the base, his army was so vast that it still extended all the way down the slope.

'An orbital strike?' Enion suggested.

'With what?' If the *Bane of Asirnoth* had still remained intact, perhaps. He headed toward the main bunker. 'Our answers will be here,' he said.

'As will the trap.'

'It will be a poor one.'

It had to be.

Some shells had fallen upon the structure, but it had withstood them. It had lost a number of its vent stacks, but appeared to be sound enough. Bolter at the ready, Ariston shouldered the doors open; they weren't barred. The corridor ahead was deserted. Lumen globes lit a silent path and the air was thick with absence.

'There is no one here,' Enion muttered.

'If they were all aboard their strike cruiser, they are worse than fools,' replied Ariston. The unease was still there, but also rage. His great triumph would be an embarrassment against an enemy this incompetent.

But no, that was impossible. The Iron Hands were fools in their dogmatic loyalty to the Emperor. But they were still tacticians.

The corridor led to a massive open area at the centre of the block. Here a shaft descended deep into the tortured crust of Galeras.

'A risky endeavour,' Enion commented.

'Agreed.' Sulphuric fumes rose from the depths. Even inside the walls, Ariston could hear the distant, endless rumble of the moon's volcanoes. Dust, shaken loose by the trembling rock, floated down the sides of the shaft. One solid quake would be enough to trigger a collapse.

'It's deep,' said Enion. There were lumen strips at regular intervals as they disappeared deeper into the gloom.

'Whatever is down there, they went to considerable effort and risk to reach it,' said Ariston. He gestured to an elevator whose tracks appeared to descend the full length of the shaft. 'An open invitation.'

'Bait?'

'Of course it is. They didn't refuse ours. I won't refuse theirs.'

'We have a choice.'

'Do we? If we want to finish them off, we have to know where they are. We have to know what they're doing.' Ariston thought for a moment. 'One squad with me,' he said. 'And I want the fleet ready for emergency embarkation.'

'What could they do against us?'

'I don't know. They think they can do something. I won't give them the chance.'

Ariston, Enion and the eight brothers in the command squad entered the conveyor carriage – it was a rapid one, but the descent was long, the shaft going much deeper than Ariston would have guessed. The violent life of the moon followed them down. Profound vibrations thrummed down the walls. They plucked at the conveyor's tracks. The deck of the platform buzzed.

Down. Down. No branching tunnels. No mining. Just down, down and down through the crust.

'What were they looking for?' Enion wondered.

And how did they know it was here? Ariston thought. There was only this base. This one shaft. This was the work of certainty, not exploration.

The temperature was rising. There was a glow coming from below now.

It was red. Molten.

The answer came to Ariston just before he saw what waited in the depths.

'They weren't looking for anything,' he said to Enion. 'They were placing something.'

'What...' Enion began, but then cylindrical shapes resolved in the gloom. They were fastened to the walls of the shaft, waiting for a distant signal to begin their brief but terrible flowering.

Cyclonic torpedoes.

Ariston opened his mouth, but he had no voice. It had been throttled by the noose that had tightened around his fleet.

SUCH WEAPONS COULD crack a planet in half, given the right circumstances. The 85th Clan-Company had removed the element of chance. *Rigour*, Khalybus thought, as he witnessed the culmination of his work. *Precision*. That was where the Iron Hands found the sources of perfection.

The torpedoes detonated. Their immense power multiplied the stresses that sought to pull the moon apart. Galeras's death came all at once. The moon exploded. The fire of its ending was dull and ugly, a volcanic fist lashing out at the near orbit. A storm of fiery crust fragments blew outwards through the Emperor's Children's fleet. The *Urthona* disintegrated, and its blast was bright, as proud as a star. It was surrounded by the smaller pyres of other ships.

Collisions and shockwaves built upon each other. Vessels many thousands of metres long were mere fragments in the holocaust, battered to nothing as the moon's fragments were propelled outwards. Mountains tore through hulls. There was no time to react. There was no evasion. The only escape came from blind chance.

As the shockwave passed, a few survivors pulled away from the disaster. None were undamaged. Few would have made the jump to the immaterium.

Aboard the Iron Hands frigate *Sthenelus*, which had lost its captain during its own ordeal over Isstvan, Atticus directed their extermination. His squadron was small. There were no capital ships. But it was more than enough to smash what was left of the enemy. The Emperor's Children had one cruiser remaining – the *Hypsous* – and it was already burning when the *Sthenelus* came for it. A gaping hole ran through the centre of its span. It was barely moving. Its drive was likely about to go critical. Khalybus made sure that it did.

The light from the *Hypsous*'s end washed through the bridge of the *Sthenelus*. Khalybus watched until there was only void again, then left the bridge. He was heading for his new quarters – the chambers of a dead warrior, now occupied by the captain of a dead ship.

Levannas was waiting in the corridor just outside. Khalybus hadn't seen him on the bridge, but that didn't mean the Raven Guard hadn't been there.

'I'm curious to hear your thoughts, captain,' Levannas said.

'I am glad of our victory,' Khalybus said. 'I regret that we suffered a significant loss, too.' The *Bane of Asirnoth* had no longer been void-worthy when they had reached Delium again. The Iron Hands had abandoned it, leaving only enough servitors aboard the strike cruiser and at the base to make a show of presence by firing the guns.

'The Emperor's Children suffered a much greater blow.'

'Perhaps.' The III Legion had been hurt. Nothing much more than that.

'Do you see what we might be able to accomplish?' Levannas asked, and at that moment, Khalybus heard his carefully suppressed desperation. The Raven Guard needed to continue the war as badly as the Iron Hands did.

'Yes,' Khalybus said quietly. 'Yes, I do see.'

Incorporating the Raven Guard's methods into the Iron Hands' strategy had borne fruit. Shattered, fragmented and wounded though they were, they could still strike at the enemy, and hit hard.

They were still in the war, and they would exact their payment of blood.

And yet...

He had assured the Iron Father that he would keep to the path of the Iron Hands. He believed he had done so.

And yet...

So many shadows. So much subterfuge.

Change had come. Caught by tragedy and necessity, the Iron Hands were becoming something other than what they had been when Ferrus Manus had led them. Khalybus could see the transformation happening before his eyes.

It disturbed him that what he could not see was where it would end.

UNSPOKEN

Guy Haley

'THIRTY MINUTES TO extraction. I will be entering vox silence, commander. Confirm?'

Captain Sulnar held his breath to hear the voice in his earpiece. The Thunderhawk pilot spoke softly, as though he feared to be overheard.

And well he might be. Their furtive communications were conveyed over clandestine frequencies unique to their clan, but the Warmaster seemed to know everything.

'*Confirm. We're close to escaping this death trap, so I'm not taking any chances.*'

'Acknowledged. Leave your beacon active or I'll be coming in blind.' *A click, small but definite, came over the vox.* 'Engaging wide band vox suppression in five... four... three... two... one...'

The vox crackled out. Sulnar set a chrono-counter running in his helmet display. The numbers ran down, hundredths of a second tumbling, seemingly frantic to be spent.

Still, too slow.

He searched the sky for some sign of their extraction craft, but nothing moved up there. Somewhere beyond the blank night sky, vessels still loyal to

the Imperium orbited the world. How, he had no idea. He decided it best
not to question miracles.

There were five of them left, the survivors of the attack at Purgatory. He
sat propped up against a rock, his mangled legs projecting in front of him.
The others were secreted in the rocks overlooking the beacon they had taken
from the gunship.

They operated on a closed vox-net, at the shortest range and narrowest frequency. Their identification markers were deactivated, their armour powered
low. They were taking no chances.

Tarkan cursed.

'Report,' Sulnar ordered.

'Movement five hundred metres up.' Tarkan spoke quietly, with minimum
exhalation. His battleplate would prevent any disturbance to his aim, but
Tarkan was meticulous. 'Four, maybe five or six. We tagged them on the
motion sensor.'

'And?'

'We lost them. And the sensor.'

Sulnar breathed out through his teeth. Traitors. They had found their sensor and blinded it. He blink-clicked his long-range vox open again. He did
not use his neural interface to activate it. It was working, unlike so many
of his armour's systems. He felt so limited without the use of his legs, and
blinking the vox on was at least a physical act he could perform. It made
him feel like he was doing something, not simply lying out of the way like
so much dead meat while others watched over him.

'Spear of Truth, come in.'

Did he warn the pilot? If he were in his position, he would not risk an
approach if there were traitors on the way. The decision was irrelevant. There
was no reply. Not even static hiss. The jam held.

He checked the positions of his men. With their markers deactivated, the
only thing he had on his visor's tactical display was their last locations. Slight
energy spikes and mild thermal differences told him that they were still there,
but had he been unaware of their presence he would not have found them.

Unless he were looking very carefully. He hoped that the traitors were not.

The irony of the current situation was somewhat ridiculous. They had set up the trap for their enemies, only to guide friends to them for one final, desperate rescue attempt. And now, the efficacy of their trap threatened to kill them just as they seemed to have found a way out.

'Vogarr, I can see your energy signature too easily. Power down your motive systems a further twenty per cent.'

'My apologies brother,' said Vogarr. 'I have erratic power delivery. I will see to it when we are safe.'

Yes, thought Sulnar. *Like I will repair my bolter, and see to my legs.* He longed to be back in the fight.

There was a tension in them all. Rescue had seemed impossible for so long. They had given their all to destruction and to vengeance, and now this... They were on edge, far more than when only death had awaited them.

They waited now in turn.

'How long?' asked E'nesh, the Salamander. *The other four of their group were all Iron Hands, all members of Clan Sorrgol. E'nesh was an outsider, but he was their brother. They all had the clock running. Perhaps E'nesh asked because he did not believe it. Sulnar was not certain he believed it himself.*

'Nineteen minutes,' he said.

Kortaan, the last of their number spoke. 'I think I see something. Movement, coming down the slope. Can you get a shot, Tarkan?'

'I could, but they'll scatter,' replied Tarkan. 'That's a Scout's grasp of tactics, Kortaan. Keep it together. We open fire as we planned, when they are close and grouped.'

'Yes, brother.'

Information rolled across Sulnar's visor. He patched through to Kortaan's visual feed. Three shapes, still small in the view, picking their way to the ravine floor. They had no identification markers.

'Should we hail them?' asked Tarkan.

'Negative,' said Sulnar. 'Might be a scouting party. Could have blind-hunters waiting, up behind.'

'The slope is too steep for constructs,' said Kortaan.

'No, it is not. If it was, then we'd never survive. Take them by surprise, Tarkan.'

The figures disappeared from sight, enhanced or otherwise. They were coming to the beacon's position now, drawn in by the lure. It was ten minutes at a cautious pace.

When they came, they were dealt with, and Captain Sulnar discovered that Isstvan V had one last horror to inflict upon him.

The Thunderhawk arrived three minutes after that.

I HAVE BEEN sleeping. I have been dreaming of the massacre, and have brought my dreams into the waking world. I am fully awake now, at this moment. The events of Isstvan V are still with me. They do not fade as nightmares will, for they are not nightmares. Oh, how I wish they were.

I cannot speak. I do not know why. The words will not come.

I sit upon the edge of the examination table and await my fate. My wounded arm is hot where the regeneration clasp works upon torn flesh. Already I can move my fingers again.

The warriors of the Iron Hands stand in judgement over me, discussing me as though I were a broken machine. Like a machine, I can say nothing in my defence, and I do not know why.

The Apothecary gestures to me. 'No, captain, I am not saying there is anything the matter with him. I am saying that there is nothing wrong with him at all.'

Upon the glass overlay are displayed parts of my anatomy. They are naked, revealed to plain sight by the artifice of the medical scanner. Part of me wonders how it works. A little of the hunger for the craft is within me yet, then, but it is an ember, dying under a black, sodden weight of persistent realisation. Realisation should be a transitory state. What was not known before becomes known, and is processed accordingly.

But the enormity of the knowledge that chokes my soul will not allow its easy resolution. Each moment, I relive that first instant of sickening revelation.

Vulkan is dead.

Every time I think upon this truth, a wave of nausea and... fear? It cannot be. I have forgotten fear.

But I never forgot grief. That I feel keenly, and I know it for what it is.

Our father is slain. Ferrus Manus also. These Iron Hands have suffered the same loss as I have. Those around me speak and operate, performing their duties with the cold efficiency their Legion is known for. It is not obvious that they are damaged, but they are not *undamaged*. Far from it.

'Do you understand me?' one of their leaders asks. His insignia is that of a commander, I think. Their rank system differs from ours. His armour is battered, his countenance fierce, twisted by pain and fury, like a dragon in a trap. He has a bionic arm – the right. It is uncovered by his battleplate, displayed for all to see, as is their custom. This too is damaged. The gleaming metal is torn and blackened around the elbow, heat bloom surrounding the wound to the prosthetic, purple fading through green to yellow. It is an iridescent bruise. When he moves his hand, it clicks. The three lower fingers no longer flex.

I nod without hesitation, but only once. I blink, putting out the forge-light of my eyes for a second, to show deference. What happens over the next few minutes is of the utmost importance.

The captain turns to the Apothecary. The medicae chamber of a strike cruiser is small and cramped, and this one is full of wounded Iron Hands. More wait on gurneys outside.

'He will not answer you, brother.'

'I can see that.' The commander turns again to the Apothecary, impatient. 'I do not care if he can speak or not. What I need to know is whether he can fight, Brother Vraka.'

Vraka glances at me. His eyes have been replaced with augmetics; a medical diagnostic model. They whir as they focus on my face.

'Commander Tayvaar,' says the Apothecary patiently, 'they found him with two others. He would not have made it that far up into the mountains if he could not. I'd say he can fight.'

'The others?' asks the commander.

Vraka shakes his head. The news of what happened to Go'sol and Jo'phor is too shameful to voice.

I cannot speak, but yes, I can fight. I grip the edge of the examination table with my hands. It is strange to be out of my armour after so long. If I could, I would put it back on again.

The captain looks down at me. It takes all my effort of will not to look away. I nod. I so desperately want to *fight*.

'Very well,' Tayvaar says abruptly. 'When he is rested, send him to me. All who can fight in the Shattered Legions will do so. And send for Brother E'nesh. Get him assigned.'

E'NESH WAS ONE of our ambushers. I follow him down the spinal corridor of the ship. Its unwieldy name is the *Voluntas Ex Ferro*. Before I left the apothecarion, a wild-eyed Iron Hands legionary explained to me that the ship arrived late in the fleet chasing Lord Manus to the system, after the Avernii were all but annihilated and the primarch slain. The Warmaster had his victory and eventually moved on, leaving the dregs behind to finish us off on the surface. And so the *Voluntas* was one of the few that managed to creep back, months later, looking for survivors. He was crazed as he recounted all this, evangelising an unpalatable truth, as if he still could not believe that he had not died alongside his father.

There are one hundred and sixty-seven Space Marines on board. The *Voluntas Ex Ferro* is designed to support just over half of that, and so it is crowded. There are not enough quarters for all, and many of those on board are wounded.

I suppose I am one of the lucky ones. My body is whole, even if I cannot speak.

This is a Legion ship. There are few human serfs left on board. They are the indentured servants of the Medusans and of a phenotype unfamiliar to me. The Imperial Truth holds that humanity is as one, but one only has to look to see that humanity is many. Seeing the unenhanced suffering the shock of betrayal makes me wonder if we were right ever to try and reunite them. They do not meet my eyes. The Warmaster's actions have affected them more than us, at least superficially.

On a deeper level it may be worse for us in the long term. They are weak, and therefore pliable – what is bent can be returned to shape. But the strongest metal does not bend, it shatters. I look into haunted transhuman faces as we walk to the gunship launch deck, and see so much broken iron.

Brother E'nesh leads me to Hangar Two. This is to be my berth.

'The other hangar,' he says, the first words he has uttered since he collected me from the infirmary, 'is full of the wounded.' He smiles, knowing of my affliction. He is trying to put me at ease, but his smile is full of pain and shame. 'They have only two operational Thunderhawks remaining.'

We pass them. They are scored by weapon impacts and re-entry wounds, and crowded around by servitors. Three Ironwroughts and an Iron Father minister to them, directing the cyborgs and a dozen of the less technically-gifted Iron Hands to heal the machine. Brilliant blue sparks shower onto the deck as damaged armour is cut free.

I think on ceramite. It is durable and versatile. But it will crack. The heatshielding armour of this Thunderhawk, for example, subjected over and over again to the stresses of re-entry, will begin to fail. It may look whole to the naked eye, but the molecular structure will be host to a thousand micro-fractures. It will serve and serve and then, one day – perhaps suffering the smallest impact, and for no obvious reason at all – it will shatter.

That is why we have the rituals of maintenance. This is why all components are tested and replaced when they have been subjected to out-parameter stresses.

There is no one to replace these Iron Hands. Not any more.

A third Thunderhawk is not currently flight capable. The deck around it is torn, the result of a hard landing. The gunship has

been turned around, cradled by cranes, supporting it where its feet
no longer could. From the right, missing landing claws aside, it
appears fine – less marked, even, than its brothers. As we pass, I
turn my head to see the port engine and wing assembly missing. I
silently salute the skill of the pilot who brought it in. I wonder if it
can be salvaged at all.

Beyond the crippled gunship the other five landing bays are empty.
With the *Voluntas* so crowded, the area has been temporarily rigged
as a barracks. There are places for us to sleep. Many cots, and a work
bench next to each one. The Medusans are kin to us Salamanders in
their love of mechanisms. Just as well, for not one of the legionaries I
have seen has a fully functional set of wargear. It would take the few
adepts on this ship years to repair it all.

E'nesh leads me to a repurposed administrative desk. I can see that
it is intended for me, for my armour is there. The plastron and left
vambrace are neatly laid out on the work surface. The rest is upon an
arming frame.

He is embarrassed. 'I am sorry that your battleplate is not within the
armoury or martial chambers,' he says, 'but, as you will have guessed,
there is no space.'

I run my hand over the breastplate. It has been polished free of carbon
bloom. Deeper marks in the metal have been smoothed and prepared
for repair. I look to E'nesh, and his eyes drop.

'Forgive me. I thought to make a start on your wargear while you
were being seen to in the infirmary. I had only the night. It was the
least I could do after...' His voice trails away. The fire-light of his eyes
has an odd colour to it.

I scratch around the regeneration unit bound to my arm. The wound
was grave, nearly enough to necessitate amputation. I was lucky it did
not. It will heal. My muscles itch maddeningly as the cells replicate. The
shot might have come from E'nesh's own gun. My three comrades –
Go'sol, Jo'phor, and Hae'Phast – are all dead. Two of them slain by
our allies, after having survived so much.

If I believed in such things, I would say fate was cruel.

I would thank E'nesh for the work he has done on my armour. It is neat and precise. But I say nothing. The silence between us yawns, a gulf I cannot bridge.

'Well,' he says. 'I will see you. My cot is there. There were already half a dozen of us on the ship. We Salamanders are all berthed together.'

I nod, though I cannot smile to reassure him. It is not his fault, the deaths of our brothers. He turns away, unsuccessfully trying to conceal a shame that I know he will carry forever.

It is already killing him.

TIME PASSES, TIME I spend working on my armour. If this were the old days, when we travelled in glorious fleets that laid the galaxy at the Emperor's feet, I would junk half of what is here and request replacements from the armoury. That is no longer possible. Materials are in short supply. I am, however, given another helmet, as I lost mine shortly after the massacre. It is brought to me by Osk'mani, one of my six brothers here, while I work. The helmet is newly forged, dull metal. It is of an unfamiliar pattern and inferior manufacture to my original, but the armour is thick. Three additional layers, with lamination achieved through the use of molecular bonding studs.

Osk'mani feels the same way about it as I do. He rests a hand on my shoulder. 'It is all they can do, brother. The internal systems are poor things, but the thickness will provide additional protection against mass reactives. Be thankful the rest of your armour is salvageable.'

I set the helmet on the stand, looking at my work.

I wish I could work faster. My brothers are all armoured, at full battle readiness. I can finally wear my plastron and backplate. I have replaced the power cabling running over my plackart and repaired the interfacings at the chest and spine. Luckily, the circuitry required only minor repair, for the complexity of the machinery there is such that a full renewal would require the knowledge of a Techmarine or Mechanicum priest. I am merely an artisan.

My right arm is also finished. This I leave off so as not to hamper my work. But the fibre bundles of both legs need replacing; it is intricate work, but not beyond me. The rerebrace of my left arm assembly is beyond salvaging. My power plant is open. One of the cooling coils is black and friable to the touch. Osk'mani looks over my shoulder at it all, making a noise in his throat as if to say he would not wish to undertake this task himself. He leaves me alone.

I am still working on my armour six weeks later when we are hailed by other survivors, and we join them.

In the following week, still more come, joining a flotilla that hides itself in the raging photosphere of a dying red star.

COMMANDER SULNAR STRODE across the docking tube, his new legs clanging on the deck plates. He felt empowered, full of grim purpose. Commander Tayvaar strode beside him. Behind them came eight legionaries, four from each of their clan-companies. The commanders saluted the Avernii guarding the entry hatch to the other ship.

'Commander Ishmal Sulnar of Clan Sorrgol.'

'Commander Rab Tayvaar of Clan Vurgaan.'

The veterans inclined their heads, and shifted the bulk of their Terminator-armoured bodies aside to open the way. 'Be welcome, Commander Sulnar, Commander Tayvaar.'

Representatives of four clans crowded the briefing room. Elements of twenty-two companies of the X Legion were present in the fugitive fleet, but together added up to little more than eight in actual fighting strength. A Raven Guard ship flew alongside them. There were also a demi-company's worth of Salamanders scattered across the various ships. None of them, however, had been invited to the meeting.

Three Iron Fathers held the floor. Their leader, Frater Juraak, addressed the lost sons of Ferrus Manus.

'There should be no hastily appointed leader,' he proclaimed. 'For the duration of this crisis, the Iron Fathers will advise each company-level commanding officer individually. There will be a moot of all the clans called on Medusa, and there it will be decided who shall lead the Legion. Though not now, and not here. Not like this.'

'Why?' asked a grim-faced captain of Clan Ungavarr. 'There are warriors who are up to the task.'

A commander of Sorrgol stood and banged a bionic hand hard on his chestplate. 'I will not be dictated to by Ungavarr!'

'Nor I,' growled another.

'And that, Commander Uskleer, is precisely why our warriors are divided and scattered,' said Frater Grivak. 'To set one clan over another at a time like this will lead to dissension.'

'Or open conflict,' added Frater Vrayvuus.

'There is one who could reunite us,' came a voice from the back of the chamber. 'Shadrak Meduson!'

'Meduson? He acts without forethought and without guidance!' said an Ironwrought in Grivak's retinue.

'And yet I have heard that many already follow him,' Sulnar whispered to Tayvaar.

'Most of the clan-fathers are gone,' said Juraak, raising his staff. 'Only we Iron Fathers may now stand outside the Legion's structure, in accordance with the old laws of Medusa. Rashness doomed us. Listen to our wisdom. This is how Warleader Meduson would have the Iron Tenth prosecute this war.'

'Then what are we to do?' asked Tayvaar, speaking up for the first time. 'You bring us news of Meduson and others of our Legion. Where are they?'

'We do not know,' said Vrayvuus. 'Deliberately so.'

'This is the wisdom we bring,' said Grivak. 'All survivors of the Isstvan Massacre are to divide into splinter cells. Battle-brothers from any Legion are welcome in our ranks, if they can prove their commitment to the cause. We cannot attack the traitors directly, but we can harry them. We shall spread ourselves far and wide, attacking their supply lines and depots, and bringing news of the treachery to whoever we can.'

Sulnar's hand involuntarily tightened. To be separated once more from his brothers would be too much. 'Frater, we have little strength in such small numbers,' he said. 'What can we do?'

'Ask yourself instead, Sulnar, what could we do all *together*? Our Legion is a fraction of its former strength. Much of the 52nd Expedition is lost, and the rest of us are scattered widely. If we all came together, in one place, we could still likely do nothing useful against the enemy's superior numbers.'

'We would instead present Horus with a single target,' said Grivak. 'We would be pursued, and annihilated.'

'Our father is dead – do not let his legacy die too,' Vrayvuus urged them all. 'If you would follow Shadrak Meduson to war, then do it on his terms. You must fight *for* him, but not *with* him.'

Tayvaar agreed. 'There is sense in this plan. Separately, we are more agile, harder to pin down and attack. Spread out across a broad front, we will tie up as many of the enemy by forcing them onto their guard as we will by actually attacking them.'

'As it should be,' said Juraak. 'Our disposition will be examined and reordered. We will not expose the warriors under our command to the truth of our Legion's inherent weakness. It is a secret shame that we will not share.'

'And that weakness is what?'

'That our primarch was wrong.'

Silence fell, full of foreboding.

'Very well then,' said Sulnar, keen to break the moment. 'What is our first move?'

'This,' said Vrayvuus, producing a data-slate.

Sulnar took it, and frowned.

'A staging post?'

'An astropathic relay station, and Legion supply point. Theta-class planetoid with attendant base units. At the time of sending, fifty-three fleet resupply vessels were there. We have coordinates. It was discovered by a small contingent of Clan Atraxii fleeing the battle at Isstvan.'

'Sending?' asked Uskleer. 'Have them return to us, and share their findings in person.'

'There are multiple command structures operating in parallel,' Grivak explained. 'It is taking time to gather intelligence upon all the disparate elements of our Legion. Not all of them are heeding our call – Clan Atraxii are particularly intransigent. Iron Lord Hrottaavak openly defies Warleader Meduson, in fact.'

'But not this company?' asked Sulnar.

'Our brothers appear to see sense,' said Grivak.

Sulnar passed the slate on, and Tayvaar looked over the information. 'Is not the key in such asymmetrical warfare to keep each cell in ignorance of the actions of the other?'

'Yes,' said Frater Juraak. 'And among those of us who chose to work with Meduson before we came to you, there is a prohibition on contact in all but the most exceptional circumstances.'

'Such division suits our temperament,' Uskleer murmured.

'And these are exceptional circumstances?' Tayvaar persisted.

'Lone elements reach out to the rest of the Legion, as though it were still whole. They too seek to slake their thirst for revenge. They cannot do this alone, or without guidance.'

Tayvaar nodded. 'The outpost is well defended by the Twentieth Legion.'

'Bombardment?' suggested Sulnar. 'We have the ships.'

'We can't waste those supplies on the ground,' said Uskleer. 'We should launch a full combat drop. Boots on the ground.'

Tayvaar smiled unpleasantly. 'And what if it is a trap?'

Grivak waved a hand dismissively. 'If it is, we will surprise them. We have sufficient numbers in this group to destroy them outright, and scatter any ambush. It is the wish of the Iron Fathers that we proceed to our brothers' aid, and turn any trap back upon the traitors. We have fought our way out from harder places.'

'The time for weakness is over,' said Juraak. 'We will charge into peril

as our father did. They expect it. Let us run at them. Let them underestimate us, and we will turn it to our favour.'

MY ARMOUR IS almost repaired by the time we go into battle. All systems check out perfectly. I am pleased with my work. I have repainted
most of the plates, but not my left shoulder. There, I must renew my
Legion heraldry. I sit down in my new arming chamber several times
to do this, but find that I cannot.

It is still incomplete, scorched by the betrayal of Isstvan, when we
attack.

We come out from the warp like rage itself, right on top of our target without thought for safe distances, matter interlacing or proximity
translation interference. The Iron Hands are eager to destroy the enemy,
and will have the element of surprise at all costs. The bow-wave of our
emergence sends the tenders around the asteroid wallowing as space
convulses about them. Several are caught in brutal temporal eddies
and are torn into fragments.

The guns of the station are upon us quickly, tracking the *Voluntas
Ex Ferro*, high-rate macrocannons casting ultra-high explosive rounds.
They aim at where we will be. Our path and theirs intersect, void combat's geometry of destruction executed as expected. Explosions bloom
all along the ventral facing of the ship. Void fields flicker with other-
worldly energy.

They hold, and my brothers and I are away, the *Voluntas* falling up
above us.

Our Thunderhawk – the third I saw, somehow coaxed back to life –
hurtled at the station without restraint or caution. The surface of the
station rushes up to us. Forty per cent of its mass is of human construction. The rest is rock into which the artificial components are
embedded. A thin regolith of pulverised stone coats the surface, fine
as lapping powder.

Our target is the astropathic relay. It arches up on a soaring buttress,
fantastical architecture that would be impossible on a Terran-standard

world. The gravity of the asteroid is negligible, but I feel it pull none-theless, a growing heaviness as we approach.

Ships explode in the sky around us. This is the work of the Raven Guard, stealing ahead. Our commanders play to our strengths.

'Stand ready!' commands Chosen Vra'kesh. There are twenty of us now, brought together from all over the flotilla, and we have a leader in the Terminator-clad Vra'kesh of the Firedrakes. 'We will secure the relay station. Our primary target is this access port.'

The port flashes on our visor displays. We know it well. We have studied it and every battle possible contingency for the last three days.

'We will rendezvous with the Iron Hands of Clan Vurgaan,' says Vra'kesh. 'It is an honourable duty.'

There is tension amongst their clans. They hope, I am sure, that over-tures from another Legion will be better received.

Ten of us bear breaching shields. These are loan-gifts from the Iron Hands. There has not been time to repaint them, and so we bear their emblem. Vra'kesh has a small shield of his own crafting, an ingenious device around which crackles a power field, its discharges as lively as lightning. In his right hand he bears a power maul in the shape of a roaring salamander's head. I smile to myself, and imagine the killers of our kin smashed down by it.

There is a determination to us. Vulkan told us to endure, and so we must. But there is a grim joy also. The newcomers to our group brought news...

The primarch's body was never found. He might live.

I am sure he does. I know it somehow. I feel it in my chest, a truth that warms both my hearts, like a growing fire in a forge left cold for too long.

The Thunderhawk touches down for a handful of heartbeats. The pilots blow open the assault ramp without venting the atmosphere, and we emerge rimed in void-frozen gases. Our guns are firing before the ship takes off again, blasting the dust around us. Between the gas cloud and the debris, we are blind for crucial seconds.

'Lock shields!' calls Chosen Vra'kesh.

'Distance to primary target, thirty metres,' E'nesh reports.

Those of us in the first rank bring our shields up as the mess clears, carried off by momentum. We run in a shuffling gait, skating on the loose material cloaking the surface. To push down too hard here is to risk death. The gravity is so weak it would not hold a shove from power-armoured legs. Our feet kick up more dust that moves outwards in strange burst patterns, unrestrained by atmosphere.

'Contact! Contact!'

Threat indicators in my helm go wild. Seven of our traitorous kin are moving to engage.

I hold my shield in front of me and brace. Bolt-rounds burn at us, their propellant loads bright in the vacuum. They rattle across our front like hail, the noise of their impact and detonation conveyed to my ears through the metal. Their combined impetus threatens to knock us over. Osk'mani stumbles. I move my breaching shield to cover him a fraction, saving him from the next volley. The rounds batter against the plasteel. He offers no thanks as he rights himself. Brothers-in-arms do not need thanks.

We return fire. The Alpha Legionnaires of the XX are arranged loosely, and we pick them off with concentrated fire. Only one of ours falls. A good exchange.

Our formation tightens again, and we are at the door. It is plain plasteel, a modular design common across the Imperium. It is set at an angle into the ground. In less terrible times, I have visited many such places but I never thought that I would have to fight my way into one.

Chosen Vra'kesh pushes his way forward. Bolts spark from his heavy armour. They veer into space; some become embed and explode in the ground, others are caught and detonated by the energy field of his small shield. He has mag-locked his power maul to his thigh, and in his other hand he hefts a melta bomb. He marches through a storm of bullets and slams it hard at the join in the centre of the doors. The rest of us form a semicircle around him as he sets the charge.

Battle rages across the surface of the planetoid. The Iron Hands fall upon the Alpha Legion with terrible savagery. They ever were furious in battle, and the death of their primarch has made them more so. But where once the Iron Hands would have marched in step with us, their allies, now they run ahead, as careless as Angron's World Eaters.

I realise for all their grimness and rigid comportment, their Legion has changed. They fight here as if they do not care for their own losses, so long as they kill the enemy. Their lives have become meaningless. Their attack began in unity, but their vanguard is soon fragmented. They assault singly or in small groups. I see a wildness in them. They barely keep themselves in formation, and fight with unrestrained violence.

A lightning flash of an explosion comes from the torus of the station, and a docking array floats away as if gently nudged. Short-lived fire spews into space. Two tenders decouple violently, trailing strands of metal. Bodies shoot from the gaps – unarmoured, human crew. Particulate matter wreaths them in shining clouds.

Bolt-rounds streak across the airless battlefield. All I hear is brought to me by vox, but my augmented hearing and my suit systems work hard to damp it down. The cacophony of battle is more disorienting when delivered secondhand.

The bulk of the traitor force is on the surface. Many wear void harnesses, or Anvilus power packs with spread venting arms, directing the out-gassing of their cooling coils through their stabilisation jets to manoeuvre. This gives them an advantage in agility, but we have the advantage of fury. The Iron Hands fight with the strength of the insane.

'Clear!' shouts Vra'kesh.

We admit him into our shield circle and withdraw. The fusion bomb glows white-hot. A large part of the door follows suit, collapsing inward like melted plastek. The charge gives out, the metal cooling slowly. Space is cold, but with no medium to carry the heat all must be lost via direct radiation.

Venting air rushes from the breach. A spray of blood and matter as someone is sucked through the too-small hole. Bolts streak outwards after it. We cover ourselves with our shields as Tu'vash and Juphat move up to force the doors wide with spreading claws. Displaced items and screaming Legion thralls are sucked into the vacuum's silence, bouncing from our shields. They wheel away to join the cloud of debris growing about the station.

Then we are inside.

The station has white corridors, brightly lit by lumen panels in the roof. Colour coded banding designates the sector. Here it is red.

Gravity plating gives an approximation of Terran norm. We do not rely on it, and engage our boot mag-locks in preparation for its failure. Sure enough, it is deliberately disengaged by the enemy the moment we are through and into the complex.

The inner voidlock has not been sealed. There are five Alpha Legionnaires within. We can advance only three abreast, so cannot easily bring our numbers to bear. They back away from us, firing as they go.

It is a stately assault. We proceed in slow formation behind our shields, leaning into the decompression winds. The traitors retreat to match our pace. We pass humans gripping onto emergency grab-bars, struggling against the gale. Their eyes are wide with fear and their faces purple. I wonder if they understand what they do. Do they follow the Alpha Legion through loyalty or through fear? Do they even know what is happening at all? Not all of them could have the black hearts of traitors, surely? These thoughts came to mind during the Crusade from time to time, but I put them aside as we cleansed one non-compliant world after another. They seem more pressing now. The unwitting humans might be saved from themselves, if they knew the truth of this war.

These questions do not trouble our Iron Hands kinsmen. They pour in through the breached doors behind us and slaughter everyone they come across.

The wind drops. This section has breathed its last.

Two of the remaining enemy legionaries break for a side corridor, covered by the last of them. One ducks back, his bolts punching holes in our breaching shields. They may be traitors, but they are still Space Marines and their combat discipline is impressive.

My suit systems find something of interest in the vox chatter and present it to me. Voices from both sides jabber away in our helms. The station has been breached in several areas.

'Proceed to the main objective! Let the Iron Hands finish clearing this area,' orders Vra'kesh. 'Secure the astropathic relay.'

Resistance is light. We pick up the pace. We pass through an unlocked door into an area with thin residual atmosphere. The difference is mostly aural. Sounds are carried by more than just the vox here.

'This way,' says Vra'kesh, pointing with his power maul.

The corridor opens out. We enter an armourglass dome looking out into the void. The relay post is visible through the curved roof. The Emperor's eagle finials on the relay have been beheaded, and baleful red lights shine from its windows. Burning ships and wreckage tangles frame it.

There, at the double doors that lead to the access spur, Iron Hands fight with Alpha Legionnaires. Iron Hands who were not of our assault group.

'To their aid, brothers!' Vra'kesh orders.

We break into a run, shouting out the newly-minted battle-cry of our Legion.

'Vulkan lives!'

Shoulder to shoulder with the Iron Hands, we slaughter the enemy. There are seven of them, bearing the sigils of Clan Atraxii. Standing amongst the dead, their armour is battered. They are the ones, then, who brought word of the installation to us. Two of them turn away and walk through the door leading to the relay without a word.

Their leader steps before us. 'Thank you for your assistance,' he says, earnestly.

And then the rest of them turn their guns upon us.

Brother Kraydo goes down, his helmet hollowed out by a bolt. Juphor falls, hands failing to stop the crimson gushing from his ruined gorget. Once, we would have reacted to such an attack with shock and disorientation.

No longer. We have become inured to treachery.

We are close in. We grapple. There are more of us than them, and we are tired of betrayal. Vra'kesh proves the leveller. His power maul swipes wide, caving in the breastplate of one. A flaring of his shield's power field halts the downward arc of a chainsword, and another of their number dies.

I wrestle with my opponent. Our guns are gone. I pin his right arm, and he kicks my legs out from under me and we both fall, he on top of me.

Through his red helm lenses, I see a fervid glee in his eyes. He grips at my shoulder guard and shakes it hard. 'I am the Alpha and the Omega, you fool,' he growls. 'And we are not your enemy.'

I see the krak grenade in his hand just in time. Twisting, I throw him hard enough to send him into the armourglass beyond. The detonation obliterates his left arm and the window.

The corpse is sucked outwards by the explosive decompression. I follow, but E'nesh grabs my arm. He is mag-locked to the floor and holds me easily. Klaxons blare and blast shielding clangs shut over the shattered window pane. The gale drops with it.

The false Iron Hands are all dead. But they have achieved their apparent goal.

At the end of its slender white bridge, the astropathic relay goes down in flames.

Vra'kesh is stunned by the sight, his power maul sinking to the floor.

'I do not understand,' says Brother Ki'shen.

'Infiltrators,' says Da'eev. He kicks one of the corpses. The rest appear to be wearing actual Iron Hands plate, but not this one. The paint is new. Revealed by scratches, Alpha Legion blue shines.

'But why pose as Iron Hands to get us to attack their own outpost?' asks E'nesh incredulously.

'Perhaps ours are not the only shattered Legions, brother,' mutters Ki'shen.

Vra'kesh shakes his head. 'If they were loyal, why then turn their guns on us? It makes no sense.'

'He said something to Brother Donak,' says Da'eev. 'What?'

'I did not hear, brother,' said Ki'shen.

The others reply similarly.

'What did he say?' Vra'kesh demands of me.

I do not reply. The Firedrake marches up to me. In his Terminator plate, he is taller and far more imposing.

'What. Did. He. Say?' he asks again.

But I cannot say, and so the truth of it remains unspoken.

For now at least.

AFTER MORE DELAY, I settle to finish painting my second pauldron. Once this is done, then my armour will be compliant with my Legion's heraldic code. It is an important moment. Clad in this battleplate, I will be the Donak of old on the outside. But I fear that I will never be the same within, and so do not stop in reverence or contemplation.

I key the brush on. The pistons of the pump chirr quietly. Spray mists the air.

Within a few seconds, the pauldron is a glossy Salamander-green, as it should be. I feel something within me – a budding optimism, perhaps? I key the paint to a yellow, wait for the brush nozzle to clean itself, then begin to rough in the stencilled outlines of flames along the bottom edge.

This takes me a quarter of an hour. I am lost in my work.

When I am done, I stop. I should add the great emblem now. The drake's head.

I pause. Something is not quite right.

I set the paintbrush down and take up my combat knife from the table. Gripping the pauldron as hard as I can, I dig into the metal with the tip of my blade. The paint scratches, but I must go deeper, I must mark the metal as I have been marked. The blade squeals on the ceramite skin covering the plasteel beneath. The metal is strong, but I am

stronger. I clench my teeth as I force the point into the otherwise flaw-
less metal, ruining what only minutes ago I had set to rights.

The ceramite curls beneath the blade. Millimetre by millimetre I etch
the salamander's head into the metal directly. Of course, I could use
my engraving tools and have the emblem done in minutes, but that
is not the point.

The struggle is the point.

'Brother, what are you doing?'

I turn, Osk'Mani is behind me with E'nesh. They appear troubled
that I am vandalising my wargear, but I ignore them and turn back
to my work. I am nearly finished. I do not care if they do not understand. They must also do this.

The last scruff of metal drops away. I hold up the pauldron. The
emblem is sound, albeit rough. The hard scratches of it catch the light,
making it appear to move.

It is what Jo'phor would do, I want to say. On Isstvan, he carved salamander heads such as this into the armour of our enemy, to make them
aware that those faithful to the Emperor still lived, and would bring
vengeance for their treachery. I do it to honour him, and to remember
our cause. Jo'phor was right. We stand now in numbers, and together
we might conclude what we began on Isstvan V.

It is a fitting tribute, and the renewal of a promise to pursue vengeance.

But I cannot speak. Not yet.

I look at my brothers, imploring them to understand. E'nesh nods
and rests a hand upon my shoulder.

'Vulkan lives,' he whispers.

I nod. Whether it is true or not, we shall endure.

I turn back to my work.

I have blunted my knife. I must sharpen it again.

THE SEVENTH SERPENT

SERPENT

Graham McNeill

'Youth is easily deceived because it is quick to hope.'

– attributed to Arystotle of Stagira

'Unless a serpent devours a serpent,
it will not become a dragon.
Unless one power absorbs another,
it will not become great.'

– proverb, circa M1

ONE

The Bird
Thamatica
For the Emperor

ULRACH BRANTHAN HAD called his cyber-eagle Garuda. The name was that of a mythical devourer of the silver serpents said to dwell in the Land of Shadow – a noble hunter whose birth fires consumed the ancient gods of Medusa.

The Iron Hands aboard the *Sisypheum* knew it simply as 'the Bird' and, since its resurrection, hope had spread that their fallen captain might also rise from his icy sepulchre.

The eagle's golden body was wrought from exquisite clockwork mechanisms and lost ingenuity, more a work of art than engineering. One wing was gold, the other silver, and where one leg was articulated ivory and brass, the other was pressed steel and polycarbonate resin.

A scar-faced bladesman of the Emperor's Children had shot Garuda from the air on Iydris, but Sabik Wayland and Frater Thamatica had worked on the cyber-eagle with all the care and attention an Apothecary would bestow upon a wounded Iron Lord.

They had restored its broken wing and twisted leg, somehow managing to restart the arcane mechanism within its heart – though neither could quite settle on *how* they had done it.

Thamatica claimed Garuda was an artefact crafted by the first settlers of Medusa, but Wayland disagreed, believing the avian automaton to be a relic from an even earlier epoch. Long would they debate the provenance of their fallen lord's golden eagle.

While Ulrach Branthan hovered near death in his frosted casket, Cadmus Tyro was Garuda's current master, and he cared nothing for its origins.

All he cared about was killing traitors.

GARUDA FLEW THROUGH the ruin of the strike cruiser's starboard embarkation deck, alighting on the wreckage of a blazing Stormbird. Warning lumens painted bulkheads crimson. Klaxons filled the air with mechanised screeching. Violated integrity fields sought to keep out the frozen vacuum of space.

The *Zeta Morgeld* howled in fury at its attackers.

They marched from the belly of a screaming Thunderhawk, shields locked and weapons blazing, thirty giants in black battleplate. They pushed into the smoke of their explosive entry like obsidian ghosts, ice-white gauntlets glittering on every shoulder guard.

Ship-to-ship boarding actions. Brutal, bloody affairs. Merciless killing in confined spaces. Firefights waged at arm's length. No room to manoeuvre. Hammering shields, barging body work.

Fighting that only the Legiones Astartes could endure.

The kind of fighting at which the Iron Hands excelled.

Bearing a heavy shield and clad in void-hardened plate of scarred black, Cadmus Tyro was first onto the deck of the enemy ship – a pitiless veteran of the infamy at Isstvan with a flint-hard soul.

His warriors followed him onto the stricken *Morgeld*.

They slammed into the deck's defenders – ravager packs of weaponised servitors armed with energised piston-hammers and hook-halberds. Behind these monstrosities, dark-robed adepts fled for transit arches leading into the heart of the ship.

The combatants slammed together with a thunderous clamour of metal on metal. Shields bludgeoned, blades stabbed. Explosive shells punched into flesh and armour at point-blank range. The Iron Hands leaned into the advance, pushing the foe back with inexorable force.

Bolters fired with metronomic regularity. Legion swords cut like the threshing blades of an industrial harvester. Tyro shot a pallid-fleshed combat-servitor in the throat then barged it to the deck with a blow from his shield.

Septus Thoic had refused a boarding shield in favour of a heavy bolter. The veteran braced himself at the head of the Thunderhawk's assault ramp and swept the deck with heavy-calibre mass-reactives. Combat-servitors were pitched back, reduced to scraps of meat and reinforced bone.

Beside Thoic, Ignatius Numen hefted the volkite he had acquired on Iydris, and leaping beams of searing heat cut down the fleeing adepts with cold efficiency.

'Secure those transit arches,' said Tyro, and the column of Iron Hands split to capture the flanking routes.

Speed was paramount in a boarding action.

Secure a bridgehead, push out and keep moving. Always moving.

Tyro's bolter slammed hard against his grip with each squeeze of the trigger. Each shot fired in time with his relentless lockstep. His shield took the battering impact of three explosive shells.

'Bolter fire,' he said, recognising the power of heavier shells. He turned in time to see a warrior launch himself through the smoke. Rich indigo-blue armour edged in silver. A hydra-glyph on the left shoulder guard.

Alpha Legion.

A gladius thrust for his gorget.

Tyro gave a quarter turn and pistoned his shield forwards. The incoming blade shattered. He snapped his bolter from the firing slot and rammed it through the faceplate of the traitor's helm. No need to pull the trigger, but he did anyway.

'Reckless fool,' said Tyro, stamping over the headless corpse.

Hardened blast shutters were coming down in the transit arches, but ground to a halt less than halfway into their descent.

Tyro grunted with grim amusement.

'Well done, Thamatica, well done indeed,' he said.

From its perch atop the burning Stormbird, Garuda watched the killing impassively. The flames of war reflected from its compound eyes, chips of sapphire limned with hazy winter's light.

THAT SAME LIGHT shimmered beneath Frater Thamatica's eyelids as he sat in a specially constructed vault deep in the *Sisypheum*. His eyes darted back and forth as he watched the fighting on the enemy ship's embarkation deck via an MIU cable slotted into the socket drilled at the nape of his neck.

The Bird sat on the remains of a Stormbird that Tyro's Thunderhawk had gutted with its dorsal battle cannon upon breaching the embarkation deck's integrity field. Then the Bird cocked its head to the side, and Thamatica fought the urge to alter his own posture. It was no proxy cyber-creature, and Wayland was not in control of this experience.

'Hold still, you wretched thing,' said Thamatica, but the Bird paid him no mind. It did what it wanted, lending – as far as Wayland had been concerned – further credence to his belief in its pre-Medusan origins.

Through its eyes, Thamatica watched Cadmus Tyro's warriors eliminate the defenders of the embarkation deck and push deeper into the *Morgeld*. He blinked his visual feed over to the link with the *Sisypheum*'s main cogitator engine. The view through the Bird's eyes vanished, replaced by a glowing schematic of the *Morgeld*'s interior structure. Obsessive attention to detail, an eidetic memory and the decades he'd spent training on Mars had allowed Thamatica to stock the *Sisypheum*'s cogitators with accurate schematics of every currently listed traitor vessel.

According to Martian launch dockets, the *Zeta Morgeld* departed Mars twelve years ago, making it one of the newest ships in the Imperial fleet registry.

The Iron Hands aboard the vessel were picked out with golden skulls enclosed in toothed cogs. Where their positions were known, Alpha Legionnaires were hydran green.

Cadmus Tyro was advancing deep into the guts of the *Morgeld* from the starboard embarkation deck, a knife thrust to capture the bridge. To keep the Alpha Legion from escaping, Vermana Cybus fought his way towards the engine spaces.

'Captain Tyro,' said Thamatica. 'A choke point approaches fifty metres to your fore. Advise you take the lateral companionway ten metres perpendicular to the axis of your advance to reach an upper transit.'

'*Understood,*' came Tyro's clipped response. He was a man of few words, and even more so in a combat situation. Bolter fire echoed over the vox, together with the clanging impacts of mass-reactives on boarding shields. The Alpha Legion fought hard to defend their vessel with a ferocity that surprised Thamatica.

It shouldn't have, of course.

With their love of indirect means of war, it was all too easy to forget that the sons of Alpharius were still a Legion of transhuman fighters.

Thamatica monitored the battle through the feeds of Iron Hands' strike teams and remote telemetry from the Bird. It kept pace with Cadmus Tyro, affording Thamatica a scouting view ahead of the boarders. He issued real-time warnings of Alpha Legion counter-attacks and alternate routes to target.

As the attack progressed, the engine spaces fell swiftly and Tyro's warriors swept up the vessel towards the bridge. With the fall of the main axial route a sharp screech, like a nail down a slate, dragged Thamatica from his battle-management.

Veils of informational light fell away from his sight and the stolid weight of the chamber re-established itself around him. Fresh-cut walls of bare iron, newly built and many-layered.

Banks of humming machinery surrounded the Ironwrought, and a host of heavily insulated cables were connected to the room's only other occupant.

It – Thamatica couldn't bring himself to think of it as a *he* – sat opposite him, bound to a bare iron throne with fetters of adamantium at its wrists and ankles.

Thamatica knew there was little need. The Kryptos wasn't going anywhere, but ever since Sabik Wayland and Nykona Sharrowkyn had captured the code-breaking cypher creature on Cavor Sarta, Cadmus Tyro had insisted it be kept immobile.

The flesh of its horrific face was corpse-pale, its jaw an obscene arrangement of articulated parts, augmitters, vox-grilles and sound-producing elements that made a mockery of anatomy. The creature's skull was a grotesque amalgam of a cogitator's punch-interface and biological specimen jar: a brass-and-flesh arrangement of xenos-formed anatomy suspended within a crackling glass compartment.

Its eyes were unblinking orbs – dull and insensate for the most part, but now filled with desperate need and pain. A wet stream of garbled machine noise brayed from the clicking, chewing, spitting mouth, meaningless to anyone without the correct augments or a form of wetware that violently resisted any attempt to duplicate it.

Thamatica glanced at the data-slate implanted on a lectern bolted to the floor in front of the Kryptos. Streams of information cascaded across it.

Gibberish and nonsense code for now.

'Wayland,' said Thamatica.

'*I see it, Frater,*' said Sabik Wayland from somewhere aboard the *Morgeld*. '*An encrypted transmission.*'

'You are closer to the source, can you jam it?'

'*I already am,*' said Wayland. '*I wasn't made Iron Father yesterday, you know.*'

'Ah, but when measured next to my experience, you might as well have been,' said Thamatica, as the enemy transmission washed through the blasphemous mechanisms engineered and gene-spliced into the Kryptos.

'*Have no fear,*' said Wayland. '*Their cry for help has been strangled at birth.*'

'Good work, lad…' said Thamatica, his words trailing off as he read the words on the data-slate.

'Frater? What is it?'

Thamatica shut off the link to Wayland, calling up the glowing schematic of the *Morgeld*'s interior.

'Cadmus!' he said, fighting to keep the excitement from his voice. 'You need to get onto the bridge and seize it right now! Do whatever it takes, but get in there.'

'What in the name of Ferrus do you think I'm doing, Frater?' snapped Tyro.

'Whatever it is, do it faster,' said Thamatica. 'They'll be trying to delete the log and astrogation data.'

'So? Why do I care where this ship has been?'

'You don't understand, young Tyro, it's where it's *going* that matters,' said Thamatica. 'By the looks of it, the *Morgeld* is en route to rendezvous with Alpharius himself!'

ACCESS TO THE bridge of a warship was intentionally difficult, and the *Zeta Morgeld* was no exception, a long and narrow approach that began at a cramped Y-junction.

'No projecting stanchions, bulkheads or places to hide,' said Cadmus Tyro, ducking back as a hail of autocannon fire from the emplaced door turrets filled the approach with searing traceries of shells.

'You expected any different?' grunted Septus Thoic from the opposite side of the junction.

'I hoped different,' he shrugged. 'It's Alpha Legion.'

'Going to have to run the full gauntlet,' shouted Ignatius Numen, finally reading Tyro's words on his helm visor. 'Shields locked tight, shoulders down and take the pain.'

A plasma grenade on Isstvan had given Numen an artificial sheen to his skin and taken his eyes. It had also partially deafened him, a wounding that one of Fulgrim's debased followers had finished.

Tyro nodded. No time to do this any way other than directly.

'Only wide enough for three abreast,' said Thoic.

'Then you and Numen are with me,' said Tyro, bringing his shield about. He mag-locked his bolter to his thigh. He'd need both arms to keep the shield steady. 'Ready? Upon the anvil.'

'And by the Iron,' finished Thoic. Numen nodded a second later. Both had handed off their heavy weapons and hefted borrowed shields – monstrous sheets of Avernii blacksteel emblazoned with the argent gauntlet of the Legion.

Tyro moved first, stepping brazenly from cover and planting his shield down hard on the deck. Shellfire from the twin turrets immediately slammed into the metal, percussive impacts like hammerblows an inch from his visor. Thoic and Numen took station either side an instant later, shields vibrating with clangs of detonation.

'Go!' shouted Tyro, and the three of them pushed into the hurricane of fire.

He gritted his teeth as the relentless impacts numbed his arm in seconds. Step by step they pushed down the approach, the noise deafening. Heads and shoulders down, legs braced and wide, bodies angled towards the streams of fire.

'Like walking into the teeth of a Medusan ash storm,' roared Numen as though he were enjoying the experience.

'Keep going, don't slacken the pace!' yelled Tyro. 'Momentum is everything.'

Thoic stumbled as a ricochet clipped the side of his helm. A gap opened. Tyro grunted as sudden fire roared up his arm. A hit. He ground his teeth, blocking the pain.

No weakness, not now.

Thoic hauled himself upright with a bellow of self-reproach. He thrust his shield back into line, pushing even harder. Tyro saw a gouge just to the right of Thoic's eye lens. A millimetre to the left and his helm would be a sloshing vault of bone and pulped brain matter.

A booming impact behind him made Tyro turn.

A heavy blast shield, like something he'd expect to see on a gunnery deck, now filled the corridor, cutting them off from the rest of the assault force.

And that wasn't the only unwelcome surprise.

Portions of the coffered wall panels were moving on either side of the corridor, veils of gunsmoke drawn towards areas of negative pressure. Gaping voids instead of pressed and riveted steel. A pair of indigo-armoured warriors stepped into view with heavy, thudding footfalls.

Vast, vaguely humanoid shapes that filled the passageway.

Tyro's heart sank as he recognised the deadly silhouettes.

'Terminators!' he shouted. 'Plant your shields! Turn and engage.'

All three slammed their shields down again as Tyro freed his arm. He spun and dropped to his haunches, his own shield locking tight to his back as he thrust his arms to the side. He gripped the handles of his brothers' shields in support as repeated impacts forced him down. Heat enveloped his shoulders as the armour's servo muscles fought against the storm of shells.

Thoic and Numen snapped their bolters free and opened fire on the Terminators, full auto. Shells blazed down the corridor, detonating against their impossibly thick armour.

It didn't even slow the titanic killers.

They might as well have been shooting a Land Raider.

The jade hydra icons glittered in the half-light of the corridor, the ruby eyes of their serpentine heads alive with wicked intent. Each warrior's helm was grotesquely horned, their shoulder guards mockingly draped with scraps of war-banners torn from the standards of their former kinsmen.

'For the Emperor,' the Terminators said in unison, and their combi-bolters filled the corridor with mass-reactive shells.

TWO

Shadow and Iron
Spoils
The sepulchre

THOIC AND NUMEN pressed themselves hard against the walls, but there was no escaping the fusillade of mass-reactives. Two shells struck Thoic's gorget and visor, spinning him into the path of two more. He dropped to the deck with blood arcing from his ruptured plates.

Numen bent low into the storm, taking the brunt of the fire on his shoulder guards. Miraculously, every shell ricocheted from the curved plates without detonating. With a roar of hatred, Numen threw himself at the nearest Terminator.

A clubbing fist of elephantine proportions picked Numen up and slammed him hard against the bulkhead. Numen's strangled cry over the vox was grating with shattered bone and wet with blood.

The Terminators stepped forwards together.

'Captain Tyro,' said a voice that seemed to whisper over the vox. *'Drop to the deck. And hold on to something.'*

Tyro knew that voice and knew better than to argue. He released the shields and dropped his exhausted arms, throwing himself flat on the deck plates.

The fire from the turrets pummelled the Terminators, halting their advance. Tactical Dreadnought armour was proof against most things, but even it had its limits. A combi-bolter exploded as its magazine took a hit and the Alpha Legionnaire staggered as his arm disappeared below the elbow.

The second Alpha Legion Terminator bent low and lumbered towards Tyro. High-calibre shells exploded against his armour, cracking the plates and drawing blood. Not enough to stop him, but he was hurting.

The turrets' targeting augurs abruptly disengaged upon registering friendlies. Tyro looked up to see the second Terminator poised to crush him beneath its giant boot.

Above the emerald hydra symbol, a fulminate-bright halo of light appeared on the ceiling. Tyro knew of only one weapon that could cause that effect.

Lascutter.

He gripped the mesh decking hard enough to bend the steel.

The Terminator looked up in time to see a three-metre section of the ceiling blow out in a rush of detonation. Hurricane-force wind rammed up through the ceiling, and Tyro saw a series of concentric holes above it, leading all the way to the void of space.

Not even the immense mass of a Terminator could compete with the force of explosive decompression. The Alpha Legionnaire flew up through the ceiling, like a bullet shot from a gun as he was hurled out into space.

Tyro was lifted into the air and spun around by the decompressive storm. His boots slammed into the wall and he activated the magnetic clamps. He saw Numen and Thoic farther down the corridor, also mag-locked against the bulkhead.

The wounded Terminator had been too far from the hole to be dragged into the void. He too was mag-locked. The sudden drop in pressure abruptly equalised, the hull breach sealed somewhere above.

He fell to the deck as a dark shape dropped through the hole in the ceiling. A warrior, armoured in black plate, but a black that seemed utterly non-reflective and which actively repelled light. His bulk marked him a legionary, but one who moved like no other warrior Tyro knew.

The warrior vaulted towards the Terminator, kicking off the wall and triggering a compact jump pack. Blue-hot jets carried him over the Terminator's shoulder in a graceful parabola.

A black-bladed gladius that reflected no light plunged down into the Terminator's weakest point, the sliver of flex-seal between his gorget and the base of his helm. A squirting geyser of blood fountained from the traitor's neck as the obsidian-edged gladius severed his carotid artery.

It kept pumping even as the Terminator halted, the warrior within dead, but kept upright by his armour's weight.

Nykona Sharrowkyn of the Raven Guard landed lightly behind his victim as another figure dropped through the hole in the ceiling. He landed hard, cratering the deck plates, and Tyro saw he bore a pair of heavy breaching charges under each arm. Diffuse light from an energy field above limned his armour in pellucid blue illumination.

This warrior was also armoured in black, but his was the black of the Iron Hands, and bore the mailed gauntlet.

'Wayland?' said Tyro.

Sabik Wayland didn't answer and moved past him to affix the breaching charges to the blast shutters securing the bridge. He slammed his palms on the activation triggers and ran back to Tyro.

He picked up Ignatius Numen's shield and hunkered down behind it. 'Right now would be a good time to lift that shield again, Captain Tyro.'

WITH THE FALL of the bridge, the battle was won and the stripping operation on the *Zeta Morgeld* went into full effect. Weapons, ammunition, spare parts, fuel, tools and raw materials, even a pair of Stormbirds on the port-side launch rails. Nothing would be wasted. The thrall crew of the *Sisypheum* would leave this ship a gutted hulk before casting it and its dead crew into the nuclear heart of a star.

The detritus of battle had been cleared from the embarkation deck and cargo haulers from the *Sisypheum* were being loaded by bulk-servitors that had once served the Alpha Legion.

Cadmus Tyro walked slowly along the line of bodies dumped at the edge of the embarkation deck. Stripped of their armour, the Alpha Legion corpses were a stark reminder of how thoroughly hate could dismantle flesh – even that of a transhuman.

'Mass-reactives account for less than half of these kills,' said Tyro, pointing out the wound patterns and apocalyptic damage wrought on the bronzed, knotted flesh of the dead. 'The majority are pure close-quarter kills.'

'It's visceral,' said Vermana Cybus, spitting caustic saliva at each corpse as they passed. 'Cathartic. Personal. No one else has more reason than us to hate these turncoat bastards.'

Tyro couldn't argue with that.

Ferrus Manus, the Gorgon, their gene-sire, was dead. Murdered on Isstvan by a brother in a moment of unimaginable betrayal.

And in his death were the seeds of madness sown.

The primarch's end had been so terrible, so shocking, it had carved an abyssal void in the Iron Tenth's psyche that might never heal.

Grief had almost ended their defiance in the weeks since the bloody black sands of the Urgall Depression, but that grief had long-since curdled into hate.

And hate was the twisted cousin of bloody retribution.

'And we're sure this is all of them?' asked Tyro.

'Aye,' said Cybus. 'I've been through every hidden corner and secret passage of the ship myself. Twenty legionaries, all told.'

'There's only fifteen here.'

'Tarsa's taken five back to the *Sisypheum* to cut up.'

'What for?'

'How should I know? I'm not an Apothecary.'

'Fair enough, but twenty warriors isn't many for a strike cruiser.'

Cybus shrugged, and his bare metal limbs clattered against his armour. None of the *Sisypheum*'s crew could match Cybus in zeal for chimeric augmentation. Even before the atrocity on Isstvan, Cybus had embraced the nascent creed of self-mortification with the fervency of a zealot.

'Probably someone hit them in the years since Isstvan,' said Cybus. 'We're not alone fighting them out here in the dark.'

'Perhaps, but this didn't feel like a ship operating below strength,' said Tyro, pausing as the Alpha Legion's operational methodology struck a disquietingly familiar note.

'It's a strike-cell,' he said. 'A single ship with a small crew, flying off-grid. It's what we're doing.'

Cybus nodded, accepting Tyro's logic.

'You really think they were en route to Alpharius?'

Tyro sighed. 'We'll know for sure once the Kryptos finishes with the logs Wayland exloaded.'

'But can we trust anything it might tell us?'

'I don't know, Vermana,' said Tyro. 'But if it's true... the chance to strike back at the traitors in such a meaningful way, to hurt them as we were hurt. We *need* this, Vermana.'

'Aye, captain, we do, but that's for Captain Branthan to decide.'

Tyro nodded stiffly. Cybus was right. Despite resting in an ice-locked stasis casket, Ulrach Branthan was still the captain of the *Sisypheum*'s warriors.

'Have you–'

'No,' said Tyro, already regretting having told Cybus what he'd seen – or what he *thought* he'd seen – in Branthan's cryo-chamber. 'The captain remains as he always has.'

'And Tarsa? What does he say?'

'Nothing,' snapped Tyro. 'What do you expect him to say? The captain is locked in frozen stasis. Wounds do not *heal* within a stasis field. No one miraculously heals mortal wounds. No one rises from death, no matter how much we would wish it.'

WITH THE WOUNDED stabilised in the apothecarion, Atesh Tarsa bore the honoured dead down into the frozen sepulchres of the *Sisypheum*. His reductor gauntlet weighed heavy with the genetic legacy of six brothers of the Iron Hands, six heroes who would no longer stand against the arch-traitor.

The passageways this deep were crusted frost-white, like a cave system within an ancient glacier. It made sound and light behave strangely. Echoes of Tarsa's footsteps travelled ahead of him and his fractured reflection writhed in the ice. Easy to understand how rumours of spectral apparitions and phantom voices in the depths had spread through the crew, Space Marine and Legion serf alike.

Nonsense, of course, but even brains as augmented and disciplined as a legionary's were prone to pareidolia.

The sterile air glittered with white flakes, and gleaming icicles hung from structural beams like glassy daggers. Tarsa passed the sepulchre where the shattered Dreadnought frame of Brother Bombastus lay interred. He paused and pressed a gauntlet against the cold metal.

He moved on, deeper into the cold heart of the ship. Tarsa's deep-green armour bled hot vapour, inuring him to the cold, yet he shivered as the airlock sealing the last cryo-vault slid aside.

Sub-zero air sighed out like breath.

Tarsa chided himself for employing such metaphors, but he was a native of Nocturne, raised in a culture of legends passed down from father to son around the hearthfire. Tales of war, tales of helldrakes, and tales of the undying fire-souls beneath the world.

Such ingrained habits were hard to break.

Ulrach Branthan's vault was a tomb in all but name, an icy cave of airless chill and hissing, wheezing machinery. Thermal tarpaulins covered the most sensitive mechanisms, and insulated cables pulsed on the deck plates like dormant serpents.

At the centre of the chamber sat the glass-topped casket in which lay the mortally wounded captain of the *Sisypheum*. Its surface was all but obscured by layers of blue-white frost that scattered winking reflections in the half-light. As had become his habit of late, Tarsa reached out to touch the glass, wiping away the frost over Ulrach Branthan's recumbent form. Familiarity had not dulled Tarsa to the horror of the man's wounds.

Missing limbs, fist-deep craters torn by mass-reactives, dreadful canyons of chainblade impacts and hideous phosphex burns.

Enough to kill a man thrice over, yet Branthan endured.

In most other Legions, such wounds would have seen him allowed to die or be interred within a Dreadnought. But the time Tarsa had spent aboard the *Sisypheum* had taught him that the Iron Hands were not *most other Legions.*

The Heart of Iron still squatted on his chest like a parasite, a vaguely arachnoid machine of brass and silver that was simultaneously healing and consuming Branthan. Thread-fine tendrils extruded from its segmented body to penetrate Branthan's flesh. Where they were going or what they were doing within his body was a mystery. None of Tarsa's equipment could map the paths they took.

In the brief moments where they risked rousing Branthan to seek his counsel, it appeared the archeotech device was remaking his catastrophically damaged organs. But only at the cost of the captain's, for want of a better term, *life-force.*

Tarsa leaned close to the casket, the coal-dark skin and red eyes of his proud Nocturnian heritage reflected in the frosted glass.

'You cling to life with a determination that goes beyond all reason,' he said, his voice little more than a whisper. 'The sons of Vulkan are proud and courageous, but we know when to advance and when to retreat. It is time to let go, Ulrach.'

Cadmus Tyro would kill him for such words. The acting captain of the *Sisypheum* believed Branthan could be made whole again, but Tarsa's efforts were only prolonging Branthan's suffering.

Decades spent training in the apothecarion told him Branthan could not possibly hear his words within a stasis field, but the part of his soul that wanted to believe in miracles wished he could.

He turned from the casket and took a deep breath, his eyes widening as blast-chilled air filled his lungs. So different from the volcanic home world he never expected to see again.

Turning from Branthan's casket, Tarsa busied himself with the safe
interment of the progenoids he had extracted from the fallen warriors. Each loss was a grievous blow to the *Sisypheum*. They had not the
numbers to suffer such losses easily.

Years spent fighting on the ragged edges of this war had taken its
toll on the already diminished crew of the strike cruiser. The expedition into the warp tempest in pursuit of the Phoenician and the Lord
of Iron had cost them dearly.

As had their escape.

With a mere forty-two warriors and a fast-diminishing stock of supplies, the time was approaching when their continued presence in the
wilds of space would become unsustainable. Soon, Tarsa knew, someone was going to have to convince Cadmus Tyro it was time to return
to the Imperium.

He sighed, knowing that duty would fall to him. Sharrowkyn was
Raven Guard to the core and relished this form of war. He would never
suggest it. And none in the Iron Tenth would shame themselves by
admitting they could no longer continue this campaign of guerrilla war.

'I have seen the same behaviour in pyrogharials,' said Tarsa to the
silent casket as he sterilised the interior of the reductor and sealed its
cylindrical sample-chambers.

'They're fiercely territorial lava-swimming lizards that dwell in the
caldera of Nocturne's volcanoes,' he said by way of explanation.

Tarsa stepped over the hissing cables on the deck to sit next to Branthan's casket. He rested a hand on the glass as he continued. 'When an
earthquake or the lava flow from a fresh eruption brings two lizards
into competition for burrows, they will not stop until the fighting is
done and one of them is dead.'

He sighed.

'From an evolutionary standpoint it is self-defeating behaviour that
appears to serve no purpose, yet still they do it as though it is hard-
wired into their reptile brains, leaving them incapable of change. I
remember climbing into the fires of Mount Kagutsuchi on the eve of

my ascension to the Legion and seeing two such beasts in battle. It was an incredible sight, Ulrach – two basalt-scaled monsters tearing at each other for the sake of a lava pool barely large enough to hold either one of them. Yet fight for it they did.

'But as I watched them battle, a great sorrow filled me at such senseless waste. What need had they to fight for this particular pool when there were many others within easy reach? Yet the beasts knew no different, so what else could they do? In the end, the bloodied victor did not enjoy his spoils for long. A third beast came down from a magma vent higher up the caldera and devoured him. If there's a lesson to be learned it is the clumsy, wasteful, blundering, low, and horribly cruel works of nature that govern all living things.'

Tarsa's head sank to his chest and he said, 'Ah, forgive me, Captain Branthan. Memories of Nocturne are making me melancholy. I miss the russet skies of my birth world and the fiery winds that sweep its blackened mountains.'

He looked into the shimmering ice coating the casket, and it seemed he saw a reflection of himself. He blinked. The Salamanders legionary in the ice sat before a casket of gold, at the head of which burned a solitary memorial flame.

Tarsa stood suddenly, his heart thudding in his chest.

He looked around the sepulchre.

He was alone.

'Just a distorted reflection,' he said. 'That's all it was.'

Yet, just for an instant, Tarsa thought he'd heard the faint sound of a distant heartbeat.

He put a hand on the ice-covered glass of Branthan's casket as sudden certainty filled him.

'Vulkan lives,' he said.

THREE

Not alone
Crossfire
Son of Medusa

ONLY THE FAINTEST glimmer of starlight illuminated the bloodstained deck of the *Zeta Morgeld*'s bridge, reminding Frater Thamatica just how far out they were. At the edge of the system, light reflecting from the dead surface of its outermost planet was the merest haze. And beyond the smear of the Oort cloud, distant light from far-off systems was already tens of thousands of years old.

He sat at the helmsman's station in a faint pool of radiance given off by a slowly rotating holographic subsector map. Septus Thoic was down on the engineering deck, stripping out the last of the *Morgeld*'s fuel and capacitors, so power cables ran from the rear of Thamatica's servo-harness to an open panel beneath the avionics cogitator.

The Alpha Legion vessel had been reduced to little more than a vast slab of cold metal adrift in the void.

Soon it wouldn't even be that much.

The map's ghostly light threw Thamatica's craggy, age-worn features into stark relief as his agile eyes darted over the three-dimensional geometry of its celestial notations.

'*Frater,*' came the voice of Cadmus Tyro over his helm vox. '*Are you and Thoic done yet?*'

Thamatica leaned back into the helmsman's seat, the articulated arms of his servo-harness wheezing as they moved to accommodate his movement. His red cloak billowed in a gust of exhaled gases.

'You do realise, captain, that plotting a course to ensure the *Morgeld* burns up in the system's star is akin to threading a needle.'

'*Just point it in the right direction and fire the damn engines.*'

'Ah, if only it were that simple, Captain Tyro,' said Thamatica. 'The dance of intersecting planetary orbits, asteroid belts and rogue celestial bodies makes plotting such a course a fascinating exercise in complex four-dimensional mathematics.'

'*Just get a move on, Frater,*' said Tyro. '*I want that ship scuttled and us on our way as soon as possible.*'

'Then allow us to get on with our work,' said Thamatica, shutting off the vox.

He'd overstated the complexity of the task, of course. The entirely predictable motion of this system's planets made plotting the *Morgeld*'s last voyage simplicity itself.

A single burst of power to the engines, then time and momentum would do the rest.

But like any savant of the Machine, he hated to destroy technology. Like a remembrancer forced to discard the written word or an artist painting over an old canvas, Thamatica felt such acts were somehow profane.

What might the generations to come say of such wilful destruction? Would they look back at him as at the book-burners of Narthan Dume, destroying in blind ignorance that which might empower the future?

But what other choice was there?

Barely enough Iron Hands were left to crew the *Sisypheum*, let alone a second vessel. Thamatica had explained how infinitesimally small were the chances of anyone ever finding the *Zeta Morgeld* in the emptiness of wilderness space, but Cadmus Tyro wasn't about to take the chance it might one day be salvaged by the traitors.

With deft keystrokes across the helmsman's slate, Thamatica laid in the course for the *Morgeld*'s last voyage. A journey of two months to the system star.

A soft chime from the adjacent auspex panel made him frown.

He waited. It didn't come again.

'Power bleed,' surmised Thamatica, but just to be sure, he routed power from avionics into the surveyor array. The console flickered to life as data from the passive surveyor arrays in the *Morgeld*'s prow filled its slates.

There. A return.

So faint that on any other ship Thamatica might have dismissed it as a ghost reading.

Yet the *Morgeld* had recognised it.

'Asirnoth's blood...' he cursed, now seeing the ghost reading for what it was.

He reopened the vox to the *Sisypheum*.

'Captain Tyro!' he shouted. '*Sisypheum* to battle stations, immediately!'

'*What is it, Frater?*'

'There's another Alpha Legion ship out there,' said Thamatica, 'and it's right on top of us!'

A CRITICAL OBJECTIVE in any sphere of battle was to detect the enemy while avoiding detection in return. And never more so than in void war. Naval commanders throughout the Imperium, from primarchs to lord commanders, agreed that, as in all forms of warfare, the element of surprise was paramount.

The Alpha Legion ship was named the *Theta Malquiant*, launched less than a year after the *Morgeld*. Tyro saw its service record was patchy, its honour roll of victories thin. Even a quick scan of its registry revealed a ship dogged by ill-fortune.

Was this the turn of its luck?

Beyond surprise, three things mattered in void engagements between gross-displacement vessels: position, conservation of momentum and a well-trained gunnery crew.

From Tyro's vantage point on the *Sisypheum's* command throne, the *Malquiant* had the advantage in all three arenas. The Alpha Legion vessel had unmasked high in their starboard rear quarter, moving abeam at a stately pace and with its broadside gun decks already launching.

Red light bathed the *Sisypheum's* command bridge as its deck crew of human thralls and Space Marines fought to make the strike cruiser battle-ready. Tyro was not a natural shipmaster, and had delegated helm control to Sabik Wayland, but even against an ill-starred vessel the odds were stacked against them. Once the initiative passed to a competent enemy, it was next to impossible to regain.

But the *Sisypheum* was a tough ship. It had rammed *Andronius* to destruction. It had survived an attack from the Lord of Iron himself and endured all that the warp could throw at it in the seething tempests that engulfed Iydris.

It would survive this.

'How in the name of Medusa did it get so close?' asked Vermana Cybus, struggling to bring the weapons systems online.

At the combined helm/engineering station, Sabik Wayland said, 'A question probably best saved for *after* we fight clear of this ambush?'

He hauled back heavy levers and spun brass dials on the panel before him, distributing the available power to those systems that needed it most. The deck tilted under his feet as he threw the ship into a hard turn.

'Ambush?' said Tyro. 'This vessel was here all along?'

'No,' said Sharrowkyn, stepping from the shadows behind Tyro. 'It was not.'

Tyro swallowed his irritation at Sharrowkyn's unannounced presence on the bridge. For all that the Raven Guard warrior had proven himself time and time again, he wasn't Iron Tenth.

'How can you know that?' demanded Tyro.

'Because it would have fought when we attacked the *Morgeld*. The *Malquiant* is here to rendezvous with its sister vessel.'

'Incoming ordnance,' said Wayland.

'Void shields?' said Tyro.

'Ignition sequence under way.'

'Will they light in time to stop this volley?'

'Omnissiah willing...'

'Then give me power to the weapons!' demanded Cybus.

'Weapons can wait,' said Wayland without looking up. 'Engines and shields first. If we survive the next few minutes, we'll see about fighting back.'

The ship groaned in protest as its keel was stressed to the limits of its design parameters. In tandem with a surge to the main drives, the manoeuvring jets were also firing – portside aft and starboard prow – pushing the ship around its central axis and presenting its rear quarter to the incoming ordnance.

'Blood of Medusa!' Tyro cursed. 'What are you doing, Wayland?'

'Keeping us alive long enough to fight back!'

Tyro watched the rapidly elongating parabolas of incoming ordnance on the main viewer and knew there was no way the *Sisypheum* could avoid a punishing series of strikes.

'Brace for impact!' he shouted.

'Belay that!' countered Wayland with an upraised fist.

'You're going to kill us all, Wayland!'

Sabik Wayland shook his head. 'The art of void-gunnery is in unleashing fire where a vessel *will* be in the time it takes ordnance to travel to its target,' he said. 'Their Master of Weapons is trying to anticipate our evasive momentum even as I attempt to confound that anticipation.'

'Then let's hope your art is superior,' said Tyro.

This time Wayland deigned to look up and Tyro saw he was grinning. 'Did you ever doubt it?'

Tyro was unsure of the Iron Father's meaning until he looked back at the rapidly unfolding tracks of the engagement. He now saw what Wayland intended and drew in a hissing breath at the colossal risk he was taking.

'Dorsal voids igniting,' said Cybus.

Collimated blinks of ablating lasers played over the shields like flashing strobes. The sheer weight of fire stripped them back and blew out a dozen ignition vanes. Blossoming explosions enveloped the vessel's topside, turning metres-thick plates of armour to bleeding streamers of molten metal.

Superficial damage. The *Sisypheum* had survived worse.

The hundreds of hyper-velocity shells following hard on the heels of the lasers were the real ship-killers.

But Wayland's ultra-rapid manoeuvre had turned the *Sisypheum*'s blazing engines into the face of the incoming bombardment. The strike cruiser's plasma-wake raised the temperature differential of the void immediately behind the *Sisypheum* by thousands of degrees. That heat bled off rapidly, but was still searing enough to cook off every warhead a safe distance from the strike cruiser.

A cascade of silent detonations painted the void in a pyrotechnic blaze.

'Bones of the Avernii,' said Tyro. 'You took a big risk there, Wayland.'

'A calculated risk,' countered Wayland, driving the vessel towards the *Morgeld*. 'One that has bought us a chance to counter-attack.'

'They're coming about again,' snarled Vermana Cybus. 'Get me into a firing position and I'll blow them to the warp and back.'

'All in good time,' said Wayland, burning the engines hard and throwing the ship into another violent turn. Strike cruisers were fast and manoeuvrable, but they weren't designed for the kinds of vector changes normally seen in a sub-atmospheric dogfight.

'Incoming,' said Cybus, reading his threat board's assessment of this latest attack. 'Prow bombards – macro-cannons, mass-drivers and hyper-grasers.'

Travelling at the speed of light, the grasers danced over the *Sisypheum*'s flanks and Tyro felt the vessel shudder as portside compartments blew out into space. A score of damage sigils scrolled across his slate.

'Hard to port!' shouted Wayland. 'Full burn on ventral thrusters!'

Once again the *Sisypheum* groaned in protest, a wounded beast desperately trying to outrun a faster predator with sharper claws. Conduits split in the vaulted space above Tyro and a series of alarm klaxons brayed. Thralls ran to shut down damaged systems.

Wayland silenced the alarms and kept on driving the vessel hard.

Tyro swore as yet more tracks of incoming ordnance slid across the display towards them. The movement on the slate was almost sedate, though the lethal shells were slashing through space at hundreds of kilometres every second.

He gripped the armrests of the command throne as the *Sisypheum*'s violent turn continued and the main engines flared. The *Malquiant* was coming about, turning rapidly in order to keep its guns on target.

Then the display lit up with multiple impacts, electromagnetic pulses and the nuclear violence of detonating ordnance – enough to level a city from orbit.

'What just happened?' said Tyro. 'Were we hit?'

'No,' said Cybus, looking over in grudging admiration at Sabik Wayland. 'They hit the *Morgeld*. Wayland put it between us and the *Malquiant*'s guns.'

The image on the main viewer dissolved and changed to show the stripped Alpha Legion ship. Ablaze from end to end, plumes of crystallising oxygen burned fiercely. Explosions marched along the length of its hull as over-pressured compartments blew out one after the other.

Its death was swift as the overwhelming power of the *Theta Malquiant*'s barrage tore it apart. Its keel split as a final detonation ripped through the heart of the vessel and turned it into a seething corona of expanding debris.

Sharrowkyn leaned forwards and gripped the brass rail behind Tyro's throne. His alabaster features were set in an expression of tight anger.

'Aren't you forgetting something, Wayland?' he snapped.

'What?' asked Wayland.

'Septus Thoic and Frater Thamatica are still aboard the *Morgeld*.'

TWISTED SPARS OF heat-softened hull ribs, glowing red from graser impacts, blocked the *Zeta Morgeld*'s main arterial. Fire filled its radial corridors, rapidly reducing the number of possible routes to an embarkation deck.

The ship shook like an ocean-going vessel in a storm. Septus Thoic staggered through the flames and collapsing corridors of the *Morgeld*. He slammed into walls as the superstructure heaved and bucked with yet more shells blasting through its hull.

Atmosphere was non-existent, the first thing vented into space. The satisfying corollary of that was the extinguishing of the vast majority of fires burning along the vessel's length.

'Septus!' said Thamatica. *'Methinks it is high time we got off this ship. I'm at the torpedo rails. Looks like that's the only way off this wreck. How close are you?'*

'Lower gunnery deck,' said Thoic. 'I'll take the main transitway and use the–'

'No, the transitway is ablaze,' warned Thamatica. *'A plasma storm burst up from the reactor deck. You'll need to reroute.'*

'Hellfires,' said Thoic. 'So the only blaze that won't die is the one blocking the route I need to take.'

'Indeed, it is most perturbing. One might almost be tempted to think this ship is taking its revenge against us.'

'Can you find me another route?'

'Route to starboard deck blocked. Options limited. Ah, there… that's it.'

'Got it,' said Thoic, as an escape route flashed up onto his helm's visor. He turned and ran for a smoke-filled companionway. According to Thamatica's schematics, it led down to a munitions sub-deck with a maintenance duct that ran parallel to the main transit. Its lateral access points should still be useable.

And from there it was a short sprint to where Thamatica waited at the ventral launch tubes. A boarding torpedo wasn't the usual way to depart a dying vessel, but Thoic would take what he could get.

He reached the companionway just as a pair of shells from a battery of macro-cannons struck the *Morgeld*'s hull less than thirty metres aft of him.

Metres-thick armour plating peeled back like the foil on a ration pack. Thoic had a fraction of a second to see the atomic hellstorm raging beyond the breach.

Then he was gone, wrenched out into the fire-filled void.

BROADSIDE TO BROADSIDE, the two vessels squared off against one another. The *Sisypheum* had been hurt and was cornered, but it still had teeth. If the *Malquiant* wanted this Imperial scalp, it was going to have to earn it in blood.

'Gun decks firing,' shouted Cybus. 'Target lock holding.'

Space was awash with electromagnetic flares from the burning corpse of the *Morgeld*. They fouled the targeting mechanisms of the weapons and threw phantom images of duplicate starships across every slate.

Wayland applied every filter he knew to keep the enemy ship solidly within the auspex sights. The *Malquiant* was arcing over the topside of its burning sister ship, rolling on its long axis to present its starboard batteries.

Even in the midst of combat, Wayland had to admire its helmsman's nerve in flying so close to a dying vessel that might go critical at any moment.

Yet, even in his admiration, he saw the enemy make their first mistake. The *Malquiant's* arc was going over too high and too fast, carrying it beyond the trajectory of its broadside guns.

It was a basic helm error, surely too basic for any Legion commander to have made, but Wayland wasn't about to squander the opportunity.

'Hard to starboard, full burn,' ordered Wayland. 'We'll cross the topside and Cybus can rake them from stem to stern.'

Before the deck crew could enact his order, the filters Wayland had set to wash out the ghost images on the auspex slate finally completed their cycle. Half a dozen false returns vanished, leaving only the *Theta Malquiant* on the screen.

And one other vessel.

Plunging straight through the blazing firestorm engulfing the *Morgeld*. Striking into the heart of the battle like an assassin's blade.

'Gorgon's blood, no...' he whispered.

The electromagnetic backwash from the *Zeta Morgeld*'s destruction made identification of the ship impossible. It knifed into range, powering through the space between the *Sisypheum* and the *Malquiant*.

'What in the name of Ferrus...' began Tyro, rising from his chair as he too saw the image on the auspex for what it was. 'Another warship?'

'It's firing!' shouted Cybus.

'At who?' demanded Tyro.

That question was answered definitively when the *Malquiant*'s flanks erupted in a sequential cascade of explosions. Glassy rods of las-fire tore its shields away like tissue and point-blank barrages from multiple gun decks disembowelled the Alpha Legion vessel with the thoroughness of a butcher's hook.

The new arrival matched speed with the *Malquiant* and thunderous broadsides punished the traitor ship over and over, an overwhelming weight of fire that crushed the helpless vessel in moments. A final spread of torpedoes finished the job, leaving the *Theta Malquiant* nothing more than an expanding cloud of radioactive debris.

Wayland had never seen a starship die with such speed and efficiency.

'Whoever commands that vessel is a master of the void kill,' said Cybus, in awe of the vessel's brutal slaying.

'Who the hell is it?' asked Tyro. 'Wayland? What Legion flag does it fly?'

'Sending a hail now,' said Wayland, cocking his head to the side as a static-washed response came through the vox-bead in his ear.

At first he thought that he had misheard. Perhaps electromagnetic distortions were twisting the words of the ship's commander, or interference was making him hear what he *wanted* to hear.

'Sabik,' said Sharrowkyn. 'What is it?'

Wayland looked up in amazement.

'It's Meduson,' he said. 'It's Shadrak *bloody* Meduson...'

FOUR

We stand alone
Treachery in the blood
Back from the dead

STUNNED SILENCE GREETED Wayland's pronouncement. Shadrak Meduson of the Sorrgol. Warleader and Bringer of the Clans. Fragments of rumour reaching the *Sisypheum* claimed that the will behind a series of retributive hammerblows against enemy forces throughout the Oqueth, Instar and Momed sectors had been Meduson's.

But Dwell was the beginning of the end.

The cornerstone of Meduson's line, its loss had broken his self-perpetuated myth of invincibility. The shadow network linking the Shattered Legion forces told conflicting tales of Meduson: that he had died on Dwell, that he still fought the traitors, that the Sons of Horus had cut his heart out...

Now this.

'Meduson,' breathed Tyro, almost unwilling to believe it. 'Are you sure?'

'The orbicular structures of the vox encryption match exactly,' said Wayland, reading fresh information from the ship's auspex. 'It's the *Iron Heart*. It's him, it *has* to be.'

Tyro heard the need in Wayland's voice. It matched his own.

The years since Isstvan had been harder than any he had known, the hardest that *any* of the Iron Tenth had known. The death of Ferrus Manus had stripped them of every certainty, and this new form of war denied them the greatest strength their gene-sire had wrought in them: brotherhood.

'They're requesting permission to come aboard,' said Wayland. 'A single Thunderhawk.'

Nykona Sharrowkyn stepped down to the deck.

'Deny them,' he told Wayland. 'Shut off the vox.'

'What? Why?'

'Shut it off and get us out of here.'

Tyro rose from the command throne and said, 'This is an Iron Hands vessel, Sharrowkyn. You have no voice here.'

The Raven Guard turned to fix Tyro with his oil-dark eyes.

'We don't know who that is,' said Sharrowkyn, jabbing a finger towards the fuzzed outline of the *Iron Heart* on the main viewer. 'Yes, it could be Shadrak Meduson or it could be an enemy vessel looking to draw us into a trap.'

'The codes check out,' said Wayland. 'They couldn't be faked. Only a true son of Medusa would know them.'

'Have you forgotten everything we've done, Sabik?' said Sharrowkyn. 'We have the Kryptos and can break the traitor's encryption. Who's to say the enemy haven't done the same?'

Tyro knew Sharrowkyn was right, but the void within every heart of the Iron Tenth cried out for the Legion to be reforged.

'You could be right, Sharrowkyn,' he said, 'but if there is even the smallest chance that this is truly Shadrak Meduson, we have to be sure.'

Sharrowkyn shook his head. 'No. We stand alone, we fight alone. That's how this form of warfare works. That's the *only way it works.*'

'This isn't the mines of Lycaeus, Nykona,' said Wayland.

'You're right,' said Sharrowkyn. 'It's not. It's worse. Back in the darkness of Lycaeus it was easy to know who you had to kill. Out here, how can we be sure?'

'Enough, Sharrowkyn,' said Tyro. 'Hold your tongue.'

'Branthan would never allow this,' said Sharrowkyn.

'*Captain* Branthan isn't here,' snapped Tyro. 'I am. The *Sisypheum* isn't a democracy and I will not have you second-guessing my orders. Wayland, send word to the *Iron Heart*, we will receive them in the fore embarkation deck.'

'You're sure they're dead?' boomed Ignatius Numen, hefting another corpse into the airlock. 'Maybe I should cut their heads off just to be sure.'

Tarsa wasn't sure whether the Iron Hand was joking or not. A safe assumption that he wasn't, but the veteran's flash-burned skin and red targeting optics made knowing for sure difficult. Numen was one of the few who had actually witnessed the death of Ferrus Manus, and his armour was etched with the names of his fallen battle-brothers.

Isstvan had robbed the Emperor's sons of any desire to smile – the Iron Tenth most of all. At least Tarsa now had hope he might yet live to see Vulkan again. He had no basis in logic for this, save that no one had *seen* his primarch fall.

That, and the vision of a brother Salamander...

Precious little hope, but still precious.

'Well?' said Numen, his combat blade half drawn.

Tarsa shook his head. 'I assure you, Brother Numen, they are quite dead. An autopsy tends to have that side-effect. But I agree, even in death, their skin retains a ruddy bronze hue.'

Numen read Tarsa's words on his optics and grunted in acceptance. He nodded and sheathed his blade. He gripped another body in one iron-sheened arm and dragged it towards the airlock.

'Tell me something, Apothecary,' said Numen. 'Do the Alpha Legion come from a volcanic world like yours?'

'Nocturne is a hot world, yes,' said Tarsa, kneeling beside one of the dead legionaries to examine his blandly nondescript face. 'But that is not the cause of my colouration.'

'It's not?'

'No,' said Tarsa. 'The particular background radiation of Nocturne reacts vigorously with the melanochrome zygote of our primarch's gene-structure to radically alter the skin pigmentation of his sons.'

'Even recruits from Terra?' asked Numen.

'Every Salamanders legionary, whether he is from Terra or Nocturne, will have skin like mine,' said Tarsa, blinking and making his eyes shine crimson. 'And he will have furnace eyes like mine.'

Numen considered this.

'You didn't answer my question,' he said at last.

'I cannot answer it, for in truth, I know nothing of the Alpha Legion's home world,' said Tarsa.

'Nor I, is that strange?'

'Strange how?'

'I know of Fenris, of Nocturne and Cthonia,' said Numen. 'But I know nothing of the world that shaped the Twentieth.'

'Why is that important?' asked Tarsa.

'Each Legion makes its culture part of its war-making, and knowing where a warrior is from helps you fight him,' said Numen. 'I have tasted the ice of Fenris, so I know the wild heart of Russ and his *Rout*. Macragge taught me of Primarch Guilliman's practical warriors. But of Alpharius and his sons... I know nothing.'

'I think the Alpha Legion carefully cultivate that mystery,' said Tarsa. 'The only ones I met were maddeningly ambiguous. Every answer they gave spawned two more questions.'

'Is that why you had these ones brought on board?' asked Numen.

'Yes,' said Tarsa, standing to wipe his fingers on the plates of his armour. 'Studying what *literally* made them, might teach us something of what drives the Alpha Legion.'

'You think treachery was in their blood?'

'I wouldn't put it as ritualistically as that,' said Tarsa. 'But, yes, perhaps there is something in their genetic structure that made them more predisposed to betrayal.'

Numen shook his head. 'It was not blood that damned the Alpha Legion, but actions. Their treachery was inevitable.'

'What makes you say that?'

Numen paused in his work and stood straight. 'For nearly two centuries we cleansed the stars of enemies, but in all that time did you ever learn what the Twentieth were doing?'

'Every war has shadows and those that must fight in them.'

'Aye, there's truth in that, Atesh,' agreed Numen, tossing yet another body into the airlock. 'But foul things hide in shadows, and I do not fully trust any warrior who goes in so deep that he loses sight of his illumination.'

Numen slammed his palm on the lock mechanism and the reinforced door slammed down as amber light flashed above it. He turned and knelt by the body Tarsa had just examined.

'You don't want this one in there too?' asked Numen.

Tarsa shook his head. 'I think we ought to take this one back to the apothecarion.'

'Why? Will his blood not tell you all you need to know?'

'Not everything, maybe nothing,' said Tarsa. 'Something in his bone structure now strikes me as unusual.'

Numen grunted and returned to the airlock, disengaging the safety protocols and twisting the venting mechanism. Warning sigils flashed and moments later a short-lived hurricane ripped the airlock's contents into space.

Tarsa watched through the armourglass port in the inner door as the bodies tumbled away from the *Sisypheum*. He watched them until the outer door sealed shut. It made no sound, but he felt the vibration of the heavy portal.

Tarsa considered Numen's cold words about those who made war in the shadows. 'Do you trust Brother Sharrowkyn?'

Numen hesitated before answering.

'Trust is in short supply, Brother Tarsa.'

'That's not an answer.'

'It's the only one I'll give that won't make me a liar.'

'Brother Sharrowkyn has fought and bled alongside us all.'

'As I say, those that work in the shadows sometimes grow to love the darkness more than the light,' said Numen, hefting the last Alpha Legion corpse onto his shoulder. 'He put a bullet in that bastard Fulgrim's head, so I'll call him brother, aye, but he is not Tenth. He has not suffered as we have suffered.'

'Nor am I Tenth,' said Tarsa. 'Do I enjoy your trust?'

Numen slapped a heavy palm on Tarsa's shoulder guard.

'You come from a land of fire, brother,' he said, turning and all but marching him from the airlock. 'You lived in the light of burning mountains. Aye, you I trust.'

Tarsa nodded, but remembered a world very different to the one Numen imagined. Skies darkened by ash, scorched plains swept by cinder-storms and a life lived in the shadows of pyroclastic clouds.

Nocturne was a world of shadow as deep as any.

THE WALLS OF the embarkation deck still bore the scars of the traitors' combined attack before Iydris. Bolter impacts and deep gouges from the monsters the Phoenician's Legion had unleashed were a reminder of just how hard the crew of the *Sisypheum* had fought to save their ship.

Cadmus Tyro had chosen this particular deck for its symbolism as much as its scale. The captain was toweringly clad in a suit of Terminator battleplate hung with a cloak of silver steel links. He carried his helm in the crook of his iron-gauntleted arm and his combi-bolter hung in a plated sheath locked to his thigh. Wayland couldn't help but notice that the weapon's arming switch was locked in the firing position.

Wayland, too, had come in the full panoply of his position, with a blood-red mantle and the articulated arms of his servo-harness folded around his midriff. Thamatica wore the white cloak of mourning, in honour of the lost Septus Thoic. He'd had wrecked the aft embarkation deck by flying a defective boarding torpedo straight into the *Sisypheum* in a bravura display that had earned Tyro's anger and admiration in one fell swoop.

Vermana Cybus stood at the head of fifteen veterans, every one of whom was armed as though mustered to repel boarders.

If Sharrowkyn was right, perhaps they might have to.

The Raven Guard warrior did not stand with them, but was surely here somewhere. Wayland scanned the darkest portions of the deck's vaulted roof, but saw nothing. Nor had he expected to. Nykona Sharrowkyn had been trained by the legendary Shadowmasters of the Ravenspire. If he chose not to be seen then he was, to all intents and purposes, invisible.

'Here they come,' said Cybus.

Wayland looked out through the integrity field, seeing a spot of light moving against the backdrop of stars. He followed its trajectory as it resolved into the angular, threatening profile of a Thunderhawk.

'Meduson,' said Tyro, his excitement palpable.

That same sense of anticipation filled the deck, a potent sense of longing which Wayland fought to contain. Someone had to remain objective, for there was merit in Sharrowkyn's belief they should remain isolated.

Isolation kept them safe, but Wayland knew the Iron Hands aboard the *Sisypheum* were slowly going mad. Grief at the loss of Ferrus Manus was turning inwards. More and more of the ship's crew were self-mortifying and embracing ever more extreme modifications to their flesh.

The crew of the *Sisypheum* needed this. They needed to know they were not locked in a slow spiral to extinction, punctuated only by brief bouts of excoriating vengeance.

The Thunderhawk grew larger until it passed through the integrity field. Wayland felt the momentary breath of equalising air pressures as the permeable barrier re-established its seal.

Heat bled from the gunship's engines and ice dripped from its frozen surfaces. Wayland ran an appraising eye over the craft, surprised to find that it was one he recognised.

Malleus Ferrum.

He'd last seen this vessel on One-Five-Four Four.

Its scarred hull was pitted with impacts and the iron gauntlet on its forwards glacis was blast-scored. The time since the war against the eldar had not been kind.

The assault ramp lowered and the Iron Hands of the *Sisypheum* took a collective intake of breath. Vapour condensed from the gunship's interior as a single warrior limped down the ramp.

Thamatica took a step forwards in shock.

'Gorgon's Oath!' he cried. 'Septus?'

'Bet you thought you'd seen the last of me, eh?' said Septus Thoic, his voice hoarse and dry.

Wayland's surprise was total. Thoic's armour was burned back to bare iron and scorched metal.

'How...?' began Wayland, but before Thoic could answer, another figure emerged from the gunship. He stopped at the end of the ramp and swept his gaze over the warriors facing him.

His build seemed enormous, though in truth he was only slightly taller than average, and wore only standard-issue power armour – black in the main, but scored silver by multiple impacts from solid slugs, mass-reactives and toothed blades. One shoulder guard bore personal heraldry of a coiled silver wyrm devouring its own tail, the other the proud fist of the X Legion. A long, twin-bladed snake-spear with leaf-shaped blades of porcelain white was slung at his shoulder.

The warrior reached up and removed his helmet.

The face beneath was a mask of hideous burn scars and augmetics. One eye was red with blood-trauma, the other a shimmering blue bionic. He was a warrior ravaged by war and tempered by loss. Yet there was strength in that blood-filled eye, a power and charisma no defeat could crush and no loss diminish.

This was the face of a warrior who had tasted bitter defeat, but refused to let it break him. He was every inch an Iron Hand, and all who looked upon him knew it.

'Permission to come aboard?' asked Shadrak Meduson.

FIVE

The mission
Awakening
Orders

As WAS CUSTOMARY when two clans met to draw up plans of war, they shared *dzira*, a fiery spirit that served many purposes between the tribesmen of Medusa. It was drunk when old grudges needed settling, when war was afoot or upon the death of a firstborn son.

Vermana Cybus sourced a *piyala* bowl, and they drank to this meeting of brothers. With the emptied bowl making its way back around to Cadmus Tyro, they drank again, this time to Septus Thoic's incredible survival.

Cast from the wreck of the *Zeta Morgeld*, Thoic's battleplate withstood the worst of the barrage-storm and sealed itself tighter than a Dreadnought's sarcophagus. Its saviour beacon had been picked up by the *Iron Heart* and *Malleus Ferrum* had retrieved him en route to the *Sisypheum*.

Thoic flatly refused any notion of treatment in the apothecarion, claiming that any Avernii veteran who couldn't take the pain of a few radiation burns wasn't worthy of the rank.

At Meduson's suggestion, the Iron Hands withdrew to the training chambers adjacent to the embarkation deck. Rather than enter the ship proper, he would speak to the *Sisypheum*'s master in the shadow of its arming chambers and sparring cages.

'Trust me, I understand the need to compartmentalise battle-cells more than most,' he said, tapping the corrugated burn scars covering his left cheek. 'A Sons of Horus warleader named Tybalt Marr and a burning flagship reminded me of that.'

'Then why are you here?' said Sharrowkyn, who had been waiting for them in the gloom of the chamber. 'Your presence here endangers us all.'

Ashur Maesan bristled at Sharrowkyn's lack of respect. His hand slid onto the wire-wound hilt of his scabbarded *hiebmesser* until Meduson raised an open hand.

'Easy, Sergeant Maesan,' said Meduson. 'The Ravenlord's son asks a fair question.'

Cadmus Tyro had granted Meduson permission to bring an honour guard aboard the *Sisypheum*. The first was Ashur Maesan, a squad sergeant whose taut posture reminded Tyro of the scarred warriors he'd seen in the XII Legion's fighting pits. A threaded ring of rusted service studs hung from the pommel of his *hiebmesser*, a disembowelling knife more often favoured by Scouts of the Night Lords.

Meduson named the second warrior as Gaskon Malthace, his equerry. Tyro liked the look of Malthace immediately. His left fist was an iron gauntlet with an implanted flail and chain of cold iron. He never strayed more than a metre from his clan-leader.

'I don't know you, raven,' said Meduson. 'Brother...?'

Sharrowkyn didn't reply and the silence between the two warriors hung heavy until Tyro answered.

'His name is Nykona Sharrowkyn of the Nineteenth Legion,' he said, unaccountably feeling the need to rise to Sharrowkyn's defence. 'A fellow veteran of the black sands of Isstvan. But not one that yet has a voice aboard this vessel.'

The Raven Guard warrior shot Tyro a hostile look as Meduson nodded and said, 'Tell me, Brother Sharrowkyn. How do you think the *Iron Heart* was close enough to fight alongside the *Sisypheum*?'

'You were hunting the Alpha Legion,' said Sharrowkyn.

'*Following* them,' corrected Meduson.

'Why?'

'Let me ask another question in return. Do you know the hardest part of cryptography? It's not breaking a code, it's using what you learn in a way that doesn't let the enemy *know* you understand their communiqués. But sometimes what you learn gives rise to a mission that makes such a risk worthwhile.'

'What mission?' asked Tyro.

Meduson grinned, but puckered scar tissue around his ravaged cheek and lips turned it into the death mask of a corpse.

'Killing Alpharius.'

No one said anything, too stunned at the prospect of what Meduson suggested. Killing a primarch? Horror had taught Tyro such a thing was entirely possible, but for so few of them? Even led by one as mighty as Shadrak Meduson?

'Just us?' said Tyro at last. 'Alone, without calling in any support?'

'Yes.'

'Kill Alpharius? *Primarch* Alpharius?' said Tyro.

Meduson nodded and said, 'The one and only.'

'How could you know for sure that these ships would lead you to him?' asked Sharrowkyn. 'We only learned of the *Morgeld*'s destination in the course of our attack.'

'Careful, little raven,' said Meduson, leaning forwards. 'You are a survivor of Isstvan, so you have my respect, but not my leave to offer insults. Maesan and Malthace take a very dim view of such things.'

'Brother Sharrowkyn means no disrespect,' said Tyro. 'But his question is valid.'

Meduson paused and Tyro saw him look over at Malthace, who gave an almost imperceptible nod.

'My apologies, Brother Sharrowkyn,' Meduson sighed. 'You are right to ask. Past losses have made me wary of those whose worth I do not yet know.'

Sharrowkyn nodded, accepting the apology, and Tyro saw the

bone-deep weariness behind Meduson's disfigurement. This was a man with only this one last throw of the dice left, one chance to avenge all those he had lost. As though coming to a decision within himself, Meduson nodded.

'You are not the only ship with access to a Kryptos,' he said, and once again the crew of the *Sisypheum* were stunned to silence. Meduson filled that silence with a grating sound that might once have been laughter, but was now a bitter emphysemic rattle.

'You honestly believe I'd come this far out and risk so much for the head of anyone less than a primarch?'

'You have a Kryptos on the *Iron Heart*?' asked Wayland.

'We did,' said Meduson with a wheezing sigh. 'An unknown pyro-necrotic self-destruct genome that escaped our Iron Father's augurs burned it alive from the inside out four months ago. But not before decrypting some high-level vox trace we managed to intercept. Couched in riddles and argot, of course, but it all pointed to an imminent conclave of senior Alpha Legion commanders. It seems they were heading for a prearranged rally point to receive orders in person from their primarch. The *Morgeld* was en route to rendezvous with the *Malquiant* before travelling to this conclave, but–'

'We killed it,' finished Tyro.

'You killed it,' agreed Meduson. 'And our best chance at making these traitors suffer as we have suffered is gone.'

'Not necessarily,' said Cybus, and Tyro cursed him for his loose tongue. 'Sabik Wayland was able to exload the *Morgeld*'s avionics logister before the crew could destroy it.'

'Truly, Brother Wayland?' said Meduson, slamming a fist into his palm as he circled the nearest of the sparring cages. His blood-red eye flared, reminding Tyro of Atesh Tarsa. The clan-captain's excitement filled the training hall.

Wayland nodded. 'I haven't been able to unlock it entirely, but I know the *Zeta Morgeld*'s next waypoint was this system's third planet.'

'Then the prey's still in the crosshairs,' said Meduson, gripping the reinforced steel bars of the cage. The iron of his gauntlet creaked with pressure as he bent the bars back on themselves.

'We must fight alongside Meduson and his warriors, Cadmus,' demanded Cybus. 'The primarch taught us to alloy our power to augment our strength. What better way of striking back is there than killing the Warmaster's brother?'

Tyro saw the sense in this, but his anger at the presumption Cybus had shown held him back from agreeing immediately. He *wanted* to fight with his brothers, of that there was no doubt. His heart cried out for this vengeance.

Shadrak *bloody* Meduson himself was offering a chance to slake his thirst for traitor deaths.

Meduson saw his hesitation and released the twisted bars of the sparring cage. 'Know that I would welcome the strength of your warriors, Brother Tyro, but there is more you must hear before making any decision. I plan to go up against a primarch. The runt of the litter, it's said, aye – but a primarch nevertheless.'

'What must I hear?'

Meduson tapped a finger against his chin. 'Tell me, have you heard the term *doppelgänger*?'

'No.'

'I have,' said Sharrowkyn. 'It's a Teuton word from Old Earth. It means "twin walker". A double. We used doppelgängers when we wanted to deceive the overseers' kill-teams in the mines. It made it impossible for them to know for sure which one was Primarch Corax's main attack.'

'Exactly,' said Meduson, snapping his iron fingers so hard that they cast sparks. He arrived at a rack of wire-suspended combat-servitors, lifeless flesh-mannequins equipped with a mix of blades and close-quarters blastguns. He pulled one along the rails as he completed his circle of the sparring cage. He held the part-organic, part-machine thing out before him like a prop.

'One of the last things we learned from the Kryptos before it self-combusted was that Alpharius has taken to using doppelgängers to throw hunters like us from his scent,' said Meduson. 'He seeks to weave a web of obfuscation around him like a shroud of invisibility.'

Meduson gave another of his death-rattle laughs.

'They say that not even his own Legion know where he walks now.'

Tyro could feel the weight of expectation pressing in on him from those Iron Hands standing in the training chamber. They wanted this. They *needed* this.

Meduson tapped an oath-seal on his shoulder guard, and Tyro saw the icon of a hydra pressed into the wax – a hydra with its many heads severed.

'I am oath-sworn to the mission,' said Meduson, 'but there is no shame in you and your warriors continuing to fight as you are.'

Tyro saw the truth in that, but what better chance would there be to hurt the traitors? Yet even as he formed the words to bind his fate to Meduson's, Sharrowkyn's caution lodged like a stubborn shard of hot metal in his hammer hand.

No, this was a decision requiring wiser counsel than any here gathered could offer.

'I will take your mission to Captain Branthan,' he said.

'WE DON'T NEED to do this,' said Cybus as they approached the captain's cryo-sepulchre. 'It's clear what we have to do. You know I'm right. Tell him, Thamatica.'

The Ironwrought looked up at the mention of his name.

He nodded and Tyro saw Thoic and Numen were also in agreement with Cybus.

'Most likely you are, Vermana,' replied Thamatica, 'but Ulrach Branthan is still captain of this vessel. He needs to know what is at stake.'

'You know what he'll say.'

'Aye, I believe I do,' said Tyro. 'And I would hear it from his lips, not yours.'

Cybus fell into a brooding silence as the blast-shielded door opened at their approach. Garuda, who'd been following them down through the ship, flew in as a wall of icy mist rolled out.

Tyro followed the Bird inside, and cold hit him like a blow.

He imagined this was what Fenris was like. Medusa knew ice, but nothing like that which the Sons of Russ boasted of their home world.

Truth be told, the frozen air no longer bothered Tyro. He had little enough flesh left on his frame for it to affect. The numerous chimeric augmentations he and Vermana had undergone over the decades rendered them immune to most weaknesses of flesh.

But not even centuries of training, discipline and bio-conditioning could entirely remove weakness of spirit.

Garuda perched on icicle-hung ductwork near the ceiling, looking down at Tarsa, who was bent double over an opened panel on the side of Branthan's frost-limned casket. A host of blinking lights and stripped wires were bound together with saw-toothed clips.

'Is there a problem?' asked Tyro.

Tarsa looked up from his ministrations as the Iron Hands entered, and shrugged.

'No more than usual,' he said, dragging numerous heavy cables from the machinery beneath the casket. 'Fluid reservoirs need to be filled, capacitors recharged and burned-out wires replaced. It takes a great deal of effort and resources to keep the captain alive.'

'Whatever it takes,' said Tyro.

The Apothecary nodded and plugged the cables into devices whose function Tyro could not even begin to imagine. It seemed the humming pitch of the casket changed, but it was impossible to be certain.

Once, in a rare moment of introspection, Tyro had confessed his doubts to Branthan's unmoving body. He had spoken of how he was unworthy to lead the crew of the *Sisypheum*. That conversation haunted him still, and every moment since had been spent trying to prove those self-pitying words wrong.

Septus Thoic moved past Tyro to stand at the end of Branthan's icy prison. He stared down at the captain, his features raw and gleaming from radiation exposure. The scars the III Legion swordsman had given Thoic still looked painful. He bore his hurts stoically, but his strained features and bloodshot eyes told a more honest tale of his suffering.

'You should let me examine you, Septus,' said Tarsa.

Thoic coughed and shook his head as though dizzy. 'There's no need, Apothecary,' he said, straightening and waving Tarsa away. 'I am fit enough to perform my duties.'

'Leave him be,' said Cybus. 'We've more important matters to discuss than Thoic's burns.'

Vermana Cybus was a warrior of great skill and courage, who excelled in battle, but lacked for any trace of empathy in the times between war-making.

But in this case, Cybus was entirely correct.

'How much time will we have, Apothecary Tarsa?' he asked.

'Two minutes,' said the Salamander. 'Give or take.'

'That's longer than normal.'

'Against all reason, every reading says Captain Branthan's injuries are lessened,' said Tarsa. 'He now seems to be winning the fight for life.'

'The Heart of Iron?' said Tyro.

'Perhaps.'

Tyro looked through the web of hoarfrost coating the curved glass. Ulrach Branthan's features were frozen in the last instant of consciousness he'd known. Like a waxen effigy or a servitor with the data-wafer yanked suddenly from its skull, his features were bereft of anything suggesting life.

'I thought you said it was killing him?'

'It was. Or at least I believed it was.'

'Don't you know?' said Cybus. 'You're the damn Apothecary.'

For a warrior whose heart pumped the molten blood of Nocturne, Atesh Tarsa remained calm in the face of hostility. He met the veteran's gaze with his own blood-red stare, and it was Cybus who looked away first.

'The Heart of Iron predates the Imperium by thousands of years,' said Tarsa. 'How it interacts with Legion anatomy is a mystery only the Emperor, beloved by all, could fathom.'

Cybus wasn't about to let the uncertainty of the captain's fate lie. 'What about you, Thamatica?' he said, waving a hand at the cyber-eagle. 'You've dealt with artefacts from the Land of Shadows before.'

Thamatica stared at the Bird before returning his scrutiny to Branthan. His lips pursed as he tapped his chin thoughtfully.

'I have, it's true,' he said. 'But this is beyond even my experience.'

Thamatica turned his attention to Tarsa and said, 'Perhaps, if the captain is indeed healing, it might be possible to remove the device for examination.'

'Remove it? Impossible. You'll kill him.'

Thamatica shrugged. 'Then I can offer no explanation.'

'Never mind explanations,' said Tyro. 'We're here to speak to the captain. Bring him up.'

Tarsa bent back to the casket and slotted home an activation key from his narthecium gauntlet. A panel slid out from the side of the cryo-tube with a number of ivory sliders and cog-rimmed dials of black plastek.

'Disengaging stasis field,' he said, turning the leftmost dial down to zero.

The field keeping Ulrach Branthan trapped in a sealed pocket of time was invisible, but Tyro knew the instant that the power was cut. Air from the past was released, frozen and stagnant and freighted with the reek of putrefaction. For all Tarsa's talk of healing, the mass of the captain's body was still hideously broken.

'Raising core body temperature.'

Frost melted on the captain's skin, running down his cheeks like tears. His features softened and gained a measure of colour as blood began flowing around his body. That same blood leaked in glutinous, oozing clots from the wounds on his chest and the ragged stumps of his thighs.

Branthan's eyes moved beneath their lids. His lips parted and a rancid exhalation misted the air before him.

'Brain activity increasing,' said Tarsa, reading the cascade of information on the slates inset on the casket's steel-panelled flank. 'Alpha wave amplitude nominal. Theta wave activity increasing. Neural oscillation building rapidly. You can speak to him now, he'll hear you.'

'Ulrach,' said Tyro. 'Something's happ–'

'We failed.'

As always, Ulrach Branthan's filtered voice sent a shiver of dread down Tyro's spine. It came from a place of unimaginable pain, where that pain was all-encompassing and sealed inside him for what would feel like an eternity. It spoke of tortures that no man should endure.

Past experience had taught Tyro that Branthan's first moments of wakefulness were often difficult as his mind reassembled its disordered fragments, fighting through the agonies clouding his thoughts. All he could do was press on.

'Captain, we've linked with Meduson of the Sorrgol Clan,' said Tyro. 'He has a mission and needs our help.'

Branthan's head rocked back and forth on the bloodstained mat beneath him. The flow of blood from his ruined extremities waxed strong. *'We failed. We failed at Isstvan, and we failed at Iydris.'*

'No, we were betrayed,' said Tyro, gripping the edge of the casket. The heat from his iron fist melted deep grooves in the ice. 'The Warmaster betrayed us all.'

'We are no longer worthy. The Angel Exterminatus was born and generations uncounted will curse our names for eternity.'

Tyro and Cybus exchanged glances. Of all the things they expected from their captain, self-recrimination wasn't one of them. Rage and a thirst for vengeance, yes, not ominously prophetic words.

'Meduson believes we should join forces,' said Tyro. 'I would hear your counsel.'

Branthan turned his head towards Tyro.

'Join forces? Why?'

'He believes we can kill Alpharius.'

'Kill Alpharius?'

'Yes.'

'Kill a primarch...'

'We will have revenge,' said Cybus, joining Tyro at the side of the casket and pouring all his hatred and grief into every syllable. 'Not on the Phoenician, but his time will come.'

Branthan's eyes opened: sunken milky orbs, veined red with dead blood and yellowed with necrosis. Tyro recoiled from the madness he saw there. A riot of insanity made sport behind those hollowed orbs. *'Revenge... Aye, revenge. Salvation in blood.'*

'Thirty seconds,' said Tarsa.

Tyro rallied his thoughts in the face of Branthan's pain and desperate hunger for atonement. He wanted no counsel from a mind torn to pieces by pain and an eternity of recrimination.

He felt Tarsa's gaze upon him and saw the Apothecary was just as horrified by the toxic rage in Branthan's eyes.

Silent understanding passed between them.

The tears on Branthan's cheeks froze instantly, but he had one last order to give before icy eternity swallowed him.

'Do it. Kill Alpharius, and purge our weakness of failure.'

SIX

Purpose
Digging
Wraith-slip

HEAT AND SPARKS filled the air of the forge – one hazing it, the other lighting it with fat orange fireflies. Furnaces burned with infernal light as steel stripped from the *Zeta Morgeld* was rendered useable.

Rivers of molten metal flowed into weapon moulds and Iron Hands stripped to the waist beat at fire-blackened anvils with shaping hammers. Hissing smoke arose from water that was too old for tempering, and seasoned smiths spoke of weakness being blended into the metal.

Soot-stained banners swayed in rising thermals, each one emblazoned with the sigil of a master armourer. The coffered walls of the forge had once been hung with the great works of those masters, warriors who had toiled in its blistering heat to work wonders with metal. Booming songs, destined to become part of every masterpiece, had once echoed from its walls.

Now none remained to shake the soot from the banners, the songs were stilled and few wonders remained.

Beyond the muttering smiths, two figures worked at an anvil in a halo of ruddy light. Like the Iron Hands, both were stripped to the waist, but there the similarity ended.

Nykona Sharrowkyn had skin of alabaster white, an albino but for the shock of glossy black hair in a short scalp-lock. Angular eyes set in an aquiline profile were pools that reflected little of the furnace light or flaring sparks.

Atesh Tarsa was his opposite in every way, dark of skin and red of eye, with a shaven skull like an orb of black obsidian. Much more than Sharrowkyn, the son of Nocturne looked perfectly at home.

Two days still remained until the ships of the Iron Hands would reach the waypoint that Sabik Wayland had identified from the *Morgeld*'s avionics. Sharrowkyn and Tarsa had spent the time since the union of the *Iron Heart* and the *Sisypheum* training, sparring and, now, forging.

Tarsa held a glowing orange sword blade upon the anvil as Sharrowkyn worked a hammer along its length.

'Careful,' warned Tarsa. 'You will fold the metal at the edges. You've taken two days to harden and straighten the steel already. It would be a shame to break it now.'

'How is it that an Apothecary knows the secrets of steel as well as those of flesh?' asked Sharrowkyn.

'All Nocturne's sons have an affinity with smiting. I have only a passing skill.'

Even Sharrowkyn's limited understanding of a forge told him that Tarsa was being modest. He knew better than to press the issue. The Salamander was a humble warrior, one who was quietly content to let his skills speak for themselves.

'It's more than I have.'

'This anvil has more skill than you,' said Tarsa, though there was no malice in his words. He shook his head. 'And to think you were born in a mine.'

'I was a salt boy,' said Sharrowkyn, his jaw hardening and the hammer speaking to his deep-rooted anger. 'As soon as I could walk, I was sent to the tidal pools of Lycaeus's deepest caves. Along with a hundred other children I spent my time scraping crystals from the rocks with a blunted mattock. The tool-making factories used it to salt their tempering water.'

Tarsa nodded as he turned the blade. 'Salt water conducts heat more efficiently and makes harder steel than pure water. Though in truth there's few tools need to be that hard. Dangerous work, I imagine.'

'It was,' said Sharrowkyn. 'Children drowned all the time. A surge tide could pour back into a cave without warning. There was a saying that the best salts came from the bones of the dead.'

'Enough hammering,' said Tarsa, moving the blade away from Sharrowkyn's blows. 'Any more will turn the edge against you.'

The Salamander lifted the sword by the point of its tang and sighted down the bevels. 'The symmetry is not perfect, but there is no warp or screw.'

'Will it do?'

Tarsa nodded and handed the blade to Sharrowkyn, who wiped it clean before working it smooth with fine-grained pumice.

'Next polish the blade until it gleams the blue of a summer's gloaming.'

'I never saw the sun until my thirteenth year,' said Sharrowkyn.

'Then think of the blue of Eighth Legion plate.'

'I'd rather imagine it red with their blood.'

'That will be when you quench it.'

Sharrowkyn nodded and put the blade upon the anvil. 'Quenched in a killing thrust. I like that.'

'If you like, I will fit a grip for you.'

'I would be honoured, Atesh,' said Sharrowkyn.

'The honour is mine, Nykona,' said Tarsa.

'Something simple, mind. I'm not given to gaudy weaponry.'

'Two palm plates of lacquered ebony?'

'Perfect,' said Sharrowkyn. 'Apologies, my heart is not in the craft this day.'

'The mission still bothers you?'

Sharrowkyn looked over his shoulder at the toiling Iron Hands. Wreathed in the steam of their labours and the fire of the furnaces, they were grotesque silhouettes, ogres of the deeps toiling at their forges.

'Yes, the mission still bothers me.'

'You don't think it's a good one?' asked Tarsa, taking up the pumice and giving the blade an even keener edge.

'That's the trouble, it's almost *too* good,' said Sharrowkyn.

'An eye for an eye as a principle of justice is as old as time itself,' said Tarsa. 'And you must agree it has a certain *operatic* quality to it.'

'Operatic?' said Sharrowkyn with a raised eyebrow.

'The One Hundred and Fifty-fourth Expeditionary Fleet had its share of playwrights and composers of verse among its remembrancers. I was privileged to hear a performance of *The Symphony of Banished Night*. The scene where Cardinal Tang is imprisoned within Nusa Kambagan and his former victims murder him is one many believe to be a cornerstone of early Imperial policy.'

'Regardless of your appreciation for opera, it's still feeding into what the Iron Hands *want* to be doing,' said Sharrowkyn. 'And killing Alpharius? Unless I get Fulgrim in my crosshairs again, there's unlikely to be a more perfect mission for the Tenth.'

'It has given our kinsmen purpose,' pointed out Tarsa. 'And a warrior without purpose is a dangerous thing. Violent impulses must be given an outlet, or men bred to kill turn them on themselves. And there are few as prone to violent self-mutilation than the sons of Ferrus Manus.'

'We *had* a purpose,' said Sharrowkyn. 'We *have* a purpose. Don't underestimate the damage we and others like us are doing. Those who fight for Meduson are far more than the sum of their individual efforts.'

'How can you know that?'

'Because it's how we won the war against the Overseers. The rats claw and bite the monster's heels until it can't keep going forwards. Eventually it has to turn, and *that* is when the real killing blow falls.'

'Surely joining our forces with Meduson makes us stronger?'

'No. Gathering our strength when our numbers are so few doesn't make us strong, it makes us vulnerable.'

'So what are you suggesting?'

Sharrowkyn wiped a hand across his brow and rolled his shoulders.

'I'm going to see for myself.'

'See what?'

Sharrowkyn grinned.

THE SYSTEM'S THIRD planet was unlisted in Imperial cartographae, which didn't surprise Sabik Wayland. Typical of the Alpha Legion to choose waypoints so far off the beaten track they hadn't even been named.

The *Sisypheum* and the *Iron Heart* orbited the third planet while Wayland sought to break the fiendish encryptions securing the *Morgeld's* astronavigation data.

The two innermost planets danced an elliptical path around their star that periodically brought them dangerously close to collision and left them monstrously geologically unstable. All were too hot to support life, though that had nothing to do with their stellar proximity. Corrosive atmospherics had boiled the worlds to death beneath poisoned skies over thousands of years.

Had there been life there once? Impossible to know for certain. Perhaps, in another future, one not hijacked by the Warmaster's treachery, worlds like these might have been explored and their mysteries revealed.

Such a future seemed all but impossible now. What hope was there for exploration for its own sake when the drums of war beat at an ever-increasing tempo? Everything he had learned on Mars told Wayland that the cost of victory over Horus would not be measured in what was won, but in what had been lost.

Wayland sighed, rubbing the heels of his palms over his eyes and blinking away the afterimages of scrolling alphanumerics. He'd spent the last thirty-six hours locked in this cell with the Kryptos.

The cunning of the Alpha Legion did not surprise him. He'd long known that the XX Legion were not to be underestimated. The bloody fight to capture the *Zeta Morgeld* had reminded them all that this Legion of vipers did not rely solely upon subtle venoms.

Frater Thamatica had made no offer to assist his code-breaking efforts. True, it had been Wayland's void-tactics that almost killed Thamatica, but his continued absence seemed needlessly petty.

Locked into its throne and linked to Wayland's cogitators by invasive neural pick-ups, the Kryptos churned through billions of code permutations with a stream of burbling static. Grating at the best of times, Wayland's nerves were now stretched to breaking point.

A concealing hood was drawn up over the creature's gnarled skull. Wayland couldn't see its face, only glistening hints of the raw lesions on its neck. Tarsa had examined the creature's grotesquely hybridised xenobiology, but could find no cause for the lesions. Were they precursors to the fate that had overtaken Meduson's own Kryptos?

Wayland turned away, disgusted by its very existence. There was something disturbingly unwholesome in the animalistic noises it made, something grotesquely and profoundly *wrong* in the arrangements of its maxillofacial anatomy. No sane force of evolution could have shaped such a creature. This was an abomination birthed in a chaos of desire and madness.

None would gainsay him were he to put a mass-reactive through its skull. He would have done so already, but for the fact that it was useful to them. Even Cybus, who could be counted upon to kill anything that didn't fit his rigid idea of the Imperial Truth, had seen sense in keeping the Kryptos alive.

Wayland estimated another three hours would see the Kryptos complete its decryption cycle, revealing the *Morgeld*'s ultimate destination.

While it did so, Wayland turned his attention to the void-log of the battle against the *Morgeld* and the *Malquiant*. He'd already used the Kryptos to pull Alpha Legion challenge codes from the vox passing between the two vessels, but something unusual had caught his eye.

'Now what are you?' he murmured, studying the battle's electromagnetic fallout.

A trace in a lower spectroscopic bandwidth he would expect to see. Nothing unusual on its own, and probably part and parcel of the violent outpourings of electromagnetism unleashed in a void engagement. But the constancy of the trace was uncommon enough to pique his interest and suggested something other than weapons discharge.

He scrolled back through the battle to find the first incidence of the emission. But with atomic detonations surrounding the warring vessels and bursts of macro-lasers spiking the readings every other micro-second, it was going to take time. He assigned a backscatter subroutine to sift through the radiation spectra as his throat-vox chirped with an incoming communication.

'This is Wayland.'

'*Can you talk?*'

'Nykona?'

'*Yes.*'

Sharrowkyn's conspiratorial tone spoke volumes and Wayland imme-diately switched to a more secure channel.

Dreading the answer, he asked, 'Where are you?'

SHARROWKYN EASED HIMSELF deeper into the shadows of the tertiary axial transit. He let the air of the *Iron Heart* fill him, gauging whether it would work with him or against him.

Hot oils, lubricant and the breath of toiling machinery. This was a vessel of war. It seethed with bellicose intent.

Sharrowkyn felt fury vibrating in its bones.

Every vessel had its own unique character and the defining one of the *Iron Heart* was, unsurprisingly, anger.

Anger and darkness.

Power came at a premium on a warship. Where to distribute that power was crucially important. Clearly Shadrak Meduson valued other systems over ship-wide illumination, which suited Sharrowkyn perfectly.

He had reached the *Iron Heart* by secreting himself atop a Thunder-hawk transporter on a supply run between the two vessels, sealing his warplate against the vacuum and deep cold of the void. In the instant before the craft entered the *Iron Heart's* supply deck, he launched him-self from its back and used micro-bursts from his modified jump pack to guide his trajectory towards a ventral battery.

From there, it was a simple matter to locate one of the louvred vents used to expel the corrosive residue of weapons fire from the gun decks.

Simple for one trained by the Shadowmasters.

It didn't hurt that, like the *Sisypheum*, the *Iron Heart* was woefully under-crewed. He'd encountered only a few legionaries, and only a handful of grey-skinned thralls who might as well have been sleep-walking for all the attention they paid him. None of them looked up or even suspected that one of the shadows gliding through the sepulchral iron corridors didn't belong there.

Though the two strike cruisers were superficially similar, the internal structure of Meduson's vessel was markedly different. Sharrowkyn had explored every hidden corner of the *Sisypheum*, but that proved no help in his exploration of the *Iron Heart*. Constructed to ancient plans, each ship was unique and every Legion stamped their own traits onto those that bore their colours. But so profound a difference? That raised the hackles of his suspicions.

Sharrowkyn slipped onwards through the darkness. Sometimes he used the floor, sometimes the roof spaces. The interior of the *Iron Heart* was a twisting labyrinth, a mass of intertwined blind alleys and passageways that spiralled back upon themselves. Every wall was seamed with weld-scars and fusion-arc stitching.

The overall impression was of a starship that had been completely rebuilt from the inside out. Nothing in Sharrowkyn's experience was of any help in navigating its interior. Every time he divined one route's solution, two more conundrums presented themselves. He paused in his exploration, and opened a secure vox channel, one he'd established before leaving the *Sisypheum*. A quick-burst transmission with an encryption key he'd copied from the Kryptos.

'Sabik?'

He received an answer with a fractional delay.

'This is Wayland.'

'Can you talk?'

'Nykona?'

'Yes.'

'Where are you?'

'Aboard the *Iron Heart.*'

Sharrowkyn heard Wayland sigh. *'Of course you are. Where else would you be?'*

'You have the structural plans of the *Iron Heart*,' said Sharrowkyn, not posing it as a question. 'Updates and refit history.'

'I do,' said Wayland. *'Everything up to Isstvan Five.'*

Sharrowkyn pictured Wayland surrounded by blooming entoptics of the vessel's interior.

'Link with my armour,' said Sharrowkyn. 'See what I see.'

He heard the clicking interface with Wayland's visor.

'Done,' said Wayland. *'But break connection before you wraith-slip again. Experiencing that over a link almost blinded me last time.'*

'Understood. What do you have on the *Iron Heart*?'

'Commissioned in 808.M30, the tenth year of the Great Crusade, as reckoned from Terran sidereal time,' said Wayland. *'Keel laid down in the tenth month of the tenth year.'*

'Appropriate.'

'Some called it a good omen,' said Wayland.

'I'd be inclined to agree if I believed in things like that, but I was hoping for more immediately useful information.'

Wayland wasn't to be discouraged. *'Void-trials began six years after the keel's sounding. Entered operational service nine months later. Two centuries of the highest honours, including trophies taken at Gardinaal, and also during the Compliance of One-Five-Four Four and the Diasporex Scattering. Listed in Tenth Legion fleet registry as occupying a vanguard position in the Gorgon's retribution fleet en route to Isstvan Five. No record of the* Iron Heart *exists subsequent to Isstvan.'*

'Hardly surprising.'

'Agreed,' said Wayland. *'What are you hoping to find?'*

'I'm not sure,' said Sharrowkyn, hearing the *Iron Heart's* plasmic heartbeat, but little else. The sense of abandonment was palpable. 'This ship is like an ore-mine of Lycaeus when its seam was played out.'

'*And where is everyone?*' whispered Wayland in his helm.

'Just what I was wondering,' said Sharrowkyn, moving deeper into the vessel.

Wayland offered commentary on the ship as he saw through the Raven Guard's helm. Sharrowkyn didn't answer, keeping his mind fixed on the artes taught to him in the darkest spaces of the Ravenspire.

'*You should be approaching the main axial now.*'

Sharrowkyn nodded as the passageway before him widened, becoming a vaulted narthex with ironwork mesh flooring and panelled walls worked in beaten metal. The external bulkhead was entirely new, a curving arc of fresh-welded steel that ran from beneath the level of the floor to a point near the apex of the chamber.

'Are you seeing this?'

'*I am,*' confirmed Wayland. '*Blast damage from battery fire. And look at the other walls. Mass-reactive craters.*'

'Broadside at close range, and then they were boarded.'

'*A common enough fate at Isstvan.*'

Sharrowkyn nodded. Few enough vessels had escaped the traitor's trap, and even those that broke through the blockades and escaped pursuit were often little more than barely functioning wrecks.

'A tough fight, judging by the number of impacts,' he said.

'*Meduson said his flagship took a beating from the Sons of Horus,*' said Wayland. '*Looks like he undersold how* much *of a beating.*'

'They were lucky to survive.'

'*Luck has nothing to do with Iron Hands surviving,*' said Wayland.

Sharrowkyn grinned, but it fell from his face as he sensed the presence of others. He vaulted onto the wall and sprang up towards the ductwork overhead, rolling over onto a perforated conduit run.

'*What is it?*' Wayland asked.

Sharrowkyn looked back down the corridor as three warriors appeared, dark shapes against the bare steelwork of the restored bulkhead. Their battleplate grated and hissed, but they walked with the sure swagger of warriors confident in their invincibility.

One carried a meltagun, another a volkite charger. The third carried a weapon that Sharrowkyn didn't recognise – a tubular construction with multiple glass-tube barrels that crackled with cerulean fire. They paused in the narthex as though looking for something, and Sharrowkyn had the powerful sense they knew he was there.

'How coul–' began Wayland, but Sharrowkyn cut the link.

The shadows around him expanded, becoming darker than the blackest night, seeming to flow around him, welcoming him into its fuliginous embrace. Sharrowkyn knew that was how it would appear to anyone who might actually see him anyway.

To wraith-slip was to become one with the darkness, to own the black and let it enfold you. Its embrace was cold and solitary, for it came from a time when there *was* no light. Years of training in the deepest mines of his birthrock had given Sharrowkyn an affinity with darkness that few beyond his Legion could match. To live sightless in the depths, with the black, slithering *things* closing in at every turn, soon taught a warrior how to hide.

He became a ghost, a rumour of movement and a whisper of belief. One of the Iron Hands glanced up, but looked away just as quickly, convinced by his hind brain as much as his eyes that he had seen nothing out of place.

Sharrowkyn soon left the three warriors behind, and felt the darkness melt away as he eased himself into a side passage. He was alone, and rolled from the conduit, swinging down to the deck and landing with a barely audible thud of boots on metal.

'You're good, I'll give you that,' said a voice at the end of the corridor.

Sharrowkyn spun around, dropping to a crouch and automatically reaching for his pistol. He halted his hand a hair's breadth from the grip as he saw the broad-shouldered silhouette.

'My ship fought tooth and nail to stay alive after Isstvan, Brother Sharrowkyn,' said Shadrak Meduson. 'Did you really think I *wouldn't* know when there's an intruder aboard?'

SEVEN

Empty threats
False flags
The best at what I do

'I SHOULD THROW you both in the brig,' snapped Cadmus Tyro, pacing the metalled floor of the embarkation deck. Wayland at least had the good grace to look guilty, but Nykona Sharrowkyn managed to impart an unrepentant insouciance to his stance.

'Him I can understand,' said Tyro, 'but you, Sabik? What do you have to say for yourself?'

'I would say that Brother Sharrowkyn's actions should be classed as due diligence,' said Wayland.

'What?'

'He was simply ensuring that what Captain Meduson told us was true.'

Tyro looked over at Shadrak Meduson, who'd brought the trespassing Raven Guard back aboard the *Malleus Ferrum*. The captain of the Sorrgol Clan was impassive, his scarred face giving nothing away as to his humours. Was he enraged at this impugning of his honesty or might he see this as Wayland did?

'You doubted the word of a fellow Iron Hand?'

'Didn't you?' countered Wayland. 'Just because you *want* to believe Captain Meduson is our ally doesn't make it so.'

Tyro expected an outburst from Meduson at this insult to his honour, but the scarred warrior said nothing.

'And did he find anything?' demanded Tyro, not even bothering to address the question to Sharrowkyn.

Wayland glanced at the Raven Guard, who kept his eyes fixed forwards.

'No,' said Wayland.

'I should strip you of rank and position, break you back down to the ranks.'

'I heard Iron Hands didn't make empty threats,' said Sharrowkyn.

Tyro struggled to keep his temper. He'd faced down the worst horrors the galaxy had to throw at a man, but Sharrowkyn didn't blink. The Raven Guard's ebon eyes stared back, and Tyro saw the mirror of his own unflinching nature.

'What did you say?'

'You shouldn't make threats you're not going to carry out.'

'You think I won't?' said Tyro.

'I know you won't.'

'And why not?'

'You need me,' said Sharrowkyn. 'I'm the best at what I do, and you don't have anyone aboard like me.'

'I *need* someone who can't obey orders? I *need* a warrior who sets his own rules of engagement and conduct?'

'Yes,' said Sharrowkyn. 'That's exactly what you need.'

'He's right, Cadmus,' said Shadrak Meduson. 'And, were our circumstances reversed, I'd have done the same.'

'So why didn't you?' asked Sharrowkyn.

Meduson grinned his burn-skewed grin.

'Who says I haven't?'

'You think I wouldn't know?'

'So sure of yourself, little raven,' said Meduson, closing the distance between him and Sharrowkyn. Though there was little difference in their height, Meduson somehow managed to tower over the Raven Guard. 'You've spent a few years aboard an Iron Hands vessel and you think you know all there is to know about us? You're good, Brother Sharrowkyn, *very* good, and the shadows bend to your will like no one I've seen before, but these are vessels of steel and stone, the twin flesh of Medusa. And none know that flesh better than the sons of Ferrus Manus.'

'I'd have known,' repeated Sharrowkyn.

'Really? Then how is it that Ashur Maesan was able to gain entry to your vessel and see your Kryptos beast for himself? Quite a setup you have down there, Wayland. Tell me, is it really necessary to bind the thing with fetters?'

Not even Sharrowkyn's inscrutable features could hide his shock at Meduson's words.

Tyro was just as shocked.

'You put a man on my ship?'

'I did,' said Meduson. 'And while I regret such a gross breach of trust was necessary, we both know trust is in short supply in such times as we find ourselves.'

Meduson's words stoked Tyro's already well-banked anger, but this wasn't a discussion to be had before his crew.

He shot a glance at Sharrowkyn and Wayland, saying, 'You're dismissed.'

They turned to go, both vindicated and chastised.

'Wayland,' said Tyro. 'How long until the Kryptos finishes decrypting the *Morgeld*'s avionics log?'

'Any minute now,' said Wayland.

'Then get me a heading before next watch bell.'

Wayland nodded, and he and Sharrowkyn marched from the deck. Tyro didn't give them a second glance.

'I'm not happy you put a man on my ship,' he told Meduson when they were gone.

'I could say the same thing.'

'Sharrowkyn acted without my authority.'

'You should have *given* him authority,' said Meduson. 'I'm just surprised it took him this long to board my ship. I think he waited out of respect for you, hoping you would give him that order. Does the *Sisypheum*'s crew lack resolve, Cadmus?'

Tyro was stung by the rebuke, just as much from the fact that it had been given as he was in knowing it was entirely justified.

'No, it does not,' he said.

'Good,' said Meduson. 'This coming fight will test us all, and only men of resolve will survive it.'

'You'll not find us wanting,' promised Tyro.

'See that I don't.'

FIFTEEN DAYS LATER and three isolated star systems over, the *Iron Heart* and the *Sisypheum* drifted silently towards a world the astronavigation charts named Eirene Septimus. A scaled orb of jade and umber, everything about it told Wayland that it was plunging towards a slow and inevitable doom.

Its image sat in the centre of the *Sisypheum*'s main viewer, wreathed in banded layers of corrosive atmospherics. Inset at each corner of the screen was a slowly degrading pict from the servitor drones launched thirty minutes previously.

Each revealed planetary topography that would soon be submerged beneath acidic oceans as torrential chemical rains spilled in an unending deluge from the impenetrable clouds.

'*A death world if ever I saw one,*' said Shadrak Meduson.

A holographic representation of the *Iron Heart*'s master stood at Cadmus Tyro's right hand, arms folded across his broad chest. Though Tyro sat in the captain's throne, the dynamic of who exactly was in command was hard to fix.

'Deadlier than most,' agreed Wayland. 'But it's those clouds that make Eirene Septimus valuable.'

'Valuable to who?' said Tyro, looking like he was imagining how it would be possible to fight within such a biosphere.

'To anyone who knows its truth,' said Wayland. 'Eirene Septimus was entered into the Carta Imperialis by the Twentieth, yet the aestimare describes it as a dead world of no value.'

'Keeping it for themselves,' sneered Meduson, his image wavering with static.

'So how exactly is it valuable?' asked Tyro.

'The atmosphere is incredibly dense and seeded with crystalline deposits of promethium from some earlier epoch of geological upheaval.'

'Useable promethium?' asked Thamatica.

'Only in the last decade,' said Wayland as a fresh graph appeared on the screen. 'Over millions of years, as the seventh planet's orbit carried it fractionally closer to the star, its atmosphere has now absorbed enough heat for those suspended promethium crystals to melt. Hence the planetary deluge.'

'How would you harness that resource?' asked Tyro.

'Like this,' said Wayland, and the display changed to reveal an airborne colossus sitting at the very upper limits of the breathable atmosphere, like one of the great orbital plates of Terra. Its size was difficult to judge, but it resembled the industrial powerhouse of Rodinia and possessed the monumental scale of Vaalbara.

The first metaphor the mind conjured was of a vast jellyfish or flattened octopus drifting serenely across a fiery ocean of blazing clouds. Its underside was hazed by immense repulsors between which thousands of flexible siphon tentacles plunged deep into the promethium-rich soup below.

The platform's upper surface was wreathed by an umbra of tar-black exhaust gases and lit by the hellish glare of flame-belching vent towers. Beneath this sullen shroud, its deck was encrusted with titanic refineries, thundering pump structures and vast silo towers. The spaces separating these structures were tangled lattices of iron spars, air processors and thousands of kilometres of pipework that leaked toxic exhalations.

Even through the sickly fog it was possible to make out the hydra-headed icons atop the platform's many towers.

'As best I can make out from its *very* few emissions, its designation is Lerna Two-Twelve,' said Wayland.

'Throne of Terra...' breathed Tyro at the sight of this nightmarish vision of industrial madness.

'It's an all-but-limitless supply of ship-grade promethium, and processing manufactories capable of refining engine-ready plasma,' said Wayland. 'A coaling-station, as such places were once known.'

'*Messy,*' said Meduson. '*Inefficient. Primarch Guilliman would not approve.*'

'So a sizeable Mechanicum presence, yes?' said Tyro.

'An estimated thousand priests and servitors,' agreed Wayland. 'But most of the facility will be self-regulating. If it were ours, I'd set it to harvest enough promethium to fill the silos and then shut down. Which would explain why no one has seen it before now. When it goes dark, it's next to invisible in the atmosphere.'

'*Is that a ship?*' said Meduson, bending to study his own vessel's surveyor input.

'Good eyes, Captain Meduson,' said Wayland, and moments later, another image appeared on the main viewer. A ripple of unease spread around the bridge as the clouds parted and the prow of a warship bearing the hydra of the Alpha Legion became momentarily visible.

'Yes,' said Wayland. 'A rapid strike cruiser, designation, as you'd expect, unknown. It's taking on fuel and looks like it's being kept synchronous with Lerna Two-Twelve by a number of very precise e-mag tethers.'

The picter moved in, and the shadow of hose-lines could be seen through the vapour clouds: huge semi-rigid pipes transporting megalitres of fuel to the vessel's cavernous tanks every minute.

'We can see it,' said Cybus. 'Can it see us?'

'No.'

'How can you be certain?'

'Do you think I would be getting this close if I wasn't certain?' said Wayland. 'If that ship knew we were here it would be blasting its fuel lines clear and the e-mag tethers would already be disengaged.'

Tyro rose from his seat and bent over the guard-rail.

'And the rest of the Alpha Legion ships?'

The *Sisypheum* and the *Iron Heart* had traced separate, spiralling routes to the seventh planet of the Eirene System, seeding their wake with passive surveyor drones. The idea had been Wayland's, and was already bearing fruit.

'All three emissions from the Mandeville circumference are moving inwards on steady bearings,' said Thamatica. 'At least three ships, maybe four. Impossible to be certain.'

'*What* is *ever certain with the Twentieth?*' replied Meduson. '*Displacement?*'

'All at least cruisers, with one capital ship.'

'*Designation?*'

'Unknown, but I'm guessing it's the *Alpha* or *Beta.*'

'Are the astropaths hearing anything?' asked Tyro.

'They concur with the long-range passives.'

'How long until they get here?' asked Cybus.

'Current estimates put them over Lerna Two-Twelve no later than fifteen hours from now,' said Thamatica.

'Then we need to move fast,' said Cybus. 'What do we know of any Alpha Legion presence down there?'

'Nothing with any certainty,' said Wayland.

'So you keep saying. Just give me a damn estimate I can work with.'

'Vessels like that don't normally carry Legion forces as standard,' said Wayland, 'but we have to assume this one does. Given its limited crew spaces, its complement would be perhaps two or three squads. Thirty warriors at most.'

'Too many to take face to face with certainty,' said Tyro.

'*But we don't need to take them face to face,*' said Meduson, his image sharpening as if by the force of his will.

'What do you mean?' said Tyro, not liking the sickly grin on Meduson's ravaged features.

'*It's time to play the Alpha Legion at their own game.*'

DESCENDING THROUGH THE planet's upper atmospheric layer was easy until the Storm Eagle hit the tropopause. This was one of the roughest descents Tyro had ever known, and he had made more combat drops than most.

Heat blooms from the platform below were mixing with the colder air above in roiling storms. Squalling temperature differentials slammed the gunship in all directions. For once, the grav-harnesses securing the legionaries were entirely necessary.

'No use in chastising the pilot, I suppose,' grunted Vermana Cybus as his head slammed into the crossbar of his restraints.

'Sabik Wayland has picked up some bad habits from Sharrowkyn, but he's still the best pilot we have,' said Tyro.

Cybus leaned forwards as much as he was able, hands clasped before him as though in prayer.

Tyro knew what was coming next.

'You should be leading us,' said Cybus.

'We went over this, Vermana,' replied Tyro. 'I can't wear the armour convincingly, not with my cybernetic bodyplan. You need to lead. I will go in with the second wave alongside Meduson and his warriors.'

Cybus glanced down the length of the gunship with distaste. 'This isn't the kind of war I was built to fight.'

'Nor was I, but it is the kind of war we face. We either fight it or get out.'

Cybus recoiled as though Tyro had struck him.

'The Iron Tenth end wars, we don't leave them unfinished.'

Tyro nodded and held out his fist. 'Upon the anvil.'

'And by the Iron,' finished Cybus, looking down the fuselage and at his own armour. 'But I still don't like... *this*.'

Tyro let his eyes roam across Cybus's armour and was forced to agree. Fourteen other warriors of the Iron Hands sat locked into drop-harnesses, but instead of black they wore the salvaged indigo and silver of the XX Legion.

'Using the armour of the enemy,' said Cybus, staring at his armour in disgust and spitting on the deck as though to cleanse his mouth of the idea.

'Unpalatable, I agree,' said Frater Thamatica, making his way down the swaying crew compartment and using the arms of his servo-harness to stay balanced, 'but total surprise is our best chance of capturing the platform intact.'

'But to have our warriors bear the colours of another Legion sits ill with me,' said Tyro.

Thamatica said, 'As it should, but the rigours of war make such demands on those that fight on its ragged edge. At least the extent of your augmentations spares you that burden.'

The Ironwrought moved on with a rolling gait that matched the lurching motion of the gunship. He reached the rear assault ramp, where Nykona Sharrowkyn crouched like the shadow of a gargoyle. The Raven Guard warrior needed no restraints and no harness, keeping his balance with the poise of a warrior in perfect harmony with his body.

Thamatica's servo-harness unfolded and slotted home into the mechanism at the side of the ramp. No sooner had it done so than a trio of bulbs on the panel changed from red to amber.

Sabik Wayland's voice came over the helm-vox.

'*Landing zone approaching. Claws down in ninety seconds.*'

Tyro, Cybus and the rest of the Iron Hands lifted their stolen helmets and fitted them to their gorgets. Tyro's vision swam for a brief second as his senses meshed with those of his armour. Targeting reticules, functionality icons, waypoint markers and objective icons surrounded him as the visor filled with inputs.

'One pass, low and slow,' said Thamatica. 'Then we land.'

The grav-harnesses securing the disguised Iron Hands lifted from their locking bolts as the rear ramp descended. Searing black fumes rammed into the gunship with hurricane force.

'At least they're not shooting at us,' shouted Thamatica over the din, leaning into the tarry clouds. Vortices of particulate-rich air ripped through the compartment.

'I'd almost prefer it if they were!' replied Tyro, rising to his feet with the rest of the Iron Hands.

Shadrak Meduson's Stormbird followed them, barely visible through the dark umbra of smoke. Without the benefits of Wayland and Thamatica's modifications it was having a rougher time in the turbulence.

'*Sixty seconds.*'

Tyro and his Iron Hands turned to face the open ramp.

'I might not be in with the first wave, but I'll damn sure be the first to put boots on the ground,' said Tyro.

'Where's Sharrowkyn?' asked Cybus.

Visibility was nil, but Sharrowkyn knifed through the obscuring pall of cindered darkness like a turbo-penetrator through bare flesh. With arms tucked in tight to his sides, legs straight, he angled his course as a red-orange fireball bloomed below him.

He passed through its outer edges, tasting the promethium-fyceline mix. The ground was near, his every sense told him so, even if his armour didn't. Too much metal, too many emissions confusing its machine senses.

Another gout of fire reluctantly lit the surfaces of his armour and the matt-black needle carbine strapped across his back. This time he saw its source, a flared tower of chained girders. Its heat washed over him, the anchored base out of sight.

He was at terminal velocity now, clouds rushing past him.

They thinned, and he saw the colossal floating structure of Lerna Two-Twelve below, spreading out in all directions like a melted hive. Stalactites of steel rose from a vaporous gruel of toxins and ash: refineries and ore silos, pump towers and vent mouths like vast sinkholes.

Two hundred metres.

Sharrowkyn saw moving things: lumbering giants he recognised as Mechanicum battle engines retrofitted with engineering claws, fuel pumps and lifter rigs. Battalions of masked servitors and automated machines attended upon them like devotees. Tracked fuel-bowsers the size of leviathans traversed vast highways of steel.

His hunter's eye quartered the ground, then quartered it again, looking for real targets.

One hundred metres.

There. Over by the edge of the platform, where the fog glittered with electrostatic discharge in the repulsor field.

Two warriors with transhuman bulk moving along a suspended walkway. Alpha Legion colours. They marched from an outflung fantail platform upon which rested a battered looking Fire Raptor. Caustic rains had taken most of its paintwork, but the hydra sigil remained inviolate.

Fifty metres.

He rolled in midair, bringing his legs around to angle his descent. This close to solid ground, rogue thermals competed to tear him this way and that. Micro-bursts from his jump pack kept him on course.

Ten metres.

One target looked up. Red eye lenses flared in alarm.

'Too late,' said Sharrowkyn, drawing his black-bladed swords with a near-silent whisper.

Five metres.

They separated, but Sharrowkyn wasn't aiming for both of them. Snap-shot mass-reactives punched the air. None close.

His boots smashed down on a helmet that broke apart like glass. He triggered his jump pack again – not enough to get him airborne, just enough to survive the impact. He rammed down through the collapsing body, buckled the decking and rolled.

He was up a second later. A bolt shell slashed past him with a flat bang of displacing air. Sharrowkyn slipped, using the shock of his arrival to confound the senses of his target. It was harder now that the legionary was aware of Sharrowkyn, but not impossible. He spun low and reversed the grip on his left-hand sword, stabbing it hard into the flex-seal joint at the back of the traitor's knee.

Even a legionary had to respect a wound like that.

The warrior dropped as his leg gave out. His arm swung around, looking to draw a bead with his bolter, but Sharrowkyn cut it off at the wrist. The weapon and its attached hand flew free of their owner, but still the legionary fought. He reached for his combat blade, but the fight was already over.

Sharrowykn rammed his sword into the base of the legionary's neck, twisting its edge and severing the spine. The warrior fell forwards without a sound. Sharrowkyn retrieved his second blade from the corpse's leg. He checked for any sign an alarm had gone out – a braying siren, or a host of weaponised servitors converging on his position.

Nothing.

Sharrowkyn tipped both bodies over the edge of the walkway, watching them fall long enough to see them convulsing as the repulsor field caught them and ripped them apart.

Their remains vanished into the corrosive fog, and Sharrowkyn set off at a run, following his instincts as much as the overlaid schematic on his visor.

Lerna Two-Twelve's control hub was five kilometres away.

He kept his swords bared.

He would kill again before reaching his raven's perch.

EIGHT

Heads held high
Kill gauntlet
Revival

BARELY HAD THE gunships touched down on the platforms than their jets were screaming to be airborne again. Iron Hands debarked from the assault ramps. As soon as they were clear, the aircraft surged into the fog.

Tyro, Cybus and Meduson met in the eye of the hurricane their ascent left behind. Clad in black war-plate and with his helm locked tight to a wide gorget, Meduson seemed more vital, more energised than before. The prospect of bloodshed and what might be won was invigorating them all.

What had seemed a flight of fancy, a mere dream of vengeance, was now within their grasp, so close Tyro felt he could reach out and pull it tight to his breast.

'Sharrowkyn's already down,' he said.

'I know, I saw him drop.'

'Then you've good eyes,' remarked Cybus.

'The best,' said Meduson. 'Or one, at least.'

The circle of clear air blasted by the Storm Eagles shrank to nothing around the gathered Iron Hands: forty from the *Iron Heart* and twenty-one from the *Sisypheum*, fifteen of whom were clad as Alpha Legion. They spread out across the platform, weapons extended, though there was no sign their rapid insertion had been detected or observed.

Gaskon Malthace emerged from the toxic fog to stand by his captain. His implanted flail described a tight circle on its chain of cold iron. Ashur Maesan let the ring of rusted service studs clink against his metalled forearm as he dragged his *hiebmesser*'s edge along the vambrace.

The gesture irritated Tyro, but this was not the time to chide another captain's chosen man. Septus Thoic and Vermana Cybus were unconsciously mirroring the positioning of the two warriors, but where Meduson's honour guard proudly wore the black of the X Legion, Tyro's men were clad as the enemy.

Affixed to the edge of their metal-rimmed shoulder guards were crimson oath-seals, a throwback to a time when going into battle with a shared oath actually meant something. The wax paper fluttered in the strong wind.

'Everyone filter in non-visible spectra,' said Thamatica. 'You should see the icons in the millihertz range.'

Tyro blinked in a filter over his visor rendering the seals as shimmering blobs of mercurial silver. Thamatica had fashioned the icons to differentiate between these faux Alpha Legionnaires and the true traitors. The Iron Hands would see them, but the traitors would not.

'Ready?' Tyro asked Cybus.

'I am, brother-captain,' said Cybus, slamming a fist to his chest in the old Unity salute.

Septus Thoic repeated the gesture a second later, adding, 'Today, a primarch falls!'

To hear a warrior clad as a betrayer say that gave Tyro the strangest sensation. Warriors clad as Alpha Legionnaires talking of killing their own gene-sire. That a schism existed between the Legions was bad enough, but the idea of it *within* a Legion – even an enemy one – sent a chill down Tyro's spine.

Thamatica pointed along the suspended walkway leading from the

platform with his servo-arms. The blurred outline of an enormous promethium silo was just visible, vast as a hab-stack and just as volatile.

Pluming vent fires belched from its summit. Lightning drizzled its
flanks.

'Follow that line of silos for three kilometres until you reach an eight-
fold nexus of pipes and cables. Take the northern route onwards that
will lead to a pumping station after another kilometre. That's where
you'll find the control hub, on the coreward side of a refinery built in
the form of a stepped ziggurat.'

'Like a temple?' asked Cybus.

'Yes, I suppose you could argue that it has something of the fane
about it,' said Thamatica. 'Strange how often that happens.'

Cybus nodded and clenched a fist above his shoulder. Tyro extended
his hand and they gripped arms as warriors of the X Legion had for
two centuries. Wrist to wrist, iron to iron. It felt strange not to actually
feel the touch of an iron gauntlet, but even that had to be concealed.

'We'll follow you,' said Tyro. 'Five hundred metres.'

Cybus nodded and said, 'Do you remember what I said on Iydris
after we'd faced the Lord of Iron?'

'I do,' said Tyro, taking the veteran's hand. 'That after facing a primarch any other death would feel small. And do you remember what
I said to you?'

'Don't die. Live forever,' said Cybus. 'Was good advice.'

The Avernii champion turned and led the warriors of the *Sisypheum*
into the chemical-rich fog.

'March with your heads held high,' Meduson shouted after them.
'Here you are Alpha Legion. Let the enemy see that and this will work.'

The disguised Iron Hands vanished into the fog.

'You heard, Thoic,' said Tyro. 'Today, a primarch falls!'

DESPITE BEING CLAD in full armour – something his cybernetics barely
permitted – Vermana Cybus had never felt more exposed. Only now,
denied the black of the Iron Hands, did he truly understand how much

of his identity was bound up in circuits and gears, oil and electro-motive power.

This armour felt *wrong*. On every level.

It moved differently and the invasive link-cables burned in his sock-ets where they entered his flesh. The visor display glitched with static, as though it knew Cybus were not its rightful wearer.

That he was an imposter.

He and his warriors followed the metalled roadway that Thamat-ica had indicated, moving through writhing fogbanks that made their footfalls echo strangely. Shadows twisted in the heavy smoke. Mechan-icum adepts and packs of roving servitors moved through the mist, but upon seeing his armour, they turned away.

The route took them between vast, cyclopean structures that throbbed with mechanised heartbeats, and gigantic columns of iron that exhaled noxious fumes. Hissing pipes threaded overhead and vulcanised cables transmitted vast quantities of power throughout the platform.

A fuel-leviathan rumbled on a parallel course, two hundred metres in height and a hundred wide. Its cliff-like flanks were layered with a patina of rust and corrosion, its interior spaces filled with an ocean of promethium. Cybus tried to imagine the scale of the blast were a high-explosive round to penetrate its armour.

'Up ahead,' said Thoic.

Cybus dismissed thoughts of the leviathan's destruction and fixed his gaze forwards once more. Ahead, the roadway approached the eight-fold confluence Frater Thamatica had told them to look for.

It wasn't empty.

Two Mechanicum adepts were held aloft on an ornate palanquin of ivory and jet by six servitors in full rebreather-kit. Both worked on a pared back cable-run as thick as a Vindicator's cannon with hooded plasma cutters that wreathed the assembly in a spectral blue light. Crackling brass wires linked them to a hunched brute of a masked ser-vitor overburdened with boxy generator apparatus.

Neither adept appeared to be armed with anything ranged, but with most of their hybrid anatomy concealed beneath ragged black robes it was hard to be certain.

'Work detail?' he said.

'Looks like it,' replied Thoic. 'Do we kill them?'

'Much as I'd like to, not unless there's no choice.'

One adept looked up, and Cybus saw the red gleam of multiple optics. A bark of static screeched from under its hood. Could its auspex see beneath his stolen armour? His visor tried and failed to translate the scrappy binary. Meaningless symbols scrolled across the display.

Were they already undone?

His hand slid towards his bolter.

The second adept raised a skeletal arm of bare bronze and jade ceramic. It too gave an unintelligible bark of static.

'For the Emperor!' said the first adept in grating, artificial tones. 'Alpharius!'

'For the Emperor!' repeated Thoic, punching the air with his bolter. 'For the Emperor!'

Both adepts bowed and returned to their work on the opened cable-run, and Cybus gritted his teeth as he copied Thoic's gesture of camaraderie.

'This way,' he said, marching from the nexus of cables via its northern exit. His soul felt sullied by allowing the traitorous adepts to believe he shared their loyalty. Every fibre of his being wanted to kill them, to make them suffer, but his orders were unambiguous.

They soon left the adepts behind, worming their way deeper into the maze of slab-sided edifices and intestinal loops of pipework. Thus far, every structure Cybus had seen on Lerna Two-Twelve was of stolid Mechanicum character, blocky and purely functional. Closer to its centre, he saw buildings whose form seemed to have no function.

In an octagonal plaza, a pyramid of mirrored glass stood at the centre of a golden circle of inscribed alchemical symbols. Nebulous congeries of light twisted at the pyramid's centre like a miniature galaxy. From somewhere nearby Cybus heard a strangely musical sound, and for the briefest instant he thought he saw a host of unblinking eyes at the centre of the galaxy.

He caught a glimpse of himself in the glass. The indigo blue of his armour disgusted him, and his iron heart rebelled at the treachery of his appearance.

'Why do they say it?' he asked.

'Say what?' said Septus Thoic.

'For the Emperor. Why that? They've betrayed him, so why retain their battle cry?'

Thoic considered the question.

'It mocks the loyal Legions,' he said. 'It tells us that no heart is unsullied. It reminds us of who they once were – our kin. They're saying that, for the right reasons, any one of us might have chosen their path.'

Cybus stared at his reflection as he considered Thoic's words.

'No, *not* any one of us,' he said at last. 'We all had a choice, Septus. No one forced the Alpha Legion to betray the Emperor, no one put a gun to their head and said they had to do what they've done. I don't know why, but they *chose* betrayal over loyalty.'

'There's the rub,' said Thoic. 'You don't know. Maybe it's best you don't know.'

Cybus nodded and turned from his treasonous reflection.

'Medusa's blood,' he swore.

Floating on cushions of repulsor energy, ten metres apart, were a pair of armoured speeders with forwards gun-mounts bearing heavy bolters. Their frontal plates were dented and dripped with condensed promethium residue. Dust devils danced in the vortices of their intersecting drive wakes.

Two Alpha Legionnaires sat in the bucket seats of each speeder, one at the controls and the other with his hands on the firing grip of the heavy bolter.

'Brothers,' said Septus Thoic, holding up a hand.

Cybus read their hostility. These warriors didn't know them, and a raised hand alone wasn't likely to win them over.

'Spread out,' he whispered, letting his hand drop to his side. Thoic guessed his intent.

'You can't draw and shoot before those gunners press the triggers,' said Thoic. 'Remember what Meduson said. March with our heads held high. Here we're Alpha Legion, brothers all.'

Cybus forced his fingers to open.

He took a breath and swallowed, walking towards the nearest speeder with what he hoped was the confident stride of someone who had every right. One speeder slipped laterally through the air, putting another five metres between the two vehicles.

'*Sethar muttax, vetheen ranko?*' said the gunner.

The words were gibberish, an unintelligible argot. Cybus had no idea what the warrior had just asked him. He slowly raised his left hand, tapping it on the side of his helmet.

'Bad vox,' he said. 'I can't hear you, brother.'

Cybus kept walking, closing the distance.

'*Sethar muttax, vetheen ranko?*' repeated the gunner.

Cybus shook his head and tapped his helmet again, glancing over at the flanking speeder. Its guns were aimed at his warriors. If he acted now, men would die and the mission would be compromised.

'*Shoot when I shoot,*' said a voice in his helmet.

Cybus paused. He knew that voice.

The gunner on the flanking speeder jerked to the side as the eye lenses of his helmet imploded. His driver's throat blew out in two silent impacts. Blood sheeted his chestplate in red and the speeder turned a slow spiral as he slumped over its controls.

Cybus didn't have time to rationalise what had just happened. He had a fraction of a second before the crew of the speeder in front of him recovered.

A fraction of a second was all Vermana Cybus needed.

His first shot exploded within the chest cavity of the gunner. He took a step to the side and put a mass-reactive through the driver's helmet.

His warriors spread out to secure the speeders and make sure their crew were dead. Cybus knew for certain they were.

'Sharrowkyn?' he said. 'Where are you?'

'Somewhere I can see what a bad Alpha Legionnaire you make,' said the Raven Guard. *'Throne, you're a terrible liar.'*

'I'll take that as a compliment,' said Cybus, turning a slow circle and scanning the surrounding towers and rooftops for any sign of Nykona Sharrowkyn.

'Please, Cybus. You really think you're going to find me?'

'No. By the way, good shooting.'

'They made it easy for me. Now get the bodies and speeders out of sight,' said Sharrowkyn. *'They'll be missed soon enough, but no sense in pre-empting an alarm.'*

The Iron Hands dragged the dead Alpha Legionnaires from their vehicles, dropping them into the smoking vent stacks.

'And, Cybus?' said Sharrowkyn. *'Hurry, the Alpha Legion ships are here.'*

Cybus looked at the speeders.

'Hurry, you say?'

WORKING IN THE apothecarion, Atesh Tarsa was never alone. The insistent hum of Ulrach Branthan's casket in the adjacent chamber was a constant reminder of another life. His other companion was the Bird. It sat on a cabinet of empty oxygen-cylinders, silent save for the occasional metallic clatter as it rearranged its wings.

'So why didn't you go planetside with Cadmus and Vermana?' Tarsa asked the Bird. It didn't answer, of course, and he shook his head. 'I don't blame you.' Cybus is a man whose company is more endured than enjoyed.'

Tarsa worked in an antechamber just off the main vault where Ulrach Branthan lay in repose. The naked body on the slab before him possessed the same transhuman bulk, but was of a different stripe altogether.

Bronzed skin marked him as Alpha Legion, though in truth there was little else to differentiate his outward appearance from that of any other legionary. One arm was a painfully crude augmetic, and his right eye was similarly bionic. The disconnected arm sat beside its stump of a forearm, the eye pried loose and hanging over one cheek.

The traitor had died painfully, that much was obvious.

Mass-reactives had taken his right leg, but the real killing blow had been a chainsword rammed up and under the plastron to tear through his heart and lungs.

Humming genetic sequencers processed blood and tissue samples, marrow cores and brain matter. Initial blood testing had detected curious anomalies in the warrior's neural structure as well as elevated quantities of neurotransmitters. Tarsa would have a full neuro-genetic workup for the dead warrior in a few hours, but in the meantime, he'd got his hands bloody.

Numerous disembodied organs surrounded him: the biscopea, the surviving heart, a shredded scrap of lung and other esoteric biological hardware. He'd examined them all with scalpels and microscopes, but so far all he had found was exactly what he'd hoped *not* to find.

That this Alpha Legionnaire was anatomically identical to him and the rest of the *Sisypheum*'s crew. He turned to face the Bird.

'Not one deviant trace within his internal structure,' said Tarsa, lifting the glossy mass of an oolitic kidney from a blood-spattered bowl. Ruddy and smooth, it was an organ of engineered perfection compared to what evolution wrought through trial and error. 'I thought, no, I *hoped* I might find some physiological marker to explain why he turned traitor. Some clue that he was different on some fundamental level.'

The bird cawed, a grating bark. Thamatica and Wayland had fixed its body, but it seemed they'd forgotten to upgrade its augmitters.

'Not in this particular organ, of course,' said Tarsa, returning the glutinous mass of the kidney to its bowl. 'A trace or mutation that might make sense of this madness.'

He sat back as the Bird flew from its perch behind him and disappeared into Ulrach Branthan's chamber. It cawed again, sounding somehow admonishing.

'Yes, I know,' said Tarsa, hearing the Bird's metal beak tapping on Branthan's casket. 'Given the last command Tyro issued before boarding the Storm Eagle, I ought to be on the bridge, but even the least among the Iron Hands knows more about commanding a starship than I do.'

Cadmus Tyro had assigned temporary command of the *Sisypheum* to the astonished Tarsa. Technically, Ulrach Branthan still commanded the vessel, but necessity forced Tyro to cede a degree of control to someone not of the X Legion. Foolish, and an obvious move to justify his and Cybus's simultaneous absence from the ship.

He sighed and let his gaze travel the length of the dead Alpha Legionnaire. Leaving aside the ruination of his chest, the warrior looked almost peaceful. Tarsa recalled something Ignatius Numen had said, questioning if the dead of the *Zeta Morgeld* were truly dead.

The warrior's skin was still bronzed, the pallor of the grave not yet draining him of colour. The melanochrome regulated a Space Marine's pigmentation, but like all living organs, it would cease function when its host was killed.

'Even my skin will pale when I die,' said Tarsa, bending over the corpse and running his gaze from head to toe. 'So why hasn't yours?'

He paused as his gaze lingered over where the warrior's arm had been severed just below the elbow. A temporary piece – that was how Thamatica had described the augmetic. Something wrought in haste and without care that it would bond to its bearer.

'Then why is the amputation scar much older and much cleaner?' said Tarsa, teasing the flesh open with a fine-bladed scalpel extruded from his narthecium.

Tarsa considered possible explanations for this, but before he could reach a conclusion, the Bird cawed again. He ignored it, but it kept squawking. Again and again, it filled the apothecarion with its strident cries.

'What is it?' demanded Tarsa, pushing away from the dead body and marching into Branthan's sepulchre. 'What do you want? I have better things to do than...'

The words died in his throat.

The stasis field sealing Branthan within his casket had disengaged. Temperature readings were spiking across the board. Every single data-slate was in the red, all of them vibrating with silenced alarms. Tarsa stared at the cyber-eagle, its sapphire eyes inscrutable as it perched atop the casket's control mechanisms.

'What did you do?' cried Tarsa. 'Throne, what did you do?'

NINE

Decapitation
Execution
He's coming down

THE ZIGGURAT WAS just where Thamatica said it would be – vast and monolithic, with spired towers that burned the fog rising from its corners. Caustic rain streamed down its bronzed metal facades. It squatted like a sacrificial fane at the edge of an open platform upon which stood two gargantuan figures.

'Titans,' said Thoic.

Cybus felt his chest tighten.

But these engines were adapted for labour and engineering purposes, not war. Instead of carapace-mounted missile launchers, they bore lifter rigs. Fuel connector and grappling limbs took the place of plasma annihilators and gatling cannons.

Sharrowkyn was probably already here, but Cybus didn't bother to try and guess where the Raven Guard might be hidden.

The bulk of the central platform housed the refuelling column, a conflation of monstrously thick cylinders of flexsteel that speared into the clouds like the corded trunk of the mightiest tree imaginable. Vapour-tugs that were little more than colossally powerful engines with a pilot's cab bolted on top, kept tight to the column, ready to begin the refuelling operation. Cybus couldn't see the Alpha Legion ships yet, but they were on their way. Already the sky was raging with atmospheric tempests caused by the inhuman bulk of the descending vessels.

A thousands-strong host of dark-robed Mechanicum adepts, servitors and loaders stood in ordered ranks. Wind and rain lashed them, but they didn't move so much as a muscle.

Cybus ignored them. They weren't his objective.

'Up there,' he said, pointing to a cantilevered control hub jutting from the ziggurat's upper reaches. 'That's where we need to be.'

Thoic nodded.

'We don't have much time,' he said, looking over at a stepped switchback climbing the ziggurat's rain-slick flanks. 'And that's a long way up.'

Cybus looked back at the two captured speeders.

'Sharrowkyn did say to hurry,' said Cybus. 'But first I need you to do something, Septus.'

'What's that?'

'I need you to shoot me.'

CYBUS SLAMMED INTO the armoured bulkhead, leaving a trail of blood down the metal. Blood poured from a shallow gash where a bolt shell had creased his arm. Behind him, warriors in torn and battered armour crowded the gantry, firing bolters down the switchback. He hammered a fist on the bulkhead.

'Open up!' yelled Cybus. 'They're right behind us.'

Mass-reactives exploded against the bulkhead. Cybus ducked and fired a three-round burst from the hip. A grenade detonated somewhere below. A legionary bellowed in mock pain.

'Sethar muttax!' he roared. 'Sethar *bloody* muttax!'

He had no real idea what the words meant, only that it was some kind of code phrase. He just hoped it wasn't one that would get him killed.

More warriors backed onto the gantry before the bulkhead. Like Cybus, their armour bore blast scars, tears from chain weapons and was smeared with blood. All self-inflicted, but the effect was strikingly convincing.

'Come on, come on,' muttered Cybus, dropping to one knee and firing over the heads of his men.

Magnetic locks disengaged within the ziggurat, and the metres-thick bulkhead split at its middle. Hot air, thick with incense and oily sweat, gusted out on a wind of positive pressure.

Cybus rose to his feet and backed into the control hub, yelling at his warriors. He turned as soon as he was in, a mental map of the hub's interior imprinting on his mind. Angles of attack, threat vectors.

Two Alpha Legionnaires flanked the opening door, another in each corner, two more in the centre of a semicircular arc of cogitators. A high bank of air-traffic control terminals ran the length of the glass-fronted facade.

Eight warriors.

'Get in!' he shouted back to his warriors. 'Before they rush the damn gate!'

More of his warriors ran in through the opened bulkhead.

Cybus counted them in as an Alpha Legionnaire hammered a fist against his shoulder guard. It took every fragment of willpower Cybus possessed not to immediately rip the bastard's head off.

'Who's out there?' demanded the warrior.

'The Nineteenth,' gasped Cybus.

'Raven Guard?' said the warrior with grating disbelief. 'Impossible.'

Cybus heard an edge of doubt. He could practically see the legionary's thought processes. If any Legion could have infiltrated the platform secretly, it would be the XIX.

The warrior came to a decision.

'How many of them?'

Cybus grinned within his helmet as the bulkhead closed behind the last of his warriors.

'And Sharrowkyn said I was a terrible liar.'

'Who?'

'The man who's hopefully about to kill you.'

✠ ✠ ✠

SHARROWKYN OBLIGED AND put a cluster of crystalline slugs through the Alpha Legionnaire's skull. The warrior standing over Cybus fell and Sharrowkyn immediately switched targets. The mercury-bright icons worn by Cybus's men made picking kills simplicity itself. Almost too easy.

Sharrowkyn shot the two warriors in the centre of the hub, one through an eye lens, the other in the throat. A classic side-by-side kill. The Alpha Legionnaires in the corners of the hub dropped and found cover, moving beyond his sight.

Fine. He'd done what he could from here.

The rest was up to Tyro and Meduson.

Tempting to remain *in situ*. Targets of opportunity would likely present themselves.

He shook his head. That kind of thinking got a sniper killed. Time to displace.

Find another shooting location.

Kill more traitors.

CYBUS ROLLED INTO cover as mass-reactives ploughed the deck. He rose to his knees and ripped a burst of shells over to where the shots had come from. Detonations glanced from the metal walls and banks of machinery. Slates exploded in storms of smoky shards.

The weakened armourglass window blew out and petrochemical winds ripped into the hub. A blizzard of loose ticker-tape streams and dust filled the air.

Thralls and implanted servitors sat oblivious or uncaring at the slaughter going on around them. Most died at their stations. Those with autonomy of thought and movement tried to run. They didn't get more than a few steps before being torn apart in the crossfire.

Horizontal streams of gunfire ripped back and forth across the hub. Two of his warriors were down, proving that even with the element of surprise, nothing was certain. Cybus still had enough warriors left to finish the job. He crawled to the edge of his cover, a shattered bank of logic engines.

Thamatica would likely berate him for the destruction he'd caused, but let him take this place without a shot! Cybus let a rare grin rest on his lips.

Most warriors hated fighting in confined spaces, but these were the kinds of fight the Iron Tenth relished. With a boarding shield, he'd be in among the Alpha Legion right now, elbow deep in entrails and bloodied to the waist.

Cybus gripped the dead Alpha Legionnaire, the one he'd spoken to, and hauled him upright with a grunt of effort. A transhuman warrior in full armour was still heavy, even to another genhanced physique. He lifted the body over the edge of the console and a burst of shells punched through the corpse's chest with cracks of shattered ceramite and bone.

Cybus released the body and surged to his feet.

Alpha Legionnaire, to the left.

He squeezed the trigger, and the enemy warrior fell with most of his shoulder and half his skull missing.

Four down, four left alive.

With more men, the advantage lay with Cybus, and the enemy knew it. He could have killed them all by now, and laughed as he imagined their confusion. He let them call for aid. He was counting on it.

'Septus!' he yelled. 'Go low around the right flank. They'll be keeping clear of that window, so drive them hard against the far wall. Then keep down for the hammer strike.'

Thoic nodded and moved off, drawing three more Iron Hands to him. Cybus waved his remaining warriors over as relentless volleys of suppressive fire punished the Alpha Legion. With nowhere else to go, they fought with their backs to the wall.

One of Thoic's men fell, his helmet a bloody bowl of sopping matter. Cybus felt his rage coalesce into something primal.

'The ingot is upon the anvil!' he roared. 'Now let the hammer fall!'

On his last word, every one of the Iron Hands dropped to the floor.

A hurricane of impacts blew the back wall of the hub inwards. Heavy calibre mass-reactives sawed through the steelwork behind the Alpha

Legion. Shredded metal flew like bronzed decoy chaff and the light
from the storm-wracked sky poured inside.

The enemy legionaries were ripped apart by the blitzkrieg of explosive shells. Armour and flesh were obliterated as thoroughly as any
abattoir's thresher blades could manage.

Cybus saw the two captured speeders through the ripped steel wall
strafing left and right, booming muzzle flares and high-velocity explosive rounds chugging from their heavy bolters.

'Stand down,' ordered Cybus. 'They're dead.'

The heavy bolters ceased fire, and Thoic rose from cover an instant
later to make sure of that. He went from body to body, systematically
putting a bolt round through the skull of every fallen Alpha Legionnaire.
Somewhere in the fighting, Thoic had removed his helmet, and Cybus
saw the hate in his eyes, a well that seemed utterly depthless. Ferrus
Manus was dead, and for many of his proud sons only hate remained.

Yet beyond that hate, Cybus saw regret. It surprised him, because he
had not thought Septus Thoic capable of regret. But wasn't that the
truest expression of this war? Regret for what the Warmaster had driven
them to, and all that would be lost by its ending.

'Clear,' said Thoic, and Cybus nodded, his moment of introspection
already forgotten.

He bent to wrench a fallen Alpha Legionnaire's ruined helm from his
head. Frantic tinny vox-chatter echoed from within, rapid-fire questions
in the enemy's rancid, serpent tongue. Cybus couldn't understand the
words, but the meaning was obvious.

He switched frequency.

'This is Cybus. We have the hub,' he said. 'Enemy inbound.'

A KEY OBJECTIVE in any ambush was to get as many of the enemy as
possible within the kill-box before opening fire. Another principle of
ambush was to render what appeared to be the most promising escape
route a death trap.

In both respects, the Iron Hands ambush was textbook.

Two demi-squads of Alpha Legion, approaching from the east and south, moved onto the platform. They converged on the ziggurat refinery with all the caution, skill and aggression to be expected from Legion warriors. Flashes of sheet lightning burst within the tortured clouds. Rolling peals of thunder echoed from the cliff-sided silos.

Sharrowkyn took the first kill as a crack of thunder slammed over Lerna Two-Twelve. Headshot. A lieutenant, by the rank markings. The headless corpse keeled over as his warriors broke for the switchback to the control hub.

Bolter fire chased them to where the warriors of Cadmus Tyro and Shadrak Meduson were waiting, and no bastion of the Imperial Fists ever had a more complete system of enfilades. Interlocking fields of fire allowed even relatively unskilled gunners to lay down killing volumes of firepower and shred an enemy advance.

When the gunners were as skilled and vengeful as the Iron Tenth, there could be no escape.

The enemy warriors died in seconds, swiftly bracketed and pummelled by explosive rounds. With the first volley, they knew they were dead, but fought back anyway. The Alpha Legion were traitors, but they were still armoured transhumans and died as hard as any.

In minutes, all but one Alpha Legionnaire was dead. The last enemy warrior had survived four mass-reactives that blasted most of his torso clear. His left arm was missing from the shoulder, yet still he fought. He killed two of Meduson's men before Cadmus Tyro finally put him down with a shot to the side of the head.

Vermana Cybus appeared at the top of the switchback, the jade hydra on his shoulder guard now defaced with a bloody X.

He pointed skywards, where the vast, lightning-wreathed belly of a starship parted the yellowed clouds like a ploughshare through poisoned soil. The void made it difficult to grasp the inhuman scale of the strike cruiser, but Lerna Two-Twelve's towering silos made it all too clear. Plated in stained indigo, the warship's bulk was awe-inspiring, its very simplicity speaking of the grand complexity within.

'He's here,' said Meduson.

THE RAIN WAS unending, all but drowning the refinery in an instant deluge. It poured in waterfalls from the silos and sent foaming rivers of pollution gurgling in the spaces between the platform's metallic structures.

Two more warships now held station over Lerna Two-Twelve alongside the strike cruiser, their reflections wavering in the rainbow-streaked mirror of the platform below. Smaller vessels, to be sure, but each with firepower enough to send the platform crashing into the planet's growing acid oceans.

Circling Fire Raptor gunships kept on station with their carriers, ready to pounce on anything that dared approach in a way they didn't like.

'Throne, Vermana, did you have to destroy so much of this place?' snapped Thamatica as he fought to restore more than one bank of cogitators. 'There's barely enough functionality to keep a pretence that Lerna Two-Twelve is still operational.'

The Ironwrought's servo arms worked furiously at his back, like the legs of a spider furiously weaving its web.

'Did you think the Alpha Legion were just going to surrender once I got in, Frater?' answered Cybus. 'I had to kill them, and killing legionaries in a confined space is messy.'

'Yes, but speeders? Was that *really* necessary?'

'It got the job done,' said Cybus.

'Not exactly subtle, though, was it?' said Thamatica through what sounded like gritted teeth.

'You should know by now that subtle isn't part of Cybus's tactical lexicon, Frater,' said Ignatius Numen with a booming laugh that rivalled the thunder.

Picking his way through the ruins of the control hub, Tyro was forced to agree. Cybus never did anything by half, but this felt extreme even for him. On the opposite side of the smashed hub, Meduson stood over a dead Alpha Legionnaire.

'That it should come to this,' he said with real regret.

'What's that?' asked Tyro.

Meduson shook his head. 'Brothers killing brothers.'

Tyro had no answer. Brothers had been killing brothers for years since Isstvan. Had its absurdity and horror only now struck home with Meduson?

Gaskon Malthace shadowed his war-leader, but Ashur Maesan made his own way through the hub. He knelt beside each corpse, and his *hiebmesser* carved the service studs from its brow in quick, bloody strokes. Tyro was not above taking war-trophies, but mutilating the dead left a bad taste in his mouth.

'Is that really necessary?' Tyro asked.

Meduson looked over to his sergeant's gruesome labours and shrugged. 'We all have our ways of dealing with betrayal. Maesan has his, you have yours and I have mine. I'll not stand between a man and the means he chooses to slake his vengeance.'

Tyro turned away from his fellow captain's indifference to Maesan's acts and returned to Thamatica's side.

Cybus and the Frater were still remonstrating against one another.

'Subtle doesn't get the job done quickly,' said Cybus.

'But it would have made *this* much easier,' grumbled Thamatica as a last parting shot.

'Enough,' said Tyro. 'We're still on mission.'

This was Thamatica issuing commands to the servitor-crewed Titans on the platform and vectoring the dozens of vapour-tugs lifting enormous fuel pipes to the vessels above. Ignited contrails, plasma-bright and falling like droplets of phosphor, painted the clouds over Lerna Two-Twelve with arcing lines of fire.

The strike cruiser had accepted the challenge codes Wayland had lifted from the *Zeta Morgeld*'s log and, as far as anyone on the ships above was aware, nothing was awry.

'Any word yet from Wayland?' asked Tyro.

'Nothing yet. The Kryptos is still parsing the vox traffic passing between the ships,' said Thamatica, his face lined with concentration. 'I would surmise that it should be easy enough to deduce which ship the primarch is on.'

'*If* he's even on one of them,' pointed out Cybus.

'The nature of the vox traffic should tell us that too.'

'And once we know?' said Cybus.

Thamatica pointed to the throbbing fuel lines arcing up to the strike cruiser.

'What's going up those pipes is a highly volatile fuel-air mix, together with a timed chemical detonator,' he said with more than a hint of pride. 'When that ship triggers its main drive unit, a virtually instantaneous chemical cascade will begin within its fuel tanks that will blow it to its component atoms.'

'Why not just do that to them all?'

'Because we will learn of the success or otherwise of this mission by their reaction,' said Meduson, picking over the debris to look up through the shattered window at the front of the hub.

'Meduson,' said Tyro. 'Get back. If any of those Fire Raptors see you...'

'If they look that closely, it won't matter,' said Meduson. 'They'll see the broken window and the shot-up walls.'

Before Tyro could say anything more, the panel beside Thamatica lit up with incoming vox. The speaker grille was smashed, so Frater routed it directly to his helm. He listened closely and nodded, before finally transmitting a binaric reply.

'What was that?' asked Tyro. 'Trouble?'

'Cybus, you need to get down to the platform right now,' said Thamatica. 'And this time you *have* to be subtle.'

'Why?' asked Cybus. 'What's happening?'

'*He* is coming down,' said Thamatica.

'Who?'

'Who do you *think*?'

✠ ✠ ✠

THE UNWAVERING DOT at the centre of Sharrowkyn's crosshairs followed
Cybus and Thoic as they led their combat squad through the hundreds
of labouring Mechanicum adepts and servitors. Half a kilometre from
the central fuelling rig, a cruciform pattern of blinking lights was guiding a Thunderhawk through the downpour.

He watched from the shadows of a vent tower three hundred metres
up from the deck of the platform. With good fields of fire all around
and a view of both the landing platform and the control hub, it was
a perfect sniper's nest.

Sharrowkyn eased the rifle back, spotting the two covering squads
of Meduson's Iron Hands moving across the platform in support.
They were good, Sharrowkyn had to give them their due. Each man
moved swiftly and silently, keeping Cybus and his warriors in sight
while keeping clear of the hundreds of milling tech-priests and
vassal-thralls.

The roar of the gunship's engines was loud enough to hear over the
thunder and Sharrowkyn eased his eye from the rifle's sight to look up.

An anonymous aircraft. Unremarkable, but that was only to be
expected. Not for Alpharius the vanity or ostentation of a signature
aircraft, just whichever flyer happened to be next on the rotation. Sharrowkyn admired the sentiment.

Of all the men Tyro could have sent to meet an enemy primarch,
Cybus was least suited to acts of guile. As direct a man as it was possible to be, yet here he was marching to meet a master of deception
and misdirection.

Sharrowkyn let his crosshairs drift over the five warriors accompanying Cybus. He knew them all – years spent confined aboard the same
starship left no other choice – but he knew them beyond just their
names and shared history.

He'd trained with these men and fought alongside them. He knew
how they moved, where their skills lay and to which of them he might
teach his own skills. He'd learned their strengths, their weaknesses and
their individual pathologies; the ones prone to despair, those who

turned their grief inwards and those who expressed it as pure hate. In this respect he knew them better than they knew themselves.

Even in their Alpha Legion plate and without knowing which warrior wore which suit, Sharrowkyn could identify each man by the way he carried himself, the way he walked or the tilt of his head. Cybus marched chest first, thrusting himself at the world, and Septus Thoic had a bullish aggression that practically dared those around him to test his strength.

Brother Gavril favoured his left side, his hips fractionally out of balance. Vedran carried himself loosely, both shoulders always in motion, ready to fight. Radek had taken a mass reactive to the spine on Isstvan and now walked with a barely perceptible limp. Olek's left hand was locked in a fist after an electromagnetic pulse fused the mechanisms of his bionic, and he'd refused to let Thamatica or Wayland replace it.

Sharrowkyn's crosshairs returned to Thoic and Cybus. The instincts that had brought him to the attention of the Shadowmasters told him something was awry with what he was seeing. His instincts were almost never wrong and his finger curled around the trigger of his needle carbine.

What was he seeing?

The rain had washed the blood from their armour, but it was clear they had both been wounded in the fight to take the hub.

Was that all it was? That they were bearing wounds?

The Thunderhawk rolled in on a fast combat drop and the howling jetwash wreathed both Iron Hands in sheets of vapour. The gunship's wings flared and its landing claws hit hard enough to drive it into a short skid. The assault ramp dropped a moment later and ten legionaries emerged at speed. Guns tight to their shoulders, scanning all around for threats. Just the kind of behaviour Sharrowkyn would expect if Corax were about to set foot from a gunship.

Not that the Ravenlord would ever be so obvious.

Behind them came a warrior in the same unadorned plate as the combat squad. Lustrous indigo, gleaming in the rainwater streaming from its curved surfaces.

Alpharius.

Taller than his warriors, but not so much as to render him godlike. He reached up to remove his helmet and Sharrowkyn's finger tightened on the trigger. Enough to slip a needle cluster into the breech of his carbine, but not enough to activate the laser designator.

Sharrowkyn eased his finger from the trigger guard.

He had put a round into Fulgrim's skull on Hydra Cordatus, but the Phoenician yet lived and had become something beyond mortal understanding.

No, this was Cybus's moment.

TEN

On station
Adrift
Fratricide

WAYLAND PUT THE Storm Eagle into a slow leftwards bank, keeping a constant thousand metres between him and Lerna Two-Twelve. Meduson's Stormbird copied his turn, holding to his right wing on his rear quarter.

He kept his altitude lower than the platform, knowing the distortion effects of the platform's vast banks of repulsors would keep both gunships from the prying auspex aboard the Alpha Legion ships.

The slate on the avionics panel was awash with data inloads: a mixture of vox traffic analysis by the Kryptos, the electromagnetic emissions surrounding Lerna Two-Twelve and his own backscatter subroutine and inloaded surveyor sweeps from the *Sisypheum*. His divided consciousness processed them all.

The Alpha Legion strike cruiser had recently launched a gunship, and transmissions passing between the vessels overhead had just spiked with activity. Half a dozen Fire Raptors were detaching from their normal combat patrols to escort the gunship to Lerna Two-Twelve.

Only one conclusion presented itself.

Alpharius was inbound.

The corollary of that extra volume of transmission was an increase in baseline encryption. Sure enough, the Kryptos now had enough comparative data-sets to interpolate the strike cruiser's designation.

'The *Sigma*?' said Wayland in surprise.

He scanned back through the archives of his eidetic memory of ship rosters and fleet registries.

'Keel laid in the Bakkan graving docks,' said Wayland. 'Part of the 455th Expeditionary Fleet under the nominal command of Shipmaster Solveig. Fleet affiliation revoked several years ago on the orders of Legate Chaitin of the Twentieth Legion, just prior to the Isstvan atrocity. No extant records since then.'

The avionics panel chimed a proximity alarm. Wayland ignored it as he had ignored it every few minutes over the past few hours. Without the particular modifications he and Thamatica had made to the Storm Eagle, Meduson's pilot was finding it difficult to keep a precise distance.

Now that his attention was fixed on the avionics panel, Wayland saw his backscatter subroutine had completed its analysis of the battle between the *Sisypheum* and the *Zeta Malquiant*.

He called the data to the front of the slate, angling his turn in towards Lerna Two-Twelve as the Storm Eagle registered the ghost of an auspex pass.

The spectroscopic analysis of the anomalous electromagnetic trace he'd detected during the battle was a stepped signal that was too regular and too persistent to be anything other than something deliberately generated.

'A highly individual signature,' said Wayland, thinking aloud. 'Something proprietary and tailored for a specific Legion or auxiliary force, perhaps?'

Only when his gaze strayed onto the upper reaches of the panel did he understand its true purpose. Partially hidden by the data-pane was the passive inload of electromagnetic emissions filling the air above Lerna Two-Twelve.

The signal was an exact match for the energies keeping the Alpha Legion ships secured in perfect geosynchrony.

'It was a bloody e-mag tether,' he said, and the only logical conclusion was suddenly and horrifyingly clear.

The avionics panel chimed again.

CYBUS HAD SEEN primarchs before and knew what it was to be face to face with a god-like being. Ferrus Manus had been the lord of stone and metal: a master of industrial labours, not a soot-smeared smiter. Primarch Guilliman was a hero of ancient times, carved from ivory and wrought in golden light.

Even Fulgrim, before his treachery, had been mighty.

Alpharius was, by contrast, something of a disappointment.

Yes, he was taller, broader and obviously more powerful than Cybus, but in a way that suggested it would still be worth a wager on the outcome of any bout between them. Beyond the negligible height difference, any one of his warriors could claim to be Alpharius and Cybus would be none the wiser.

The primarch carried his helm in the crook of his elbow, and his exposed features were ruddy and bronzed with health. Dark hair, hooded eyes, full lips curled in wry amusement. A coiled serpent tattoo around his left eye, and, barely visible above the line of his gorget, a scar in the shape of a reversed Ultima.

And yet there was *something* about him, a radiance that came from the eyes. A charisma that made Cybus want to stand taller and kneel in the same instant. He fought the latter urge until he realised he was *already* kneeling.

'My lord,' he said. 'Welcome to Lerna Two-Twelve.'

'Get up,' said Alpharius.

Cybus did so, skin reddening at how easily he had been made Alpharius's dog and not even known it.

'Who else is here?' asked Alpharius, his hand resting on the leather-wound grip of a plainly formed line gladius.

'My lord?' said Cybus.

'Don't be coy, Sergeant Daraka,' said Alpharius, his fingers tightening on the grip of his sword. 'I know there are two vessels hidden in orbit with Eirene Septimus. Tell me, which of them is it?'

The name Alpharius had used for Cybus confused him until he realised the primarch had read the visual tagging of his armour.

'Which of who?' he asked.

Alpharius looked over his shoulder at Thoic and smiled.

'You know, don't you?'

'Aye, my lord,' said Thoic. 'I know.'

BRANTHAN WAS STILL alive, but that was about all Tarsa would venture. Slathered in gore to the waist, his arms and face were thick with the captain's blood. The last two hours had drained him to the point of exhaustion.

His every instinct had been to let Branthan die, to allow this great warrior the dignity of oblivion and let the Bird's inexplicable actions mark an end to his suffering.

But Ulrach Branthan wasn't about to give up on life.

He fought for it as any Iron Hand would.

He clawed for it, refusing to be drawn into death's final embrace. Tarsa's oaths as an Apothecary forbade him to be a bystander in such a battle, and the captain's will to endure had, against his better judgement, left him no choice but to fight alongside him.

Whatever the Bird had done to the casket could not be undone, and Tarsa fought with every scrap of knowledge gained on the Imperium's battlefields to keep the captain alive.

From the outset he'd known it was a fight he couldn't win.

The captain's wounds were too deep, too mortal and too many. The stasis field refused to re-engage, and the temperature within the cryo-casket rose steadily with every passing minute. Garuda had been thorough in its dismantling of the apparatus keeping Branthan alive.

In all but one respect.

The Heart of Iron remained clamped to the captain's chest, its monofilament wires now girdling his entire torso. The mass-reactive wounds on Branthan's chest were entirely submerged beneath a weave of fine silver mesh.

His lifeblood seeped at an ever-increasing pace from his ruptured limbs. His heart rate was spiking on the cusp of colossal rupture and his blood pressure plunged to the nadir of survivability.

And he *still* refused to die.

Tarsa eventually stopped the bleeding and brought the captain's vitals back to a level that wasn't immediately fatal. Even as he'd pulled the captain back from death, he'd known that, without something more permanent, it was a temporary respite at best.

Sooner or later, Branthan's ruined flesh would succumb.

That had left him with only one choice.

He still wasn't sure he'd made the right one.

Tarsa withdrew to the adjacent antechamber, leaving the *Sisypheum*'s three part-functional medicae servitors to work alongside the dozen others he'd summoned from Frater Thamatica's workshop. Their labours were not quiet and nor were they subtle, but they offered the best chance of survival for Captain Branthan. Pneuma-hammers beat metal and crackling arc-welders seamed massive plates of adamantium together.

His medical expertise and familiarity with the mysteries of steel would be needed soon enough, but for the moment he had time to reflect on what he'd done and its repercussions.

Tarsa washed the blood from his forearms at the deep basin normally used for surgical preparation. Boiling water washed clots of gelatinous Larraman-clogged blood from his ebony skin. The pain of it was tremendous, and Tarsa gripped the basin's edge, hard enough to buckle the metal as he let out a shuddering breath.

Garuda flew in on clattering wings of gold and silver. It landed on its usual perch of the empty oxygen-cylinders and let out another grating, metallic caw. In reproach or approbation, Tarsa couldn't tell.

'Shut up, damn you!' he yelled, curling his hands into fists.

The Bird cawed again and Tarsa wanted to smash it to fragments, to rip the wings from its body and stamp its ancient mechanisms beneath his boot.

He quelled his hate with the mantras of smiting taught to every son of Nocturne, letting their repetitive, soothing cadences smooth the jagged edges that threatened to overturn his reason.

Tarsa's time with the Iron Hands had taught him that hatred's pull was stronger than almost any other emotion, and only by virtue of his Nocturnean stoicism did he turn from it.

'Revenge is a poison, not a balm,' said Tarsa, letting out a shuddering breath that tasted of his birthrock's volcanic air.

Tarsa ignored the Bird and returned to the mortuary slab that still bore the corpse of the Alpha Legionnaire killed aboard the *Morgeld*.

The machinery he'd set in motion had finished long ago, winking green lights attesting to his preoccupation. In lieu of anything else to do, Tarsa flipped the switch on the inset data-slate and studied the results of the genetic sequencers.

With every line of scrolling text, Tarsa's horror mounted as the truth of the dead body became numbingly apparent.

'Throne, no, it's impossible,' he said, pushing himself away from the slab as though distance would make the findings of the machines less repugnant. 'It's impossible.'

Tarsa gripped the edge of the slab, now seeing the truth of the warrior's severed arm.

'You didn't *lose* it,' he said. 'You surrendered it willingly.'

His breath felt trapped in his lungs, his physiology as strained as Branthan's had been in his last moments.

'I need to run the tests again,' he said, already knowing such tests would just confirm what they had already revealed. 'There must have been some specimen contamination. Yes, that must be it. It *has* to be. I need to know this isn't true...'

But genetic data did not lie. Every test confirmed the same thing independently of one another.

The warrior on the slab was not an Alpha Legionnaire.

He was an Iron Hand.

WAYLAND PUT THE Storm Eagle into a screaming climb. It shuddered as he drove it through the squalling geomagnetic fields of Lerna Two-Twelve's repulsor field. A risky manoeuvre, but this couldn't wait.

'Tyro, this is Wayland,' he yelled into the vox. 'Can you hear me?'

The speaker burred with static, thick with distortion.

'Come on, come on,' he hissed at the vox, willing Tyro to answer swiftly.

'This is Tyro, what is it, Frater?'

'You have to get out of there, Cadmus,' said Wayland. 'It's a trap!'

'What? Say again.'

'The *Malquiant*, it was on an e-mag tether,' said Wayland, the words pouring out of him in a rush. 'Someone else was remote piloting it. That's why it flew over too fast and high.'

'What are you talking about, Wayland?'

'The electromagnetic distortion being thrown out by the *Morgeld*'s destruction broke the tether between the *Malquiant* and whoever was controlling it!'

He heard only silence in response, and hoped that meant Cadmus Tyro was simply digesting what he'd told him. The other option was too terrible to contemplate.

'Who?' asked Tyro.

'The *Iron Heart*,' said Wayland. 'They were the only vessel close enough. That's why Meduson intervened when he did, to blow *Malquiant* to atoms so we wouldn't board it and see it didn't have a crew.'

Again the maddening pause before Tyro answered.

'Meduson? Why would he do such a thing?'

'So we would trust him. To make us believe he was on our side. He put us in his debt by telling us that we'd ruined his plans and then told us what we wanted to hear. A mission we couldn't refuse.'

He let the inescapable truth of that sink in before continuing. 'This whole endeavour, it's a lie. They used us to find this place, to bring them here.'

'Why would Meduson lie to us?'

Before Wayland could answer, the Storm Eagle's avionics panel lit up with threat warnings. Blood-red icons illuminated and a screeching wail of a combat alarm blared.

'Missile lock! Missile lock!'

THOIC STEPPED PAST Cybus and addressed his words to Alpharius.

'Who do you *think* is waiting for you?' asked Thoic.

Alpharius narrowed his eyes, as though he might be able to see through Thoic's helm to the burn-scarred face of the warrior beneath.

'You're not Skolova,' said Alpharius.

'No,' agreed Thoic. 'I'm not.'

'You're one of *his*, aren't you? Seyhan?'

Thoic gave a short bow. 'At your service, Legate Chaitin.'

Cybus gripped Thoic's shoulder guard.

'What is he talking about?' he demanded. 'What are *you* talking about?'

'I'm talking about a betrayal of trust,' said Thoic, with a nod towards Alpharius. 'His mainly. But also mine.'

Thoic spun on his heel and his gladius was a blur of Medusan steel. It opened Cybus's throat back to the spine.

SHARROWKYN WATCHED CYBUS die through the scope of his rifle.

He saw the catastrophic blood spray, watched the warrior of the Avernii fall with his hands at his neck, but still couldn't believe it. Thoic followed up his murderous betrayal by leaping to attack Alpharius. Gunfire erupted as the new arrivals and the disguised Iron Hands opened fire.

Mass-reactives at close range were messy. With no time to arm, each round became a subsonic bludgeon. The arithmetic of a firefight was brutally direct, and the outcome of this one was entirely predictable.

Gavril's shock at what Thoic had done cost him his life. He fell in a lake of his own blood as three rounds tore away his right arm, rib-cage and pelvis. Radek killed two Alpha Legionnaires then died in a storm of impacts, his armour cracked open and hydraulic shock drag-ging the blood from his heart in a scarlet deluge. Olek had his pistol out and fired three shots before he was gunned down. Two of his tar-gets died with him.

Vedran threw himself into the midst of the duel.

He thrust at Thoic, but it was a clumsy, rage-fuelled blow and lacked precision. Thoic trapped the blade against his side and hammered a fist into Vedran's helmet. His former comrade-in-arms reeled from the blow. Thoic spun behind him and drove his blade up through the back of his neck and into his skull.

Alpharius took a step back and fired a volley of mass-reactives that blasted Vedran apart. Thoic dropped the ruptured mass of his human shield and threw himself at Alpharius before he could shoot again.

Sharrowkyn watched their blades clash in glittering arcs. Both warri-ors were skilled and as Sharrowkyn watched Thoic fight, he understood the source of his earlier disquiet.

The warrior fighting Alpharius wasn't Septus Thoic.

He was faster than Thoic ever was, and Thoic was one of the *Sisypheum's* best with a blade. Meduson claimed to have infiltrated Tyro's ship, but only now did Sharrowkyn realise just how literally he'd meant.

Septus Thoic had died aboard the *Zeta Morgeld*.

And the warrior Meduson had returned to the *Sisypheum* was an imposter. One who wore Thoic's face and possessed his memories.

Knowing how such a feat could be achieved sent a wave of nausea through Sharrowkyn.

'Damn it, Tyro, I *told* you not to do this,' he whispered, watching the two fighting warriors through his scope. 'Similar fighting styles, funda-mentals you both learned from the same master. Which makes you both viable targets.'

He centred his sights on Alpharius, slowing his breathing and letting his instincts follow the ebb and flow of combat. Every duel was a lethal dance that moved to a particular rhythm. Chaotic and unpredictable to be sure, but if a shooter understood its grammar, then a shot into a furious combat was entirely possible.

Sharrowkyn waited, his finger loose on the trigger. External sensory input fell away until all he saw and felt were the targets before him. He understood the rhythm of this combat and let his target come to him.

A head drifted into his sights and he squeezed the trigger.

And a tripartite cluster of razor-edged needle shards punched through the orbit of Alpharius's right eye. They shattered on impact, hundreds of fragments ripping through the skull's vault in an expanding cone that pulped brain tissue to grey-pink gruel.

Alpharius collapsed instantly and Thoic dived for cover as the surviving Alpha Legionnaires ran to their fallen leader. Meduson's warriors appeared at the edge of the platform, flensing the landing platform with murderously accurate bolter fire. Sharrowkyn switched his aim to Thoic, but in that instant of disconnect between shots he heard the roar of incoming jets.

His position was compromised. Two Fire Raptors were racing to his position. No time to wonder how they'd found him.

Sharrowkyn sprang to his feet and slung the needle rifle over his shoulder. He blinked away the disorientating shift in perspective from gunsight to normal vision.

At fifty metres out, the gunships' centreline avenger cannons spooled up to fire.

Sharrowkyn sprinted to the edge of the vent tower.

Twin hurricanes of fire brayed from the gunships' dipped prows. Hellstrikes streaked from their wing pylons. Sharrowkyn leapt from the tower as its summit vanished in a sheeting blaze of explosive fire.

ELEVEN

Wheels within wheels
That's all you get
Kill them

TYRO GRIPPED THE edge of the panel, his mind racing to process Wayland's desperate vox. The transmission had been abruptly cut off, but Tyro had heard the screeching wail of a missile lock.

'You know, then,' said Shadrak Meduson.

It wasn't a question.

'I know,' said Tyro, glancing first at Thamatica and then through the shattered window.

A moment of perfect understanding passed between them.

Tyro turned slowly, his heart colder and harder than Medusan ice-diamonds. His hand slid towards the bolter mag-locked to his thigh.

'I'd keep my hand from that weapon if I were you,' said Meduson. 'Sergeant Maesan favours his *hiebmesser*, but he's the best I've seen with a bolt pistol.'

Tyro spread his fingers as he completed his turn.

Twelve warriors clad in the black of the Iron Tenth stood with Meduson in the ruin of the control hub. Each had their weapons raised. Ashur Maesan stropped his gutting knife along his silvered arm, an arm Tyro now knew to be a lie. The spiked ball of Gaskon Malthace's flail described a tight arc beside his knee.

With Cybus, Thoic and the others gone to meet the arrivals on the platform, only Thamatica, Ignatius Numen and Sulgan, Dubric and Cynan, of the *Sisypheum*, stood with him. The odds weren't good, but the Iron Hands had never been ones to let impossible odds stand in their way.

'What in the name of the Gorgon is going on?' bellowed Ignatius Numen.

'Meduson has betrayed us,' said Tyro.

He didn't need to see Numen's face to know how ridiculous that sounded. That one Iron Hand would ever betray another was utterly preposterous, a lunatic fever dream. So impossible was it that only one other possibility presented itself.

'You're not Shadrak Meduson,' said Tyro.

'No, Cadmus, I'm not.'

'Then who are you?'

'Now you're just stalling,' said Meduson, reaching up to remove his helmet. 'You already know, don't you?'

The face beneath was just as Tyro remembered it when Meduson had first set foot upon the *Sisypheum*'s deck. He regarded Tyro with a mixture of amusement and regret.

His blood-filled eye blinked, and all traces of the trauma vanished. In its place was an eye the colour of honeyed milk. Meduson took hold of the crude mask of cybernetic augmentations covering the side of his head and tore it free, taking the layer of burn scars with it.

'That was real skin, you know.'

The revealed face was handsome, with a smooth complexion of beaten bronze. A strong jawline, wide cheekbones and the merest hint of a sardonic grin lurking on the lips. It was the face of one who could command loyalty with a glance, devotion with a word.

The face of a primarch.

'Alpharius,' said Tyro.

'The one and only.'

Meduson had always possessed a dynamic physical presence, but revealed as Alpharius, Tyro saw the true power lay behind his eyes. Behind them turned schemes within schemes, wheels upon wheels. The primarch's thoughts slipped effortlessly in dimensions Tyro couldn't even begin to fathom. Inside the mind of Alpharius, the galaxy turned ten thousand times a day.

'Why?' said Tyro. 'What was this for?'

Alpharius stepped towards him, supremely confident that Tyro couldn't harm him. It would take only a fraction of a second to draw and shoot, but Tyro knew he would be dead before the weapon was even half raised.

Alpharius turned to him and said, 'I envy you, Cadmus. You know *with utter and absolute certainty* you can trust those who bear the black and silver. I am not so fortunate. When I made my choice, not all my sons agreed to trust my revelations.'

'Revelations?' said Tyro, keeping himself between the enemy primarch and Thamatica.

Alpharius waved away his question. 'It would take too long to explain, and I'm not sure your all-too-literal mind would be capable of understanding anyway.'

'Is that why you turned traitor?' asked Tyro. 'Because of your... *revelations*? Is that why you betrayed your father?'

Alpharius laughed and raised an admonishing finger. 'Do you really think you can get under my skin with such obvious barbs, Cadmus? What is it you think, that I'll get angry and make some kind of mistake you can exploit to save the day? No, there's nothing left for you to say.'

'So who came down on that Thunderhawk?' said Tyro. 'One of your captains who refused to follow you into treachery?'

Alpharius said, 'Legate Chaitin. A good man in his own way. Honourable to a fault and possessed of a great deal of sensitive information, which is why I needed to find him before he reached the Imperium. Thank you for helping me with that, by the way.'

'You needed our Kryptos to find him,' said Tyro.

'I'd have caught him eventually,' replied Alpharius, folding his arms across his chest. 'But, yes, the Kryptos definitely made things easier.'

'So the Alpha Legionnaires aboard these moored ships? Their crews still hold true to the Emperor?'

Alpharius rapped his knuckles on the console behind him and said, 'They do, yes, but if Frater Thamatica has done his job well, as I'm sure he has, then Chaitin's ship is already a floating time bomb. It's just going to go off a little earlier than planned.'

Tyro looked for an angle he could use, a chink in the primarch's aloof armour, but he had nothing. Tyro was a warrior, pure and simple; he was ill-equipped for a battle of wits against a primarch.

That wasn't a battle he could win, but as he heard Thamatica's servo arm tap thrice against the deck plates, he knew he wouldn't have to.

Alpharius saw the change in his body language.

'What is it, Cadmus?' he said with a grin. 'Do you think you have hope? Have you conceived a scheme to thwart me?'

'Not me,' said Tyro, nodding to Thamatica. 'Him.'

Tyro threw himself to the floor as the wrecking-ball fist of a Titan smashed through the control hub.

The fist was a manipulator claw, which was just as well, as a true Battle Titan weapon would have killed everyone in the control hub instantly. Detonating metal and machinery slammed into Tyro. His armour cracked open in a dozen places.

The deck fell away as the hub's cantilevered supports were torn apart by the rampage Thamatica had set the Mechanicum engine upon. The world turned upside down as he fell from the ziggurat. He smashed into a lower level, rolled and kept going on a downward trajectory, slammed all the way by the tsunami of debris falling from above.

Bodies flashed through his vision, too fast to see who they were. Hammering impacts smashed him in the chest, driving the breath from him. A spar of something sharp gashed his head. All sense of up and down was instantly lost. Even his Lyman's Ear was incapable of processing the sheer speed and ferocity of his descent.

The avalanche carried him onwards in a river of shattered steelwork that threatened to crush him at any moment. Tyro felt every impact, most violent enough to break bones. His femur shattered like broken ceramic. The ossified bone sheath protecting his chest split down its centre and his collarbone snapped in three places.

The pain was excruciating, but he pushed it down as his genhanced senses at last began to impose some kind of order upon his surroundings.

He'd stopped moving.

The wrecked side of the ziggurat reared up before him, the Titan still pummelling its sides with its clawed hands as if seeking to gouge some treasure from within. A near-constant rain of shattered plasteel and bronzed plating fell from its onslaught. Tyro fought to draw a breath, watching as a blooming explosion wreathed the structure's pinnacle in fire.

Blazing plumes of phosphor-bright promethium arced downwards like pyroclastic fireballs. Secondary blasts rocked the platform wherever they struck something volatile.

On Lerna Two-Twelve that was more or less everything.

Magma-red light bathed the platform in diabolical radiance, like the hell fires of primitive underworlds loosed upon the world. Smoke boiled from ruptured silos, flames roared to the sky from spewing pipes.

Tyro was reminded of the eternal fires of Mount Karaashi, the glowering stratovolcano where the primarch had come to Medusa. Brother Bombastus had been named for that violent peak, even before he'd been interred within his Dreadnought sarcophagus.

A sheet of steel, heat-warped like plastic, pinned him to the ground. Tyro pushed against it, but the weight of debris on top was too much for him.

His armour was inert: plates of buckled, scorched ceramite without power. His generator pack had been torn from his back sometime during his pinwheeling fall.

'I won't die here,' he grunted through the red mist of pain.

'Then shut up and help me lift,' said Thamatica, scrambling through the smoke and cindered rain. He'd had lost all but one of his servo arms, and his craggy features were a mask of clotted blood and oils.

Tyro nodded and forced his arms under the steel, squeezing his eyes shut and gritting his teeth against the pain. Tyro roared as he and Thamatica lifted together. It still wasn't enough.

Then Ignatius Numen was there, adding his vast strength to their effort.

Tyro felt the steel lift a fraction. Enough to scramble his way to freedom.

'Get out,' gasped Numen. 'Now.'

Thamatica and Numen let the sheet fall as Tyro pushed himself onto one knee. His broken leg was a fiery mass of grinding pain, but it would support his weight if he worked with it and not against it.

'Our men?' he said between sucking breaths that told him at least one of his primary lungs had collapsed.

'Cynan's dead,' said Thamatica grimly. 'Sulgan and Dubric are here.'

'Alpharius?'

'No idea,' said Thamatica. 'Hopefully dead.'

'We couldn't be that lucky,' said Tyro, shaking his head.

The motion set off a dozen explosions of pain inside his skull. At least one fracture, maybe more. He'd lost his helmet in the fall and hadn't noticed until now.

'No, you couldn't,' said Alpharius, emerging from the burning rain like a fiend newly risen from the pit. 'But that was a good effort, Frater.'

The primarch's bronzed features were no longer handsome, cut and bloodied in his tumultuous descent, yet he stood unbroken where lesser men had died. The fall had abraded most of the black from his armour, leaving him a giant in bare metal plate.

Matchless anger smouldered in those ever-turning eyes.

Ashur Maesan and Gaskon Malthace stood with their master. Unbelievably, Maesen appeared to have come through the fall virtually unscathed, but Malthace held his right arm across his chest. A knot of splintered bone jutted from the shattered elbow.

'A good effort,' repeated Alpharius. 'But that's all you get.'

The primarch lifted his bolter and put four mass-reactives through Tyro's chest.

IGNATIUS NUMEN DID not consider himself a man of much imagination, but the silent sight of Alpharius gunning down Cadmus Tyro stirred long-forgotten memories of his boyhood on Medusa. It took him back to moonless nights when he thrilled to tales of daemons wrought in silver rising from the planet's spiteful heart.

Daemons, aye, and the heroes that slew them.

Tyro fell, a fountaining arc of blood following him to the ground, and the moment passed. Once again Alpharius was simply an enemy to be killed. A faithless traitor who deserved no such grand mythologising.

Alpharius said something, but Numen's visor was cracked and no words appeared there. Instead, he read them from the primarch's lips.

Kill them.

Ashur Maesan went for Sulgan and Dubric, seeing the iron studs affixed to their helmets. Gaskon Malthace took slow steps towards Numen, swinging the tarnished steel ball on its chain in a rigidly controlled spiral.

Alpharius faced Thamatica, and words passed between them. Numen didn't bother to lip-read. He needed all his focus for his own fight. Peripheral vision registered movement, but Numen blocked it out. At times like this, when total focus was required, his deafness was a boon.

Malthace didn't say anything, and Numen was grateful. They were going to fight and one of them was going to die. What use were words at a time like this?

They circled in the chemical rain like predators sizing up a rival alpha. Malthace kept his flail in motion, the killing head fist-sized and welded with bluntly lethal pyramidal spikes. Numen ignored it and kept his battered chainsword, a weapon that had served him faithfully for thirty-seven years, held wide in a loose, right-handed grip.

Malthace feinted left, stepped right and struck for Numen's knee with shocking speed. He expertly maintained the tension in the chain, keeping the thrust of the haft perfectly in sync with the arc of the spiked head.

Numen spun away, avoiding the spiked mace-head by a fraction. Malthace jerked his arm, whipping it back and sending the ball slamming into Numen's plastron. The force was enormous, and Numen grunted as he felt flesh rupture beneath his armour.

Another blow arced inwards on another crippling parabola.

Numen managed to get his sword up, but the mace-head shattered the blade like porcelain. Serrated teeth flew from the broken sword and Numen roared as one lodged in his left eye lens. The visor fogged with distortion. He stepped away from his opponent as Malthace whipped the killing head of the mace around again.

This time he aimed for Numen's head. The blow was expertly judged, perfectly timed and, against any other warrior than one of the Iron Tenth, would have ended the fight there and then.

Numen reacted the only way he could. He raised his arm and caught the mace-head in the centre of his palm. He gripped it tightly before Malthace could withdraw it.

'Something to be said for having an iron hand,' he said.

Numen shifted his weight and lunged, the iron ball cocked to the hollow of his neck. With his entire mass and momentum behind it, Numen hammered the mace-head through Malthace's faceplate. It tore through his helm and into flesh and bone. The impact shivered up Numen's arm.

Malthace gave a gurgling cry and stumbled back as far as the taut chain links would allow. Ceramite fell from his shattered helmet, and the scale of his wounding was terrible to behold.

The iron ball had caved in the left side of the equerry's face from jawbone to brow. One eye was entirely gone, the other pressed from its orbit by the pressure. Gory runnels ploughed his skin and muscle into trenches. Broken, bloody teeth gaped through rents the spikes had torn.

'On your knees, dog!' bellowed Numen, yanking the chain like a master calling a whipped cur to heel. Malthace mewled in agony and fell to the ground before him, one arm upraised where Numen held the chain and mace-head.

With his free hand, Numen drew his bolt pistol and pressed its muzzle through the gaping hole ripped in Malthace's cheekbone.

Numen pulled the trigger just as the photonic edge of Ashur Maesan's *hiebmesser* plunged in under his ribs on an upward trajectory towards his heart.

THAMATICA WAS HOPELESSLY outclassed and knew it. That he was still alive only confirmed that Alpharius hadn't yet decided to kill him. Such behaviour flew in the face of logic and reason, but perhaps the primarch had passed beyond such things. Alpharius was cutting his armour apart piece by piece.

Sulgan and Dubric were dead, their chests and necks carved apart by Ashur Maesan in half a dozen strokes of his *hiebmesser*. Numen was on his knees over the headless body of Gaskon Malthace, struggling with Maesan who was attempting to drive a blade towards his heart.

Alpharius trapped Thamatica's arm with a twist of his blade and spun him around. The primarch twisted Thamatica's shoulder hard enough to crack bone and wrenched his head towards the storm-wracked sky.

'Do you see, Frater?' said Alpharius. 'Let justice be done as the heavens fall!'

Upon the last word, the ventral plating of the strike cruiser bulged outwards. Moments later, blazing plumes exploded from its flanks, blowing outwards in a percussive cascade of titanic detonations as the lethally volatile fuel-air mix blasted through the vessel's internal compartments.

A vast groaning of metal on metal rolled over Lerna Two-Twelve, like the lowing of a vast plains-dwelling leviathan being brought down by hunters. The prow of the strike cruiser nosed over as explosions pounded through its drive section and drove its stern into the clouds.

The massive fuel lines tore loose, spewing thousands of megalitres of promethium over the stricken vessel. It ignited a microsecond later and flashed back down the pipes to the vast fuelling tower at the centre of the platform.

Emergency shutdowns and flow cut-offs engaged, but against such calamitous speed they had no hope of sealing in time. The central tower exploded, and the entire mass of the platform shook with the power of the blast.

The heat of its detonation washed over Thamatica in a searing wave. He gritted his teeth against the pain, feeling the point of Alpharius's sword press against the underside of his jaw. Blood welled around its tip.

'Fine work, Frater,' said Alpharius. 'Look.'

The strike cruiser was falling, its wedge-shaped prow aimed squarely at Lerna Two-Twelve. It fell slowly, fighting its inevitable demise with dignity. The vessel bore the colours of the enemy, but Thamatica mourned its passing.

'An unworthy end for such a magnificent ship,' he said.

He had no wish to watch so lofty and ingenious a work of man's artifice die, and closed his eyes, knowing his own death would not be long in coming.

'You should watch it die,' said Alpharius, as though reading his thoughts. 'This isn't the kind of thing you'll ever see again.'

Thamatica didn't reply, but set his eye upon a lone spot of darkness within the vast swathes of neon-bright firestorms.

Alpharius followed his gaze, peering into the roiling skies and white-hot plasma hurricanes raging over the ruin of the central fuelling tower.

'What is it, Frater?' said Alpharius. 'What do *you* see when you look into the fire?'

Thamatica grinned.

'Deliverance,' he said.

✠ ✠ ✠

SHARROWKYN'S BOOTS SLAMMED into Ashur Maesan's shoulder guard, sending him sprawling over Malthace's corpse. He rolled as he landed, drawing his twin, black-bladed swords as he sprang to his feet.

Maesan was already up and thrust his *hiebmesser* at Sharrowkyn's throat. He parried with one blade, blocked with the other, surprised and not a little impressed at the sergeant's speed.

He blasted away from the murderous Alpha Legionnaire with a quick burst from his jump pack. Burning debris fell around them and the ground shook with the deep vibrations of platform-wide explosions.

'You're a fast one, little raven,' said Maesan, bobbing his head like a snake as he weaved towards Sharrowkyn with his knife passing from hand to hand. 'But you'll find old Maesan's faster – oh yes, faster by far. I've already claimed four scalps, but yours will be today's crowning achievement. Come closer and let me clip your wings.'

Sharrowkyn took the measure of the man. He knew nothing of the Alpha Legion's roots, where they came from, the culture that birthed them or the hardships that shaped them. Maesan's skill was great, but Sharrowkyn couldn't pinpoint its nuances. That he was fast, agile and ruthless was beyond question, but Sharrowkyn saw a well of lunacy, deep as an ocean in his eyes.

'You're insane,' said Sharrowkyn.

'Makes two of us then, little raven,' said Maesan.

They flew at one another and their blades tore like talons.

Maesan swayed aside from each killing thrust, the *hiebmesser* blocking Sharrowkyn's blows with extraordinary speed. Sharrowkyn had seldom fought faster. Only the laughing swordsman with the mask of scars he'd killed on Iydris came close.

He found himself bleeding from his hip and neck without even realising he'd been struck. Maesan's every blow was masked by a feint, every seeming killing thrust a subterfuge for a deeper wound.

Maesan danced back, his blade orange with the flames of the platform's destruction and wet with Raven Guard blood.

He wiped it on his vambrace.

'Not used to being cut, are you, little raven?' Maesan said.

Sharrowkyn took a faltering step back, letting his blades sag. Maesan grinned, thinking him already defeated.

The Alpha Legionnaire rushed him, and Sharrowkyn let one blade fall as he bent his knee like a runner at the blocks. He triggered his jump pack and launched himself at Maesan. The move caught the traitor by surprise, but he recovered with blinding speed, ducking from the path of the powered lunge.

As Sharrowkyn had known he would.

Gripping the warrior's lowered shoulder guard like a pivot, Sharrowkyn arced over Maesan like the sweeping hand of a clock. Vertical, he aimed his remaining sword and triggered the jump pack once more.

Sharrowkyn's black blade plunged into the trove of vital organs and blood vessels behind Maesan's collarbone. He twisted around to straddle Maesan as speed and mass drove his opponent to his knees.

With his sword buried hilt-deep, Sharrowkyn churned the blade like a lever. Arteries blew apart, hearts ruptured and lungs collapsed. Hot, blood-frothed breath blasted from Maesan's opened mouth. He spasmed in shock and pain, still trying to throw Sharrowkyn off. But the strength was leaving him with every passing second and every mouthful of blood clogging his throat.

Sharrowkyn kept the blade moving until he was certain no life remained.

He looked up in time to see the warrior with Shadrak Meduson's body and a primarch's face walking slowly towards him. He held Frater Thamatica in one hand as though he weighed nothing at all.

'You're Alpharius, aren't you?' said Sharrowkyn. 'The real one, I mean, not a *doppelgänger* or some homunculus?'

'I'm as real as I need to be right now,' said Alpharius, tossing Frater Thamatica to land alongside Cadmus Tyro.

Sharrowkyn rose from Maesan's corpse and circled slowly towards the fallen Iron Hands. He bent to retrieve the sword he'd dropped. Somewhere nearby, a refinery exploded. A blazing cloud of white flame mushroomed skywards.

'You're good, I'll give you that,' said Alpharius, with an appreciative nod as he mirrored Sharrowkyn's movements, 'I was sure Maesan would kill you.'

'We Raven Guard are hard to kill. Isstvan should have taught you that,' said Sharrowkyn, dropping into a fighting stance and readying his swords. Petrochemical droplets slid down each blade, cutting through their coatings of ash.

'Clearly you haven't heard what's been happening on Deliverance,' grinned Alpharius, bending to retrieve Ashur Maesan's *hiebmesser*.

Sharrowkyn tensed, expecting an attack.

'Put your blades away, Nykona,' said Alpharius, sheathing the butcher's knife. 'I said you were good, but that shadow-slipping trick my brother taught you won't work on me.'

'We'll see,' said Sharrowkyn, angling his sword blades, one low, one high.

'No, we won't,' said Alpharius, turning to walk away.

'You're not going to fight me?'

'As much as I want to, I'm not going to kill you, Nykona. At least, not today,' said Alpharius. 'Magnus asked me not to.'

'Good to know,' said Sharrowkyn, sheathing his swords.

Alpharius laughed. 'I like you, Nykona. You're a man who'll saddle a gift horse rather than look it in the mouth.'

Sharrowkyn knew good counsel when he heard it, but couldn't help himself from asking. 'Then what was all this for? Why all the secrets and lies? Why entangle us in this?'

Alpharius looked up into the firestorm engulfing Lerna Two-Twelve. 'Ask Tyro to tell you, if he survives.'

Sharrowkyn said, 'I will,' and bent to check on Thamatica and Tyro. He wasn't sure he believed Alpharius wouldn't kill them all, and kept a wary eye on the primarch. Thamatica was already stirring, the flex-seal at his neck crumpled by intense crushing pressure.

Thamatica groaned and said, 'Cadmus...' his voice little more than a shattered, wet wheeze.

Cadmus Tyro was bleeding out, four mass-reactives making his chest look like the leavings of a greenskin feast.

His eyes were wide with pain, his skin paler than Sharrowkyn's alabaster complexion. That he was alive at all was a miracle, but he expected nothing less from a captain of the Iron Tenth.

Alpharius was now just a shadow, a blurred outline in the smoke. Blazing promethium billowed and seethed around him, but did not touch him. Other shapes moved in the smoke wreathing the primarch, warriors in the dark plate of the Iron Hands, though none were as they seemed.

'I said *I* wouldn't kill you,' said Alpharius, backing away into the flames and smoke with every word. 'But I think *that* might.'

Sharrowkyn looked up.

The dozer-blade prow of the wrecked strike cruiser sliced from the tempests wracking the sky, plunging towards Lerna Two-Twelve and its doom.

'Thamatica,' said Sharrowkyn. 'Help me with Tyro.'

TWELVE

Always somewhere to go
Punch it
Equals

THOUGH THEY BOTH knew there was no escape, Sharrowkyn and Thamatica dragged Cadmus Tyro from the wreckage. Ignatius Numen followed, limping and with a metalled hand pressed to his side where Maesan's blade had sought to gut him.

They managed to reach the edge of the ziggurat refinery before the prow of the strike cruiser slammed into Lerna Two-Twelve. Its descent had seemed ponderous, almost leisurely, but its mass and momentum were devastating.

All four warriors were thrown to the deck as it lurched upwards like a tectonic shift. The noise was deafening, a roaring, grinding, crashing thunder without end. The shriek of tortured, buckling metal was the platform's death scream and a bellow of hatred all in one.

Sharrowkyn's stomach lurched as he felt Lerna Two-Twelve being dragged downwards by the unstoppable force of the strike cruiser's impact. Its repulsor banks fought to keep the platform in the sky, but that was a hopeless battle.

More explosions painted the sky and blooming clouds of ignited gases rippled outwards to the horizon like an oncoming thunderhead.

Sharrowkyn had seen mine fires like that, a cascade of ignition that only ever ended badly.

Thamatica saw it too.

'The crystallised promethium in the atmosphere has reached its flashpoint.'

Sharrowkyn sprang to his feet as a towering wall of flame rose up behind them from the ruptured refuelling tower. Billions of cubic litres of promethium blasted their confining silos to vapour in an instant, and uncapped geysers of volatile explosive material added to the mix. A tsunami of white-hot liquid flame raced towards them, blinding in its intensity and throwing their shadows out behind them.

'Come on, help me,' said Sharrowkyn.

Thamatica nodded and helped the Raven Guard warrior lift Tyro's near-lifeless body. The air began to spark all around them, as if they'd blundered into a thousand swarms of fireflies.

The chemical-rich atmosphere was starting to ignite.

'There's nowhere to go,' said Thamatica, but despite his words, he kept going.

'There's always somewhere to go,' snapped Sharrowkyn.

'Where?' grunted Thamatica, risking a glance over his shoulder. 'There's a tidal wave of molten promethium racing towards us, the very air is about to combust and this entire platform is moments away from falling into an acid ocean. I'll keep going to the very end, Brother Sharrowkyn, have no fear of that, but tell me, *where* can we go?'

'Wayland!' shouted Numen.

Thamatica shook his head. 'Sabik was shot down, Ignatius, we heard it on the vox,' he said. 'Medus... that is, Alpharius's Stormbird blew him out of the sky.'

'Wayland!' repeated Numen, pushing past Thamatica.

Sharrowkyn turned and there it was, perforated by gunfire and holed by missile detonations, but still airborne.

One of its engines was on fire, but Sabik Wayland's Storm Eagle was as much X Legion as its warriors, and it never gave up, never quit fighting and never left a man behind.

'There's always somewhere to go,' said Sharrowkyn.

LEAVING TYRO IN the care of Numen and Thamatica, Sharrowkyn fought his way through the steeply canted crew compartment of the Storm Eagle. Its hull was shaking as though ready to come apart at the seams and the scream of its tortured engines was that of a man wounded beyond any tolerance of pain.

He hauled himself upwards, using hanging stowage straps and buckled stanchions to reach the cockpit. Sabik Wayland wrestled with the controls, fighting the searing thermals trying to swat them from the sky.

Sharrowkyn threw himself into the co-pilot's seat. He strapped himself in and did his best not to distract Wayland as he threaded a needle path through the destruction of Lerna Two-Twelve. The Storm Eagle juddered, and Sharrowkyn felt sure he heard something tear loose from the hull's exterior.

The temperature within the cockpit was phenomenal and still rising. It felt like the interior of a blast oven or the heart of a rust desert. The promethium tsunami was almost upon them.

'Got to break atmosphere, Sabik,' he said. 'Quickly.'

'We can. We will,' said Wayland, the latter as much a request of the aircraft as it was an answer. 'But don't speak to me until we do.'

The gunship banked and swooped and dived, its flight path a spiralling, looping nightmare as Wayland fought to anticipate volcanic eruptions of promethium, collapsing silo towers and blizzards of steelwork caught in fire-tornadoes.

It felt like the gunship was under fire above a dropzone, but this was worse than any flak-storm Sharrowkyn had endured. Flames roared over the armourglass canopy, and he gripped the edges of the seat as the view beyond was entirely obscured.

'Throne!' cried Sharrowkyn.

'I said don't talk!'

Sharrowkyn bit back an angry response, and forced himself to watch the lunatic path Wayland was flying. He saw a gap ahead, a break in the unending torrent of debris and flames filling the sky.

He shouted and pointed, but Wayland had already seen it.

Wayland threw the Storm Eagle into a bellowing climb, and Sharrowkyn felt sure the aircraft was going to shake itself apart. Screens shattered on the avionics panel, the armourglass cracked. Heat spiked.

Sharrowkyn hammered his fist against his chest in a last gesture of defiance in the face of death.

He kept hammering until Wayland said, 'We're clear.'

Sharrowkyn opened his eyes and found himself staring into the blackness of the exosphere. The void was above, and the heat within the cockpit began dropping off rapidly. The Storm Eagle ceased its attempts to shake itself into a mass of components.

'We're clear,' repeated Wayland, and Sharrowkyn let out a long stream of breath.

'Throne, that was incredible flying.'

Wayland shrugged and said, 'Who's back there? I couldn't see clear enough against the glare.'

'Too few,' said Sharrowkyn. 'Thamatica and Numen are tending to Cadmus. He's hurt. Badly. He might not make it back to the *Sisypheum*.'

Wayland pushed out the engines.

'He's Iron Tenth,' said Wayland, as if that explained everything, and Sharrowkyn supposed it did. 'He'll make it.'

SHARROWKYN LEFT THE flying to Wayland and went aft to check in with Thamatica and Numen. The gunship's interior felt horribly empty now. The warriors who'd begun this mission with the prospect of revenge filling their bellies were now ash.

Names flashed through Sharrowkyn's mind, faces. He had lost so many brothers in the XIX Legion, and the brothers of the *Sisypheum* were no less his kin for having a different gene-sire.

Numen sat propped up in his grav-harness, and only the fractional rise and fall of his chest told Sharrowkyn he wasn't dead. He put a hand on Numen's brow, the skin oily and hot as his body diverted its energies to healing the grievous hurt done by Maesan's churning blade.

Sharrowkyn knelt beside the mortally wounded clan-captain. Thamatica had stripped the few remaining portions of Tyro's shattered plate. From the gory horror of what the mass-reactives had done to him, Sharrowkyn suspected another name would soon be added to the *Sisypheum*'s wall of the fallen.

'He lives?'

The Ironwrought looked up and said, 'Death's got his claws in deep, aye, but Cadmus won't go without a fight.'

'Can I do anything?'

'No, and though it galls me to say it, neither can I. To live or to die will be the captain's choice.'

'Then he'll live forever,' said Sharrowkyn.

'Your words give me hope, Son of Corax,' said Thamatica, rocking back onto his haunches. 'You would have made a fine Iron Hands legionary if only you'd had the fortune to be born on Medusa.'

Sharrowkyn took the compliment as it was intended, leaving unsaid the fact that he would sooner have let Alpharius kill him than not be Raven Guard.

He pushed himself to his feet and took a seat against the cold metal of the fuselage.

'So what now for the *Sisypheum*?' he asked.

'What do you mean?'

'Look how many we lost down there. With all we have left we can just about fly the ship, but can it fight?'

'So long as the *Sisypheum* has a crew it can fight,' said Cadmus Tyro, coughing a wad of bloody phlegm. 'You hear me, Sharrowkyn?'

'Don't talk, Cadmus,' said Thamatica. 'Save your strength.'

'I hear you,' said Sharrowkyn.

'I should have heard *you*,' said Tyro. 'You warned us of this.'

Sharrowkyn didn't answer. Recriminations would achieve nothing, save to tear Tyro's wounds wider.

'You now have a voice aboard my ship,' said Tyro. 'Use it when you must. As an equal. The *Sisypheum* is no longer an Iron Hands vessel. It's a ship of warriors, and every voice matters.'

'I'll use my voice, Cadmus, count on it,' Sharrowkyn promised.

Tyro turned his head, and Sharrowkyn felt the heat of the clan-captain's gaze. It bored into him like a lascutter, demanding truth to be the next thing passing his lips.

'What did Alpharius mean?' said Tyro.

'About what?'

'You know what,' grunted Tyro. 'Why does Magnus the Red want you alive?'

'I don't know,' said Sharrowkyn. 'I never served alongside the Fifteenth, let alone met the Crimson King.'

'Should I believe that?'

'Why would you not?' countered Sharrowkyn. 'Alpharius is a master manipulator – a purveyor of lies, untruths and misinformation. Nothing he says can be believed.'

Tyro nodded and his eyes squeezed shut as wracking pain convulsed him. Thamatica held his shoulders as the wave subsided.

'There's truth in that,' agreed Tyro. 'Let me cling to that on this day of lies.'

'What did he mean about Deliverance?' asked Sharrowkyn.

THE SISYPHEUM HUNG in the void like a beaten ingot fresh from the fire. Its hull was gnarled and pocked with recent impacts, its blunt, pugnacious prow still crumpled from the impact with the *Andronius*.

Wayland guided the Storm Eagle towards it with gentle manoeuvres, fearful the gunship might fall to pieces were he to move too suddenly. Even a glance told him the *Sisypheum* had been in a desperate fight since he had last laid eyes upon her.

'What happened?' said Sharrowkyn, his humours black since his return from the crew compartment.

'That,' said Wayland, pointing to where the gutted wreck of the *Iron Heart* smouldered just beyond the *Sisypheum*'s quarterdeck. Even from here it was clear to see the two ships had been tearing at one another like rabid dogs in a cage.

That the *Iron Heart* should have come after the *Sisypheum* was no surprise, but that the outcome appeared to have been so one-sided was. The *Iron Heart* had been pummelled mercilessly, disembowelled by weapons fire and emptied of life with repeated broadsides.

'Throne, I never knew that Tarsa had the heart of a void warrior,' said Sharrowkyn.

'Vulkan's sons are full of surprises,' said Wayland, guiding the Storm Eagle towards the forwards embarkation deck. The same deck upon which they had welcomed the false Shadrak Meduson. That an enemy primarch had trod the halls of the *Sisypheum* sent a horror of violation through Wayland.

The chamfered opening to the embarkation deck grew steadily in the cracked glass of the cockpit. Wayland nudged the controls, angling the gunship to pass seamlessly through the centre of the integrity field.

He felt the lurch of ship gravity and gently set the Storm Eagle down on the nearest launch rail. He let out a breath it felt like he'd been holding since realising the truth of the betrayal visited upon them. Just being back on the *Sisypheum* renewed Wayland, gave him hope that something good might be salvaged from this disastrous mission.

If not even the trap of a primarch could lay low the crew of the *Sisypheum*, then perhaps they *would* live forever.

Then he remembered Ferrus Manus and his hope was crushed.

He followed Sharrowkyn back into the crew compartment. Atesh Tarsa was already on the gunship, as were a gaggle of medicae servitors slathered in dark fluids. They lifted Cadmus onto a suspensor stretcher as Tarsa set up numerous drips and applied pressure bandages.

The Apothecary's dark skin was bathed in sweat, but after a void fight like the one that had ended the *Iron Heart*, Wayland wasn't surprised.

Tarsa glanced up, and Wayland saw wariness in his crimson eyes, quickly masked. Then the Apothecary hurried from the gunship with Cadmus Tyro upon the stretcher. Garuda perched on its edge, but flew off as soon as it began to move.

Thamatica, Wayland, Sharrowkyn and Numen followed him from the Storm Eagle, and Numen fell to his knees as soon as he set foot on the deck. The Avernii veteran bent to kiss the deck like a superstitious feral-worlder.

Wayland called after Tarsa, 'You fought well, Apothecary,' said Wayland. Tarsa shook his head and gestured to a presence just out of sight behind the Storm Eagle's smoking engine.

Something massive took a heavy step around the gunship, and Wayland retreated before the towering, armoured machine that came into view.

It was Brother Bombastus.

Who had last walked as a Dreadnought.

But this was no Dreadnought, and Bombastus was dead. This was a nightmarish fusion of technology and biology and mechanical necromancy. The towering construct had no sarcophagus, merely a cable-wound cocoon of raw sutures and bare flesh.

At its heart, bound into its workings by crude biomechanical interfaces, were the ruined scraps of meat and bone and hate that once commanded the *Sisypheum*.

'Tarsa didn't kill the *Iron Heart*,' said Ulrach Branthan. 'I did.'

HAND ELECT

Chris Wraight

HE COULD WALK again. He could raise his left arm. His blood circu-
lated, his hearts beat.

Yet Jebez Aug was a shade, a weakened element in a Legion of weakened
elements, and that was detestable. For many months he had been in the
warleader's shadow, impotent and unregarded, undergoing procedure after
procedure to restore his ravaged flesh and broken iron. Despite his stated
defiance after the Oqueth massacre, there had been nights when he had
countenanced a darker outcome – that he might yet die of his wounds,
or be rendered so weak that he would remain an encumbrance to an
Iron Hands strike force that already carried too many walking wounded.

In the end, it had not been defiance that had carried him through.

It had been shame.

A burning, gnawing desire to make amends. There was still work
to do, atrocities to be avenged, and so he lived, and he suffered the
agonies of renewal.

And gradually, his physical capability returned. Slowly, his mind
turned to what he was, and what he had been, and what he could yet
be again.

Perhaps, in time, that process could have been completed on board the *Iron Heart*, but the shortage of... well, *everything* made it doubtful. Gorgonson was a competent Apothecary, but Aug's needs went beyond mere flesh-matter and into that tangled, troubled interface with the machine. Once, the Legion could have met those needs easily, but now its remnants were forced to run from haven to haven, begging for what they couldn't steal, swallowing down their pride lest it stick in their throats.

He looked up from his meal tray then – a slab loaded with tasteless void rations – to see the blackened-steel profile of Goran Gorgonson staring at him.

'And?' Aug asked.

'We are in visual range of Lliax, lord Frater,' Gorgonson said, bowing slightly. 'I thought you would want to know.'

Aug nodded. The journey from Meduson's side in the escort frigate *Dannang* had taken far longer than he had hoped. Then again, every journey took longer now as they clawed their way through the tormented mire of the warp, so it was indeed good to know that they had reached their destination safely. Such things could not be relied upon as they had been in the past.

'Any signal from the magos?' he murmured.

'Not yet. We are hailing.'

Aug set his tray aside, placing it on the table next to his recliner couch. There was a time when addressing a battle-brother while seated would have been an unthinkable breach of decorum. Now it was just another petty humiliation. 'You are still angry with me.'

Gorgonson only hesitated for a microsecond. 'I do not know what you mean.'

'You believe you could have repaired my flesh.' Aug eased his shoulder in a half circle, feeling the steel ball-and-socket interface scrape. 'And you believe that we should not have left the warleader's side.'

'He needs you, that is certain.'

'He has his fourfold council. In any case, what use am I to him like this? An Iron Father is more than just a counsellor.'

Gorgonson didn't reply. His helm – daubed night-black, its lenses bleeding a soft red glow – gave away nothing, but his exposed face would have been equally stony. For a Terran, the Apothecary was admirably unreadable.

'You think I pursue my own aims over his,' said Aug, shifting painfully in his recliner. 'Not so. I must join him as Hand Elect again, and for that I must be restored. You could not have done it. And there is no shame in that, for you do not have the tools.'

'But these... outsiders...'

'They are no such thing. We have worked with them before. *Fought* with them before. They are among the last of our true allies.'

Gorgonson paused again, as if he was considering one final entreaty. Before he could speak, however, a click from his helm gave away a comm-burst from the bridge.

'They have responded, lord Frater,' the Apothecary reported. 'Archmagos Dominus Pharmakos Lev Termadian bids you welcome to Lliax, and extends all hospitality protocols. He has been made aware of the reason for your mission and has instructed his staff to make preparations.'

If there was reproach lurking in those words, Gorgonson masked it well.

'Good,' said Aug, flexing the muscle-bundles of his partially disassembled right-leg augmetic. He would need to walk soon, and somehow hide the pain of it. 'Send him thanks, and make preparations for planetfall. I have been a half-formed thing for too long. It is time for restoration.'

FROM LOW ORBIT, the forge world Lliax glowed like a star, swathed in a nimbus of dirty orange that turned and churned like plasma. Only once the lander had broken through the upper reaches of the atmosphere did it become apparent that the effect was created by planet-wide

palls of heavy smog, lit from within and below by the ceaseless workings of continent-wide forge complexes.

Gorgonson stared out of the lander's starboard viewport, watching
the fiery vistas swell up towards him. Jets of bluish flame burst out
from iron-capped wellheads, lost among remorseless kilometres of
criss-crossed pipe lanes. Gases plumed from the crowns of dark chim-
ney towers, each one marked with the Machina Opus emblem of old
Mars. The seamy, humid air was filled with crawling atmos-haulers,
plying their way through the murk like agri-harvesters scouring the
nutrient fields.

Aug sat opposite him in the lander's crew-bay, slumped against the
inner wall, breathing with the snapping click of a damaged helm.
The two of them were alone, bar the pilots and a skeleton honour
guard of thralls in the bay below. Meduson had been able to spare
none of his own warriors for the journey, a decision for which Gorgonson did not blame him. If Aug wished to make the perilous errand
to the domains of the Mechanicum, whose loyalty to the Throne was
now as suspect as any in a galaxy riven by treachery, the warleader
had judged that it could not be allowed to risk the fragile strength of
the clan-companies.

Below them, rapidly growing in size and clarity, was the angular bulk
of a command ziggurat, soaring over the iron forge-plains and crowned
with a circlet of red halo-beams. Taghmata macro-lifters hung above it
on smoky downdraughts like a shroud of vultures, their spewed effluent
merging with the drifting carpets of filth below them. In orbit, now lost
beyond the veils of glowing clouds, were command-arks, their arcane
weaponry trained on the *Dannang*. Lliax, like all worlds of the known
galaxy, was now on full war footing, cranking out greater volumes of
weaponry with every passing day, gearing up for the inevitable impact
of the Warmaster's all-conquering battle-front.

The X Legion lander slowed, coming under the influence of the ziggurat's grav-shunts. A cavernous hangar set two-thirds of the way up
the leading slope opened. Gorgonson watched in silence as its interior

swallowed them, marking the dim ranks of skitarii silently tracking them from flanking galleries.

The lander travelled along the entire length of the hangar, guided by the shunts, before roughly being set down. With some effort, Aug got to his feet, planting the heel of his staff against the deck to steady himself. Gorgonson waited, saying nothing, letting the Iron Father gather his strength.

The blast doors opened. Clusters of robed tech-thralls waited for them, chattering in bird-like, semi-audible binaric cant. Beyond those stood static maniples of Thallax battle-automata, bronze-crowned, their photon thrusters trained with silent accuracy. In the distance, across the vast expanse of the ziggurat's landing stage, greater constructs stalked awkwardly through a haze of red – Castellax monsters, accompanied by teams of cable-faced, arch-backed Myrmidon Secutors.

Before them all stood the lone figure of what had once been a mortal, robed in dun-red and with exposed skeletal fingers of tapered steel. From under its cowl, an insectoid cluster of lenses pulsed.

'Be welcome to forge world Lliax, lords of Medusa,' it said, in an emotionless husk of a voice. 'Your mission is known to us. Your needs will be met.'

Aug bowed. The movement was fluid enough, and Gorgonson couldn't help but be impressed by the Iron Father's sheer willpower. 'My thanks,' said Aug. 'How may we know you?'

'I am designated Shaelecta. The magos dominus is expecting you. It will be efficient for you to join him now.' The tech-priest turned to Gorgonson. 'You are intact, but your armour is damaged. I can assist. It will be efficient for you to join me now.'

Gorgonson looked to Aug, who nodded his assent.

'You have my thanks,' the Iron Father said to Shaelecta. 'Tell your master I am eager to begin.'

THE INTERIOR OF the ziggurat was honeycombed with a succession of huge chambers, all humming with the grind and crash of machinery.

Skitarii were everywhere, overseeing companies of servitors, lesser automata and mortal forge-adepts. It was hot. Punishingly hot.

Gorgonson and Shaelecta traversed through the levels, borne above the tumult by chain-draped grav-platforms, surrounded at all times by sinuous Scyllax guardians, their skulls glinting in the firelit gloom and their mechadendrites snapping around them.

Goran Gorgonson was used to forges. His Medusan brothers had practically grown up amid the sparks and hammers of their home world's hyper-industrial fortress cities, but even he, as a Terran, had seen plenty. Since the rediscovery of the primarch, the entire Legion had become a brotherhood of tech-wrights, delving ever deeper into the lore of the machine in order to hone their mastery of the many forms of battle.

So Lliax was not an entirely alien environment, but nor was it a familiar one. The air smelled strange – heavy with incense and ritual oils, as if spiced. The servitors were not merely lobotomised human stock, but bizarre fusions of neural conduits and brain-matter, some fused into the anvils they serviced, others stretched and warped into more strenuous amalgams of metal and flesh.

'The war has not reached this world,' Gorgonson observed, as they rose higher still, passing rows of metal presses stamping out boltgun casings.

'Incorrect,' said Shaelecta. 'Seven attacks have been repelled from without, each one larger than the last. Magos Dominos Pharmakos calculates the next attempt will occur within four months, Martian-standard.'

'And you have the means to defend yourselves?'

'Look around you. We create a new maniple every seven hours. Pharmakos wishes to accelerate this.'

'And... from within? Your own kind?' This was a delicate question.

Shaelecta gave no indication of offence. 'Elements within the lower grid were corrupted at the outset, before we knew what to look for. Purges have been thorough. You need have no doubt, Medusan – Lliax cleaves to the Omnissiah.'

More chambers swept by, dizzying in their number and variety. To

Gorgonson's eyes there seemed no pattern to the distribution of manu-
factoria, but every unit was operating at a furious tilt, depositing heaps
of munitions in silos, or winching steaming armour plates from cooling
vats and up towards the assembly chambers, or welding engine cases
together as they trundled along conveyor belts to waiting vehicle shells.

It seemed infinite, inexhaustible. He knew that every facility on the
planet would be working at a similar rate.

They reached a high arming chamber, as clogged with smoke and
incense as all the others, windowless and deafening. Tilt-hammers
swung down onto massive anvils, smashing out adamantium components in showers of sparks. Tech-priests with iron snouts protruding
from charred cowls hovered over their creations, rejecting any imperfec-
tions and ceaselessly monitoring the output of hundreds of labouring
forge-thralls.

Shaelecta and the Scyllax attendants came to a halt before a vast
series of altarpieces, all studded with devotional tracts. Finished armour
plates hung from thick chains above every surface, turning gently in
the fervid air. Hundreds of broad pads, vambraces, sabatons and
breastplates had been suspended over the altars, each one primed but
unpainted. Teams of servitors, their pale flesh punched through with
iron impulse-shackles, prostrated themselves before the rotating components, mumbling autoscreed through vox-emitters lodged in their
throats and chests.

'Your right pauldron and left greave are defective,' said Shaelecta.
'Allow us to rectify that.'

Gorgonson looked up at the rows of pristine armour pieces. Every
conceivable mark was represented in that gallery across a number of
variants, and he had no doubt that the artisans would be able to make
it fit him perfectly.

Shaelecta was correct: his battleplate carried a number of long-running
faults, none of which could be properly mended with the resources
they had on the *Iron Heart*. And yet, this armour was the protection
that had kept him alive on Isstvan, and which he had tended since,

and which he had promised himself he would take to Medusa for refashioning one day.

He looked down at the prostrate servitors, each still mumbling their benedictions, entirely unaware of his presence. Further down the line, out towards the far end of the arming chamber, a living thrall was being tied down to an obsidian block, stretched out under an array of mechadendrites extending from the smoke-thick ceiling. The man was mouthing some kind of litany from panicked lips, staring up at the needles hovering over his face as he was secured in position.

'What is being done to him?' asked Gorgonson.

Shaelecta's voice was impassive. 'He will serve better. He will be made passive, as the forges demand.'

Gorgonson looked away as the needle-thicket was lowered into place. Above him, the empty armour fragments hung amid their plumes of incense, ready for the application of Legion livery.

He looked back at Shaelecta. The tech-priest's metal faceplate was hidden under its cowl, masked by both shadow and coarse fabric. The thrall's screams were shrill, and went on, and on...

'I thank you for the offer,' Gorgonson said, turning away, 'but I will attend the Iron Father now.'

Shaelecta cogitated that for a moment. In the distance, the sounds of agony slowly died away, replaced by throttled gurgles as nutrient tubes were inserted. A team of dull-eyed menials shuffled up to the obsidian slab bearing impulse shackles for the new servitor.

'As you wish,' said the tech-priest, sweeping round to follow the Apothecary. 'I will locate him. I will guide you.'

LEFT ALONE, AUG waited for twenty-nine minutes and forty-seven seconds.

His Mechanicum guardians had melted away, chittering back into the gloom with their robes rustling dryly behind them, leaving him in the circular chamber to await the magos dominus.

The walls were blood-red, cloaked in shadow and marked with long binaric sequences. He studied some of them, but the code fragments were obscure, most likely obsolete. Perhaps this was a repository of old knowledge, buried in the heart of the pyramid, kept safe during the long years of turmoil. A reliquary, of sorts.

We were supposed to have put these religious trappings aside, Aug thought, flexing a pain-slug into his bloodstream. *But who would tell the Martians that?*

During the wait, his mind began to work, imagining the stature and form of his host. No doubt the magos would be some fused thing, his mortal-born body pulled and twisted into something more elevated and austere. And yet they had all been infants once, Aug reflected, these monsters of brass and lacquer. Once their pudgy fists had clenched and their soft cheeks blushed from bawling.

Then again, so had he been, in the long-forgotten past.

As the eighth second of the thirtieth minute slid down his helm's chrono, a panel in the chamber's far wall finally creaked open, hissing as a gout of steam spilled from leaking pull-pistons. Aug turned slowly to face the aperture, and saw waiting a mirror image of himself – black armour, the pale tracery of Iron Hands combat markings, a pair of red lenses glaring back at him.

'Iron Father,' came a voice that was both alike and unlike to his own.

'Iron Father,' Aug replied, bowing painfully. 'You might have given me some warning you were here.'

Frater Kernag, of Clan Garrsak, returned the bow. 'Comms signals may be tracked. These things are better done in person.'

'How did you know I would be here?'

'Like I said – comms signals may be tracked.'

Aug regarded his opposite number. Kernag occupied a roughly equivalent rank to him in the old X Legion hierarchy. The Iron Fathers had always held an ambiguous role – part guardians of the Legion's soul, part throwback to a pre-Imperial culture of machine mysticism. Now, though, who knew what their role was? The balance of power within such a scattered brotherhood had come to lie in mere force of will, or old pacts between souls, or little more than blind luck.

'I take it,' Aug ventured, 'that the warleader did not send you.'

'He does not govern our coming and our going. He never has. And that is why I am here, as you may already know.'

Aug softly ran a threat-scan of the chamber. No other life-readings were within range. Kernag held no weapon. 'No, Frater,' he said, 'I do not. Enlighten me.'

Kernag drew close, in a gesture reminiscent of old-Earth conspiracies. The movement was surely futile, as every chamber in this place was likely studded with dozens of Mechanicum listening devices, but still he did it, as if for courtesy's sake.

'How fares the warleader?' he asked quietly.

'He endures,' said Aug. 'Dwell was a setback, but the war continues.'

'And his greater task?'

'More join us every hour. He is pulling what remains of the Legion to his banner, just as we asked him to.'

'*I* never asked him to.'

Aug thought carefully before replying. 'But even you can see the victories he has brought us.'

'I see a future for the Legion even without the clan-fathers, that much is certain.' Kernag turned away from him, casting his gaze over the binaric engravings. 'Yet you did not consult us, before you passed Shadrak Meduson the mantle of leadership.'

'I cannot believe–'

'That we would not welcome it?' Kernag shook his head. 'What do you think Meduson can achieve, in truth? A few strikes on a greater enemy, buying a little more time for those who failed to aid us and creating a larger target for the enemy to locate and destroy. If you had come to me, and asked my counsel, I would have told you this.'

Aug regarded his counterpart cautiously. 'You have spoken favourably of him before.'

'Biding our time. We did not prevent any who wished to serve under his banner from going to him, but we always told them – a true council will come. We will return to Medusa, and we will decide our Legion's future there. That has not changed.'

'And so, what of the war?'

'What of it?' Kernag reached out to trace an armoured finger along the lines of nonsensical algorithms. 'We cannot end it. We cannot alter its course. Our only task is to *survive* it.'

Aug scoffed. 'Little good being alive, without honour.'

'No doubt, but do not equate honour with weakness. We owe no one, we are owed by no one.' He turned away from the binaric inscriptions and looked at Aug squarely. 'Here is the thesis, one that you know but will not admit – we were destroyed by the primarch. He was the single point of failure, the one that brought down the machine. He was not of Medusa, not truly. You know this, and it cost us all. And now, what are we doing in his wake? We retread history, and set up a figurehead, a cult of personality. We create a new single point, weaker than the old, and again born of Terra. A kind of insanity, you might say.'

'Ah, then you need say no more,' sighed Aug. 'I know what follows. You will convene your council on Medusa. The Iron Fathers will take up command of the Legion, just as the clan-fathers tried to.'

'That was always our way.'

'Until Ferrus.'

'Quite so.'

Aug rounded on Kernag then. 'And you would *never* have spoken thus, were he still alive! *Now* you tell this story of weakness, but you never gave it voice before.'

Kernag shrugged. 'We cannot change the past.'

'Meduson is not the primarch.'

'No. It is one of his few merits.'

Aug felt his anger flare up hotter, hard to quell, and had to prevent himself reaching for his blade. 'You have wasted your time,' he said. 'You have wasted the effort to track me here, and you have misjudged my mind in this. When I am restored, I will be his Hand Elect. If we are doomed to die, then so be it – but we shall do so with weapons in our hands.'

Kernag drew in a long, thin breath. 'I came to show you the path of reason, my brother. You are still an Iron Father. You would be among us, guiding the Legion.'

'No. Meduson is giving them hope again. I will not see you take that away.'

Regretfully, Kernag held his gaze, but said nothing in reply. Aug kept his gauntlet close to the handle of his short chainaxe, and tried to judge how quickly he could reach for it in his weakened state. The air between the two of them seemed to thicken, as if charged with static.

Then, slowly, Kernag relaxed. As he did so, another panel in the far wall of the chamber slid open. On the far side loomed a huge mass of bronze coils and mechadendrites and claws, all draped over and underneath a golden mask, then heaped with thick robes of deepest crimson. With a shuffle of segmented metal and a hiss of opening rebreather apertures, the magos dominus slid into the chamber, accompanied by floating censers and a swarm of nano-drones.

'My lords,' intoned Pharmakos, as emptily as Shaelecta had done before. 'I regret the intrusion, but all is in readiness for the procedure. I trust you might conclude your business speedily?'

'We have nothing more to say to one another,' said Aug, turning away from Kernag to bow to the magos.

'He will not take you back into his confidence,' said Kernag, still speaking to Aug. 'He has his own advisors now, just as Ferrus did. The Hand Elect is an empty title, bestowed to keep you leashed to him. Heal your wounds, I implore you... But it will not bring you what you wish for.'

But Aug was no longer listening. From beyond the magos he could see another chamber opening up, ringed with flesh-carvers and metal scourers. In the midst of it all he could see a medicae slab, held ready for the opening up of his battered mortal frame. There would be pain on that table, but also restitution.

'I have endured enough,' said Aug, limping towards the chamber. 'But no more – start the procedure.'

Pharmakos looked up as Aug passed him, his empty golden eyes alighting upon Kernag. For a moment, the Iron Father of Garrsak did not respond. Then, almost imperceptibly, he nodded.

Pharmakos returned a fractional bow and swung around, his robes sliding over the polished metal floor.

'As you will it, Medusan,' the magos said. 'All now stands ready.'

GORGONSON REACHED OUT to pull Shaelecta back. The tech-priest, stalking just a pace ahead of the Space Marine, stiffened at the touch.

'We did not come this way,' Gorgonson snarled.

'That is correct.'

'I told you to take me to the Iron Father.'

'I am doing so.'

'By the *fastest path.*'

The two of them were on a suspension bridge high above a churning pit of fizzing calderae. The air boiled with spark-lit smoke, tumbling from the open maws of refinery vats. Hanging chains swayed and clanked, poised to be fastened to heavy iron castings by the teams of thralls labouring below.

Shaelecta turned to face the legionary, its lens-lights blurred in the smoky gloom. 'You did not specify. The fastest path may not be the most efficie–'

Gorgonson wrenched the tech-priest to one side, nearly sending it crashing through the nearside walkway barrier. Then he began to run, his heavy tread making the bridge sway under the impacts.

'Medusan,' came Shaelecta's cry. 'Do not proceed unaccompanied. There is peril ahead.'

Gorgonson ignored the priest and broke into a sprint. He knew when he was being stalled. The two of them had proceeded through chamber after chamber, each filled with the arcane wonders of the Martian priesthood, as though the occupants of the ziggurat had wished to demonstrate their power in some bizarre cavalcade of grotesquery. In every hall and forge, he had seen more of them – cranium-dulled slaves, their minds and bodies fused to mechanical shackles, their wills gone. That was what this place was built upon: thousands upon thousands of these meat-puppets, a churn of superfluous flesh sacrificed on the altar of blind servility. That was what they *did*, the lords of Lliax, enslaving minds to the will of the machine in order to preserve them against the coming storm.

Dulling the senses, crushing the soul.

And he had let them take Aug.

Gorgonson reached a pair of bronze-plated doors and barrelled through them. Galleries extended away before him, high-vaulted and clogged with blundering automata. He smelled the foul stink of scorched gears and heard the drumbeat rhythm of forge-hammers. Tunnel entrances gaped, dozens of them, each twisting away further into the heart of the fortress. He saw servitors shamble through, watched over by troops of tech-guard. Further up, a detachment of Thallaxii turned their faceless heads towards the intruder in their midst.

The Apothecary did not stop. He picked up a locator signal at last. It was close.

Shaelecta might have been slothful, but it had been taking him in roughly the right direction. The Iron Hands legionary vaulted up a long stairway, his boots cracking the marble. He pushed through more doors, shoving blinded thralls aside in his haste.

As he neared the signal's source, he drew his bolter, still running. The corridor was barely lit and smelled of copper. He closed on the target – an iron portal bearing the sigil of Mars – and Scyllax guardians unfurled to meet him, their skull-faces lit an eerie green. He picked off the first with a single shot, exploding its metal carcass and sending it shrieking back into the shadows. The others rushed him, tentacles grasping and vox-emitters babbling machine nonsense. He felt claws rake his pauldrons, and augers pierce the outer skin of his breastplate.

Roaring now, Gorgonson threw them all off, smashing their carapaces with a hail of bolt-rounds. More came to take their place, slithering up out of the murk, but by then he had reached the portal.

He seized the joint between the clam-shell door halves. With an almighty heave, he wrenched them open. The portal's locks snapped, showering sparks across the deck, and Gorgonson crouched down, ready to leap through the breach.

On the far side was a small chamber, a cross between a medicae station and a machine-lab. Several dozen tech-priests stood before him, each one bearing a different instrument of excruciation. They did not seem surprised to see him.

He aimed his bolter at the nearest, but never fired.

The tech-priests parted, revealing a long table in their midst. Aug was half raised on it, his helm removed and his upper armour gone. Long tubes coiled around his muscles, bubbling with fluids. The Iron Father's expression was groggy, as if dulled by powerful analgesics, and blood and oil ran in rivulets from the table's edges.

But he was conscious, and he was alive.

'Brother Gorgonson,' said Jebez Aug, sternly. 'What madness is this? Put away your weapon. Do you not see me? I am restored.'

IT TOOK ANOTHER week for the deep wounds to heal. Pharmakos had remade Aug down to the marrow, replacing sinew with wire and bone with adamantium. After that his armour was returned to him, also renewed and strengthened, its livery picked out in dazzlingly fresh white-on-black.

Shaelecta repeated the offer made to Gorgonson earlier, and again it was declined.

Then Aug offered his final thanks to the magos dominus, and pledges of mutual allegiance were affirmed.

Gorgonson and the Iron Father returned to their lander, and thence to the *Dannang*, and thence back to the warp. Guided by Meduson's forward tactical data, left for them strategically in inter-cell blind drops, it took them another month to locate the *Iron Heart*.

Once returned to the flagship, Aug sought out the warleader. His movements, though still tight with pain, were more fluid than they had been in a long time. When he entered Shadrak Meduson's strategium, he walked tall, just as he had done on the eve of Isstvan.

The warleader came to greet him, cracking a rare smile. 'Lord Frater,' he said, reaching out to grasp him by the hand. 'Your return gladdens me.'

'Brother, how goes the war?' Aug was eager for knowledge now. There were things he could *do*. 'How have you hurt them?'

Meduson's gaze flickered a little. His blunt features bore fresh scars, laced over pallid flesh. 'It becomes harder. But they know my name now.' He smiled, dryly. 'They are speaking it across the sector and beyond, so we have done what we said we would.'

Aug felt like laughing. 'So we have. And wounds may heal, making us stronger yet.'

He had expected Meduson to agree with that, to give some sign of affirmation. Instead, the warleader let go of his wrist. 'Then you are yourself again.'

'Just as I was before Oqueth. Stronger, if anything.'

Meduson nodded. 'And their price, for this service?'

'We are their allies,' said Aug. 'It was as I told you – they always honour their word. A Martian pact is a strong thing.'

The warleader nodded again, moving away. 'So it would seem. You asked of the war. We will strike them again in two days, and my plans are near complete. Hamart Three is being used as a supply dump, and is lightly defended. We can take it, the others agree. Can you fight yet? I would welcome it, if you would join us.'

Aug let his hand drop. 'Surely,' he said. 'I will reap them as if new-forged, and you shall see blood flow again. But what then? There will be other worlds to plunder.'

'Of course.'

'Then tell me of them.'

Meduson looked up at him. 'In time. I have yet to consult with my council.'

Aug felt words forming upon his lips.

You need no council now. You have the Hand Elect.

But he could not speak those words, for that would be too much like begging, and the promise had already been made.

'Then what shall I do, here?' he asked, eventually.

'What do you mean?'

'My wounds are healed. We spoke of this. I wish to serve.'

Meduson's gaze moved away. 'You do not *serve*, Iron Father. Never that. You are our guide and our inspiration. Just as before.'

Our guide. Our inspiration. What words were these? Where had they come from?

Aug stood there, stiffly. Meduson said nothing more, and now held himself just as awkwardly. The silence grew between them, as thick as the forge-smog of Lliax.

'Hamart Three, then,' said the Iron Father at last. 'That is the next target.'

'It is. I would have you fight at my side then, if you will it.'

'Thus it shall be.' Aug knew then that there would be no more than that, at least not now. 'Shadrak, is all–'

'We have two days,' said Meduson, forcing a final smile. 'You will need time to prepare. We will talk again, before the attack, but it is good to see you again, lord Frater. I did not know if I would ever do so, but you were right. The Martians keep their oaths.'

Aug nearly recoiled from that, only catching himself at the last moment.

'As must we all,' he said, numbly.

HE RETURNED TO his chambers after that, alone, shadowed only by Legion serfs who dared say nothing to him. The ship was busy, filled with the sounds of impending combat. Most of the legionaries were of the Iron Tenth, going about their business with grim fortitude. Gorgonson had gone to join them, his battered armour blending well with theirs. The Iron Father stood out now, like a polished dagger amid a clutch of rusted knives.

He closed the doors behind him, then locked them.

He paced back and forth, turning over the events of his return in his mind.

Kernag's words would not leave him.

The Hand Elect is an empty title, bestowed to keep you leashed to him.

It will not bring you what you wish for...

Aug flexed his new muscles, feeling a tight interface with the new augmetic structures. He was far stronger than he had been, flesh-spare, rebuilt from the core. Was that what made Meduson cold to him now? Was he envious? Or did he see something else there, something that had not existed until Lliax?

Aug ran a scan of his internal systems, some of them housed within his armour, some in the augmetic nodes that peppered his skin. It was only then that he noticed the new relay indicator on his helm, buried deep within overlapping layers of tactical read-outs. It was insignificant, really – a tiny adjustment, gifting him a single new rune amid the screeds of them offered by his auto-sensory display.

He pondered it for a moment. The threat of it was obvious, as was the opportunity. Being manipulated was almost as anathema to him as weakness in combat, and both led to the same outcome. He should have seen it earlier, of course. Perhaps he should have seen many things earlier.

Aug withdrew to the inner sanctum of his chambers, to where the scanner baffles were complete and his new gift would be safe to use.

He remembered his own words on Lliax, as proud and defiant as they had been.

But then he had seen Meduson again, and something had changed.

Aug activated the aether-link, and for a moment his aural nodes filled with nothing but static as the connection flickered from one hidden system node to another.

They cleared, and Kernag's disembodied voice crackled across the void.

'Iron Father,' he said. *'You have something to report?'*

'You were telling me of your plans for Medusa,' said Aug, turning away from the light. 'Tell me more.'

THE EITHER

Graham McNeill

I

SHIPBOARD HOROLOGS SHOWED that three years had passed since the infamy of Isstvan. It felt longer. Much longer. Three bloody years hunting the mewling scraps of Legions culled on the black sands. A duty he hadn't relished, even as he recognised its necessity.

Three years the XVI Legion spent earning glory without him, fighting at the forefront of this new-birthed war.

That hurt. That hurt a lot.

But he was nothing if not a true son, and he knew the value of obeying orders. So much time apart from his brothers and Lupercal was akin to a hot blade cutting pieces of his soul away.

Leaving a void like the one gouged by Verulam Moy's death.

Was this what the warriors of the X Legion felt, knowing their gene-sire was dead? Hollowed out and empty. In need of fresh purpose to fill that void? Was that what drove them to keep fighting in the face of certain extinction?

A yearning for purpose when there *was* no purpose?

He had described his feelings to a flesh-spare warrior of the Iron Hands they'd captured a year ago in the airless hulk of the last remaining Momed voidhive.

His name was Tharbis of Clan Felg, but that was about all he ever
told them. Interrogating one of the Legiones Astartes through pain was
an exercise in futility. Doubly so with an Iron Hand.

Instead, he sought to break Tharbis with words of Ferrus Manus.

'I saw your gene-sire die on Isstvan,' he would say on one of his
frequent visits to his captive's cell. 'I watched the Phoenician weep
as he clove his brother primarch's head from his shoulders. And do
you know what else I saw as he fell? I saw the fight wither in the Iron
Hands still standing. They simply *gave up*. One by one, they laid down
their weapons and were slaughtered like swine. All so they might die
next to their father. Quite noble in its own way.'

All inventions, of course – he had seen nothing but dying Salamanders on Isstvan – but they cut Tharbis deeply. Over and over he sought
to break his captive with hopelessness and despair, yet even to his last,
metallic, oil-rich breath, Tharbis had defied him.

The last word to pass his lips had been a curse and a threat all in
one. A name, he had since come to learn.

Shadrak Meduson.

He had laughed as Tharbis died, leaning close so that the last thing
the warrior would hear would finally crush him.

'Haven't you heard?' said Tybalt Marr. 'I've already killed Shadrak
Meduson.'

THE SKIES OVER Dwell burned hot. Re-entry cones painted it in fire.
Tybalt Marr was bringing his ships and his warriors back to the Warmaster. They'd translated in-system seven days ago and made all speed
for the fifth planet. Only the ruins of the ship schools, battery plates
and drifting siege-hulks locked in ever-decreasing orbits forced them
to exercise more caution in their approach.

The Sea of Enna shone like an elliptical mirror of brass, reflecting the
low sun and the sky-born atomic fires. It reminded Marr of the great
amber eye at the centre of Lupercal's breastplate.

He guided the Stormbird lower, circling the haphazard collection of dwellings that made up the city of Tyjun, a disordered collection of eclectic structural forms filling a shallow rift valley like the leavings of a tsunami.

Only a vast ochre necropolis atop an overlooking plateau presented any unity of form. He'd learned it was known as the Mausolytic, and that it pre-dated the Imperium by millennia.

Fitting that this reunion would be held in the shadow of a house of the dead.

Marr overflew its blocky immensity, keeping the proud nose of the Stormbird high. A flyby to honour Lupercal and to announce the triumphant return of one of his true sons. Wasteful not to simply land, yes, but he and his warriors had earned the right to preen a little.

A dangerous warleader was dead by their hand, his host broken. That was worth a little grandstanding.

Ten Stormbirds flew in formation with Marr's craft, roaring overhead with a legacy of victory carved into their entry-hot flanks. Marr made one more circle before finally issuing the order to land. Coming in from the north, the septentrional aspect he had always favoured, he transitioned his gunship to vertical flight.

He brought the heavy craft down hard, a war landing.

Leaving the post-landing checks and protocols to a Legion thrall-servitor, Marr decoupled from the controls and made his way back through the crew bays.

Kysen Scybale already had the squads on their feet. Scybale was a sergeant, Cthonian to the core. Old guard, but with sense enough to move with the times. A man of his experience should have been made captain by now, but Scybale knew where he fitted best.

One look into his flinty grey eyes, lit from within by Cthonia's dark fire, and even captains found themselves taking an unaccounted step back.

Marr's chosen warriors formed up, eager to rejoin the Legion. Scybale stood at Marr's right hand, Cyon Azedine on his left. The Company Champion's hand never strayed from the leather-wound grip of his mortuary sword, its basket-hilt reworked to bear the death mask of the Iron Hand who had borne it before him.

'Don't we all make a pretty picture?' asked Scybale.

Marr grinned and gave the sergeant a nod, locking his transverse-crested helm into the crook of his arm as the forward assault ramp lowered with a squeal of pneumatics.

Russet light poured in on a gust of air, hot with propellant from the Stormbird's exhausts.

Marr tasted Dwell.

Dry, spiced atmosphere. Salt-rich wind from the sea and a low range of still-smouldering heavy metals. A lingering taste of acrid preservatives.

He marched down the ramp, his stride sure and confident, purposeful in a way it hadn't been for a long time. He emerged from the shadow of the Stormbird onto a newly-constructed apron of scorched plascrete at the edge of the plateau. Gunships squatted like scaled raptors in hot clouds of vapour to either side.

'The Legion *was* expecting us, yes?' asked Azedine.

Marr had no answer for him.

He hadn't expected a triumph to match Ullanor. He'd hoped, but hadn't *really* expected Horus Lupercal to be here. He'd hoped a few companies of Sons of Horus at least.

Four warriors stood at the far end of the apron. Three were known to him as brothers, the fourth a stranger. At their number, Marr felt a twinge of unease. Nothing he could identify, just a ripple of source-less disquiet.

First Captain Ezekyle Abaddon was impossible to mistake.

Towering and brutal, his shaven head and swishing topknot made him unique among the XVI Legion. Cleaving close to Abaddon was Falkus Kibre, his enormous war-plate making his already massive frame even larger.

The third warrior's face was cold and humourless, sharply angled and patrician in mien. Like the Warmaster, but without the dynamism of Horus Lupercal. A true son, saw Marr, but one that was unknown to him.

But in the face of Little Horus Aximand, Marr had his first real shock. He did his best to hide it, but the look on Aximand's face told him he hadn't been successful.

Little Horus held out his gauntlet before he could say anything.

'Welcome to Dwell, Tybalt,' said Aximand, his disfigured face moving as though the muscles beneath his skin were being worked by invisible strings. Still recognisably a true son, but somehow entirely *other*. Marr couldn't decide whether Aximand now looked *more* or *less* like their sire.

'Little Horus, what–' said Marr, but Aximand shook his head.

'Another time,' said Aximand. 'Let's just say that steel forged on Medusa has such a fine edge, and leave it at that.'

'As you say,' agreed Marr with a slight incline of his head.

'So the Either returns to us,' said Abaddon with what was probably meant to be a grin, but came off looking more like the death mask on Azedine's mortuary blade. 'Or is it the "Or", I could never tell you two apart...'

Anger touched Marr at Abaddon's poor attempt at humour.

'You never did have any skill at jests, did you, Ezekyle?' he said. 'Verulam died on Davin's moon. So I'm not the Either any more, and I'm certainly not the Or. Now I'm just Tybalt Marr. *Captain* Tybalt Marr.'

Abaddon's brow furrowed, but he refrained from rising to the barb, much to Marr's surprise.

Before that changed, Aximand took a step towards him and put a hand on his shoulder guard. He gently, but firmly turned Marr towards the polished ochre stone of the Mausolytic.

'We meet in a liminal space,' he said. 'A place where life and death are not so far apart as we might wish. It's fitting we remember the dead as we knew them. Ezekyle meant no disrespect to the memory of Verulam. Did you, Ezekyle?'

'No,' said Abaddon through gritted teeth. 'I did not.'

Aximand nodded and stepped back. 'You see? The restoration of the Mournival has given Ezekyle fresh reserves of empathy and humility.'

That made Marr smile until the full import of Aximand's words hit home. That explained the vague unease he'd felt when he'd seen there were four of them.

The others saw the realisation in his eyes.

'He didn't know,' said the unknown warrior. 'Of course, how could he?'

Marr rounded on him, taking in his inferior rank.

'Who are you, and why are you talking to me as though you're my equal?'

The warrior gave a curt bow, barely enough to show respect.

'Apologies, Captain Marr, I offer all respect,' he said. 'My name is Grael Noctua of the Twenty-Fifth Warlocked.'

'You're just a squad commander,' said Marr.

'Yes,' said Noctua. 'For now.'

'And you're Mournival? All of you?'

Noctua nodded, and Marr saw a cold glimmer of a ruthlessly calculating intelligence. He wondered if the others had seen it.

'We needed our confraternity restored,' said Aximand. 'Now more than ever.'

Marr nodded, the muscles in his jaw tight as tension cables in a Stormbird's wing.

'And Lupercal?' he said. 'He approves?'

'He does,' said Abaddon, and Marr felt the knife in his back twist just a little deeper.

Falkus Kibre stepped forward and clapped both gauntlets on Marr's forearms. He and the Master of the Justaerin had never been close, but Marr had always respected Kibre's honest and brusque to-the-point manner.

'It's good to have you back,' said Kibre. 'Took your time disposing of a few ragamuffin survivors, eh?'

'You didn't vox ahead to tell them?' asked Scybale. 'Tell them what you did.'

'Tell us what?' asked Aximand.

Marr took a breath and said, 'That a warleader of the Tenth Legion named Shadrak Meduson was alloying those *ragamuffin* survivors into a fighting force of not inconsiderable strength. We destroyed his fleet at Arissak.'

Almost immediately, Marr knew something was wrong when he saw the confused reaction to his pronouncement.

'No, Tybalt,' said Aximand. 'I'm afraid Shadrak Meduson is very much alive.'

He should have died.

That was the thought uppermost in Marr's mind as he watched grainy pict-capture of the Iron Hands' Fire Raptors strafing the Dome of Revivification with gunfire. High-velocity shells tore through its latticework structure, detonating the cryotubes within and wrecking mechanisms thousands of years old.

The Fire Raptors circled, their centreline and waist turrets braying with explosive fire, and the tower upon which the dome sat erupted like a flaming geyser.

Horus, Mortarion and Fulgrim were in that dome.

A meeting of brothers undone by an attempted decapitating strike. If it hadn't been directed at his own primarch, Marr would have admired such a gutsy approach. Especially in the wake of the White Scars' abortive assassination attempt.

To have lain in wait for so long displayed a level of patience Marr had hitherto not encountered in his dealings with Shadrak Meduson. The boarding action he'd led aboard the *Crown of Flame* had taught Marr much about the man: his cunning, his determination and his resilience. Also recklessness and the exploitable desire to strike back *hard*.

But patience? No, that wasn't a virtue he associated with the warleader of the Iron Tenth.

Could Meduson be alive? Might he have escaped the slaughter in the Arissak System? It had been so comprehensive a defeat, so thorough in its bloodletting, that it seemed impossible anything could have escaped.

He'd watched Meduson's flagship die, seen its guttering hulk tear itself apart in a lethal torsion of reactor detonations and warp implosions.

Marr shook his head and returned his attention to the pict capture, the swaying feed coming from a servitor drone attracted by the sudden noise and light.

When the end came, it came suddenly.

One of the gunships crumpled as though being crushed in the inescapable gravity of a black hole.

Then Horus Lupercal was there.

Marr's breath caught in his throat.

He'd watched this a dozen times already, and still the power of the Warmaster was astonishing. He leapt onto the prow of a gunship hooked by a chain hurled by the Death Lord. With one sweep of *Worldbreaker*, Lupercal demolished the Fire Raptor's prow, before vaulting onto the last enemy craft and breaking its spine.

It was the most incredible thing Marr had ever seen.

The pict capture exploded into static as Sons of Horus gunships finally arrived on station and shot down anything that didn't bear the Eye of Horus. Marr reached forward. He toggled the ivory switch to loop the broadcast and sat back on his bench seat as the image of the dome reconstituted itself in veils of light.

Marr sat in the central courtyard of what might once have been a wealthy merchant's villa, but was now just an empty marble shell. It sat on the upper slopes of the rift valley, within walking distance of the Mausolytic Precinct, wherein Horus Lupercal was said to be communing with the frozen dead of Dwell.

Marr had brooded within the villa for five days, the knowledge of Shadrak Meduson's survival having robbed him of the triumphant news he was to deliver. Small wonder the primarch made no time for him.

Two dozen data-slates lay scattered on the black-veined flagstones of the courtyard, each filled with notations of enemy actions over the last three years, spreading out from Isstvan. He'd studied them obsessively for those five days and his eidetic memory was fully conversant with everything they contained.

Marr picked up the nearest and scanned its contents again.

Acts of sabotage, supply lines cut, fuelling asteroids destroyed and a host of guerilla engagements where enemy forces had attacked, fallen back then attacked again.

Raven Guard through and through.

The random nature of each strike, and, more tellingly, its isolation from the others, had kept Marr – kept everyone – from registering their importance. But when viewed as being part of a greater whole, the faintest hint of an implacable, resolute and indefatigable will became apparent.

An iron will.

Marr saw nothing definitive, but each morsel was a tantalising bread-crumb that pointed to one inescapable conclusion.

Shadrak Meduson was indeed alive.

Not just alive, but raising his threatened storm with new skills and a new level of cunning alloyed in the fire of his apparent destruction.

Meduson's supposed defeat had come in the shock-spasms following Isstvan V. The Iron Hands warleader had fought as he'd always fought, the only way he knew how, gathering whatever resources he could to assemble a fresh fighting force.

That was the way of the X Legion. If a machine broke down, they did whatever it took to get it working again, replacing broken parts with whatever came to hand. Meduson had taken that credo to its logical extension by incorporating squads from the Salamanders and Raven Guard into his formations.

And it had very nearly worked.

Marr had destroyed Meduson's agglomerated fleet, but the scattered, ad hoc flotillas in the outer reaches of the system had taken much longer to hunt down.

In the end, the survivors had been too broken, too dispersed and too psychologically shattered to endure the ferocity of Marr's vengeful prosecution. Of course, there had been elements that evaded destruction, but he'd believed them to be minor irritations and barely worth notice.

The assassination attempt on Dwell was the prism that threw an entirely new and dreadful light on that belief.

He reached down and lifted a clay amphora of wine that had somehow survived the city's fall and which he'd found half-empty in the basement. It was too thin and watery to his tastes, but just drinking it stoked a fire in his belly as his genhanced metabolism countered the alcohol.

The wine tasted sour, but everything tasted sour just now.

MARR WANDERED THE empty halls of the villa, drinking from the amphora and letting his mind consider the idea that the random attacks on forces sworn to the Warmaster were not random at all.

He had to take his suspicions to Horus Lupercal, but needed to be absolutely sure that what he believed was beyond doubt.

Too much certainty and he would be viewed as paranoid, jumping at shadows and seeing threats where none existed. Too little and Lupercal would dismiss him out of hand, relegating him to the rear echelons of forgotten warriors whose names history wouldn't bother to remember.

But hadn't that already happened?

How many more times could he be passed over? How many more times could he be ignored? The Either and the Or, two nicknames blithely indifferent to the individual heroism of Tybalt Marr and Verulam Moy's achievements.

Marr knew how the Legion viewed him. Precise, efficient and workmanlike. Steady, but without the glories won by men like Sedirae, Abaddon or, apparently, Grael Noctua. Even Marr's magnificent victories in the low mountains of Murder hadn't changed that perception.

He remembered standing in the strategium of the *Vengeful Spirit* during the early stages of the war on Murder. Loken had been there, spitefully leaving him to the droning attentions of Iacton Qruze. The old warrior had been a relic from a bygone age of the Legion, a man whose counsel was rarely sought, but always offered.

'I won't be the half-heard,' said Marr, making his way down a carpeted hallway in the upper levels of the villa, a passageway replete with portraits that bore unmistakable genetic links.

Only the most recent picture had no date of death beneath it. A woman shawled with rich fabrics and draped in expensive jewellery stared back at him, handsome with rich living and what looked like subtle flesh sculpting.

'Did you own this fine dwelling?' he asked the portrait. 'How did it feel to have it taken from you? To have your dreams crushed under the boots of the Sons of Horus?'

The portrait was, of course, silent.

'Are you even still alive? Perhaps you fled to the interior countryside to wait out the war. Maybe you took refuge in another of your holdings, or in the household of a friend.'

Marr stepped away from the portrait and hurled the amphora at the wall. It shattered and soaked the picture, drenching it in wine that dripped in garnet droplets from its gilt frame.

'It doesn't matter!' he roared. 'Whatever became of you, you are nothing now. Whatever your achievements, they are as dust in the wind. All your labours, all your dedication, blood, sweat and tears... all shed for nothing.'

He turned as he heard a door opening below. Footsteps on marble. Too heavy a tread to be anything other than a legionary.

'Tybalt?' shouted a voice, echoing through the villa. 'Are you in here?'

He made his way back through the villa to the head of a fine set of marble and ouslite stairs that split apart midway down their length to curve groundwards in opposing symmetrical arcs. Below was Little Horus Aximand, standing in the centre of a mosaic floor of coloured glass tiles that depicted bucolic scenes of Dwell's pastoral antiquity.

'What do you want?'

'To talk,' said Aximand. 'As old friends do when they meet after long absences.'

Marr made his way down the stairs, much as the lady of this house must once have done when receiving guests. Aximand waited patiently, his new face regarding Marr quizzically. Belted at his waist was a huge blade of Cthonian bluesteel, its edge notched and badly in need of repair.

'I want you to know that I put your name forward,' said Aximand. 'For the Mournival, I mean.'

'But I was rejected.'

'Ezekyle knows you are a good man, and coming from him that is a superlative compliment.'

Marr reached the bottom of the steps.

'But he still rejected my appointment,' said Marr. 'Which goes some way to explaining why he didn't tear my head off when I insulted him on the landing field.'

Aximand nodded. 'I'd urged him to be sympathetic. After a while he agreed.'

Marr grinned. Little Horus Aximand had been a true friend to him over the years, but this latest wound in his pride was going to take more than consoling words to salve.

'Why was I rejected this time?' asked Marr. 'And please, don't try and sweeten the balm.'

'Very well. Ezekyle didn't think you had the stomach for the job,' said Aximand.

Marr ground his teeth at so casual a dismissal.

'He kept pushing for his own men,' continued Aximand. 'Choleric types like Kibre, Targost and Ekaddon, but we needed balance. I hoped you would be the one to bring it, upon your return.'

'Balance?' asked Marr. 'And yet you let the Widowmaker in? I wonder if you properly understand the concept of balance.'

'You know Ezekyle,' said Aximand with a shrug. 'Once he gets an idea in his head, it's next to impossible to shift.'

'So that's why you made the overture to Grael Noctua? One of his, one of yours.'

'Something like that,' said Aximand, and Marr caught a trace of something else, some other reason behind Aximand's suggestion of Grael Noctua, something he wondered if Aximand himself even understood.

He sighed and said, 'I'd offer you some wine, but I think I just smashed the last amphora in Tyjun.'

'Shame.'

'No, it wasn't very good.'

Aximand smiled, and even with his new face, its warmth was genuine. 'So what are we to do if not drink as warriors?'

'You brought a sword,' said Marr. 'We could fight.'

'Would that help?'

'Help with what?'

'To balance your humours,' said Aximand. 'Because it looks like they need balancing.'

'Aye,' said Marr. 'There's a courtyard at the centre of the villa, that should suffice for an arena. Take up that monstrous blade of yours and we'll fight.'

'*Mourn-it-All*,' said Aximand.

'What?'

'My sword, it's called *Mourn-it-All*.'

'I know how it feels,' said Marr.

II

'RIDICULOUS,' SAID ABADDON, dropping the data-slate to the gleaming obsidian table. 'That's what they want you to think.'

They gathered in one of the sepulchral audience chambers of the Mausolytic, a place where the citizens of Dwell could meet and commune with their ancestors. Octagonal, with semicircular alcoves spaced at regular intervals around the wall, the gloomy and sombre chamber had been appropriated by the Mournival for their newly instigated meetings.

At Marr's request they gathered to hear his suspicions of the growing threat of Shadrak Meduson.

Aximand sat before a glowing hololith, the light throwing the bruises on his cheek and swollen eye into sharp relief. Their sparring in the villa had been a brutal, punishing affair, of which Marr had taken the honours. Cathartic and not a little liberating, Aximand had been proven correct in that it had balanced Marr's humours.

Little Horus studied an entoptic rendering of interlinked icons. Each one was the location of an attack on their or their allies' forces, with a spreading chain of outcomes linking to other attacks and their consequences.

It looked so much like a web – Marr half expected to see the image of a glowing spider at its centre.

Or an iron fist.

'It's entirely the opposite,' said Aximand. 'If Tybalt's right, then they want us to dismiss them, to view them as a negligible threat until it's too late.'

Grael Noctua had a spread of data-slates fanned out before him, scrolling through multiple informational cascades at once.

'Or Ezekyle's right and it's all just beating the brush to make noise, to make us *think* there's a huge force out there working to some unseen plan and forcing the Warmaster to divert resources to fight them.'

Of all the Mournival, Noctua had thus far asked the most penetrating questions. Aspects Marr himself had not considered, counter-positions and *Advocatus diaboli* refutations that made him feel like he had entered a court-martial with nothing more than circumstantial evidence and hearsay to prove his case.

Abaddon paced the floor, his boundless energies keeping him from sitting in one place for any length of time. Kibre sat opposite Aximand, restraining himself from pacing as Abaddon did with visible effort.

'If this were true,' said Falkus Kibre, speaking slowly and tapping the nearest data-slate, 'don't you think Horus Lupercal would have seen it?'

Elevation to the Mournival was evidently suiting Kibre.

Much to Marr's surprise, it was allowing a maturity he hadn't suspected the Widowmaker was capable of attaining to bloom. He'd asked the one and only question that had given Marr second thoughts about presenting his findings at all.

Marr hesitated, knowing he was taking a risk in suggesting any lack on the part of the Warmaster.

'Lupercal's gaze is fixed upon Terra,' he said 'It keeps him from seeing what is behind us.'

Abaddon stopped his pacing.

'And you said he didn't have the stomach for this,' said Aximand with a chuckle.

The First Captain switched his thunderous gaze between Marr and Aximand. 'Another one who thinks he knows war better than the Warmaster,' he said, with a shake of the head. 'There's nothing here, Marr, just a lot of smoke with no fire. You were on Isstvan. You know what we did there. Do you *really* think Lupercal would have been so careless as to let enough warriors escape who might form any kind of credible threat?'

Marr knew he was on dangerous ground here. To agree with Abaddon was to openly criticise their primarch, and even Aximand would take a dim view of such open dissent.

Speculation was dangerous here, so he stuck to facts.

He leaned over the table and switched the hololith to display scrolling diagrams that looked like genealogical trees, but which were in fact Legion orders of battle.

'This is a full manifest of the enemy forces deployed at Isstvan as it was divined at the opening of the assault,' said Marr, splitting the holo into three columns, silver, green and black. 'Iron Hands, Salamanders and Raven Guard. Watch.'

One by one, the icons representing enemy squads changed from pale blue to red as Marr fed in casualty reports and recorded exterminations. Like the creeping cellular sickness Marr had once observed Apothecary Vaddon studying in the bloodstream of an infected Scout auxilia, it expanded and increased the speed of its attack.

'Even though they are our enemies, it still chills the blood to see so much Legion strength lost,' said Noctua.

'Don't be foolish,' said Abaddon. 'You don't grieve for the enemy when he dies, you give thanks it wasn't you.'

Eventually the display finished updating, leaving the estimated forces a ragged shadow of their former glory.

'As best as can be estimated through collated butcher's bills and recovered armour, this is as close to an accurate figure as I can ascribe to the number of warriors who likely escaped Isstvan.'

The red icons of destroyed Legion formations faded out, and Marr swept the remaining icons together. They didn't fit together nearly as neatly as the original diagram, but then this wasn't an order of battle, just a representation of what had likely survived the massacre.

'Look at what's left, look at what we can't account for,' said Marr. 'I'll wager it's more than you thought, yes? Perhaps twenty-two thousand warriors all told, give or take a few thousand either side. That's not a force we can just ignore.'

'So more got off Isstvan that we thought,' said Abaddon. 'It still doesn't prove Shadrak Meduson's behind all these attacks or that he has some overarching plan. He mustered some resistance here at Dwell, but we defeated him. You broke him at Arissak. If he is in command, then he's doing a pretty poor job of fighting us. These attacks, irritating as they might be, are meaningless in the larger scheme of things.'

'Are they?' asked Marr, skidding a data-slate over the tabletop towards Abaddon. 'Meduson threatened to raise the storm against us, and that's just what he's done. Look at what these *meaningless* attacks achieved. An entire company of Sons of Horus diverted from the front lines of the war. Months spent securing Isstvan's supply routes, increased security around captured systems and, more crucially, the slowing of the march to Terra.'

Abaddon slammed his fist down on the table and cracks spread across its mirror-black surface, reaching out to each member of the Mournival.

'Enough! You think because Meduson escaped you once before that he is everywhere now. You really expect us to take these guilty delusions of yours to Lupercal? No, Tybalt, go back to your company and get them ready for war. Within the week we will leave Dwell for a greater prize.'

'You won't take this to Lupercal?' asked Marr.

'No,' said the First Captain. 'We will not.'

'And the rest of you agree with this?'

Kibre nodded, as Marr knew he would. Noctua also nodded, but he had at least considered his decision.

Aximand placed his palms on the table, but any hopes that Little Horus would side with him were quickly dashed.

'I think there is some merit in this, Tybalt, but I have to agree with my Mournival brothers,' he said. 'If this threat is as dire as you believe, to divert the level of resources you'd need to deal with it would greatly weaken our thrust on Terra.'

Marr nodded slowly and switched the hololith's display from the combined survivor lists to an image of the galactic spiral. Isstvan shimmered with a faint nimbus of cerulean light, Terra with a pulsing yellow haze, a blister in need of lancing.

'Ask yourself this, *Mournival*,' said Marr, pointing to the tenebrous gulfs of space between the blue and the gold. 'Who knows how much time the remnants of these shattered Legions have bought the Emperor and his warriors to fortify, regroup and prepare? How much closer to Terra would we be *now*, if not for them?'

He leaned forwards.

'And I'll tell you another thing, if Meduson *is* behind these attacks, then he has a plan, and things are only going to get worse.'

Kysen Scybale and Cyon Azedine were waiting for him in the pillared approach vestibule beyond the Mausolytic's inner chambers. He marched past them, helm held in the crook of one arm, his other hand gripping the hilt of his sword. He kept up the swift pace until they stood on the scorched granite steps of the Mausolytic, looking out over the Sea of Enna.

'I'm guessing that didn't go well,' said Scybale.

'No,' said Marr. 'It didn't.'

'And there is no word yet from the primarch?' asked Azedine.

'None.'

'But I see you're still set on this course,' said Scybale. 'Without sanction or authority?'

Marr looked up into the burning sky and nodded.

'Now more than ever,' he said.

Sorties out toward Dwell's Mandeville point were rare, and despite the name such locations were very rarely fixed points in space. The term was equally applied to any point far enough away from the gravity well of a star to allow safe translation into the warp. In essence, any point on a notional sphere surrounding the star could be the Mandeville point, which made a mockery of any attempt to guard it.

Local system pilots and astropaths, of course, knew points upon that sphere where the angles between the Empyreal realm and real space intersected to a greater degree and allowed for a smoother warp-translation.

Occupying regions of space tens of thousands of kilometres wide, they were haunted voids, where sourceless voices muttered obscenities and ghosts lurked in the shadows.

And such points *could* be guarded.

Three Sons of Horus vessels followed a stately course towards Dwell's coreward jump point, known locally as the Azoth Gate. The two destroyers, the *Helicanus* and the *Kashin*, and the frigate *Lupercal Pursuivant*, bristled with vanes and spikes, mailed fists in the face of the void.

The small flotilla had set out from Dwell six days ago, and were making good time through the asteroid belt spread between the seventh and eighth planets. Marr commanded from the bridge of *Lupercal Pursuivant*, keeping his vessels in close formation as they navigated between waypoints towards the Azoth Gate.

The asteroids were the debris of the system's creation millions of years before, left to drift in a captured orbit around the sun. Hundreds of kilometres in diameter, each vast hunk of inert rock drifted through space like an aimless wanderer. Thousands of kilometres separated each asteroid from its nearest neighbour, making transit of the belt a relatively simple affair.

Cosmic dust and micrometeor impacts ablated the hulls of all three vessels, fouling local auspex sectors with false returns and phantom images.

If there were going to be an attack, this would be an ideal location from which to launch it. Despite that, the three shipmasters were making no attempt at stealth. A constant chatter of vox passed between each vessel and active surveyor sweeps, together with high-energy electro-magnetic pulses, lashed the void before them.

The auspex stations on every bridge revealed no trace of enemy presence.

Not that Marr expected any.

Not yet, at least.

THE FIRST SIGN of trouble came when the engines of the *Lupercal Pursuivant* stuttered with occlusion flare. The venting systems of a starship's drive systems were necessarily extensive, given the volatile plasmas employed in their reactor cores.

The fouling of venting systems with void-borne dust was something no captain could afford, carrying as it did the risk of explosive blow-back into the reactor cores.

When the Master of Engines sent word to the bridge of the *Lupercal Pursuivant* of ejection failures throughout the engineering decks, Marr immediately shut down the reactors.

A flurry of urgent vox passed between the three shipmasters as the best course of action was deliberated. The Master of Engines estimated thirteen hours for the servitors to scrub the vents clear, and thus Marr gave the order for the *Helicanus* and the *Kashin* to continue onwards.

Two vessels on station was better than none.

The *Lupercal Pursuivant* would haul anchor in the shadow of an aster-oid and rejoin the flotilla upon the restoration of drive functionality.

ELEVEN HOURS PASSED before they caught the first hint of another ship on an intercepting parabola. Marr stiffened on the command throne as the Master of Auspex lifted his fist – a withered, fused claw of a thing.

'Captain Marr,' he said in a sopping gestalt of a dozen or more inter-leaved voices. 'A vessel approaches.'

'Designation?'

'By displacement, a rapid strike cruiser. The minds aboard bear the unmistakable touch of Medusa upon them.'

Marr didn't question this last morsel of information.

More than just machines were searching the void around the *Lupercal Pursuivant*. Locked in a pitch black chamber within the vessel's prow, a host of warp-touched astropaths were linked to its sensorium via neural spikes driven into their cuneocerebellar tracts.

As it had been described to Marr, they felt vibrations in the spaces *between* real space and the warp.

Dark-robed Mechanicum adepts had modified the *Lupercal Pursuivant's* auspex systems during the three year hunt for Meduson's fleet, which had given the Sons of Horus a marked advantage against the Iron Hands.

A ship could go as dark as it was possible to go and still the *Lupercal Pursuivant's* shuttered astropaths could find it if the minds aboard burned brightly enough.

And from the look of the phosphor-bright image on the viewscreen, the minds on this new ship burned so *very* brightly.

The Master of Auspex had once been a warrior of the Sons of Horus, but now he was something both more and less than transhuman. His altered body reclined on a grav-couch, pierced through by scores of bubbling tubes and inload cables. His head was encased in a latticework scaffold and the lid of his skull was crowned by numerous invasive implants. All of which completely remodelled the synaptic architecture of his brain to better process the visions coming from the astropaths and display them in a useable fashion.

'Looks like you were right,' said Scybale, his slate-grey eyes following the glittering track of the incoming starship. 'They've been watching us. Who knows for how long...'

Marr nodded.

'It makes sense,' he said. 'We were the last of the Sons of Horus fleets coming in to Dwell, and such a muster speaks of a greater deployment to come. I can't imagine that Shadrak Meduson wouldn't want to know what Lupercal's next move is.'

'So he left a vessel lying in wait to watch our movements.'

'Yes, but whoever is in command of that ship is Iron Hands to the core,' said Marr. 'He couldn't resist a foundering vessel in an asteroid belt.'

'More fool him.'

'Who's to say we wouldn't do the same if Lupercal fell? What risks would we take to strike back at those who cut him down?'

Scybale shrugged, unwilling to concede he might make such an error of judgement. Instead, he changed the subject, gesturing towards the Master of Auspex.

'As useful as… *this* has proven, it's no end for a warrior of the Legion,' said Scybale.

Marr nodded in agreement. 'It sits ill with me also, sergeant, but the results speak for themselves.'

Scybale's vox chirruped and he placed two fingers to his ear. He nodded at what he was hearing.

'Enemy vessel five thousand kilometres and closing on our ventral rear quarter,' said the Master of Auspex.

'Coming in behind and below,' said Marr. 'Classic breaching tactics. They mean to cripple us then board us.'

'Azedine has his warriors ready on your word,' said Scybale, unable to mask his own urge to be locked in a gunship assault pattern.

Marr grinned.

'Don't worry, Kysen, you'll get your chance to fight,' said Marr. 'You and I both.'

THE PERFECT KILL. Executed flawlessly. The enemy's demise would be welcome in and of itself, but to deliver a deathblow with such machine-like precision against the Warmaster's own Legion just made this manoeuvre all the sweeter.

The *Gorgorex* was a rapid strike cruiser of the Vurgaan Clan, old and hoary even before the treachery of Horus. It had fought its way clear of Isstvan with a shell-shocked cadre of survivors; mainly Iron Hands, but with a solid proportion of Salamanders and a handful of Raven Guard.

The Vurgaan were a proud and isolated clan, and thus the crew of the *Gorgorex* were well suited to the new way of war forced upon them after Isstvan.

Its commander was an Iron Father of the X Legion named Octar Uldin, and he swung the *Gorgorex* in below the stricken *Lupercal Pursuivant* using only the smallest bursts of thrust to manoeuvre. They were operating purely on external visual feeds; the risk of the enemy ship detecting any auspex sweeps were too great to countenance.

Uldin had watched the three vessels surging towards the Azoth Gate and logged them in the ship's database, assaying their speed, armaments and quirks as they went.

Any and all information on enemy vessels was invaluable, for just as warriors had their foibles, strengths and weaknesses that could be exploited, so too did starships.

Legion registries identified the frigate as *Lupercal Pursuivant*, the destroyers as *Helicanus* and *Kashin*. All were known to the Iron Hands after news of the disastrous engagement at Arissak had trickled down through the necessarily compartmentalised network of attack cells.

The *Helicanus*, the larger of the two destroyers, was slightly slower adjusting course to port. Its armour looked to have been repaired numerous times on its starboard flank, layered plate over layered plate, making it heavy on the turn. The *Kashin* had a few seconds latency on its manoeuvring igniters, a weakness that a foe with greater agility could turn to its advantage.

And, it now transpired, the *Lupercal Pursuivant* had issues with its vent cowlings. Its reactors were burning hot, far beyond any recommended tolerances. If those vents weren't cleared soon, the ship would blow itself to pieces without any help from the *Gorgorex*.

At full magnification, the servitor crews struggling to clear the vents were like swarms of ants moving around the armoured haunches of a plains-dwelling leviathan.

Under normal circumstances, Uldin would not have engaged. His orders, passed down through secretive relays and encoded with the highest priorities, were to watch and wait. To observe and report.

That wasn't the Vurgaan way, especially when intercepted vox-traffic between the enemy ships appeared to confirm that the *Lupercal Pursuivant* was the flagship of a XVI Legion captain named Tybalt Marr.

That this was undoubtedly the same Tybalt Marr whose head Shadrak Meduson had sworn to take, made the danger of exposure worth any risk.

The dorsal launch tubes were loaded and ready.

They would kill the crew of this vessel, render it dark and then ram it out of the Dwell system with a single, high-intensity burst of acceleration. The ship would never be seen again, its disappearance a celestial mystery that would never be explained.

'On my mark, light them up,' said Uldin.

'THEY'RE MAKING READY to launch,' said Scybale.

'Counterspread on my command.'

'It's a risk letting them fire first.'

Marr shook his head.

'No, it was the only way to get them in close enough,' he said. 'Once we stir the void with enough blood, the sharks will come to feed. And you know the first rule of void-war?'

Scybale grinned and said, 'Be the shark.'

THE FIRST WAVE of boarding torpedoes raced from the *Gorgorex* at almost the same instant as a spread of countermeasures launched from the ventral guns of the *Lupercal Pursuivant*.

With a much lighter payload, the Sons of Horus missiles closed the distance between the two ships in the time it took the boarding forces to travel a hundred kilometres.

Little more than two hundred metre-long tubes filled with shrapnel, the countermeasures exploded and formed supersonic clouds of tumbling debris. The torpedoes had no chance to evade, their guidance systems locked until their terminal manoeuvres, and fully half were ripped open or sent tumbling off into deep space.

Battery fire engaged the rest and yet more were blasted to ruin before they got to within fifty kilometres of the *Lupercal Pursuivant*. Point defence guns killed the rest as they executed their terminal dive.

Only one torpedo survived to penetrate the frigate's hull.

Avakhol Hurr, one of 18th Company's most feared breach-leaders, was waiting for it with his blood-spattered warriors.

Not a single enemy warrior set foot on the *Lupercal Pursuivant*.

Realising he had been lured into the attack, Octar Uldin broke off immediately. The *Gorgorex*'s engines fired, but having drifted for so long, it took time to coax them to full power.

Time that the *Lupercal Pursuivant* did not need, having kept its engines hot to maintain the illusion of reactor cores on the verge of overload.

Marr swung the frigate around and let the multiple batteries on its prow and portside flank have free rein as it rapidly closed the distance to its prey. The hunted now became the hunter as slashing arcs of high-yield lasers raked the *Gorgorex*'s length.

Its voids were yet to ignite, and detonations marched across the dorsal armour, melting armoured plates to molten slag and explosively venting hull compartments to the void. Serfs and menials spiralled out, shock-freezing in an instant.

The *Gorgorex* shuddered in pain, but it was a vessel of the Iron Hands, proud and defiant. The voids finally lit as it took its wounding stoically, like a pugilist who knows he cannot win the fight, but will stay on his feet until the last bell. Its engines flared, ready to push it from this one-sided engagement.

Its rear quarters exploded as a flurry of torpedoes launched in its rear arc slammed home and detonated within the drive cowlings.

Swinging out from behind the moon-sized asteroids that had covered their swift turns, *Helicanus* and *Kashin* effectively crushed any hope of the *Gorgorex*'s escape. Its engines vanished in an expanding plasma corona and oxygen bled into the void like glittering silver blood trails.

The two destroyers manoeuvred into close range. Their guns flayed its voids, collapsing entire quadrants of protection in moments before targeting its point defences. They pulled away with perfect synchrony as a shadow fell across the *Gorgorex*.

Angular and deadly, an assassin's blade over the face of the sun.

Lupercal Pursuivant hove to, so close that the space between it and the *Gorgorex* danced with borealis light as the remaining void envelopes overlapped. Generator vanes blew out in flaring surges of feedback. Space burned blue and purple and crimson.

A frigate of *Lupercal Pursuivant*'s displacement normally had no capacity to launch strike craft, but its loading bays opened and three Stormbirds that had spent the voyage from Dwell chained to the deck now fell into space.

They rammed their engines to maximum thrust and powered towards the their stricken prey. Helpless, the crew of the *Gorgorex* could only watch and await the inevitable assault.

Hull penetration came two minutes later.

III

'DON'T THEY KNOW they're beaten?' said Scybale, ducking out from cover to fire down the transverse approach to the main axial. Return fire tore up the bulkhead behind him.

Shrapnel and flakes of metal drifted from the impacts, spiralling in the zero-gravity chill. Behind them, a melta-cut breach gusted with condensing air from the interior of the Stormbird locked to the *Gorgorex*'s hull.

Half a dozen Sons of Horus fired back – Marr's honour squad, positioned all around the hexagonal approach. The absence of up or down as relative terms was a benefit of combat in zero-gravity.

The vox-net crackled as Cyon Azedine replied.

'Would you yield to an enemy who thought you beaten?' said the champion, his mortuary blade poised behind his combat shield. The Eye of Horus emblazoned upon it glinted with a web of frost in the void-chilled corridor.

'No, but I'm Sixteenth,' said Scybale. 'Even the Iron Tenth can't match that.'

'They appear to think differently,' said Azedine.

'Then it's time we disabuse them of that foolishness,' said Marr, hefting a wide-barrelled weapon he'd appropriated from one of the support
squads.

All cogs, coil-wrapped condensing tubes and a tight ring of focus
blades, the volkite caliver was a weapon more suited to lightly armoured
targets, but it did have the advantage of being utterly lethal in confined spaces.

'Since when does a captain deign to wield a caliver?' asked Azedine, a
man to whom the protocols of warfare were of paramount importance.

'When he wants the job done yesterday,' said Marr and depressed
the grip-trigger.

A searing beam of tightly focused energy shot down the transverse approach. It impacted on the far wall of the axial approach and
exploded in a billowing cloud of caustic fire. Phosphor-bright trails
blazed with sudden, shocking intensity.

There were no screams in a vacuum.

'Azedine,' said Marr. 'Go. Now.'

Cyon Azedine spun out from cover, and his speed was something
uncanny. Movement in low gravity was usually slow and painstaking,
each step taken with magnetized boots.

Marr's champion had no truck with that.

Instead, he bounded from wall to wall, pushing off with limbs like
coiled springs. He spun away from incoming rounds and, with a last
piston-like thrust from the ceiling, he slammed down onto the deck
among the reeling survivors of the volkite blast.

His boots clamped the metal deck and his sword reaped lives. Sprays
of blood hung like red archways in the air.

Marr released the volkite weapon and left it floating behind him.

'Let's go,' he said, and the rest of his honour squad followed him
towards the enemy. Not that he expected to meet any resistance from
here on in, since most of the ship's fighting strength had died in the
void.

All through the enemy ship, breacher squads were converging on

strategic targets: life support, reactor cores, engine spaces. The last thing
Marr wanted was for the remaining crew to scuttle their vessel in spite.
He needed it in once piece.

A starship had numerous routes through its superstructure, but only
one to the command bridge.

And that target was Marr's.

By the time he and his warriors reached the main axial, Cyon Azedine
had killed everyone there. Six bodies floated in the axial, trailing drifting
slicks of vivid crimson. A blob of blood affixed itself to Marr's shoulder guard, painting his Legion marking in red.

He turned and moved up the axial towards the shuttered bridge interlock. Its defence guns weren't firing, which told Marr they were either
out of ammunition or no longer functional. Most likely the latter, the
arrogance of the Iron Hands leading them to believe they would never
be boarded.

Crackling voices spoke of areas seized within the ship. Resistance was
fierce, but minimal. Clearly this ship had been operating with something less than a skeleton crew.

That they had managed to fly it and fight at all was to be admired.
Schematics overlaid the visor display within his helm, his warriors
picked out in pale blue.

'Avakhol, bring your Breachers to me,' ordered Marr.

Moments later, he felt the vibration of heavy footfalls along the axial
as a demi-squad of Rukal Breachers approached.

Avakhol Hurr led them, a febrile warrior with a potent love of all
things explosive. He carried a gore-smeared thunder hammer, and
his iron armour was a filthy mix of ocean green and rust-coloured
stains.

A breacher never cleaned the blood from his battleplate and Hurr
was no exception. He'd been a line warrior during the Jubal Secundus
Liberation, but earned his command during the bloody ship-to-ship
fighting above Isstvan.

Marr jerked his thumb at the bridge access. 'Get that open.'

The Breacher sergeant nodded and hefted his thunder hammer.

'My pleasure.'

MARR STORMED THROUGH the ragged, cherry-red ruin of the entrance to the bridge. The Rukal Breachers followed, fanning out with their shields locked and bolters levelled, ready to annihilate any resistance.

The bridge was empty.

Or as good as empty, it made no difference. A single flesh-spare warrior stood at its centre, locked to the deck and with a photonic-edged war scythe. A dozen servitors flanked him, armed with a mix of clubbing weapons and tools adapted to form rudimentary firearms.

An Iron Father, if Marr wasn't mistaken.

The machinery around him was smashed and cratered, ruined beyond repair and useless. Deliberate sabotage to keep whatever data this vessel's logic engines had once held from falling into enemy hands.

But Marr had seen how much information could be retrieved from supposedly irreparable machines by the tech-sorceries of the Mechanicum, and knew something of value could probably still be extracted.

'I am Octar Uldin,' said the Iron Father. 'Which of you dogs wishes to die first?'

Marr almost laughed.

'You and I? We fight an honourable duel to the death? Is that what Shadrak Meduson is teaching you now, even after Arissak?'

Even a warrior with so little flesh left to him couldn't help but react to the name of the X Legion's new saviour.

'He teaches us that however we die, it will be with honour,' said Uldin, dropping into a fighting crouch with his scythe held to one shoulder.

'No,' said Marr, 'It will be screaming in agony when we torment what little flesh you have left, beyond anything even you can stand.'

He turned away.

'He's all yours, Azedine. Make him bleed, but don't kill him. The Warmaster will want him alive.'

✠ ✠ ✠

THEY WERE WAITING for Marr when he returned from Dwell, as he'd known they would be. They'd denied him the Warmaster, but what had they expected him to do? Sit meekly by and accept the judgement of those he knew to be wrong?

That wasn't the XVI's way of doing things.

It wasn't *his* way of doing things. Not any more.

The Stormbird's engines growled as they powered down, hissing and steaming in the rain. Dwell's atmosphere was paying the inevitable price for a ferocious war fought in low orbit. Numerous space-based gun batteries and dry-docks had finally come down, and the sky over Tyjun was lousy with distortion. Actinic thunder boomed over the mountains and electrical tempests danced on the horizon. The smell of wet plascrete and foaming ocean water was strong. Rain battered the ground and the outer hull of the gunship.

Marr, Scybale and Azedine stood at the top of the assault ramp as a strobing sheet of purple lightning lit the Stormbird's interior.

'This could be bad, yes?' asked Azedine.

'It could be,' agreed Marr. 'We embarked on an unauthorised mission, took ships without the express consent of the Warmaster. Yes. This could be bad.'

'But what we learned,' said Scybale, 'from the very presence of the Iron Hands, from Uldin, that's got to count for something. Otherwise, what was the point?'

'That's what I hope,' said Marr.

'This could be bad,' repeated Azedine, wrapping his too delicate fingers around the hilt of his mortuary blade. 'They could strip us of our rank. Our position. Our honour.'

'They could do a *lot* worse than that,' said Scybale. 'You've seen some of the changes in the Legion, the things Erebus brought with him, the old Cthonian ways coming back. I'm not saying I'm against that, per se, but some of those ways were left behind for good reason.'

Marr straightened his spine. 'We're delaying, and we're better than that. Come on.'

He set off down the ramp, finding not four warriors awaiting him, but five. Four he'd expected, but the fifth...

Horus Lupercal, the primarch.

Encased in glossy black plate of colossal dimensions, he was a titan amongst giants. The glaring eye on his breastplate seethed in amber, the dark slit at its centre seeming to regard Marr with utter indifference. A pelt of resin-stiffened fur mantled Lupercal's shoulders, the long fangs of its upper jaw splayed over one curved shoulder guard.

He held *Worldbreaker* in one hand, as easily as Marr might carry a slender data wand. It was of cold iron, its weight unimaginable. His other hand was bladed with reaper's talons, a tearing weapon as far beyond the power of a lightning claw as a legionary was above a mortal soldier.

But it was his face, a face that was both beautiful and cruel, that drew Marr in. A face that was the fountainhead of the Legion. Hadn't their renaming after Xenobia simply affirmed what they all knew?

Every one of the Mournival called themselves *true sons*, as did Marr, but they were pale imitations of the Warmaster's perfection. Only Aximand, with his terrible surgical rebirth, came anywhere close to the essence of the Warmaster.

Only now did Marr realise just how terrifying that was.

He dropped to one knee, Azedine and Scybale following his lead a heartbeat later.

'Sire,' he began, but the sensation of great weight on one shoulder stopped him from saying more.

Worldbreaker rested on his armour, kept from crushing him only by the Warmaster's great strength. He held the enormous, ultra-dense mace at full extension, a feat none gathered there could match.

'You've been busy, Tybalt,' said Horus.

'I have been fighting our enemies, my lord,' he said, keeping his head bowed.

'So I gather. Drawing up missions of your own and executing them with my ships.'

Marr finally dared look up, and a tremor ran down his spine as his eyes met those of the Warmaster. Better men than he had quailed before that iron gaze. Armies had laid down their weapons rather than stand against this mortal god. Yet even in the stormcloud fury he saw a glimmer of amusement behind this show of anger. Hoping he was right, Marr knew there was only one way to respond.

'I did, sire,' said Marr. 'To prove the broken warriors we left in our wake at Isstvan are no longer broken. They are organised, efficient. In contact.'

Horus removed *Worldbreaker* from Marr's shoulder.

'How do you know this?' he asked.

'Because he is going to tell me,' said Marr, rising and beckoning Avakhol Hurr from the Stormbird. The bloody Breacher and his fellow gutter-killers led Octar Uldin down the assault ramp, his neck clamped in the spiked collar of a man-catcher. Snapping sparks of electrical discharge burned the meat and metal of his neck, and his steps were stiff and ungainly as artificial nerves were stimulated with pain signals.

'One of the Iron Tenth,' said Horus. 'You took him in this system?'

'Him and his vessel,' said Marr. 'Lurking out by the Azoth Gate, keeping watch on our comings and goings and passing that information back to Shadrak Meduson.'

'You can't know that for sure,' said Abaddon.

'Can't I?' snapped Marr. 'While you were sitting on your complacent behinds, I took action. You were so sure of your own prowess that you never gave any other Legion credit for being as good, as resilient, as tough as us. Well, guess what? They *are* strong, and they *are* fighting back!'

Horus stepped in and took hold of Marr's shoulder guards, pulling him in tight to embrace him in a clatter of plate.

'Tybalt Marr,' he said as he released him. 'Truly you are a son of the north, the aspect of illumination, discovery, wisdom and understanding. As ancient Polaris was permanent, so too are you a symbol of the eternal.'

'Thank you, my lord,' said Marr, but Horus wasn't done yet.

'Yet the ancient peoples of Old Earth looked upon the north as a

place of darkness, an aspect regarded with suspicion and, aye, even terror. The great Shakespire spoke of daemons "who are substitutes under
the lonely monarch of the north".

'I don't understand, my lord,' said Marr, as Avakhol Hurr forced Octar
Uldin to his knees before the Warmaster.

'It means that you have been away from your brothers too long, I
think,' said Horus, a single killing claw lifting Uldin's battered chin. The
Iron Father's eyes were gone, plucked by Azedine's mortuary blade and
now nothing more than sliced cables hanging down over his cheeks.
'That you have become the lone wolf, the hunter who works best alone.'

'What are you saying, sire? Exile?'

'No, but whether you are right or wrong, Tybalt, you will cost me
dearly,' said Horus. 'If you are right, and Meduson is raising a storm in
our wake, then I must send warriors to find him and kill him. If you are
wrong, I must punish you for your disobedience. So which is it to be?'

'I am not wrong,' said Marr, certainty filling him.

Horus regarded him for a moment, as though weighing up which
option would cost him the least. But that glimmer of amusement was
still there, and Marr wondered if the others had seen it or even knew
Lupercal had made his decision long before Marr's Stormbird had landed.

'Tell me what you want, Tybalt,' said Horus. 'Do you want to hunt
down these "Shattered Legions"? Root them from their shadowed lairs
and drive them into the light? Destroy them?'

'I want to finish what we started at Isstvan,' Marr replied.

'Then you will be my hunter in the void. I will give you ships and warriors, weapons and power to do what must be done to end this threat.'

'My lord?' said Abaddon. 'The campaign...'

'Will succeed or fail with or without Tybalt,' said Horus, lifting his
Talon and stopping any further discussion.

'I go to Molech, Tybalt,' said Horus, fastening his gaze upon him
once more. 'Tell me what *you* are going to do.'

Marr stood tall and said, 'I'm going to bring you Shadrak Meduson's head.'

ABOUT THE AUTHORS

Dan Abnett is the author of the Horus Heresy novels *The Unremembered Empire*, *Know No Fear* and *Prospero Burns*, the last two of which were both *New York Times* bestsellers. He has written almost fifty novels, including the acclaimed Gaunt's Ghosts series, the Eisenhorn and Ravenor trilogies, and *I am Slaughter*, the first book in The Beast Arises series. He scripted *Macragge's Honour*, the first Horus Heresy graphic novel, as well as numerous audio dramas and short stories set in the Warhammer 40,000 and Warhammer universes. He lives and works in Maidstone, Kent.

David Annandale is the author of the Horus Heresy novels *Ruinstorm*, *The Damnation of Pythos*, and the Primarchs novel *Roboute Guilliman: Lord of Ultramar*. He has also written the Yarrick series, several stories involving the Grey Knights, and *The Last Wall*, *The Hunt for Vulkan* and *Watchers in Death* for The Beast Arises. For Space Marine Battles he has written *The Death of Antagonis* and *Overfiend*. He is a prolific writer of short fiction, including the novella *Mephiston: Lord of Death* and numerous short stories set in The Horus Heresy, Warhammer 40,000 and Age of Sigmar universes. David lectures at a Canadian university, on subjects ranging from English literature to horror films and video games.

John French has written several Horus Heresy stories including the novels *Praetorian of Dorn* and *Tallarn: Ironclad*, the novellas *Tallarn: Executioner* and *The Crimson Fist*, and the audio dramas *Templar* and *Warmaster*. He is the author of *Resurrection: The Horusian Wars*, as well as the Ahriman series, which includes the novels *Ahriman: Exile*, *Ahriman: Sorcerer* and *Ahriman: Unchanged*, plus a number of related short stories collected in *Ahriman: Exodus*. Additionally, for the Warhammer 40,000 universe he has written the Space Marine Battles novella *Fateweaver*, plus many short stories. He lives and works in Nottingham, UK.

Guy Haley is the author of the Horus Heresy novel *Pharos*, the Primarchs novel *Perturabo: The Hammer of Olympia* and the Warhammer 40,000 novels *Dante*, *Baneblade*, *Shadowsword*, *Valedor* and *Death of Integrity*. He has also written *Throneworld* and *The Beheading* for The Beast Arises series. His enthusiasm for all things greenskin has also led him to pen the eponymous Warhammer novel *Skarsnik*, as well as the End Times novel *The Rise of the Horned Rat*. He has also written stories set in the Age of Sigmar, included in *War Storm*, *Ghal Maraz* and *Call of Archaon*. He lives in Yorkshire with his wife and son.

Nick Kyme is the author of the Horus Heresy novels *Deathfire*, *Vulkan Lives*, and *Sons of the Forge*, the novellas *Promethean Sun* and *Scorched Earth*, and the audio drama *Censure*. His novella *Feat of Iron* was a *New York Times* bestseller in the Horus Heresy collection, *The Primarchs*. Nick is well known for his popular Salamanders novels, including *Rebirth*, the Space Marine Battles novel *Damnos*, and numerous short stories. He has also written fiction set in the world of Warhammer, most notably the Time of Legends novel *The Great Betrayal* and the Age of Sigmar story 'Borne by the Storm', included in the novel *War Storm*. He lives and works in Nottingham, and has a rabbit.

Graham McNeill has written many Horus Heresy novels, including *Vengeful Spirit* and his *New York Times* bestsellers *A Thousand Sons* and the novella *The Reflection Crack'd*, which featured in *The Primarchs* anthology. Graham's Ultramarines series, featuring Captain Uriel Ventris, is now six novels long, and has close links to his Iron Warriors stories, the novel *Storm of Iron* being a perennial favourite with Black Library fans. He has also written a Mars trilogy, featuring the Adeptus Mechanicus. For Warhammer, he has written the Time of Legends trilogy *The Legend of Sigmar*, the second volume of which won the 2010 David Gemmell Legend Award.

Gav Thorpe is the author of the Horus Heresy novels *Deliverance Lost*, *Angels of Caliban* and *Corax*, as well as the novella *The Lion*, which formed part of the *New York Times* bestselling collection *The Primarchs*, as well as several audio dramas including the bestselling *Raven's Flight* and *The Thirteenth Wolf*, among others. He has written many novels for Warhammer 40,000, including *Ghost Warrior: Rise of the Ynnari*, *Jain Zar: The Storm of Silence* and *Asurmen: Hand of Asuryan*. He also wrote the *Path of the Eldar* and *Legacy of Caliban* trilogies, and two volumes in The Beast Arises series. For Warhammer, Gav has penned the End Times novel *The Curse of Khaine*, the Time of Legends trilogy, *The Sundering*, and much more besides. He lives and works in Nottingham.

Chris Wraight is the author of the Horus Heresy novels *Scars* and *The Path of Heaven*, the novella *Brotherhood of the Storm* and the audio drama *The Sigillite*. For Warhammer 40,000 he has written the novels *Vaults of Terra: Carrion Throne*, *Watchers of the Throne: The Emperor's Legion*, the Space Wolves novels *Blood of Asaheim* and *Stormcaller*, and the short story collection *Wolves of Fenris*, as well as the Space Marine Battles novels *Wrath of Iron* and *Battle of the Fang*. Additionally, he has many Warhammer novels to his name, including the Time of Legends novel *Master of Dragons*, which forms part of the War of Vengeance series. Chris lives and works near Bristol, in south-west England.